JODOROWSKY - MŒBIUS - JANJETOV - LADRÖNN

DECONSTRUCTING THE INCAL

JEAN ANNESTAY AND CHRISTOPHE QUILLIEN

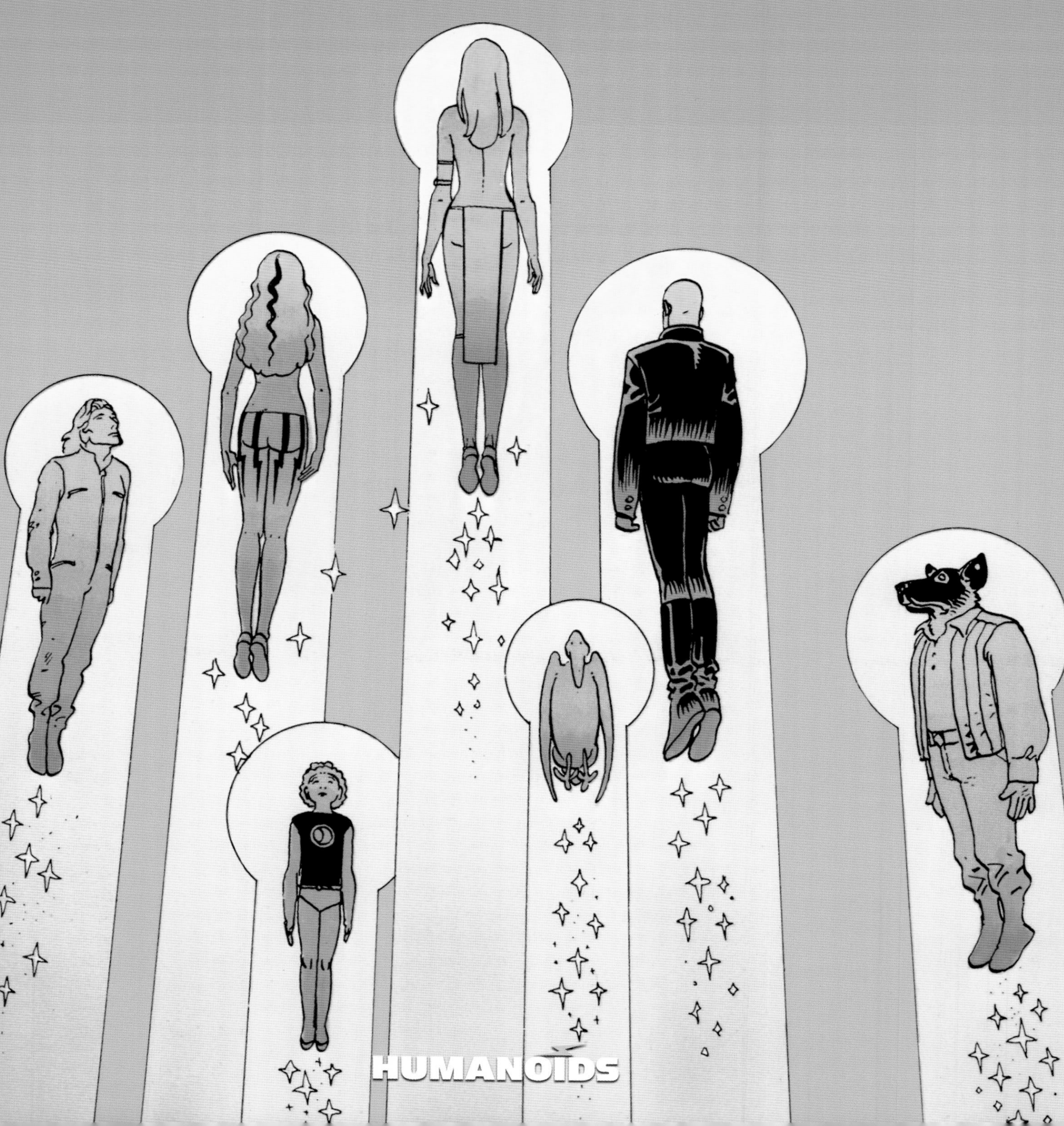

HUMANOIDS

Alejandro Jodorowky
Mœbius, Janjetov & Ladrönn
CONTRIBUTORS

Jean Annestay
& Christophe Quillien
WRITERS

Montana Kane
TRANSLATOR

JERRY FRISSEN
Senior Art Director

**ALEX DONOGHUE
& TIM PILCHER**
U.S. Edition Editors

FABRICE GIGER
Publisher

Rights & Licensing - licensing@humanoids.com
Press and Social Media - pr@humanoids.com

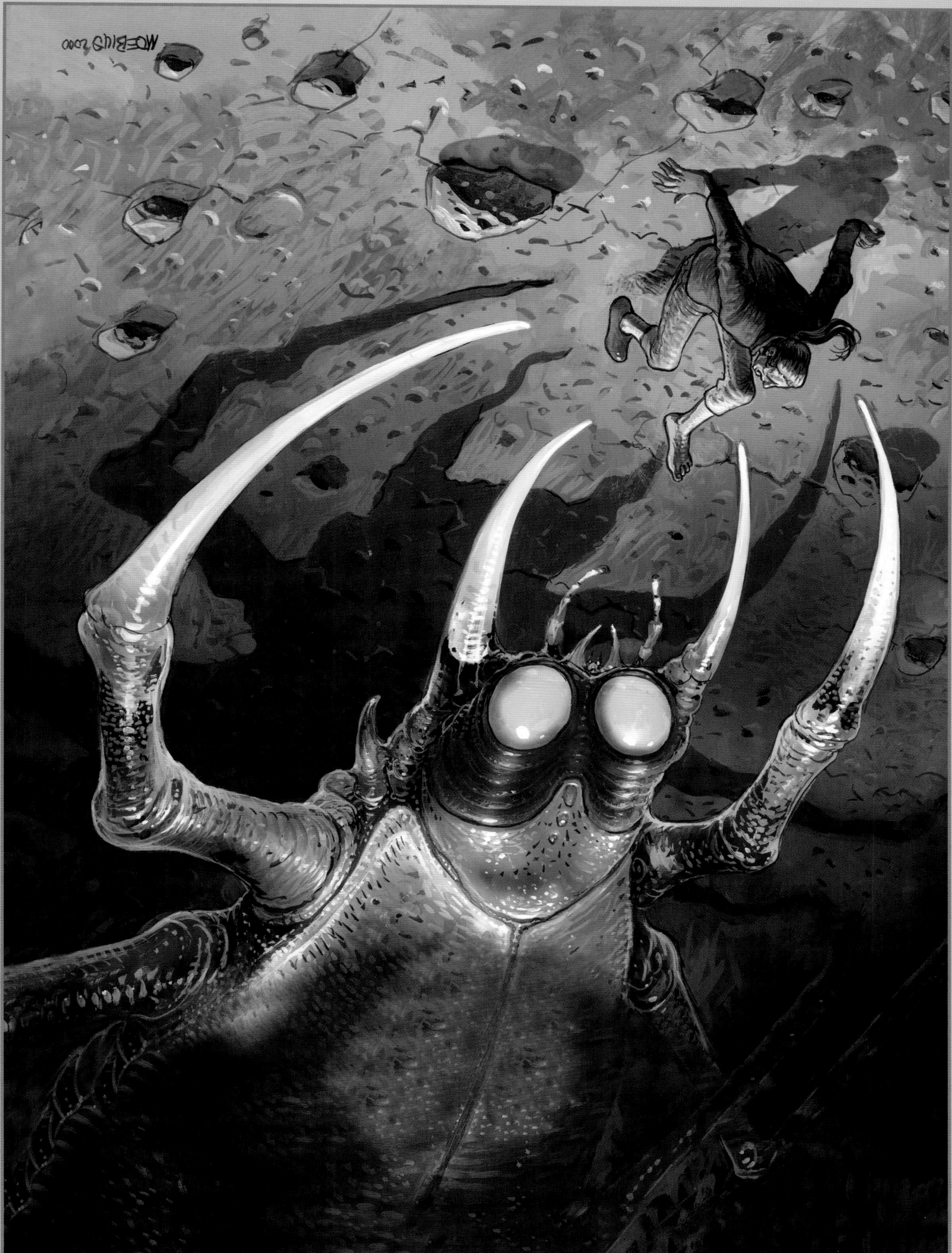
MOEBIUS 2000

IN THE SAME JODOVERSE:

HUMANOIDS PRESENTS: THE JODOVERSE
(excerpts from multiple series)
ISBN: 978-1-59465-167-0

THE INCAL SERIES:

BEFORE THE INCAL
Alejandro Jodorowsky, Zoran Janjetov
ISBN: 978-1-59465-901-0

THE INCAL
Alejandro Jodorowsky, Mœbius
ISBN: 978-1-59465-093-2

FINAL INCAL
Alejandro Jodorowsky, Ladrönn
ISBN: 978-1-59465-107-6

THE METABARONS SERIES:

THE METABARONS
(collected edition of first cycle)
Alejandro Jodorowsky, Juan Gimenez
ISBN: 978-1-59465-106-9

(trade editions in 4 volumes)
THE METABARONS: VOLUME 1: OTHON & HONORATA
Alejandro Jodorowsky, Juan Gimenez
ISBN: 978-1-59465-891-4

THE METABARONS - VOLUME 2: AGHNAR & ODA
Alejandro Jodorowsky, Juan Gimenez
ISBN: 978-1-59465-744-3

THE METABARONS - VOLUME 3: STEELHEAD & DONA VICENTA
Alejandro Jodorowsky, Juan Gimenez
ISBN: 978-1-59465-880-8

THE METABARONS - VOLUME 4: AGHORA & THE LAST METABARON
Alejandro Jodorowsky, Juan Gimenez
ISBN: 978-1-59465-390-2

METABARONS GENESIS: CASTAKA
Alejandro Jodorowsky, Das Pastoras
ISBN: 978-1-59465-161-8

WEAPONS OF THE METABARON
Alejandro Jodorowsky, Travis Charest, Zoran Janjetov
ISBN: 978-1-59465-163-2

THE METABARON BOOK 1:
THE TECHNO-ADMIRAL & THE ANTI-BARON
Alejandro Jodorowsky, Jerry Frissen, Valentin Sécher
ISBN: 978-1-59465-153-3

THE METABARON BOOK 2:
THE TECHNO-CARDINAL & THE TRANSHUMAN
Alejandro Jodorowsky, Jerry Frissen, Niko Henrichon
ISBN: 978-1-59465-680-4

MEGALEX
Alejandro Jodorowsky, Fred Beltran
ISBN: 978-1-59465-091-8

THE TECHNOPRIESTS
Alejandro Jodorowsky, Zoran Janjetov, Fred Beltran
ISBN: 978-1-59465-050-5

1. Inside The Incal: The Revelation of The Books

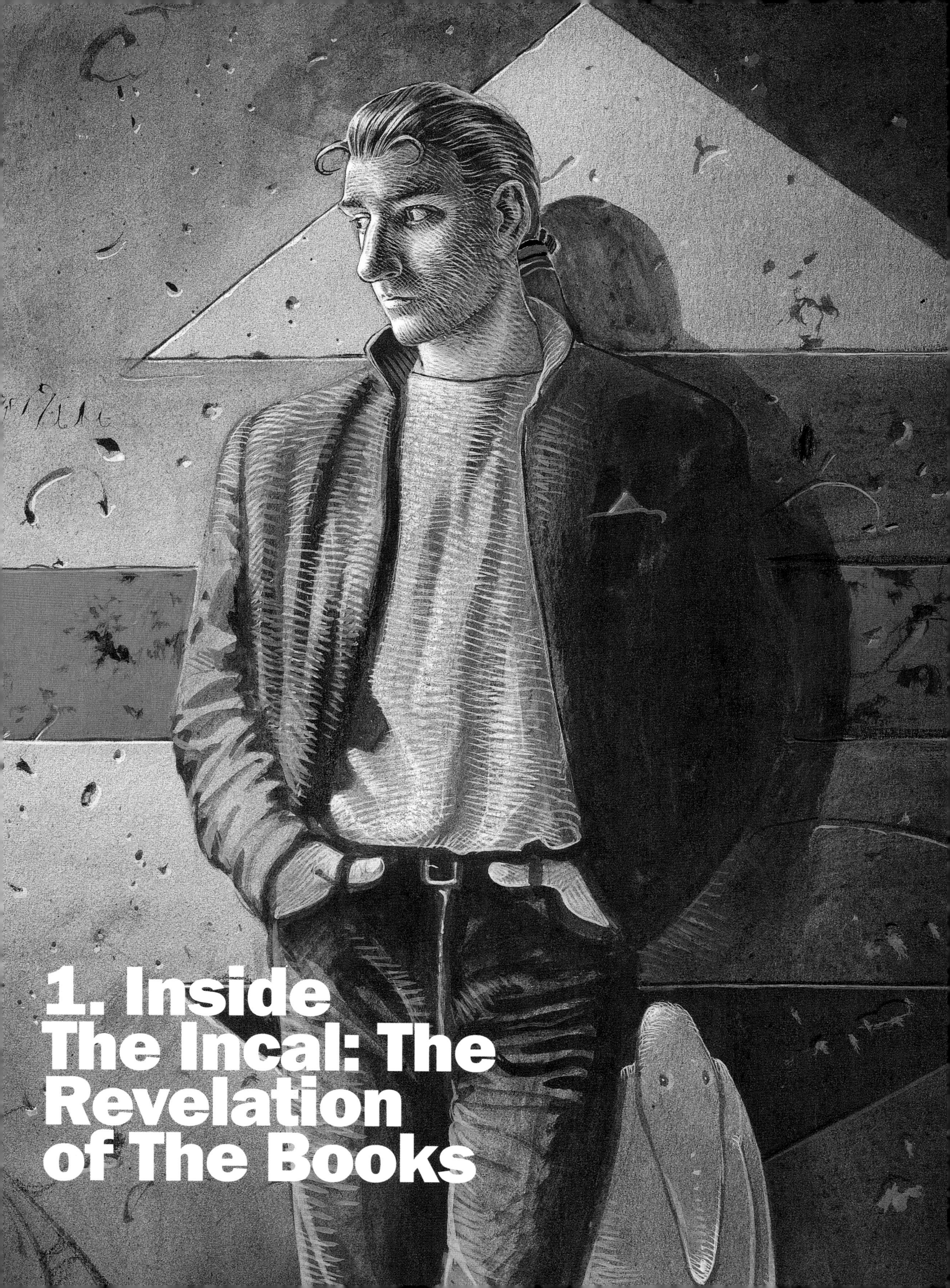

The Incal

What is *The Incal*? The title of one of the bestselling and most epic comic book tales ever. A multi-faceted work that blasted onto the '80s comics scene like an Unidentified Book-Shaped Object, filled with a wealth of imagery unlike any other and riddled with cultural and artistic references. The miraculous synthesis between ultra-modern science fiction, Jean "Mœbius" Giraud's magical touch, Alejandro Jodorowsky's gift as a storyteller, and a narrative imbued with South American magical realism. An aesthetic and thematic punch in the face that pushed the boundaries of comics as a medium. Yes, undoubtedly it's all these things. But what else?

Released serially between 1981 and 1988, and translated into more than 20 languages since, *The Incal* is made up of 291 comic pages that form a narrative circularity framed by a near-identical beginning and end: the fall of the hero eternally returned to his point of departure, just like in those repetitive dreams, filled with childish terror, where we are endlessly falling.

The six volumes that make up *The Incal* read as a single book, which can be divided into three pairs. *The Black Incal* is the mirror reflection of *The Luminous Incal*; *What Is Above* follows *What Lies Beneath*; and *The Fifth Essence* is divided into two chapters, *The Dreaming Galaxy* and *Planet Difool*. This construction reflects one of the main principles in *The Incal*: duplication and repetition. An analytic quest, a journey of initiation, a coming-of-age novel, an exploration of memory and dream, and an expanding graphic universe: the adventures of John Difool bring all these elements together. They launch a world complete unto itself, a vast system of intricate associations whose subtle cogs are activated by an accumulation of successive images in what we call sequential art.

But what we're talking about here is, of course, not just any hit comic book. Yes, it's an adventure story and a sci-fi fable, but *The Incal* nonetheless possesses the scope and scale of a masterwork of creative expression. It speaks of the world of the mind and its hidden places, of the great symbols that govern human cultures, of contemporary society, and of its own creators.

Thus *The Incal* constitutes a remarkable fiction machine, the kind the comics world manages to produce from time to time, on equal footing with classic works of literature or cinema. It has created its own autonomous universe, with its own poetic language, and, deep down, its own special secret.

For while *The Incal* offers a complete world, a narrative,

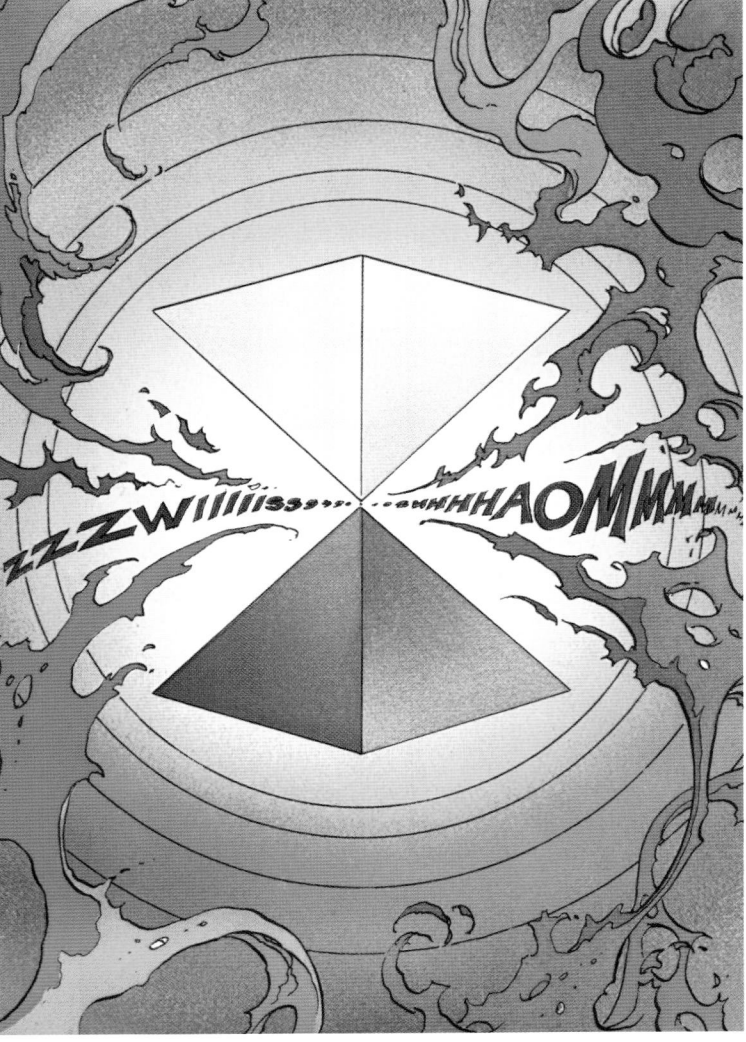

imagery, an exploration of the contemporary soul, and a work of artistic creation, it doesn't tell the reader everything about its own universe. When we get to page 311, we're back at the beginning. This time, John Difool is obsessed with a single thought: "I must remember." He's like a dreamer who, upon awakening, shakes off the fading remnants of messages from his subconscious. What is it that he needs to remember? Is it the story that he has just lived through, which the reader is perfectly aware of—the story, therefore, that is about to start all over again? Or is what he must remember a more terrible and profound secret that the reader has also unconsciously forgotten?

The Incal is not just the title of Jodorowsky and Mœbius's masterwork; it's also the name of an object—on which depends "the fate of not only the planet, but fate of the whole universe," as a Berg tells a perplexed John Difool at the beginning of *The Black Incal*. A living creature, gifted with speech—for the Incal is alive: "I am not a computer. I am alive, just like you! And destiny has brought us together to restore justice to the universe," it explains to an increasingly perplexed John Difool.

"Whoooaa! Slow down, buddy! I'm just a Class 'R' Private Detective. I've got nothing to do with justice!" he says in an attempt to get out of the situation, as it begins to dawn on him just how far he's being dragged into a "mess of galactic proportions!" In *What Is Above*, when Raïmo of Kamar inquires about the nature of the Incal ("The Incal? What is that? I've never heard of it. Is it a man? A weapon? A cult? What are its powers?"), Kill Wolfhead offers up a definition: "It was born on the Empire's most insignificant planet. It is the new light that will one day illuminate the galaxy. It is pure consciousness, a direct emanation of the divine will—the power of God incarnate!"

Perhaps it would be easiest to turn to one the Incal's co-creators, Alejandro Jodorowsky himself, to try to define it, or at least to better understand its true nature. In an 1986 interview with Frank Reichert that would be published in the French paperback edition of *The Black Incal*, Jodorowsky made an attempt to explain: "As for the Incal itself, I would say that it's the 'inner Master' everyone carries within. I would say that it was my subconscious that dictated this word to me...just like that! Perhaps it came from Inca? Or perhaps it also came from the English word incall, 'the inner call'?" As for Mœbius, in his conversations with Numa Sadoul (for the book *Doctor Mœbius and Mister Gir*), he defined the Incal as "the human dream that kills the old God." In an early draft of the story, there was no Incal. Instead, there was the "Key Eye."

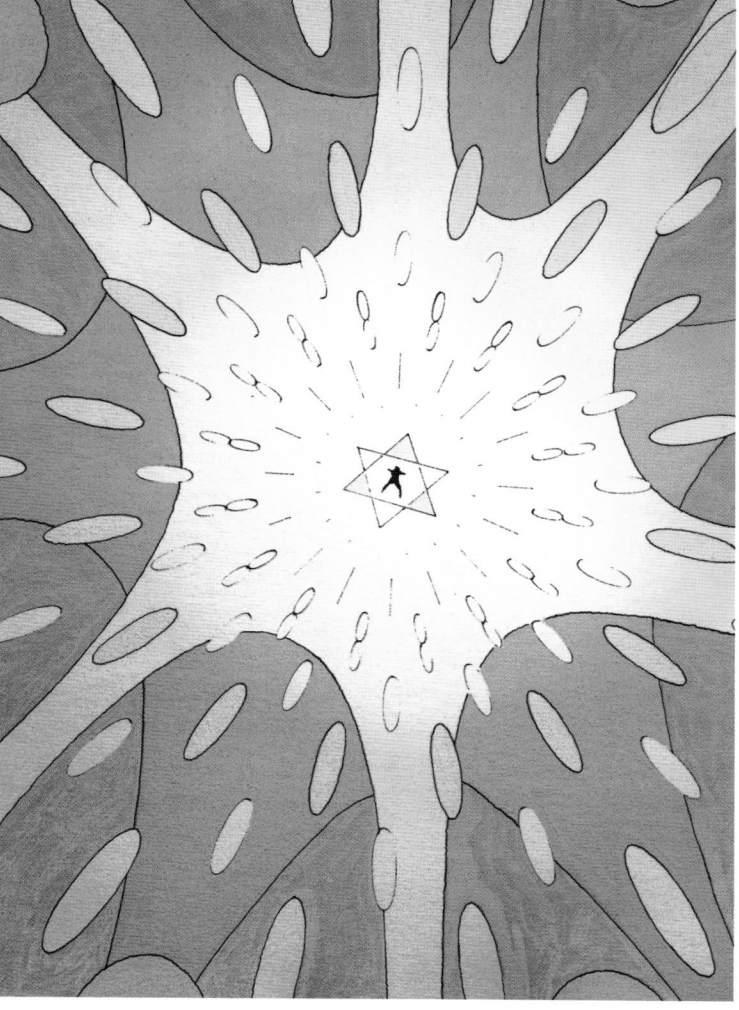

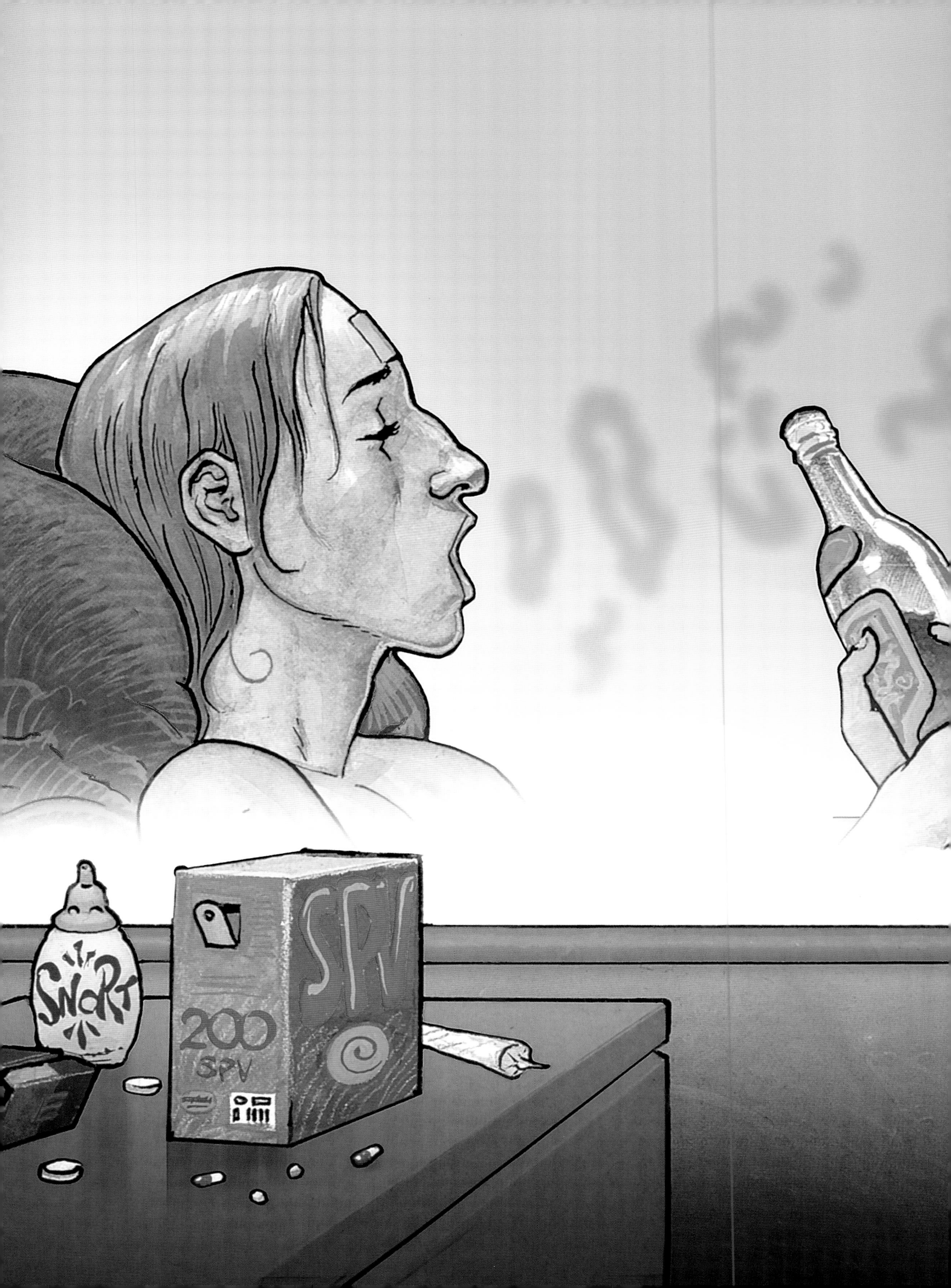
SNoRT
SPV
200
SPV

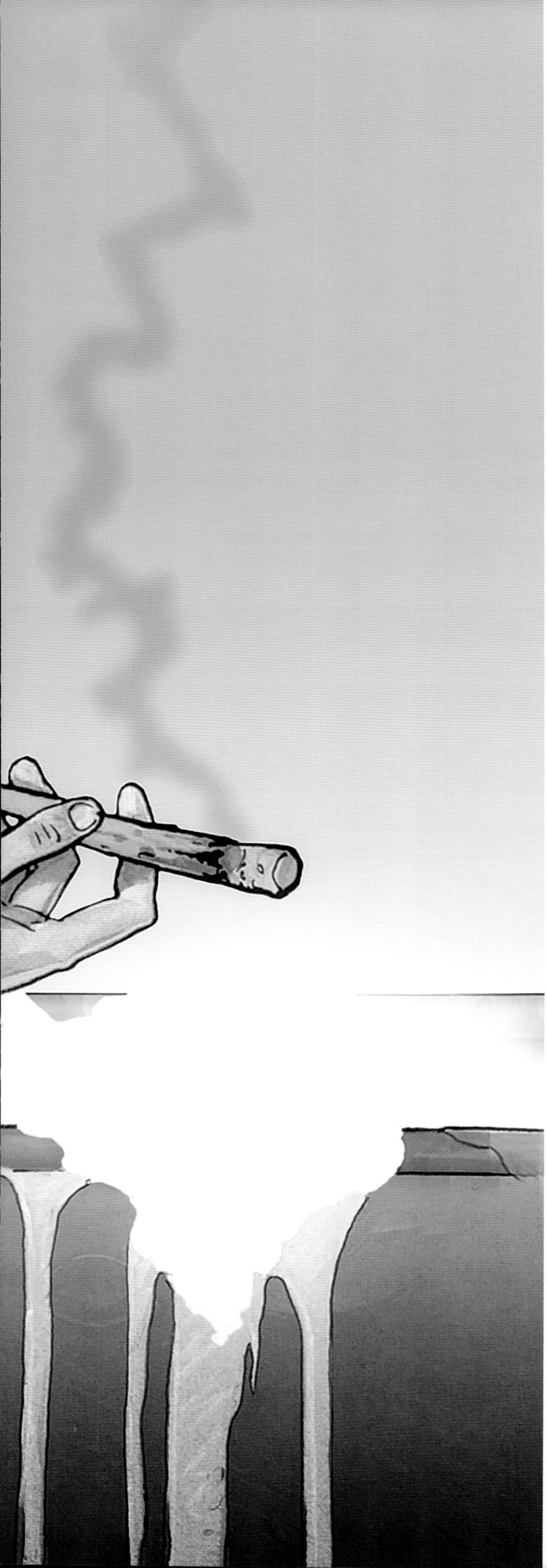

Before The Incal

The Incal is not the product of chance—neither Mœbius nor Jodorowsky believed in chance—but rather the coming together of two likeminded artists. The series' prequel, *Before The Incal,* was similarly born of a feeling of connection between two individuals: Jodorowsky and a young illustrator named Zoran Janjetov. Their first encounter took place in 1986, in Humanoids' Parisian offices. Filled with feverish enthusiasm, Janjetov had traveled from his native Serbia to show his artwork, introducing himself as a die-hard disciple of Jean Giraud/Mœbius, his creative inspiration and guru. As he studied the young man's pencil work, Jodorowsky was struck by the similarity between his line and the one Mœbius used to use before embarking on the epic *The Incal.* A line composed of the small points and the crosshatching that were so characteristic of Mœbius's earlier graphic style, and worlds apart from the purity and the sense of synthesis he had used in *The Incal.*

For Jodorowsky, this graphic kinship was a sign: since Janjetov used a "pre-*Incal*" Mœbius style of drawing, he would be the perfect illustrator for a series about John Difool's early days. Back in his home country (at the time, it was still Yugoslavia), Janjetov drew the first chapter in a state of euphoria, filled with both the enthusiasm and the stylistic flaws characteristic of youth. The pages were shown to Mœbius at a book fair in the U.S., where the illustrator had been living since the early '80s. Won over by the homage of this young disciple, the master gave his seal of approval. *Before The Incal* could proceed and John Difool could once again relive his youth—or rather, discover a new version of it.

Many have asked if the original plan was for Mœbius to draw the prequel, "Alejandro had the idea when he met Janjetov and offered him the project. Then, he said to me, 'Here, I wrote about Difool's youth, take a look at a few pages.' I thought it was great, I said OK," Mœbius recalled during a discussion with Numa Sadoul. Jodorowsky, however, offers up a slightly different version. "Numa, look at me: do I look like the kind of guy who wouldn't want to do the story with him? Of course I came to him first! But he didn't have the time, and he wasn't really feeling it. He would have liked for it to happen just like he told you, but my version of the facts is the real one!" Who knows where the truth lies? One thing is certain; the mysteries of the *Incal* series are intricate and mysterious both inside and out of its pages...

Before The Incal was originally released in six parts between 1988 and 1995. In a new edition published in 1991, Janjetov redrew the first eight pages of the first volume.

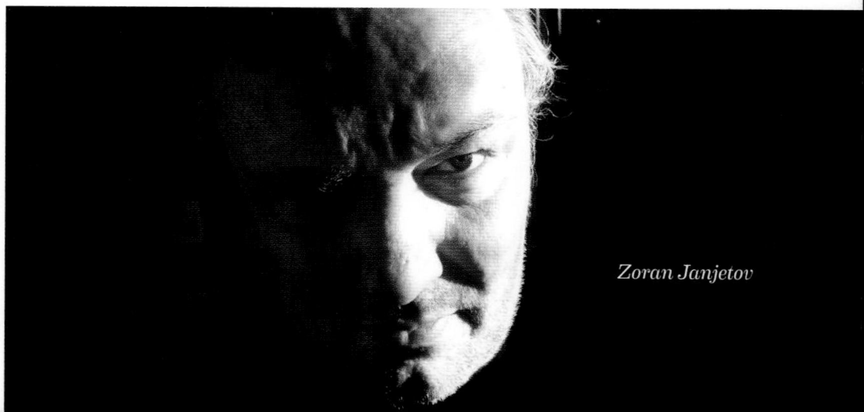
Zoran Janjetov

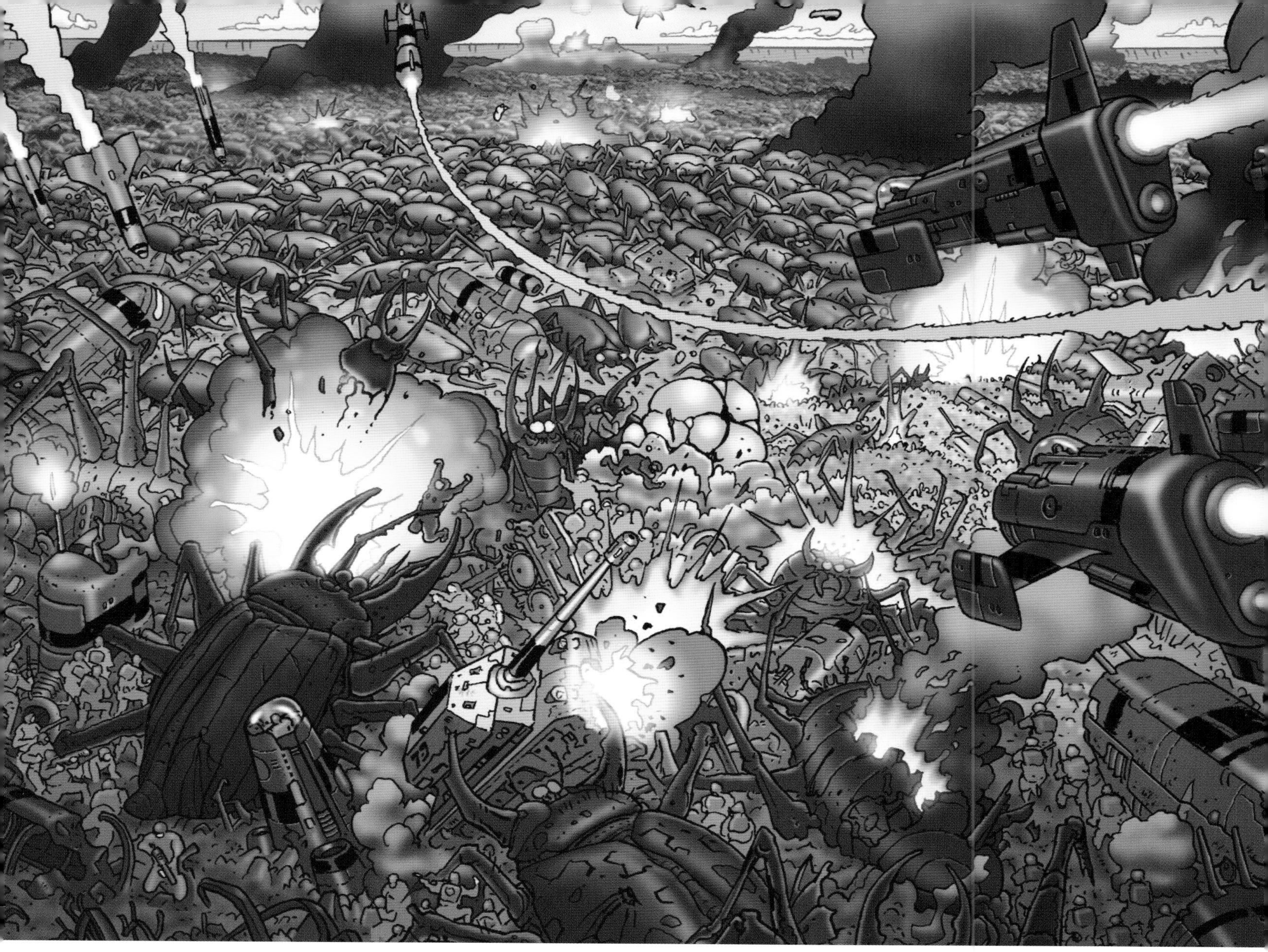

After The Incal

In 1988, Alejandro Jodorowsky and Mœbius finished their initial *Incal* saga. But their collaboration did not stop there: in 1992, they released the first part of *Madwoman of the Sacred Heart*, which, unlike *The Incal*, is firmly rooted in contemporary reality. Jodorowsky then decided to expand the world of John Difool by writing about his youth in the prequel, before giving a family to the character of the Metabaron in *The Metabarons*, a sweeping epic that unfolds in Juan Gimenez's masterful images, and continues to this day with a new generation of creators.

But the allure of *The Incal* isn't so easily denied, and the prospect of a sequel was a notion the writer toyed with on a regular basis. Jodorowsky eventually shared with Mœbius the idea of a sort of metallic plague that would appear and poison the world of Terra 2014. Twenty years after their initial *Incal* outing, the two partners in crime teamed up once again to create *After The Incal*, this time with cutting-edge digital coloring by Fred Beltran, who would go on to illustrate Jodorowsky's *Megalex*.

The story opens in Difool's conapt. Our hero suddenly wakes up from a "horrible dream" that haunts him every night: he watches himself fall from the top of Suicide Alley and plunge into the Acid Lake. But this time, unlike the opening pages of *The Black Incal*, no one comes to scoop him up in the nick of time and save him from dissolving in the green, murky waters. A question nags at him, as he struggles to regain full consciousness: in his dream, he had to remember something, but what? It remains a total mystery. "Someone" had given him a mission, but who? And what mission? Unbeknownst to him, he is being closely monitored by "Eyecops," i.e. surveillance drones sent by the Central Cranium, who wants to make sure Difool's memory is not reactivating...

The cycle only saw the publication of one volume, as Mœbius was soon swept away by other adventures and temptations. Undaunted, Jodorowsky would eventually find another artist to continue John Difool's adventures...

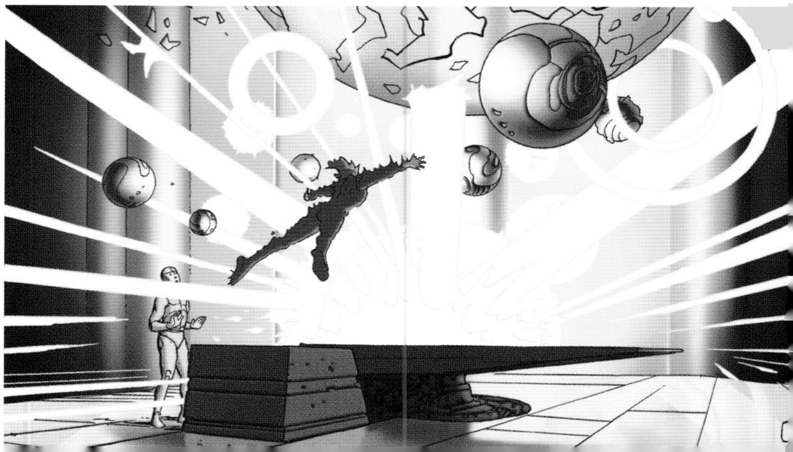

Final Incal

After Mœbius finished drawing the initial 56 pages of *After The Incal*, the story still wasn't complete. But Mœbius was busy with other projects and commitments, having moved on to another chapter of his professional life, which meant he was leaving John Difool stranded with nothing less than "the fate of the universe" hanging in the balance. On top of that, we had no idea whether Deepo—who finds himself in the unfortunate position of being caught between the claws of the new, metal-encased Prez—would be rescued in time. In short, our heroes—and the series' readers—needed someone to replace Mœbius—even though it went without saying that he was irreplaceable and everybody knew it. Coming up with a sequel to *The Incal* was not going to be easy.

Examining John Difool's early years didn't present any issues of consistency with the original story, because before he became the Class "R" Private Detective everyone knows and loves, he had obviously had a childhood that would prove interesting. But to write about what happened after *The Incal* risked undermining the very foundation of the saga, which followed a loop structure: the end of the story feeding back in on itself with John Difool forced to relive the original scene in which he's hurtling through the air toward the Acid Lake. In *After The Incal*, Jodorowsky had solved this problem by resorting to a writing trick, the artifice of the dream. So everything that happened to John Difool was just a dream? In other words, did this wonderful adventure, *The Incal*, never exist anywhere except in Difool's mind? Was it all just a product of his fevered imagination? The ruse of turning this "cosmic and comic" epic, as Jodorowsky called it, into a mere dream was later regretted by the writer, with his trademark colorful humor. "I got it wrong in *After The Incal*. I don't know what moronic notion got into me that I had to go and decide that the whole story of *The Incal* was nothing but a dream. Way too easy. After doing a purge that involved living among the Amazon Indians and eating coconuts, I recovered my shamanic insight. The wise eight-legged rats I saw in my visions asked me to start the story over again. Mœbius, who was gently upset with me, decided not to follow me down that 'schizo-mystical' path, and I had to wait eight years before I found an artist worthy of the new version. The dream turned into several parallel worlds."

Salvation was to come in the form of Mexican illustrator Ladrönn, a great admirer of both Mœbius and *The Incal*,

a series he worshiped and that he felt changed the very course of his life. Instead of just picking up where Mœbius had left off in *After The Incal,* Ladrönn started from scratch in a new story entitled *Final Incal.* On Terra 2014, the Prez has treated himself to a new body, one made entirely of metal. And he firmly intends to "destroy every last bio-cell in the City-Shaft, no matter how small," and eradicate all bio-matter so that a new life can begin. Henceforth, life will be immortal and metallic, or not at all. But to achieve his ends, he must get rid of John Difool once and for all...

In *Final Incal,* the precision of Ladrönn's line and his ability to portray a run-down universe corroded by rust and rot—both material and moral—works wonders. The illustrator succeeds in following in Mœbius's footsteps, leaving his own unique graphic signature on the story and adding new facets to the world of Terra 2014, while also enabling the reader to plunge back into familiar territory. A world in which it's thrilling to be reunited with memorable characters such as Gorgo the Foul and Kill Wolfhead, who are given more dimension here. For instance, Kill's lucidity, courage, and depth of feelings give him an unprecedented aura that's a far cry from the clichéd, vengeful, pathetic, and ridiculous soldier he embodied in *The Black Incal.*

The cycle concludes with Luz and John reunited and making tender—organic—love before setting out to sow that love throughout the metallic universe. The scene is beautiful and moving but doesn't stoop to the level of melodrama; and Jodorowsky ensures a touch of welcome humor, thanks to what Gorgo the Foul cries out: "All this galactic fuss has really given me an appetite! I could eat a whole protosaurus!" As Jodorowsky puts it, "*The Incal* isn't over! In the last chapter, John and Luz—in Spanish, 'luz' means 'light'—take off together to go conquer the universe. He, along with his wife, becomes the Solune from the prophecy. As he enters her, they becomes the Incal... For what is the Incal? It's black and white, it's the sun and the moon... The Incal is the total being! There is a rebirth at the end."

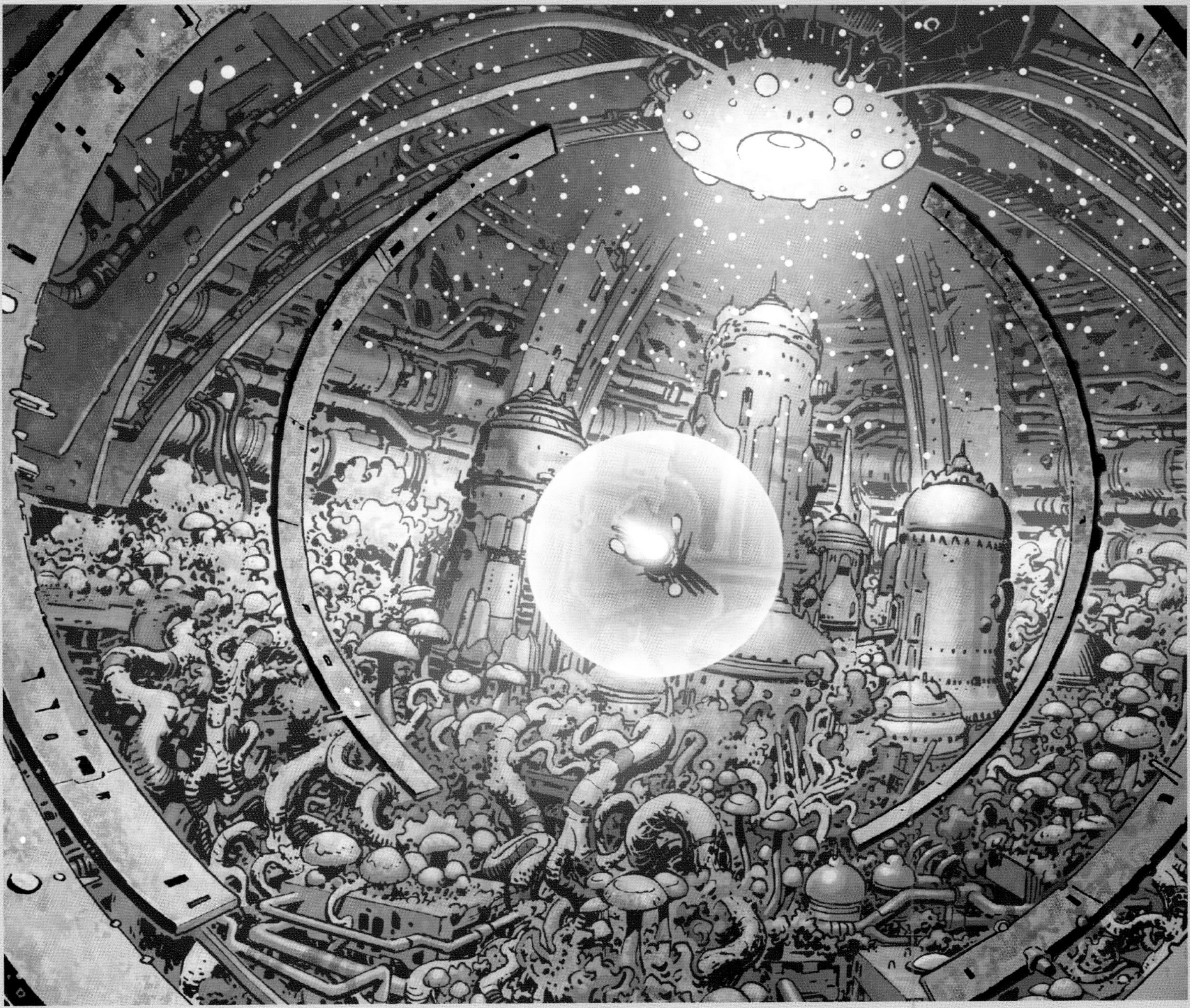

2. Behind The Incal: Creators & Origins

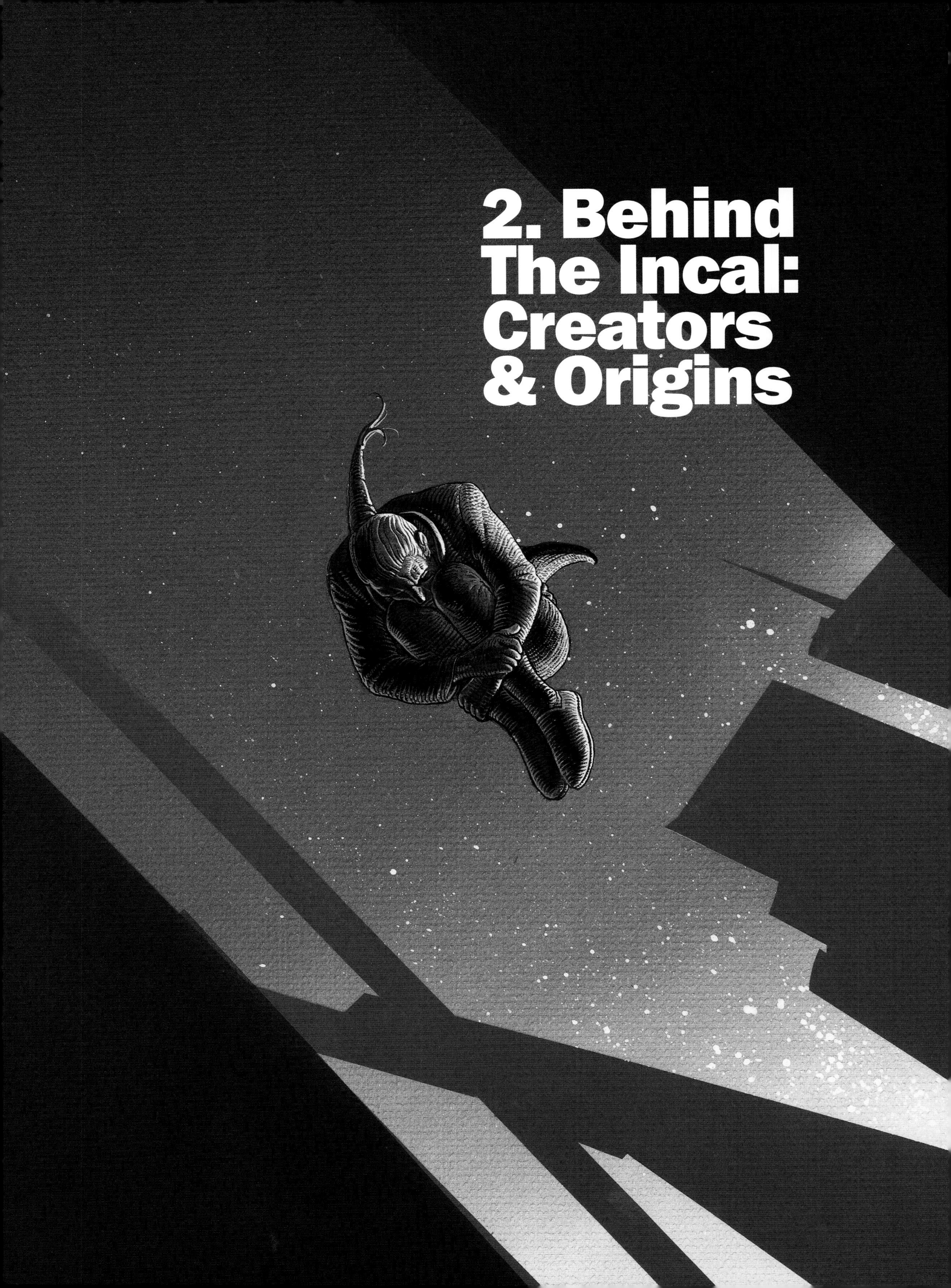

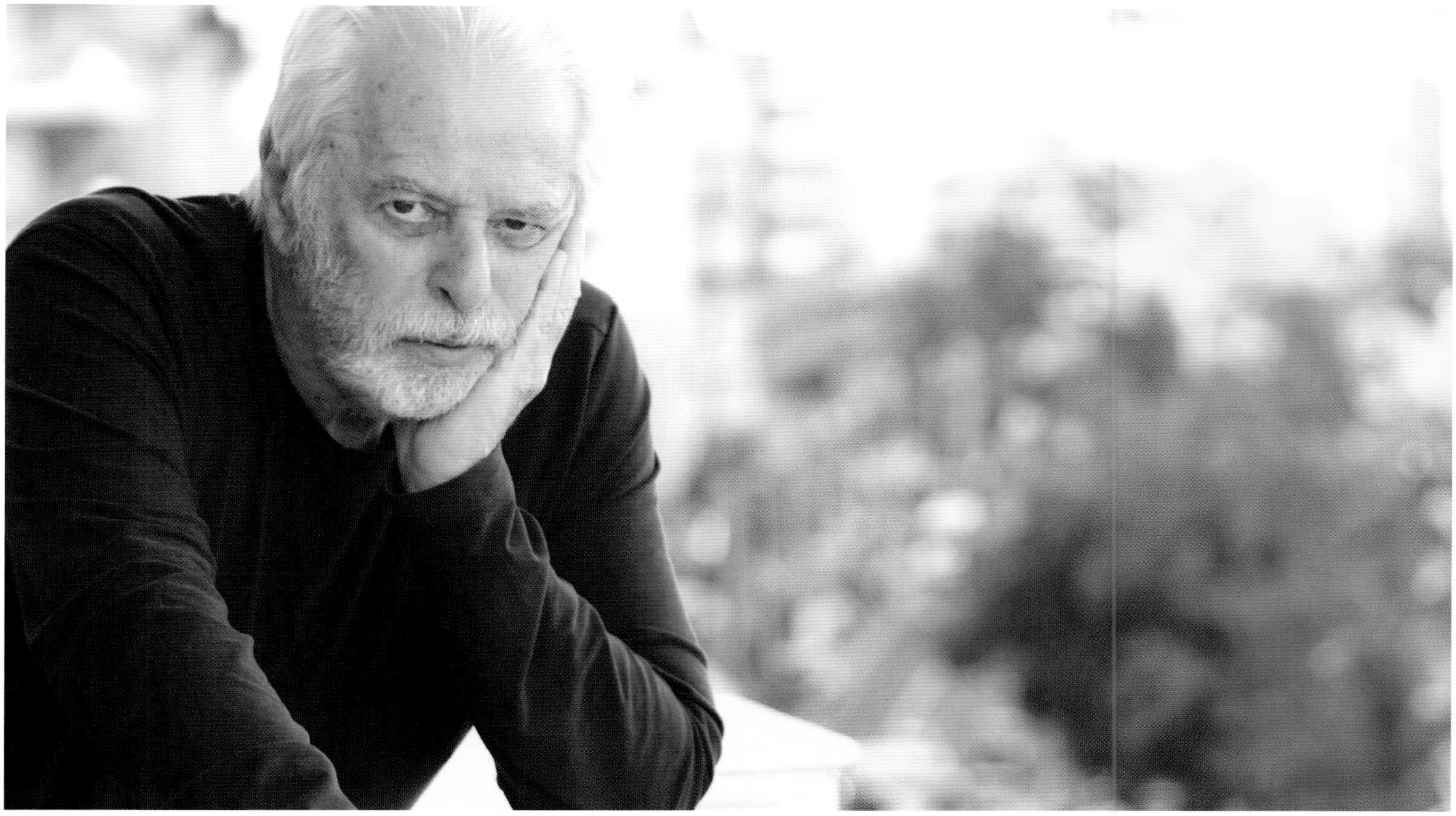

Alejandro Jodorowsky

Alejandro Jodorowsky was born in 1929 in Tocopilla, a village in northern Chile where his parents, Russian Jews, had settled after fleeing the pogroms. He left his homeland in 1953 after having roamed Chile extensively with a troupe of puppeteers—ignoring his father's wish that he become a doctor. He soon arrived in France, with a mere $50 in his pocket. In Paris, Jodorowsky became a house painter, wrote mime routines for the legendary mime Marcel Marceau, and directed musicals, namely for French cabaret singer and entertainer Maurice Chevalier. Jodorowsky also grew close to members of the Surrealist theater movement, before distancing himself from them.

In 1962, Jodorowsky, along with Roland Topor and Fernando Arrabal, founded the Panic Movement, mocking the rigid approach of the Surrealists. They put on numerous subversive performances, which fell somewhere between comedy, athletic feats, and pornography. "We didn't do much in particular, except have a good laugh together," summarized Jodorowsky.

In 1965, at Marcel Marceau's request, Alexandro rejoined the theater troupe heading for Mexico for the start of a South American tour. He would remain there for 10 years, founding the avant-garde theatre of Mexico, adapting one of Fernando Arrabal's plays, *Fando y Lis*, and launching his filmmaking career with two films that would soon become cult classics: *El Topo* (1970) and *Holy Mountain* (1973). Jodorowsky would also go on to direct *Tusk* (1980), *Santa Sangre* (1989), and *The Rainbow Thief* (1990).

It was, paradoxically, a resounding cinematic failure that would cause him to shift his focus to writing graphic novels, a medium he had briefly explored writing for a local comic book and illustrating a series called *Fábulas Pánicas* for a weekly magazine in Mexico. In 1975, Jodorowsky met the man who would later become another of the medium's most formidable figures, Jean "Mœbius" Giraud, who had just founded, along with his colleagues from *Pilote* magazine, the comics anthology *Métal Hurlant* (which would go on to inspire numerous foreign versions, including *Heavy Metal* magazine in the U.S.), and the publishing house Les Humanoïdes Associés (of which Humanoids was later created as its American counterpart). Jodorowsky dragged Mœbius into his newest project: a pharaonic, off-the-wall film adaptation of *Dune*, Frank Herbert's seminal science fiction novel. The project anticipated the epic sci-fi sagas that were to dominate the big screen from the 1970s onwards. But production on the very ambitious project was aborted and Jodorowsky and Mœbius redirected their energy and imagination to Humanoids, first publishing *The Eyes of the Cat*, an illustrated fable, before jumping into what would become *The Incal*. With *The Black Incal* (1981), Jodorowsky made his sensational entrance into the world of European graphic novels, where he would become one of the most original, and prolific, writers. Graphic novels allowed him to bring to life his most outlandish ideas without the limitations of the film medium.

And his imagination is indeed limitless; for more than 30 years, Jodorowsky has written stories for his main publisher, Humanoids, across many genres and for a wide variety of artists, from Arno (*Alef-Thau*), Georges Bess (*The White Lama*, *Anibal 5*, and *Son of the Gun*), Zoran Janjetov (*Before the Incal* and *The Technopriests*—with Fred Beltran), Juan

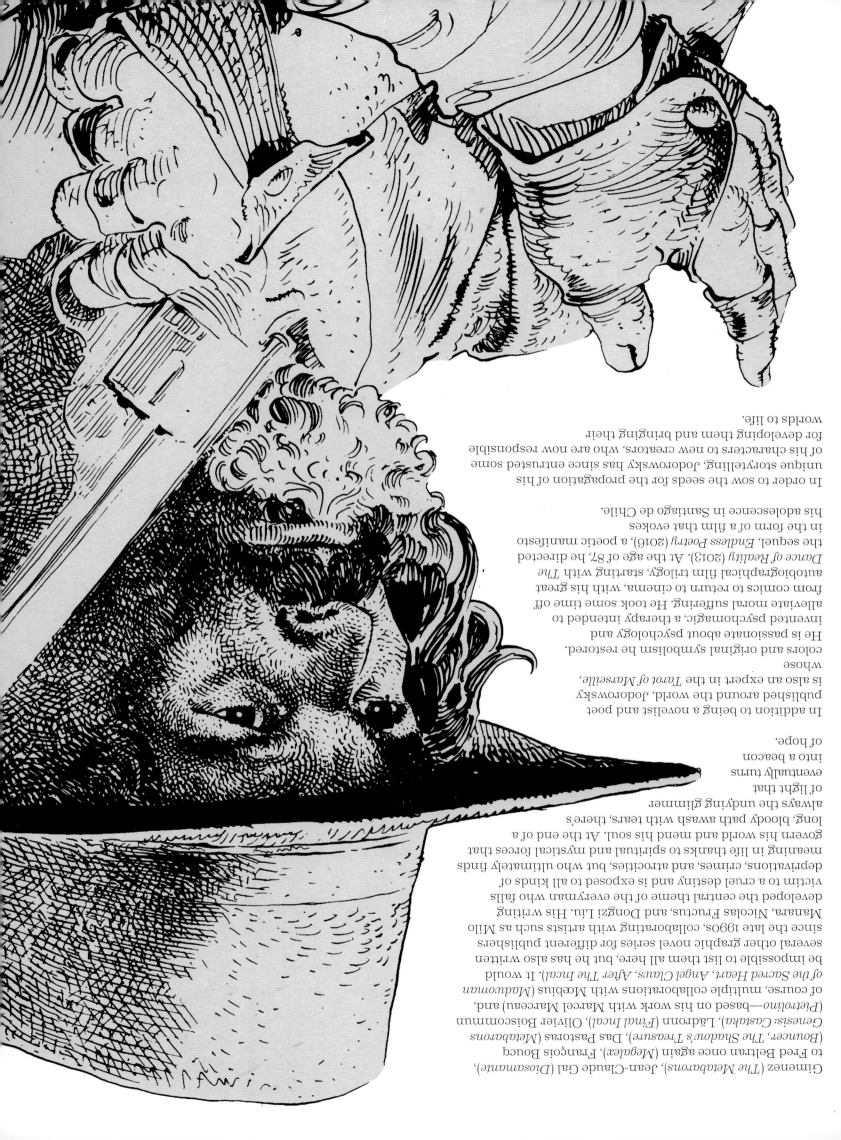

Giménez (*The Metabarons*), Jean-Claude Gal (*Diosamante*), to Fred Beltran once again (*Megalex*), François Boucq (*Bouncer, The Shadow's Treasure*), Das Pastoras (*Metabarons Genesis: Castaka*), Ladrönn (*Final Incal*), Olivier Boiscommun (*Pietrolino*—based on his work with Marcel Marceau) and, of course, multiple collaborations with Moebius (*Madwoman of the Sacred Heart, Angel Claus, After The Incal*). It would be impossible to list them all here, but he has also written several other graphic novel series for different publishers since the late 1990s, collaborating with artists such as Milo Manara, Nicolas Fructus, and Dongzi Liu. His writing developed the central theme of the everyman who falls victim to a cruel destiny and is exposed to all kinds of deprivations, crimes, and atrocities, but who ultimately finds meaning in life thanks to spiritual and mystical forces that govern his world and mend his soul. At the end of a long, bloody path awash with tears, there's always the undying glimmer of light that eventually turns into a beacon of hope.

In addition to being a novelist and poet published around the world, Jodorowsky is also an expert in the *Tarot of Marseille*, whose colors and original symbolism he restored. He is passionate about psychology and invented psychomagic, a therapy intended to alleviate moral suffering. He took some time off from comics to return to cinema, with his great autobiographical film trilogy starting with *The Dance of Reality* (2013). At the age of 87, he directed the sequel, *Endless Poetry* (2016), a poetic manifesto in the form of a film that evokes his adolescence in Santiago de Chile.

In order to sow the seeds for the propagation of his unique storytelling, Jodorowsky has since entrusted some of his characters to new creators, who are now responsible for developing them and bringing their worlds to life.

Mœbius

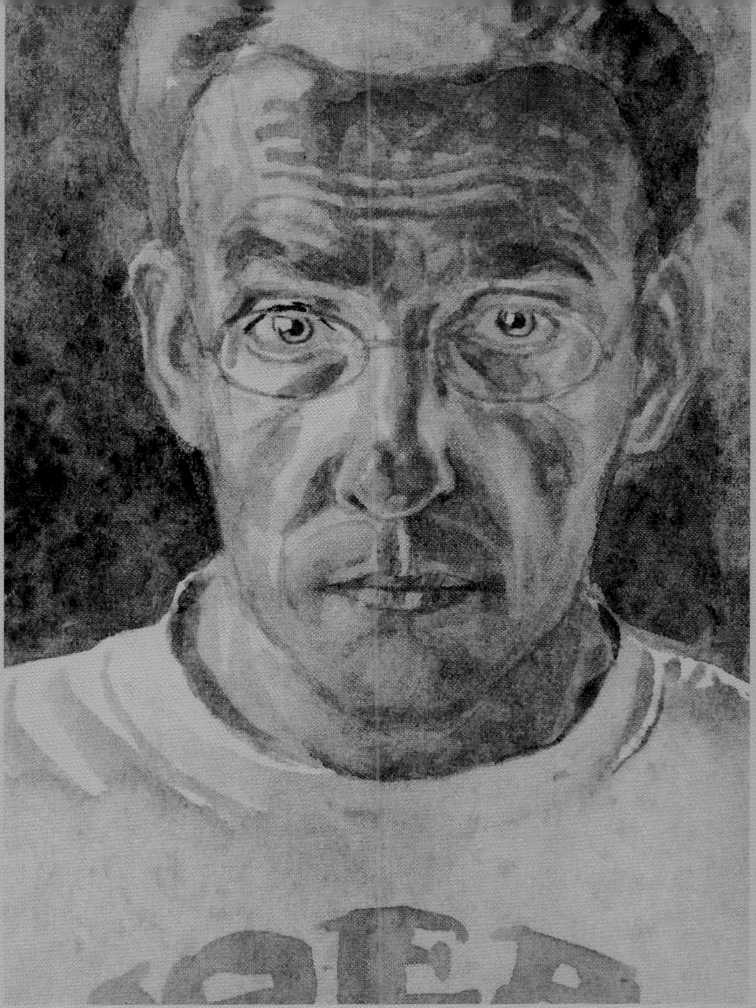

Jean Giraud (aka Mœbius) was born on May 8, 1938 in the Paris suburb of Nogent-sur-Marne. His parents divorced when he was only three years old, and he was raised by his grandparents for the first few years of his life. It was nevertheless thanks to his father that, at the age of 15, he discovered sci-fi literature, through the magazine *Fiction*. After studying Applied Arts for two years, he began his career as a professional cartoonist and worked on Catholic newspapers such as *Cœurs Vaillants*.

In 1955, he went to live with his mother in Mexico, where he discovered marijuana, jazz (be-bop in particular), and sex. The experience of the desert proved to be life-changing and would go on to leave notable impressions throughout his later work. Back in France, he did his military service in Germany and Algeria, first as a switchboard operator, then as the supervisor of an ammunitions depot. He was never called to fight and spent all his free time drawing.

After the army, he contacted Joseph Gillain, aka Jijé, one of the star artists at famed weekly Franco-Belgian comics anthology *Spirou* and the illustrator of a number of series, including *Spirou et Fantasio* and the western *Jerry Spring*. Jean Giraud became Jijé's protégé and worked with him on a *Jerry Spring* book, *La Route de Coronado*. On his mentor's recommendation, Giraud met Jean-Michel Charlier, writer and co-editor-in-chief of *Pilote*, another weekly comics magazine. In October 1963, the two men launched the adventures of the cowboy Mike Steve Blueberry in *Pilote*. Initially called *Fort Navajo*, after the fort where the character is based, the series went on to revolutionize the western comics genre.

Under the influence of Giraud, a huge fan of film in general and westerns in particular, *Blueberry* incorporated stylistic elements from the films of John Ford, Sam Peckinpah, and Sergio Leone. As such, the series features a dramatic intensity that far exceeds the usually strict framework of traditional comic books.

The "Gir" signature, which he used for *Blueberry*, embodied his classical or neo-classical style. But, gradually, Jean Giraud developed another creative side to his artistic personality. Under the pseudonym Mœbius, inspired by the works of mathematician Möbius and his "Möbius strip," he began creating darkly humorous drawings for the satirical weekly *Hara-Kiri* in 1963.

The Mœbius *nom de plume* would soon take on a whole new dimension. After a second visit to Mexico, this time marked by his introduction to hallucinogenic mushrooms and the challenging experience of solitude, Mœbius drew cover art for science fiction novels published by Opta, as part of their Club du Livre d'Anticipation imprint, as well as for *Fiction* and *Galaxy* magazines. Then he created several stories for *Pilote* that featured a different tone, imbued with newfound narrative and illustrative freedom, such as *La Déviation* (1973), which went on to influence countless comic book artists.

The launch of *L'Écho des Savanes* magazine, founded in 1972 by Nikita Mandryka, Claire Bretécher, and Marcel Gotlib, and the French "adult" comics movement influenced by the likeminded American underground one, were born out of a desire of the creators to free themselves from censorship and the limitations imposed on books for young people. In 1974, Mœbius released *Le Bandard Fou* (aka *The Horny Goof*). The following year, he teamed up with Jean-Pierre Dionnet, Philippe Druillet, and Bernard Farkas to launch a science fiction quarterly called *Métal Hurlant* and a publishing house, Les Humanoïdes Associés. In the pages of this new outlet, Mœbius went on to publish several masterpieces, including *Arzach* (1976) and *Le Garage Hermétique* aka *The Airtight Garage* (1978). That same year he met Alejandro Jodorowsky and worked with him on the *Dune* film project. After that, Mœbius was involved in the development of several feature and animated films, such as Ridley Scott's *Alien*, René Laloux's *Les Maîtres du Temps* (*The Masters of Time*), Steven Lisberger's *Tron*, and an adaptation of *Little Nemo: Adventures in Slumberland*, based on the comic strip by Winsor McCay.

Mœbius lived in Los Angeles for a few years in the '80s. During his American sojourn, he did some work for Marvel and drew *The Silver Surfer*, written by Stan Lee, the famed creator of *The Fantastic Four* and *Spider-Man*, among many others. After Jean-Michel Charlier passed away in 1989, Mœbius returned to *Blueberry* and took over both the writing and artistic chores.

A prolific writer and illustrator, Jean Giraud/Mœbius constantly reinvented himself and created countless comics, both on his own, and with many of the industry's top creators, from *Jim Cutlass* (with Charlier) to *Icaro* (with Jiro Taniguchi). There have been several solo exhibitions of his work, noteably at the Angoulême Comic Book Museum in 2000 and the *Transe Forme* show at the Fondation Cartier in Paris in 2011. He has been celebrated with a multitude of awards and honors, from the Science Fiction Hall of Fame to the Eisner Awards, as well as a lifetime achievement award from the famed Angoulême International Comics Festival.

Jean Giraud passed away in Montrouge, France, on March 10, 2012.

Zoran Janjetov

Zoran Janjetov was born on June 23, 1961 in Subotica, Serbia. Passionate about painting and comic books, and a huge fan of Mœbius, Frank Hampson (*Dan Dare*), and Carl Barks (the creator of *Uncle Scrooge*), he studied at the Academy of Arts in Novi Sad. He started doing a variety of illustration work in 1979, from album and book covers to television credits, and his art was soon published in student magazines. In 1982, he created the character Bernard Panasonik, the hero of a science fiction parody strip. In 1986, after having met Jodorowsky and the Humanoids team, and while preparing the first book in the *Before The Incal* series, he was entrusted with coloring volumes 5 and 6 of *The Incal*. Mœbius rejected Janjetov's first attempts, but agreed to show him the proper way: the result was a 45-minute lesson that Janjetov compares to a young jazz musician receiving direct advice from Miles Davis. When asked what he feels he owes Mœbius, he replies: "Everything!"

"A whole generation of cartoonists used Jean Giraud's work as inspiration for their starting point; he had the same kind of impact on the medium that Milton Caniff or Hergé did. But whereas most cartoonists start copying their influences and then evolve their own style, I endeavored to be more Mœbius than Mœbius himself. I never tried to hide it: I've put all my energy into remaining a Mœboid!"

In 1997, after completing the sixth and final installment of *Before The Incal*, Janjetov devoted himself to *The Technopriests*, a series also written by Jodorowsky and colored by Fred Beltran. In 2010, the first book in a new series by Jodorowsky and Janjetov came out, titled *Ogregod*. And in 2015, Janjetov teamed up with writers Leo and Rodolphe to create the first episode of a space opera, *Centaurus*, for French publisher Delcourt.

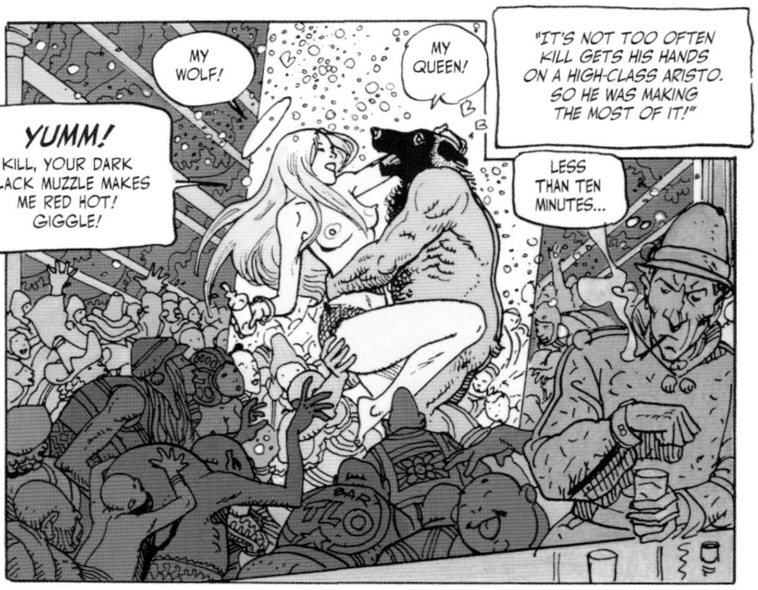
"IT'S NOT TOO OFTEN KILL GETS HIS HANDS ON A HIGH-CLASS ARISTO. SO HE WAS MAKING THE MOST OF IT!"
MY WOLF!
MY QUEEN!
YUMM! KILL, YOUR DARK BLACK MUZZLE MAKES ME RED HOT! GIGGLE!
LESS THAN TEN MINUTES...

Art by Mœbius from *The Incal*.

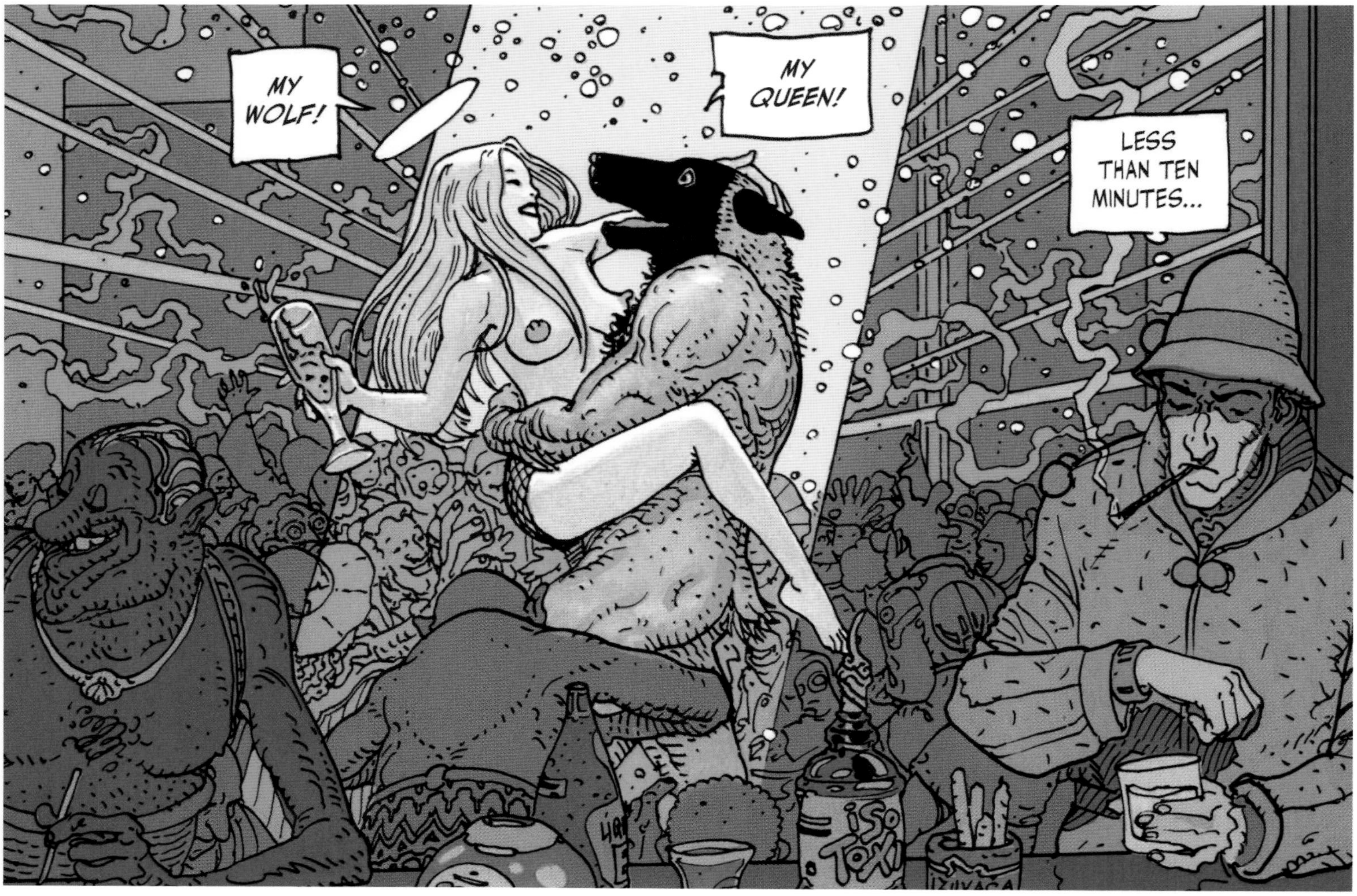
MY WOLF!
MY QUEEN!
LESS THAN TEN MINUTES...

Art by Janjetov from *Before The Incal*.

Yves Chaland

Yves Chaland provided the coloring for *The Black Incal*, the first book in the *Incal* saga. His wife, Isabelle Beaumenay-Joannet, colored the next three installments, then Zoran Janjetov took over, under the supervision of Mœbius, on the two parts of *The Fifth Essence*. Or at least that's what has always been listed in the credits of the various books in the series. The reality is actually somewhat different...

One day, while Mœbius was working on *The Black Incal,* he stopped by the offices of *Métal Hurlant*, the magazine in which John Difool's adventures were first serialized. There, he ran into Yves Chaland, a young, gifted artist and the future co-creator of the Atomic style of drawing (a stylish remake of the Marcinelle School in Franco-Belgian comics). Jean-Pierre Dionnet, then editor-in-chief of the publication, had initially recruited Chaland to do mockups. When Mœbius told him he was looking for a colorist for *The Incal,* Chaland said he was interested. When he got home, he spent an hour on the first page...before turning to his wife and asking her to take over.

The idea of coloring another creator's series didn't appeal to Chaland. Later, he would go on to illustrate realistic parody covers for *Métal Aventure*, another magazine launched by Humanoids, but at the time, he was more interested in focusing on his own stories. And because he worked long days at the *Métal Hurlant* offices and frequently brought work home with him, it was Isabelle, who was then studying at the Beaux-Arts, who ended up doing much of the coloring. But Chaland waited until preparations for *The Luminous Incal,* the second book in the series, were underway to "officially" pass the job on to his wife. Isabelle did the work following Mœbius's guidelines, but these turned out to be rather vague, although quite insightful. Isabelle Beaumenay-Joannet explains: "Mœbius didn't talk to me about colors, he described the story in terms of mood, light, or atmosphere, the same way a filmmaker would. My job was to stick to that mindset and to connect with his vision of other worlds. He once spoke to me of 'vaginal ambiances...' The timeframes were very short, I had 10 days to color a chapter of eight or 10 pages, which wasn't very long, then I would take the pages to Editorial. If Mœbius was in the office, he would look them over and give his opinion. Otherwise, he wouldn't see them until the magazine came out. He had signed off on the first book. After that, it was 'whatever will be, will be!'"

Yves Chaland went on to create such iconic humor series as *Bob Fish* and *Young Albert,* among many others, before tragically passing away in a car accident at the young age of 33. His widow Isabelle continues to carry the torch of their shared legacy through events such as Les Rencontres Chaland, a yearly *bande dessinée* festival held in Nérac, in south-western France.

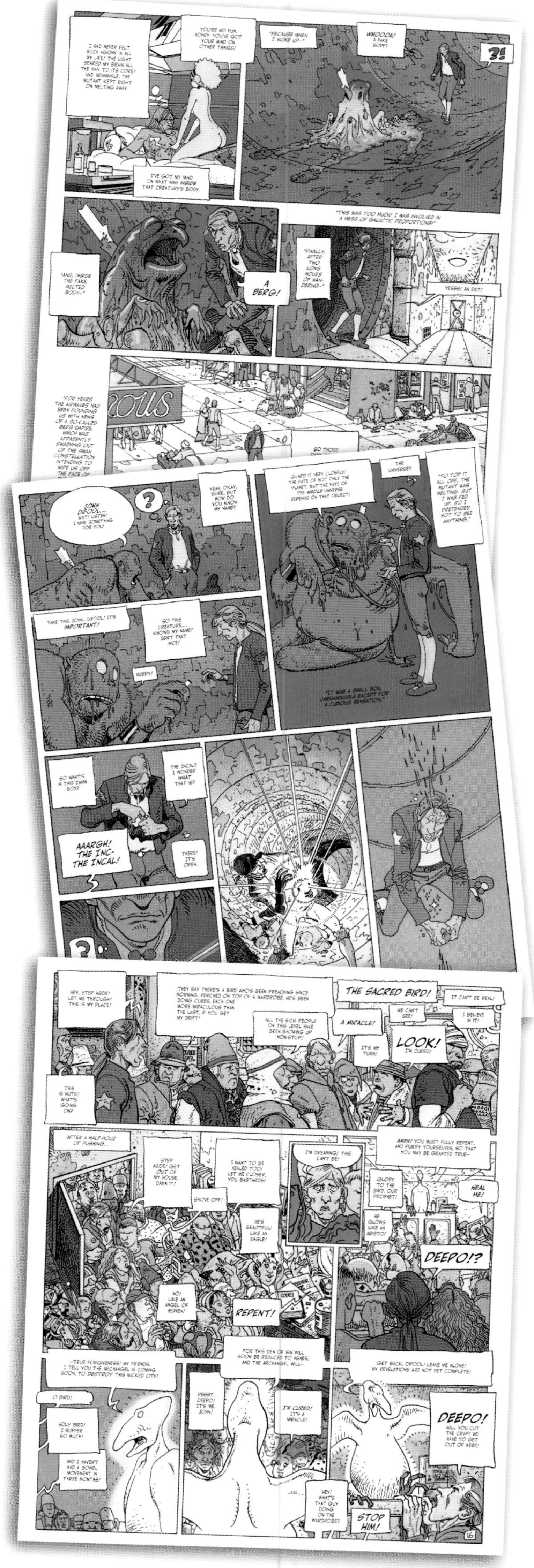

WHOOOA! A FAKE BODY?
I'VE GOT MY MIND ON WHAT WAS INSIDE THAT CREATURE'S BODY.
"THIS WAS TOO MUCH! I WAS INVOLVED IN A MESS OF GALACTIC PROPORTIONS!"
"AND, INSIDE THE FAKE, MELTED BODY..."
A BERG!
YESSS! AN EXIT!
JOHN DIFOOL... WAIT! LISTEN! I HAVE SOMETHING FOR YOU!
YEAH, OKAY, SURE, BUT HOW DO YOU KNOW MY NAME?
THE UNIVERSE?
TAKE THIS, JOHN DIFOOL! IT'S IMPORTANT!
HURRY!
SO WHAT'S IN THIS DAMN BOX?
AAARGH! THE INC- THE INCAL!
THERE! IT'S OPEN.
THE SACRED BIRD!
IT CAN'T BE REAL!
A MIRACLE!
WE CAN'T SEE!
I BELIEVE IN IT!
LOOK! I'M CURED!
IT'S MY TURN!
THIS IS NUTS! WHAT'S GOING ON?
I'M DREAMING! THIS CAN'T BE!
SHOVE OFF!
HEAL ME!
DEEPO!?
REPENT!
O BIRD!
I'M CURED! IT'S A MIRACLE!
DEEPO! WILL YOU CUT THE CRAP! WE HAVE TO GET OUT OF HERE!
STOP HIM!

Ladrönn

José Omar Ladron, aka Ladrönn, was born in 1967 in Minatitlán, in the state of Veracruz, Mexico. A comic book artist and painter, he began working on various mainstream titles for both Marvel and DC Comics in 1996. In 2000, he began illustrating the series *Inhumans* based on a script by Carlos Pacheco. Two years later, fed up with the deadlines imposed by the big publishing houses, he joined the team at Active Image to illustrate *Hip Flask*. The hippo/human hybrid was initially conceived by Richard Starkings as an advertising mascot for his online font-selling website, before being converted into a comic book character written by Starkings and Joe Casey. Winner of the 2006 Eisner Award for Best Painter or Multimedia Artist for *Hip Flask*, Ladrönn worked on several other series, including *Spider-Boy Team-Up*, *Cable*, and *Legends of the DC Universe*. Ladrönn first crossed paths with Alejandro Jodorowsky at the 1997 San Diego Comic Con, which the writer was attending along with Mœbius. Ladrönn took the opportunity to show them his portfolio. The next time they met was a few years later at the Humanoids office in Los Angeles, where the publisher was preparing to launch an American version of the *Métal Hurlant* magazine. Ladrönn recalls: "Alejandro asked me a lot of questions. He wanted to get a good sense of my personality, then he told me that he had a story idea to offer me. A month later, I received the script for *Tears of Gold*." Humanoids published the story in a 2006 anthology titled *Alejandro Jodorowsky's Screaming Planet*, a collection of short stories the writer created for *Métal Hurlant*.

But long before they met, Jodorowsky was already part of Ladrönn's mental landscape. The fact that they're both originally from Latin America and share a language and culture has helped them build a close working relationship. "I always say it's very easy for me to work with Alejandro," confirms the illustrator of *Final Incal*. "Not only because we speak the same language, Spanish, but because we laugh at the same subjects and jokes. We discuss food, cinema, actors, and even politics, sometimes. For us Mexicans, Alejandro is part of our soul. He lived in Mexico for a long time, he has been very involved in the culture of this country, he has worked here and made films here. The people of my country adore him, and his theatrical productions have become the stuff of legend. While he lived here, he helped open a window that allowed us to explore our creativity. I'm sure many Mexican artists continue to draw inspiration from his legacy."

And if he goes back even farther in time, to a period when he only knew of Alejandro Jodorowsky through his work and before he'd even thought of becoming a comic book artist, Ladrönn specifically remembers the psychological jolt he experienced when he read *The Incal* as a young man. "To me, *The Incal* is a magical book! When I read it for the first time, I was shaken: there was too much visual information for me! I was seduced by both the drawing and the story. It is pure, boundless creativity. Alejandro has written a story that goes beyond our understanding. Few works make as strong an impact as *The Incal*. I was completely blown away by that absolutely crazy universe of his!"

The Incal shook things up for Ladrönn in more than one way: reading the series was what inspired him to make his career choice. At the time, Ladrönn had no plans to become a comic book artist and was leaning more toward painting. Once of his major influences was Swiss artist and illustrator H.R. Giger, who had worked on the *Dune* project with Jodorowsky and designed the monster and spaceship in Ridley Scott's *Alien*. "I loved comics but I was very happy as a painter. I wanted to become a fine artist, like Giger. But after reading *The Incal*, I thought to myself, 'If I ever become a comic book artist, that's the direction I would want to take.'"

Given that information, one can just imagine how he must have reacted when asked to illustrate *Final Incal*, even though he had already drawn the covers for the serialized U.S. edition of *Before The Incal*. "It was totally unexpected," says Ladrönn. "Alejandro called to tell me he wanted me to draw *Final Incal* and that Mœbius, after reading *Tears of Gold*, was on board with the decision as well. I was thrilled: the Master had given me his blessing to carry on his work!" But to succeed Mœbius...? Wasn't that a stressful and incredibly intimidating challenge for a comic book artist who had been weaned on the work of the man behind *The Airtight Garage* and *Arzach*? "Mœbius is one of the greatest artists I've ever met in my life. His amazing work has always been a source of inspiration for me. It is impossible to reach the degree of beauty that emanates from his work. Before I started working on the project, I talked it over with Alejandro. He told me that *Final Incal* was a new story, that it wasn't a dream anymore, but reality. Right then, I knew what I was going to do with it. But I needed to forget Mœbius to be able to concentrate on my own work. Alejandro performed a psycho-magic intervention that consisted of burning all the shadows of Mœbius present in my subconscious, in order to free my mind." All that was left to do was for Ladrönn to achieve his goal of making *Final Incal* a story that was "huge and frightening but with a touch of reality. At the same time, I also wanted to make a book that was epic."

Now free from the mental barriers that could have prevented him from giving the book his best shot, Ladrönn embarked on the *Final Incal* odyssey. He developed an effective working method with Jodorowsky, using videochat to bridge the long distance gap between America, where the artist is based, and France, where the writer resides. "This tool gives us the ability to react in real time and make the necessary adjustments," Ladrönn explains. Jodorowsky—who'd long since given up dictating his stories, as he had done with Mœbius when they originally developed *The Incal*—would send Ladrönn the text written in screenplay format. "I'm the one who does the layout," the illustrator adds. "It allows me to control the rhythm of the story. Once I receive the text from Alejandro, I sketch the whole book and I put in the balloons with the text in them. This phase takes time, but it allows me to get an overall vision of the book and make the necessary tweaks. I then rely on these thumbnails to draw all the actual pages. All the drawing and coloring is then done digitally." Even though he loves all the characters in *The Incal* universe (or "Jodoverse" as it has come to be known), Ladrönn once confessed he had weak spot for Deepo, who he calls a "visual pressure valve... He can look realistic or like a cartoon character, he can alternate between serious and funny, and he's always easy to draw."

When asked about Alejandro Jodorowsky's contribution to the world of comics, Ladrönn responds with one word: "Ideas." According to him, the comic book industry is looking for artists and writers capable of mass producing, but that's never really appealed to Jodorowsky. "He's always tried to find new ways to push the boundaries of human consciousness and that's what makes him different," the Mexican illustrator reflects. "I think what's most important, in his eyes, is the beauty of an idea. Alejandro is a poet, he seeks to offer the reader different perspectives and visions of reality through his stories. He feeds on his experiences and his very special way of coping with life. He never rests, he works every day because he knows that's the only way to achieve great things and to transcend existence. That's the reason the 'Jodoverse' is so unique: it is part of his soul. His characters and the themes of his stories are small conceptual seeds. If you nourish them and let them grow in your mind, they will become flowers one day, and their petals will be the canvas on which you can release your ideas."

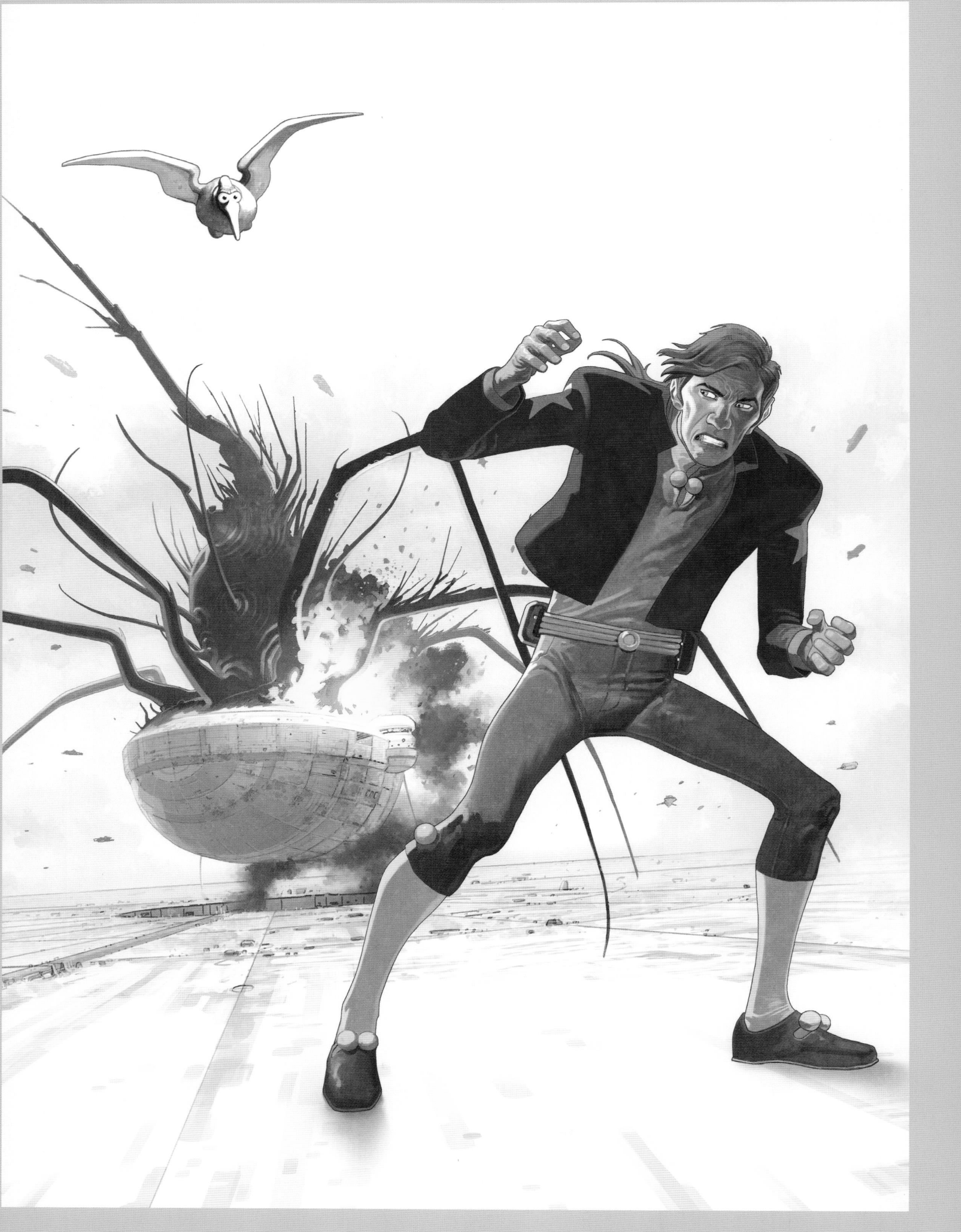

Alejandro Jodorowsky's Dune

For Alejandro Jodorowsky, the inspiration for the *Incal* series can be found, in part, in his screen adaptation of the novel *Dune*, which never came to fruition. "Everything I had come up with for the *Dune* screenplay, I transferred to *The Incal*."

I DIDN'T WANT TO REMAIN FAITHFUL TO THE BOOK

In his own words: "I didn't want to remain faithful to the book, I wanted to reinvent it. For me, *Dune* doesn't belong to Herbert, just as *Don Quixote* didn't belong to Cervantes. There is one artist, only one among millions of other artists who, once in his lifetime, by a kind of divine grace, receives an immortal theme, a MYTH. I say 'receives' and not 'creates' because works of art are received in a state of mediumship directly from the collective unconscious. The work is beyond the artist and, in a way, it kills him. Because humanity, in receiving the impact of the myth, has a profound need to erase the individual who received it and transmitted it: his individual personality is an obstacle, a stain on the purity of the message, which, basically, demands to be anonymous. We don't know who created the Notre Dame Cathedral, or the Aztec solar calendar, or the Tarot of Marseilles, or the legend of Don Juan, etc.

"We can sense that Cervantes gave us HIS—naturally incomplete—vision of *Don Quixote* and that WE carry the total character in our soul. Christ does not belong to Mark, Luke, Matthew, or even John... After all, there are many other so-called apocryphal gospels, and there are as many lives of Christ as there are believers. We each have our own story of *Dune*, our own Jessica, our own Paul. I felt fervid admiration for Herbert and at the same time, I felt conflicted (I think the same thing happened to him). He was getting in my way... I didn't want him as a technical advisor and I did everything to keep him away from the project. I had received a version of *Dune* and I wanted to convey it: the myth had to abandon the literary form and become image."

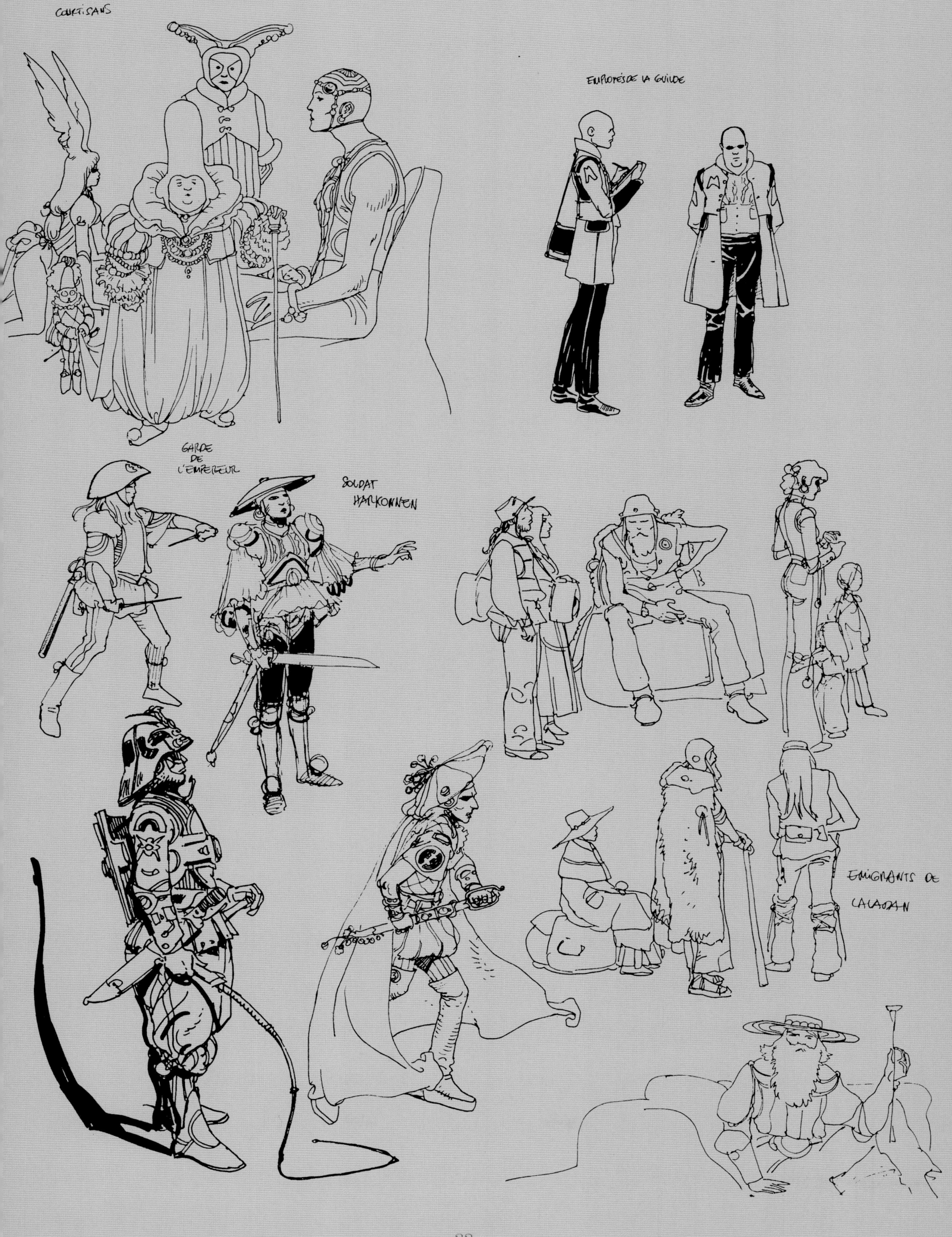
COURTISANS
EMPLOYÉS DE LA GUILDE
GARDE DE L'EMPEREUR
SOLDAT HARKONNEN
EMIGRANTS DE CALADAN

MY VERSION OF *DUNE*

"In my version of *Dune*, the Emperor of the Galaxy is mad. He lives on an artificial planet made of gold, in a palace made of gold, and according to the non-laws of non-logic. He lives in symbiosis with a robot that looks exactly like him. The resemblance is so perfect that citizens never know if they're in the presence of the man or the machine.

"In my version, the Spice is a blue, spongy drug filled with animal-vegetable life endowed with a consciousness of the highest order. This consciousness is constantly taking on all sorts of forms, constantly moving. The Spice constantly reproduces the creation of countless universes.

"Baron Harkonnen is a huge man who weighs over 600 pounds. He's so fat and heavy that in order to walk, he has to use antigravity pouches attached to his extremities. His lust for greatness knows no limits: he lives in a palace built as a portrait of himself. This enormous sculpture rises up from the ground of a miserable, swampy planet... To enter the palace, you have to wait for the colossus to open its mouth and stick out its metal tongue (aka the landing strip).

"At the end of the film, the wife of Count Fenring lunges toward Paul, who's already turned into a Fremen, and slits his throat. As he's dying, Paul says: 'Too late, it's impossible to kill me...because...' 'Because (Jessica continues, speaking in Paul's voice), to kill the Kwisatz Haderach, you would have to kill me too.' And every Fremen, every Atreides now speaks in Paul's voice: 'I am the collective man. The one who shows the way.'

"To conceive the final sequence of the transmutation of matter, I was lucky to come into contact with real alchemists... These mysterious beings (one of them seemed to be over 100 years old, yet he moved with the energy of a young adolescent despite his great age) assisted me because *Dune* could be like a philosopher's stone, the stone that changes all other metals into gold... For that sequence, they described what actually happens when they manage to transform matter in those alchemical furnaces. And for the 'guerilla warfare' that Paul and the Fremen wage against the imperial army, I was lucky to be in touch with a guerrilla expert in South America. He had fought in Bolivia, Chile, Peru, and Central America. His invaluable information helped lend a martial reality to the screenplay.

"When Jessica becomes Supreme Mother of the Fremen and has to go through initiation ceremonies, learn the medicine of the sorcerers, and contact other dimensions of reality, I was already familiar with the magic medicine of the gypsies through the late Paul Derion, with the ceremonial hallucinogenic mushrooms, and with the miraculous interventions of Pachita the witch, a being who had far more powers than the so-called Filipino psychic surgeons."

I WANTED AN ILLUSTRATOR GIFTED WITH GENIUS AND SPEED

"The divinity was kind enough to once tell me in a lucid dream: 'Your next film must be *Dune*.' I hadn't even read the novel. I got up at six in the morning and, like an alcoholic waiting for the bar to open, I waited for the bookstore to open so I could buy the book. I read it in one sitting, without stopping to eat or drink. I finished reading it at the stroke of midnight that same night. At one minute past midnight, I called Michel Seydoux in Paris (I was in New York). He would be the first of the 'seven samurai' I was going to need for this enormous project. Michel was a young man of 26 with no filmmaking experience, but his company, Caméra One, had bought the rights to my latest film, *The Holy Mountain*, and had done a great job distributing it. He had once told me that he would love to produce a film with me. I didn't know much about him, but, guided by an intuition, which, in hindsight, I find astonishing, I saw in him the greatest producer of our time. Why? It's a total mystery... But my intuition was right. When I told him I wanted him to buy the rights to *Dune* and that the film had to be international because the budget would go over the $10 million mark (an astounding sum for the time, as even Hollywood didn't believe in sci-fi films; *2001: A Space Odyssey* was an exception that would never be surpassed), he didn't flinch: 'Okay. Let's meet up in two days in L.A. to buy the rights.' He hadn't read the book... And I think he still hasn't, to this day, because he had a problem with Herbert's prose.

"We were able to buy the rights—rather easily, actually, because Hollywood didn't think the book could be adapted for the screen or that it had commercial potential. Michel Seydoux gave me *carte blanche* and huge financial support: I could assemble my team without worrying about money issues.

"I needed a very detailed screenplay, visual even. I wanted to make the film on paper before shooting it. Nowadays, all special effects movies are done like that, but at the time, nobody used this technique. I wanted a cartoonist who was a genius and who was fast, so he could act like a camera and at the same time provide me with a visual style. It was by chance that I found my next warrior: Jean Giraud, aka Mœbius (at the time, he had not yet made *The Airtight Garage*). I said to him: 'If you take this job, you have to leave everything else and fly to L.A. with me tomorrow to talk with Douglas Trumbull, the visual effects wiz behind *2001: Space Odyssey*'s special photographic effects. Mœbius asked me for a few hours to think about it.

"The next day, we left for the States. It would take too long to tell the whole story... Our collaboration, our encounters in America with strange visionaries, and our 7 a.m. conversations in the little coffee shop downstairs from our offices, which, by 'chance' was called The Universe. All in all, Mœbius did more than 3,000 drawings, all of them wonderful... The screenplay for *Dune*, thanks to his talent, is a masterpiece. You can see the characters come alive, you can follow the camera movements.

"You can also visualize the shooting sequences, the sets, the costumes, etc. All this with just a few strokes of the pencil, every single time. I would look over his shoulder and ask him for different POVs, different ways of putting the actors in the scene, etc. We were filming with pen and paper.

"For the third warrior, I needed an ingenious dreamer who could draw spaceships in a distinct way than those seen in American films. That's why I wrote to Chris Foss, an English illustrator who was doing cover art for sci-fi novels. Like Giraud, the thought of working in film had never occurred to him. He was thrilled, and he left London to come and work in Paris. The spacecrafts he designed for *Dune* left a singular mark on cinema. He managed to make semi-living machines that could transform themselves with the color of the stones of space.

He made 'parched battleships dying century after century in a desert of stars, waiting for the living body that will come and fill their empty reservoirs with the subtle secretions of its soul.'

"After that, I found H.R. Giger, a Swiss painter I had discovered when Dalí once showed me a catalog of his work. His decadent, sick, suicidal, fabulous art was just perfect for Planet Harkonnen. He came up with concepts for the castle and the planet that really captured metaphysical horror.

"For the special effects, thanks to the decision-making power Michel Seydoux gave me, I was able to turn down Douglas Trumbull. I couldn't abide his vanity, his head honcho attitude, and his exorbitant prices. Like a true American, he pretended to look down on the project and tried to make us feel insecure by making us wait, talking with us at the same time as he talked to 10 other people on the phone, and finally showing us magnificent machines he was trying to perfect. I got tired of the act, told him to go screw himself, and I went in search of an emerging talent. I was told that in L.A., that would be like looking for a needle in a haystack. But at a small, indie sci-fi film fest, I saw a film made on a shoestring budget that I thought was absolutely wonderful: *Dark Star*. I contacted the guy who had done the special effects: Dan O'Bannon. It was almost like partnering with a child raised by wolves. O'Bannon had a mindset that was completely outside conventional reality, and in my eyes, he was genius. He couldn't believe I would entrust him with a project as huge as *Dune*. But then

when his plane ticket arrived, he had no choice but to believe me. I wasn't wrong about him: Dan O'Bannon went on to write the screenplay for *Alien* and many other films that were huge hits."

WHAT ABOUT PINK FLOYD?

"Jean-Paul Gibon was head of production at Caméra One, and he was just as passionate about the project as we were. He and I went to England in search of our composer. One thing that was key to me: every planet had to have its own style of music. A band like Magma, for instance, would be great for the warrior rhythms of the Harkonnens, which would be able to crystallize the beauty of the sand planet, with its mystery and its relentless energy and the strange symphony made by the rings of the giant worms.

"Virgin Records met with us and offered us Gong, Mike Oldfield, and Tangerine Dream. That's when I said, 'What about Pink Floyd?' At that time, the band was so huge that nobody thought the idea was feasible. Luckily though, because of my film *El Topo*, the musicians knew who I was and they actually agreed to meet with us, at the Abbey Road Studios in London, where The Beatles recorded their biggest hits. Jean-Paul Gibon was very pleasantly surprised that they had said yes, but personally I had almost lost my individual consciousness by then. I was the instrument of a sacred, miraculous work, where everything was possible. *Dune* was not at my service, I was, like the other samurai I had found, at the service of the work.

"They were in the process of recording *Dark Side of the Moon*. When we arrived, what we saw was not a band of great musicians performing their masterpiece, but four young guys devouring their *steak-frites*. Jean-Paul and I had to stand there and wait for their voracious hunger to be satiated. On behalf of *Dune*, I was overcome with righteous anger and I stormed out of the room, slamming the door shut behind me. I wanted artists who knew how to respect a work of such tremendous importance to human consciousness. I don't think they were expecting that. David Gilmour was taken off guard and he ran after us apologizing, then invited us to listen to the latest mix of their album. We were in total ecstasy! After that, we attended their last public concert, where thousands of fanatics cheered them hysterically. They said they wanted to see *The Holy Mountain*. They saw it in Canada and decided to get involved with us by producing a double album they would call *Dune*. They came to Paris to discuss the finances, and after a very intense discussion, we reached an agreement. Pink Floyd would do almost all of the music in the film."

DALÍ CHARGES $100,000 AN HOUR!

"Now that we had the best music on our side, I started looking for actors. I had seen Charlotte Rampling in *Zardoz*. I wanted her for the role of Jessica. She turned down the part. In those days she was seemingly more interested in a love life than in art. David Carradine was interested in the role of Leto and traveled to Paris.

"But the actor I wanted most of all was Salvador Dalí, for the small part of the crazy Emperor. What a saga that turned out to be! Dalí very enthusiastically agreed to the idea of playing the Emperor of the Galaxy. He wanted to film in Cadaqués,

Catalonia and, for his throne, to use a toilet made of two intertwined dolphins. The tails would make up the base and the open mouths would be used to receive 'pee' and 'poo' separately. Dalí thought it was in dreadfully poor taste to mix 'pee' and 'poo.' We told him we would be needing him for seven days. Dalí replied that God created the universe in seven days and that he, Dalí, being no lesser than God, must charge a fortune: $100,000 an hour. And perhaps upon arriving on set, he would agree to shoot for more than one hour every day for the same price.

"The whole Dalí fiasco was going to set us back $700,000. We asked him to take one night to think about it and we took our leave. That night, I ripped out a page from a book on the Tarot; it had the drawing of a card on it, The Hanged Man. I wrote Dalí a letter saying that we didn't have the budget to pay him $700,000, and that for $150,000, I expected three days and not one hour and a half of shooting. I told him I also wanted to have a polyethylene replica of him made, to use as his double in the movie. Dalí was furious. He yelled 'You'll see! I'll go shoot in Paris, but the sets are going to cost you way more than Cadaqués and my museum as a set. Dalí charges $100,000 an hour one way or another!'

"Eventually he calmed down and bitterly agreed to the idea of being reproduced in plastic, provided the sculpture would be donated to his museum afterward. We decided to finalize the contract the next day. I talked it over with Jean-Paul Gibon and we came to the conclusion that it was impossible to bargain with Dalí. I thought about the dilemma at length and then made a final decision: I would cut Dalí's part down to one and a half page in the script. I would pay him his quote, his $100,000 an hour, but one hour was all I was hiring him for. I would film the rest with his robot double. Dalí would never consent to lowering his price. We went to see him. I handed him the little page and a half and Dalí accepted the proposal because he had saved face. This would make him the highest paid actor in the history of cinema, earning more than Greta Garbo. Dalí enthusiastically showed me his wooden bed with the dolphin sculpture. A worker was there, already making a cast of the dolphin to use for the toilet. For both Dalí and myself, scribbling a few words on the Hanged Man card and using it as a contract was enough. Dalí loved the aristocracy and, like any man of noble spirit, he was a man of his word."

DUNE CHANGED OUR LIVES

"Personally, I loved fighting for *Dune*. We won almost all the battles, but we ultimately lost the war. The project was sabotaged in Hollywood. The storyboard did the rounds at all the major studios and the overall feedback was that the message of the film wasn't 'Hollywood enough.' It was French after all, and not American. With that said, there was certainly some stealing of ideas. Later, when *Star Wars* came out, the look of the film bore a strange resemblance to our own visual style. When it came time to make *Alien*, they called on Mœbius, Foss, Giger, O'Bannon, et al. Despite them not wanting it, our project made the Americans realize that it was possible to make blockbuster sci-fi movies without having to adhere to the scientific rigor of *2001: A Space Odyssey*.

"All those involved in the rise and fall of the *Dune* project learned to fall down a thousand times with fierce obstinacy until they learned to stand upright. I remember my old dad, who, as he lay dying a happy man, said to me: 'Son, in life, I triumphed because I learned to fail.'"

AAHRHH!...
EN GARDE VIEILLE CASSEROLE!
DÉBUT D'ENREGISTREMENT! CKIIC!
FLUX VITAL NIVEAU A: 12 FLEX! NIVEAU B: 17 FLEX! NIVEAU C...
MÉTA BARON! FAIS TAIRE CETTE MAUDITE MÉCANIQUE!
CLICK
IL SUFFIT DE DEMANDER
APPROCHE QUE JE TE CABOSSE!
CLIIIIK!
CLICK

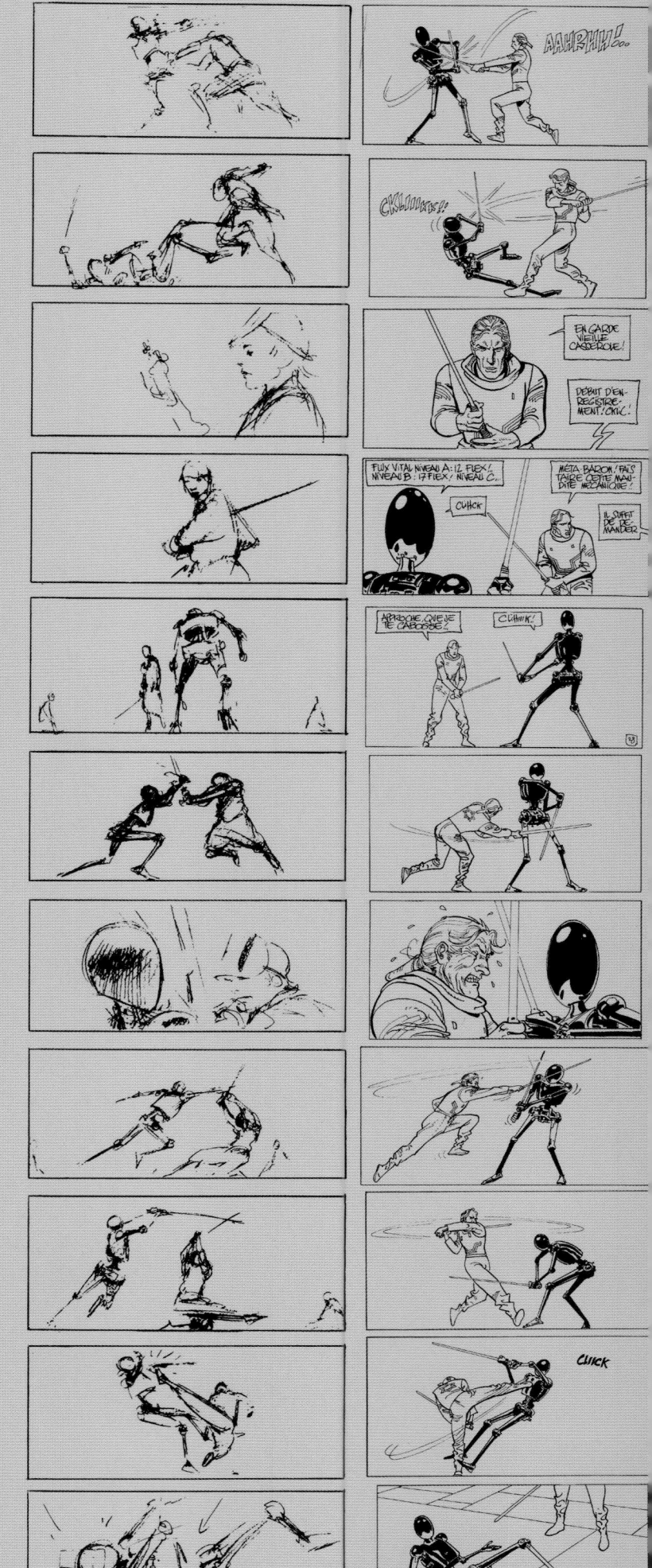

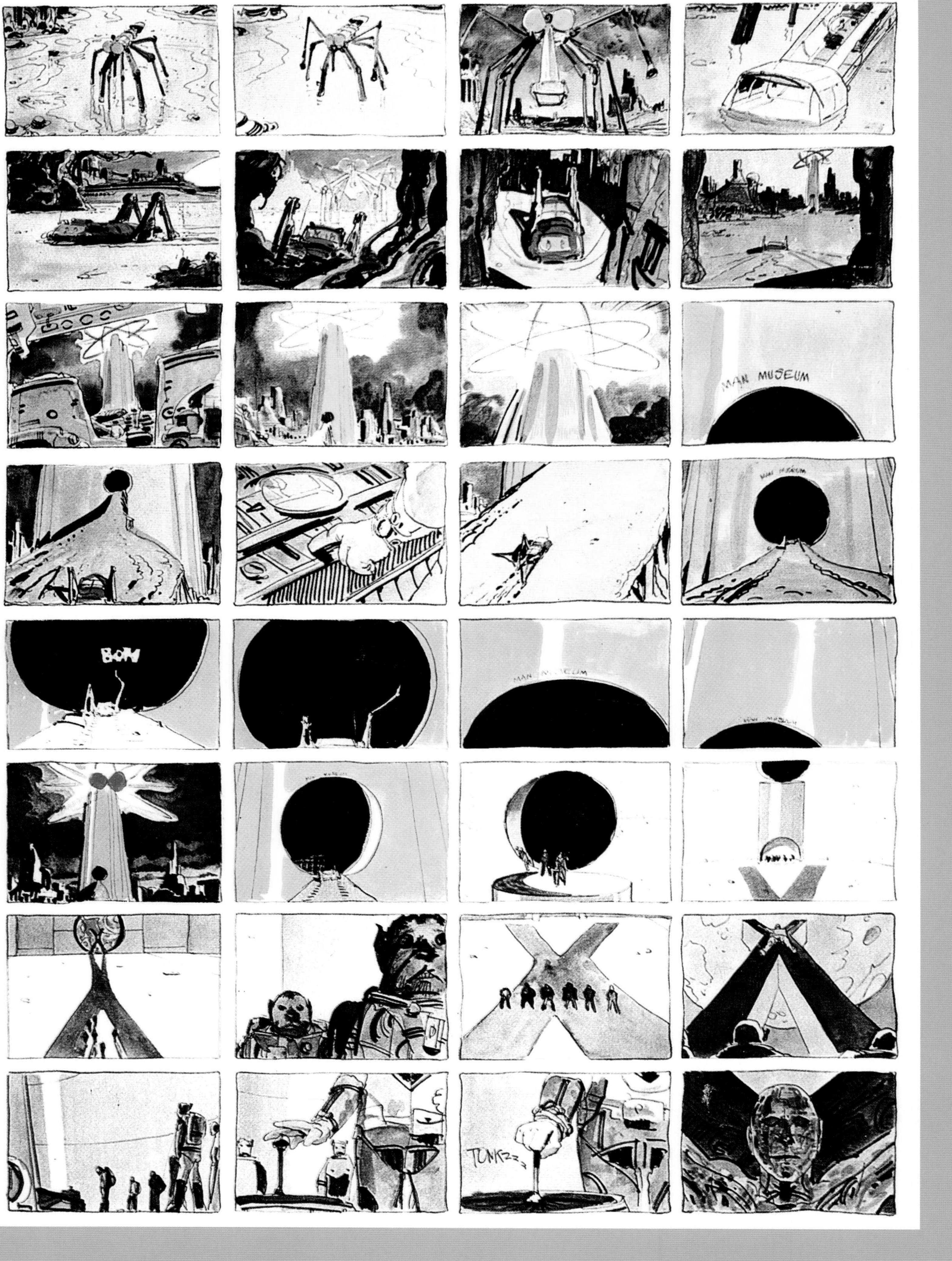
MAN MUSEUM
BOM
MAN MUSEUM
TUNKzzz

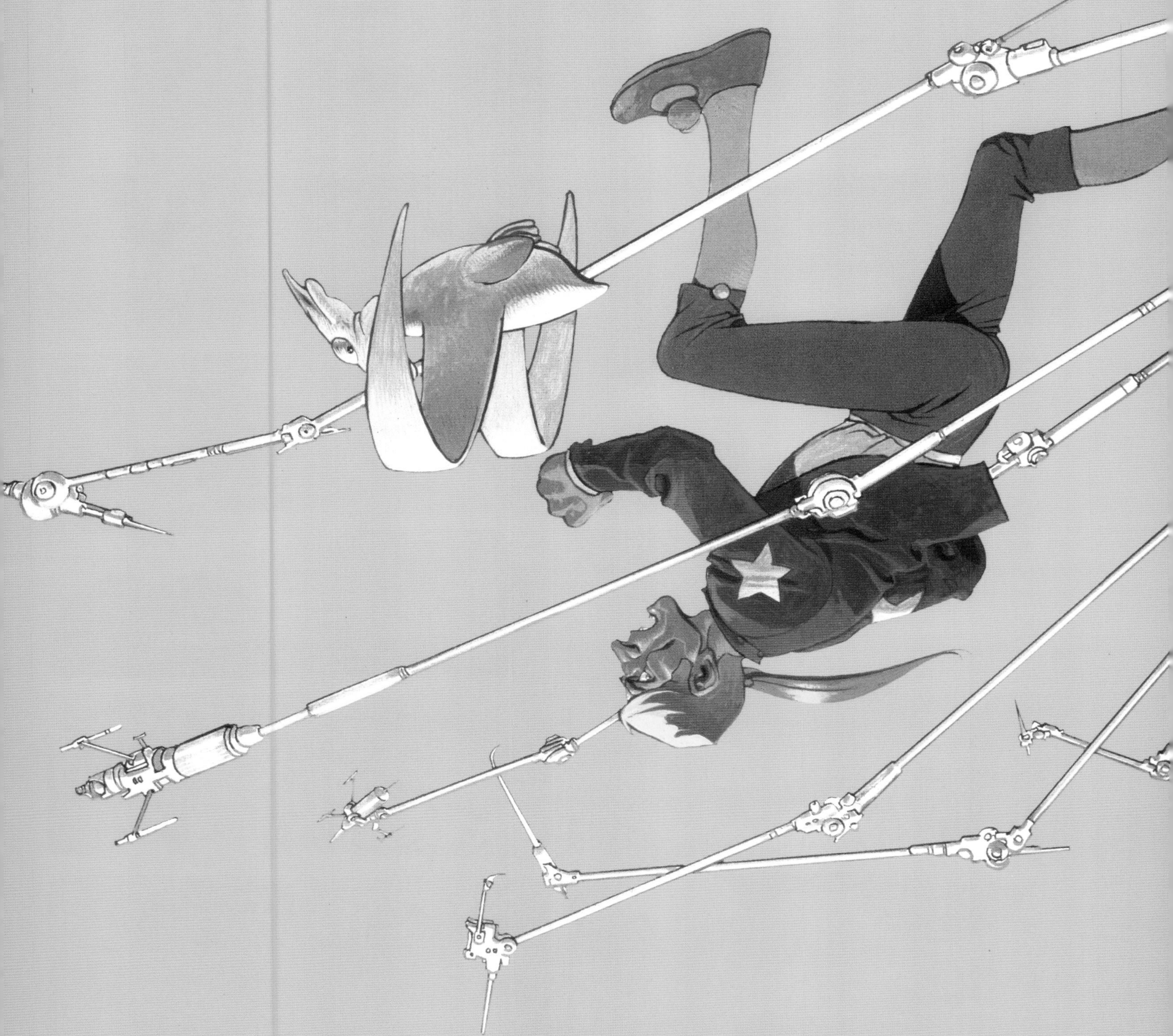

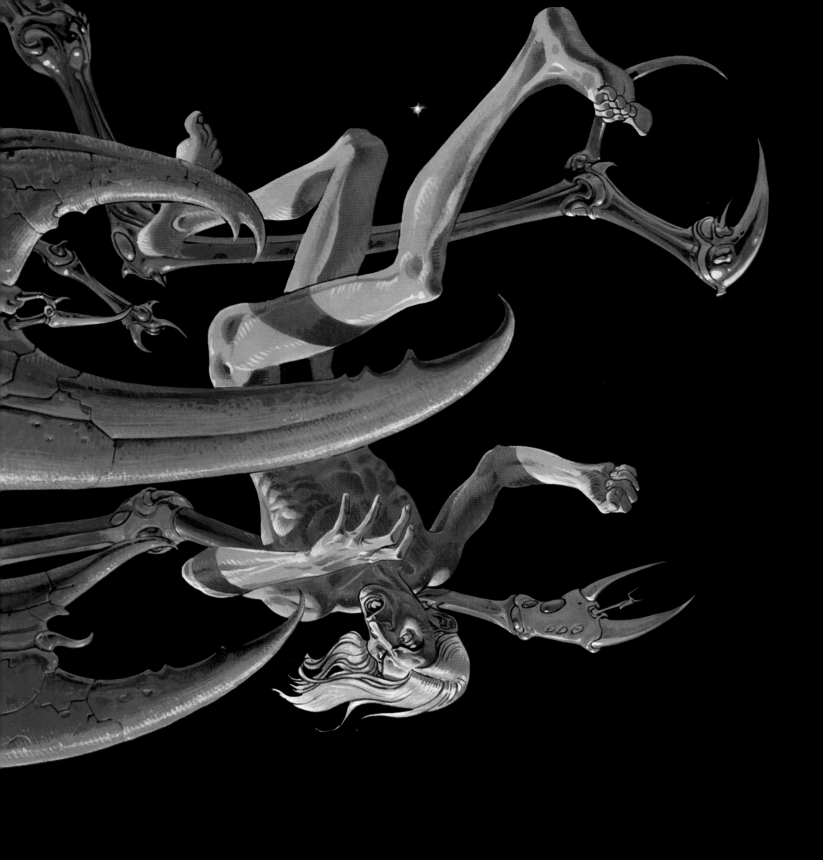

The Creative Process

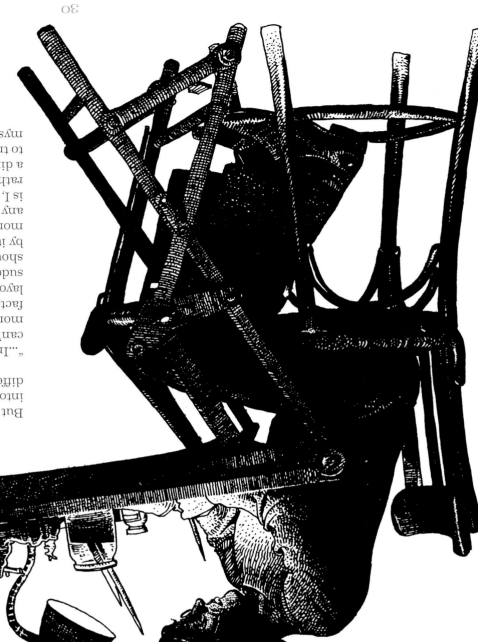

When it came to illustrating *The Incal*, Moebius gave himself an unbelievably difficult challenge: to finish each page in the space of a single day, after receiving, in the form of "art notes," the improvised script dictated by Jodorowsky. That is no small achievement considering how most Franco-Belgian comics are usually so tediously created.

A variety of graphic styles are derived from such a time constraint, which breaks with a diehard rule of the sequential storytelling genre, where the look of a character must remain consistent from the beginning to the end of a story, to avoid confusing the reader.

This freedom—which is paradoxical, since it was the fruit of limitations that Moebius imposed on himself, by creating time restrictions—is clearly expressed in the pages of *The*

Incal. Take for example the differences between the opening, immersive pages of *The Black Incal*, teeming with characters, sets, and details, and the streamlined pages of the subsequent volumes. These distinctions even include the face of John Difool himself, whose contours and expression evolve based on the initiation stages he's going through. Moebius explained this in a November 2, 1987 interview with Frank Reichert, published in the French paperback edition of *The Luminous Incal*. In it, it's not surprising to learn that the physical diversity of some of the characters is due not only to the speedy work imposed by deadlines, but also to the artist's own weaknesses and limitations, regardless of his reputation as a virtuoso of the comics genre.

Moebius: "It's a principle that governs the aesthetics of *The Incal*: I made it my rule to never take more than one day to draw a page. That time imperative is what shaped the style of the book. Everything people see in *The Incal* is my response to the pressure of this constraint. I do very little pencil work, or just very light sketches for certain characters that are problematic for me. So yes, the drawing isn't very precise, and sometimes I have a problem really 'feeling' such or such character. So, Animah, for example: she's cute, true. But I wanted her to be beautiful and gentle, and I could have done better. Or better yet, John Difool: even he ends up with a head that comes in three different styles. Some illustrators never have this problem. They render a character and then stick with it, they're very good at staying with a certain shape and look. Depending on my impulse, I might be inspired to do elongations or very tight shots, I go from one type of anamorphosis to another, in a perfectly intangible way. I have no idea what kind of pressure or trigger sets off this phenomenon. But I had to make do with this defect and turn it into quality. It was my only way out: having several different styles.

"'...In the last part of *The Incal*, *The Fifth Essence*, you can't really talk in terms of a change in style. It was more as if a sort of plughole had suddenly popped. In fact, I had always wanted to give more mayhem to my layouts, make them more dynamic. And then all of a sudden, it dawned on me, just like that. Why indeed should I remain prisoner of a certain form, trapped by it, when I feel that elsewhere things could have more movement? And that has nothing to do with any change in layers as the story itself goes. It is I, Moebius, and I alone, who is changing 'layers.' Or, rather, it is I who decides to exploit the possibilities of a different layout, a layout that I hadn't had the nerve to try until *The Fifth Essence*. Perhaps I'm now letting myself be influenced by American comics?'"

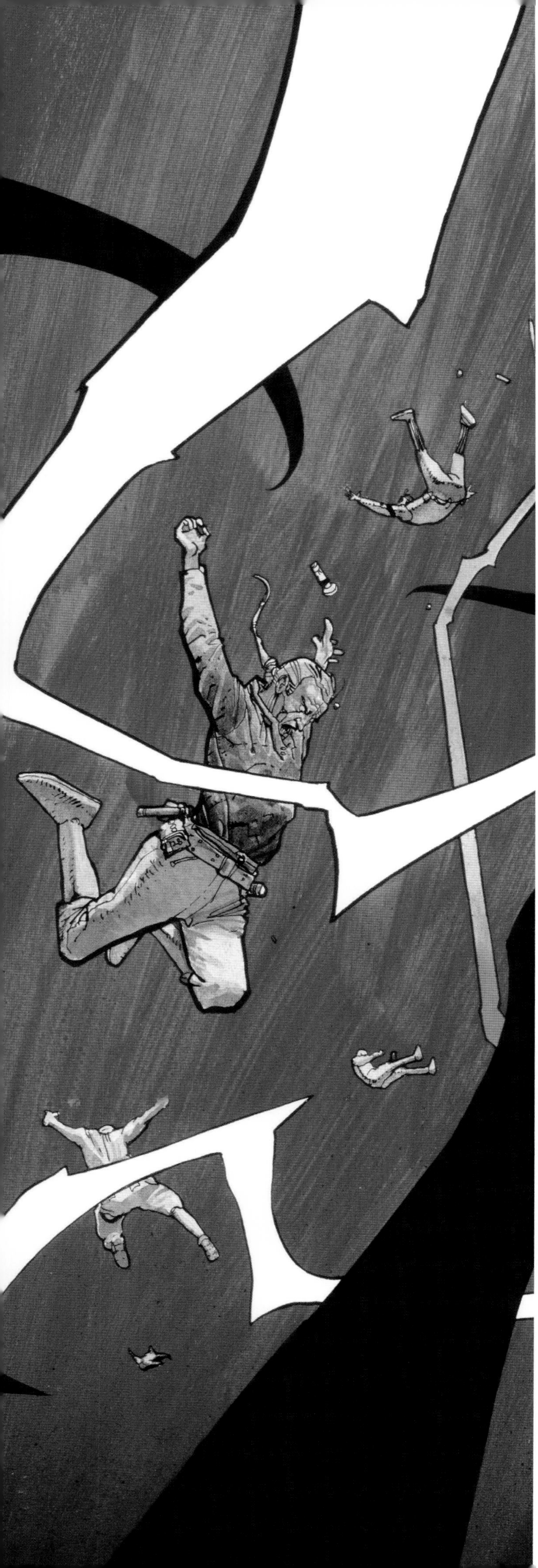

Improvisation

The freedom of tone and range found in *The Incal* owes much to its production process. The approach was oral and visual, not written down and predetermined. This story, the product of a dream coming together with a graphic universe, was produced during intense work sessions in which Jodorowsky told and mimed the story for Mœbius, who would sketch the different stages as they unfolded before his eyes. Imagine the scene: speaking and gesticulating, Jodorowsky lives out *The Incal* and reveals to his own imagination the stream of events that take place one after the other. Stimulated by this gushing creative output, Mœbius's ultra-fast hand draws all the elements in a notebook that then becomes the first draft of *The Incal*. The artist shows the writer the episodes that emerge from the sketches as soon as he finishes them, which invariably influences the course of future exchanges and subsequent creation, and so on.

This was, of course, "controlled" improvisation: the ending was known from the start. From day one, everything came together and was structured in such a way that the loop could be closed, so that the entire narrative could move toward the protagonist becoming the Eternal Witness. But no one knew the exact steps, or how the plot would actually unfold. This confession appears in the last pages of the saga, in the words of John Difool: "You've dragged us through this entire crazy adventure without once knowing the truth?" That same Difool, beholding a new manifestation of the Darkness, reflects in a defeated way: "This is never going to end!" (in *The Fifth Essence Part One: The Dreaming Galaxy*). Or, in the third installment, *What Lies Beneath*, seeing right through his mischievous creators: "It certainly seems to be full of ramifications."

While *The Incal* does achieve the creators' objective of following the tradition of the novel—albeit one that uses a very loose approach—the way the work was produced is more in keeping with the tradition of verbal storytelling. It integrates the possibility of randomness rather than the classic linear storyline typically found in novels, where the need for every element to have its place allows for less freedom and pure invention.

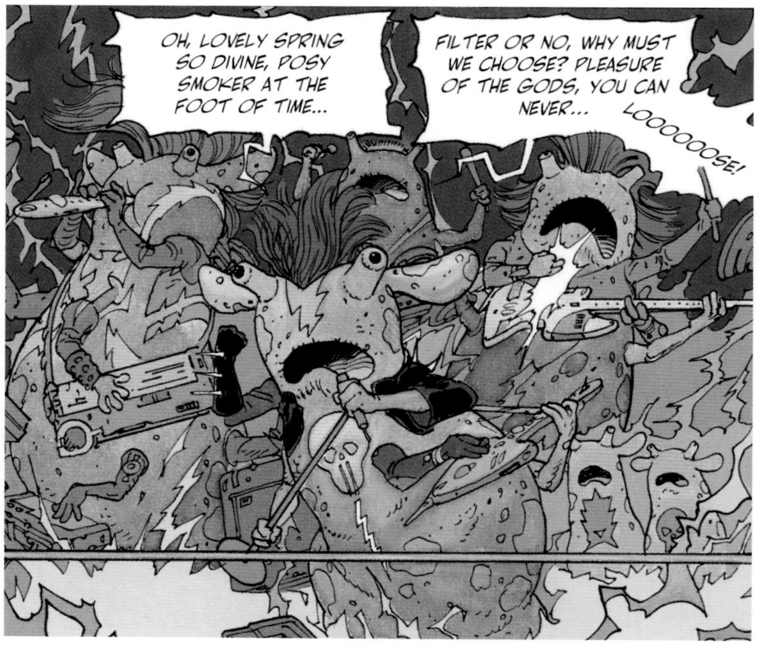
OH, LOVELY SPRING SO DIVINE, POSY SMOKER AT THE FOOT OF TIME...
FILTER OR NO, WHY MUST WE CHOOSE? PLEASURE OF THE GODS, YOU CAN NEVER...
LOOOOOOOSE!

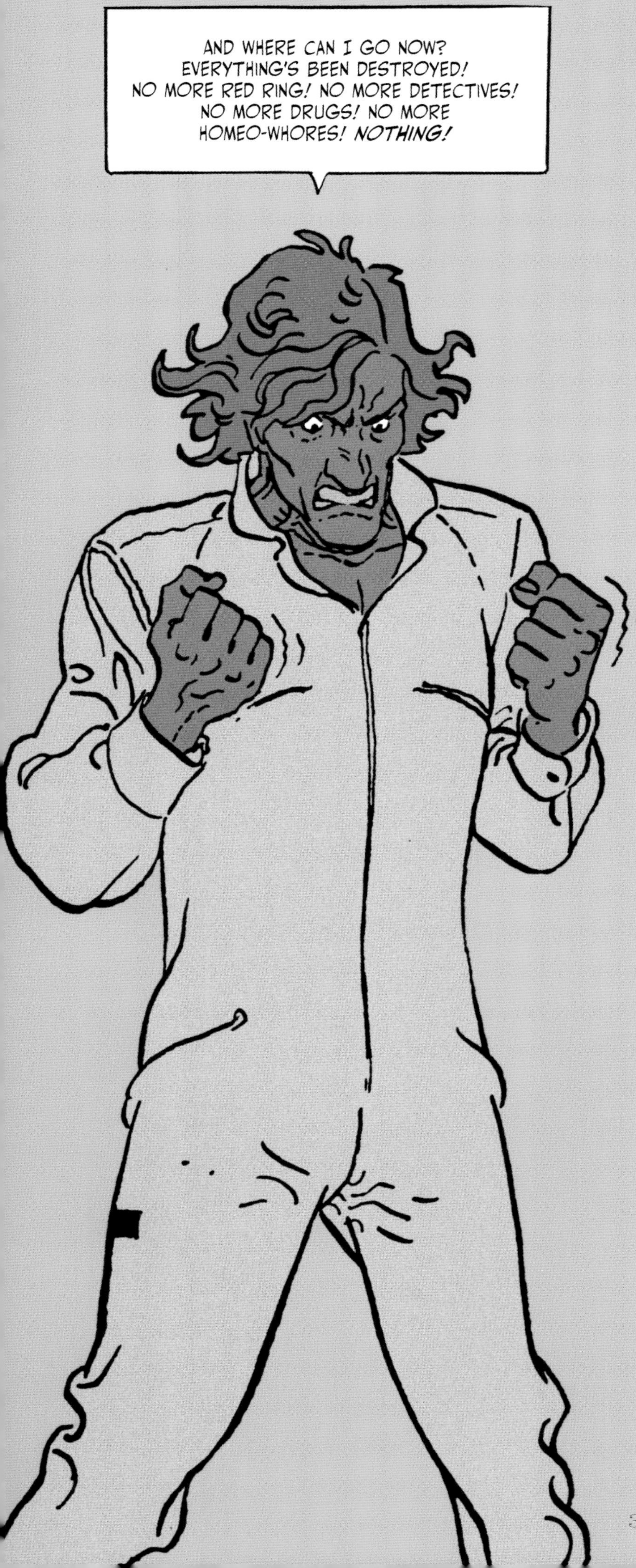
AND WHERE CAN I GO NOW? EVERYTHING'S BEEN DESTROYED! NO MORE RED RING! NO MORE DETECTIVES! NO MORE DRUGS! NO MORE HOMEO-WHORES! *NOTHING!*

Collaboration

The first collaboration between Alejandro Jodorowsky and Mœbius took place long before *The Incal*. As far back as 1955, on his first trip to Mexico, Jean Giraud produced various illustrations for the poems of a Chilean writer named... Alejandro Jodorowsky. But it wasn't until 20 years later, and in a seemingly fortuitous way, that the two men met face to face. Mœbius: "I met Jodorowsky in an office where I had come to deliver a movie poster. He saw me and said, 'Ah! Giraud, I'm a big fan of your comics. How would you like to work on my *Dune* film?' Well, I said yes, of course! That was in March of 1975."

Back then, Jodorowsky was familiar with Gir's western series *Blueberry*, but it was actually more the Mœbius than the Gir side of the illustrator that ended up working on the storyboard, sets, and costumes for *Dune*. This is because the collaboration between the two was dependent on more of an internal level. "The first few times I met with Alejandro, he would bombard me relentlessly with information and I would put up this incredible resistance. He was always telling me about symbolism, Tarot cards, the Kabbalah, and all that, and I refused to play his game. But after a while, I couldn't resist anymore: it all came crashing through, and shook me to my core..." A literal collaboration for the ages.

Frustration

Alejandro Jodorowsky: "To write *The Incal*, I attempted, first and foremost, to erase my intellectual need to define, so I could put myself in a position to 'receive' the story, directly from my subconscious. Kabbalah means, 'That which is received.' I always thought that true art is art that is received. I don't think a human being could write John Difool's story. It wasn't I who wrote it..."

Would Jodorowsky have written *The Incal* on his own?

"Never! Mœbius and I worked eight hours a day for a year on the adaptation of *Dune*. It was an idyllic period, during which a friendship developed. A period where we could afford to lock ourselves in to work on that specific project. And that project failed. That failure left us very frustrated.

"What was important is that Mœbius and I reached the point where we vibrated in unison. Because Mœbius possesses such subtlety, such adaptability... Mœbius is like water! And I too am like water! And the result is a double river: when there's an obstacle, we go around it. As soon as I had the story in my head, I went and found Mœbius to tell him about it. And I never had to change anything about it. At first he said, 'I don't know where you're going with this, but this story is probably already written somewhere!' I already knew the general direction of *The Incal*, as well as the key details. The things that were still hidden in my subconscious revealed themselves gradually. So, in reality, I 'wrote' *The Incal* by telling him about it," explained Jodorowsky to Frank Reichert.

Design

"Convoys, tanks, fighter robots... It's an all-out war!" John Difool cries out in *Final Incal*, transfixed by the sight of thousands of spacecraft preparing for a conflict on Terra 2014. The reader is just as captivated: Ladrönn's impressive drawing style gives scale and power to the multitude of machines of all kinds that unfold across his pages. As such, the artist joins the ranks of the master illustrators of science fiction.

The armada of ships flying over Terra 2014, the epic combat scenes between "millions of machines against millions of insects," the frightening spectacle of the presidential palace covered by the Benthacodon's black mass, the striking image of the Elohim embedded in a kind of giant wheel, the entrance gate on Tortuga Island or the Techno-Mushrooms floating in space: so many powerful images offered up by Ladrönn, worthy of a big budget sci-fi film. He took a gamble and decided to use a realistic style for the structures and machines born of his and Jodorowsky's imagination, and it paid off. His reinterpretation of the City-Shaft is a model of the genre: to present a new vision of the universe initially portrayed by Mœbius while remaining faithful to the spirit of the architecture is a sure sign of Ladrönn's fertile imagination and artistic talent. His City-Shaft emerges as a colder, more run-down, rustier, more inhuman—in a word, more "real"—version of Mœbius's original creation, which had retained a touch of poetry and whimsy that made it less frightening than the one offered up in the pages of *Final Incal*.

This impression is reinforced by the stunning way Ladrönn plays with light. His lighting gives a more pallid and morbid tint to Suicide Alley—a place that didn't exactly need it to begin with—which has now become invaded by City-Shaft residents whose flesh is under attack by the Biophage 13-X Virus. His depiction of the Acid Lake, over which hovers a messy tangle of beams that bring to mind an abandoned, dilapidated version of Paris's Pompidou Center, seems to deter some potential suicide candidates for good. Ladrönn has succeeded in following in the master's footsteps while making his own distinct mark on the material and giving full expression to his personal artistic vision.

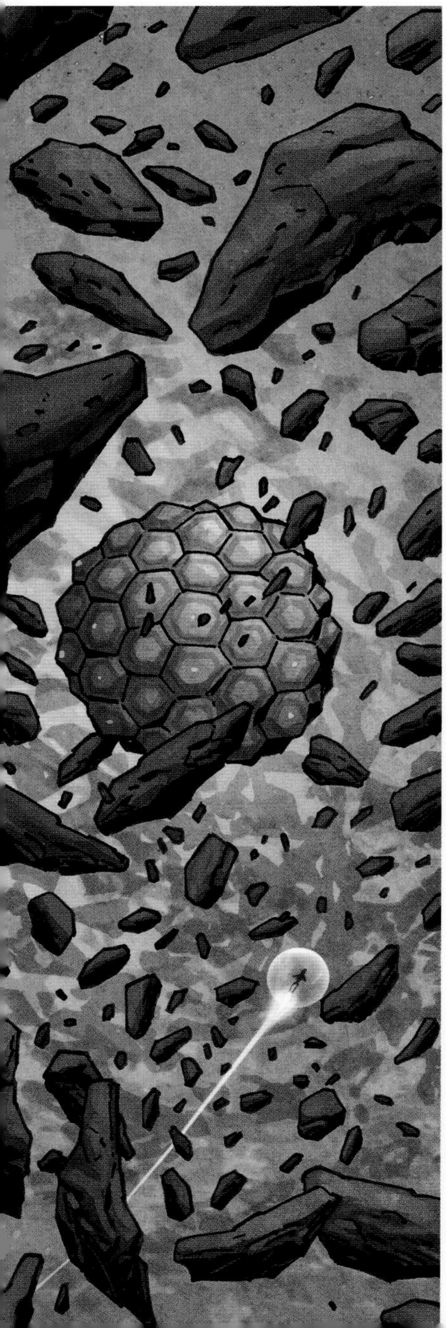

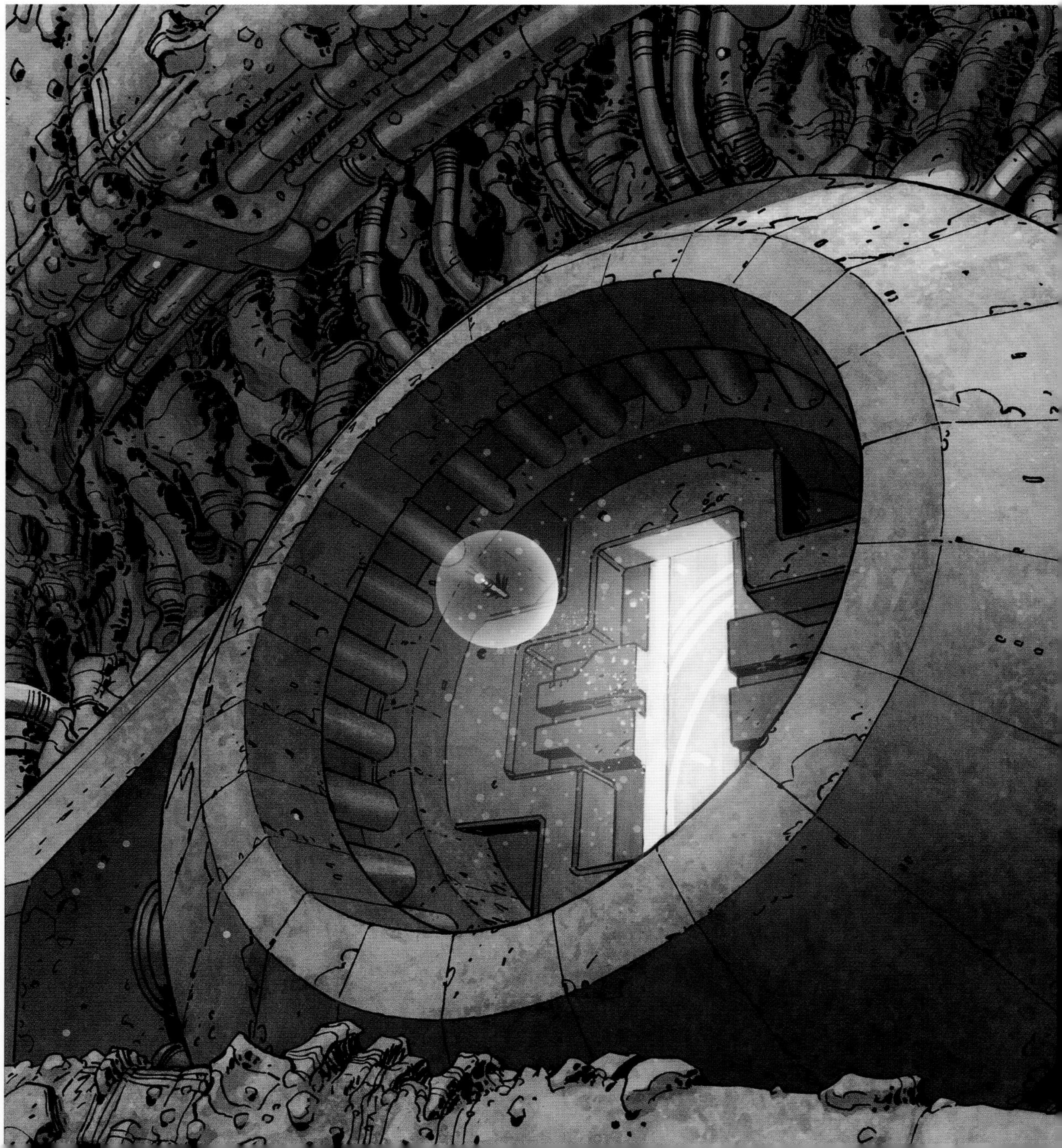

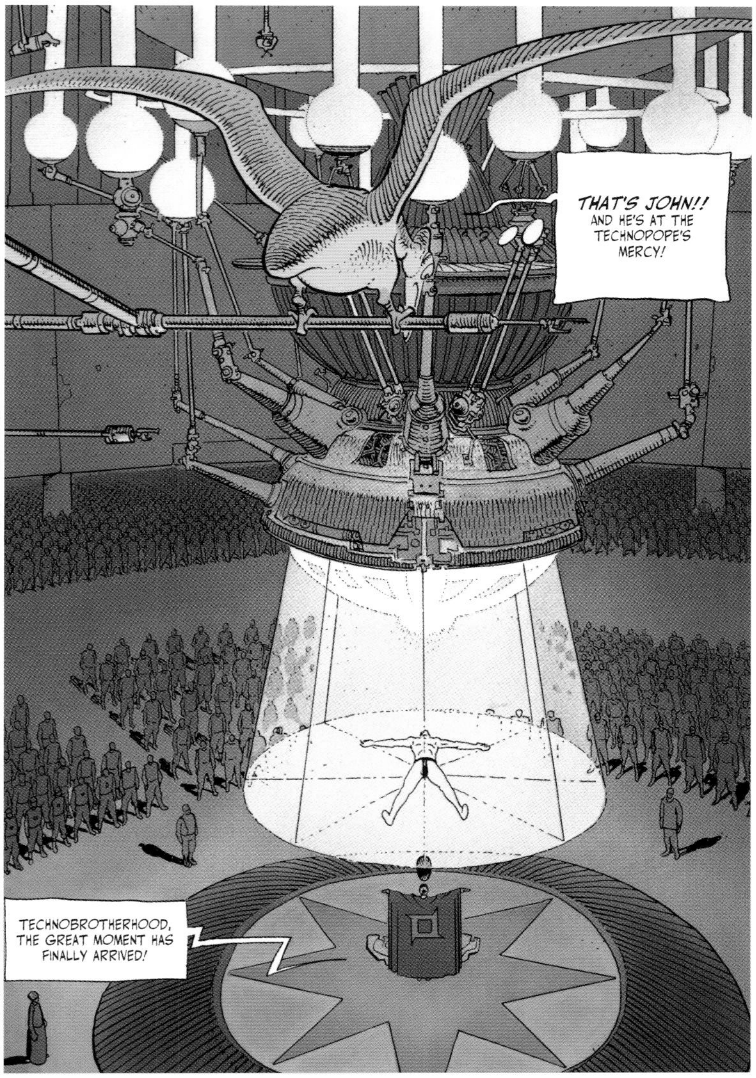
THAT'S JOHN!! AND HE'S AT THE TECHNOPOPE'S MERCY!
TECHNOBROTHERHOOD, THE GREAT MOMENT HAS FINALLY ARRIVED!

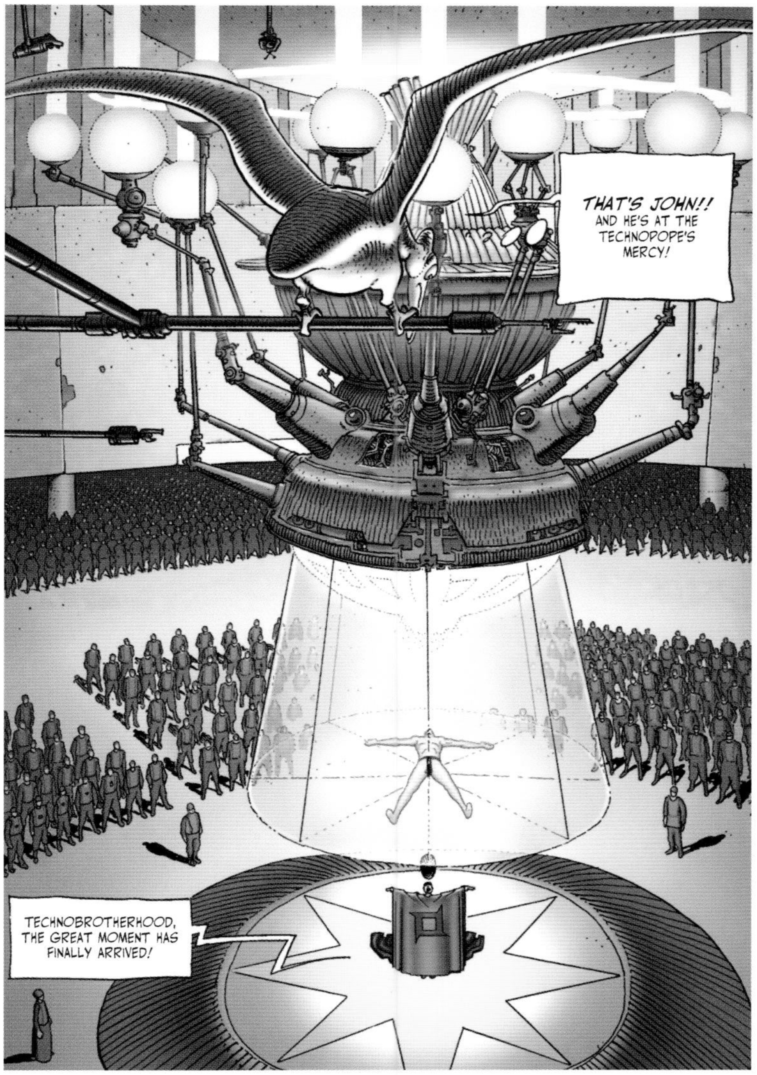
THAT'S JOHN!! AND HE'S AT THE TECHNOPOPE'S MERCY!
TECHNOBROTHERHOOD, THE GREAT MOMENT HAS FINALLY ARRIVED!

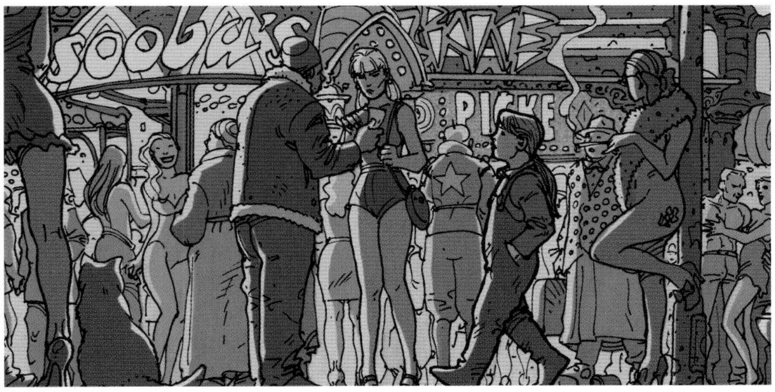
PICKE

Re-Coloring

THE INCAL, A REFLECTION OF ITS TIME

In the early days of computer coloring, *The Incal* and *Before The Incal* were re-colored digitally by Studio Beltran (namely Valérie Beltran), which changed the series' aesthetics considerably. These versions were released between 2002 and 2004 and stayed on the market for a few years before eventually being replaced by the original colors once more, which were restored by Humanoids team member Léonor Pardon, thanks to advances in technology.

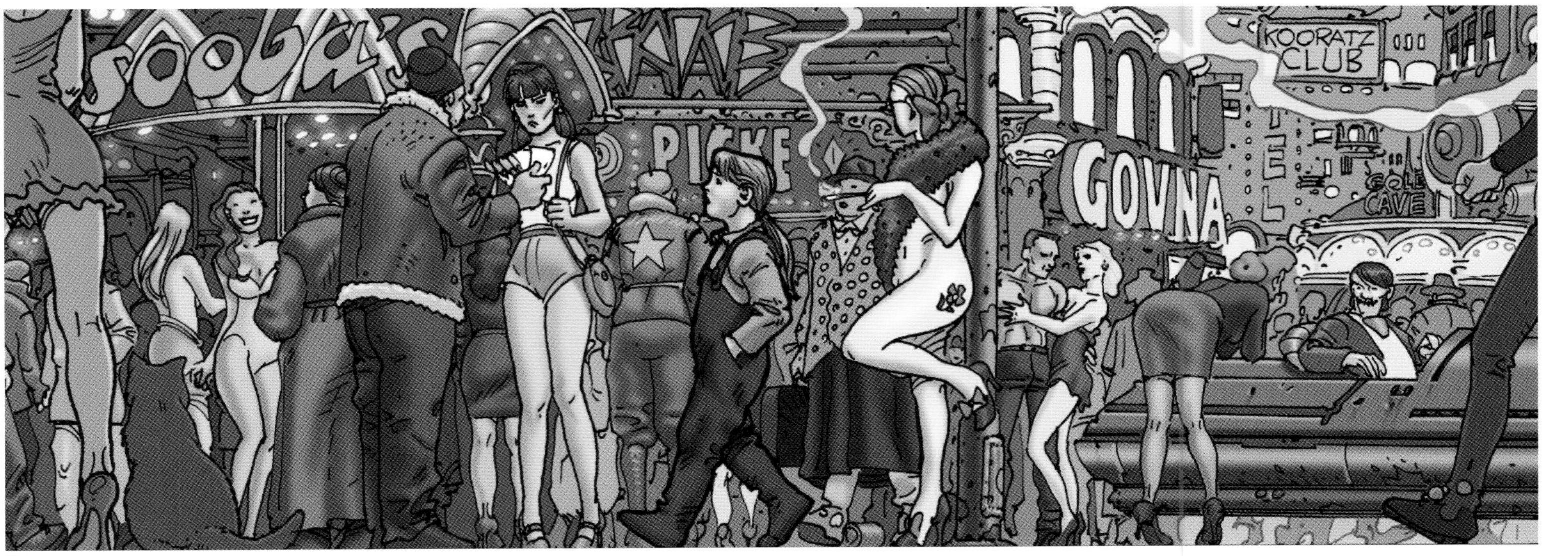
PICKE
GOVNA
KOORATZ CLUB

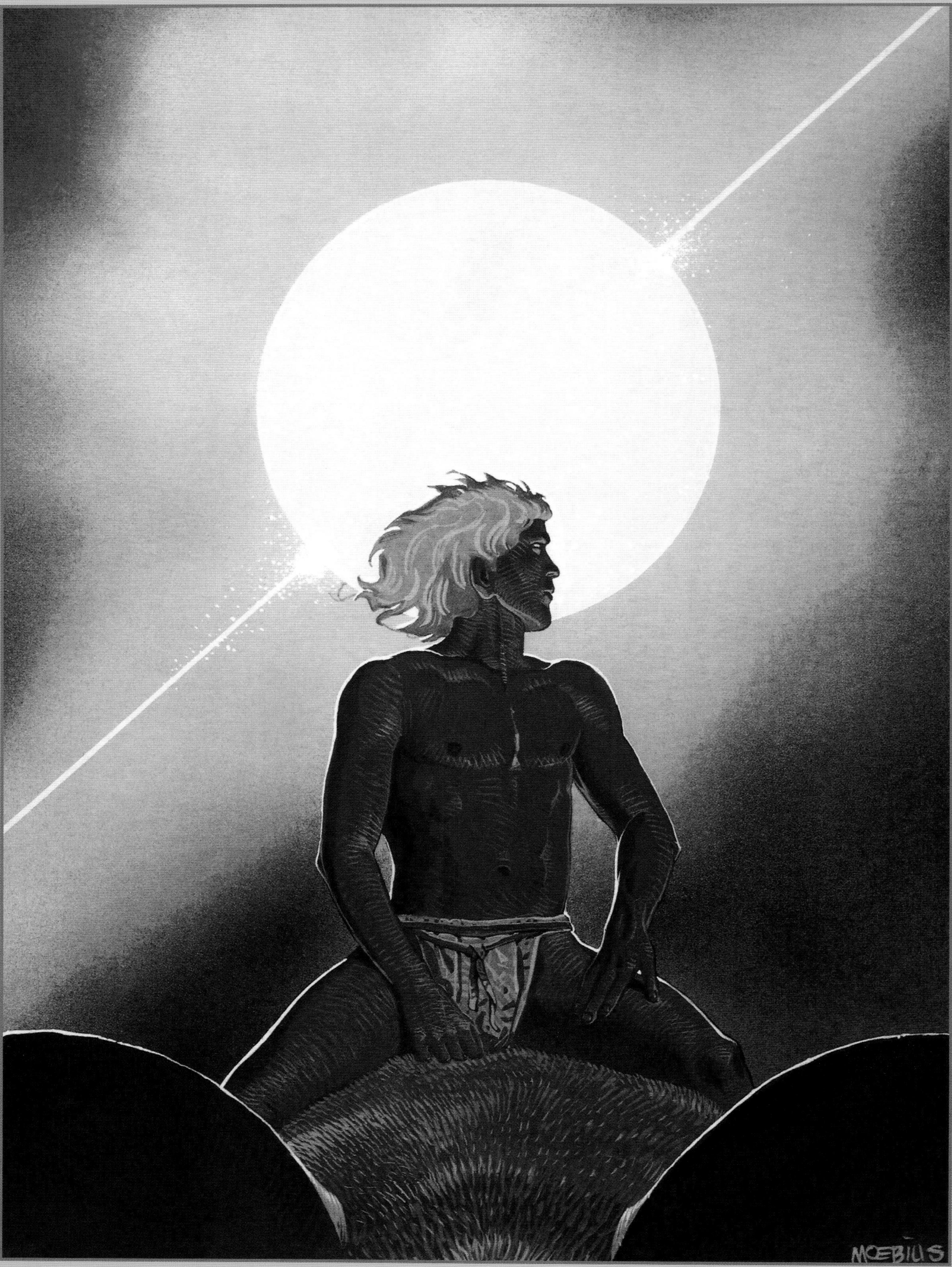
MOEBIUS

Dialogue

The dialogue in *The Incal* is undoubtedly a key reason readers find the series so engrossing. It is anything but stereotypical, and it reflects the twists and turns of the narrative and the successive transformations of the characters, which occur in perfect harmony with the development of the saga. In turn humorous, filled with wisdom, or imbued with a relatable vulgarity, the dialogue captures both the story's setting and the personality of the individuals talking. Drawing part of his inspiration from the hardboiled writing of Mickey Spillane—author of *Kiss Me, Deadly*, among others—Jodorowsky succeeded in injecting the first few pages of *The Black Incal* with a tone worthy of the best crime fiction that's perfectly in keeping with the spirit of the story while making the reader feel like they've just been kicked in the head. In fact, the author himself put it in similar terms: "That's how *The Incal* starts out, with a punch in the face!" The writing is yet another product of the close and unique collaboration between the writer and the artist. Jodorowsky explained this process to Frank Reichert during their 1986 interview: "While Mœbius takes hand-drawn notes, I dictate as I write. This way, he can show me the episode right after I finish narrating it to him. Then we polish up the dialogue. I come up with the plot on my own, but Mœbius works on the dialogue when he feels like it. In my opinion, the writer should not force dialogue on his artist. A drawing can suffice to communicate dialogue, while dialogue can allow for a simplified illustration. The writer must not hinder the work of the artist and must instead allow him to give free reign to his imagination. That is how *The Incal* was created, in a state of ecstasy and freedom!"

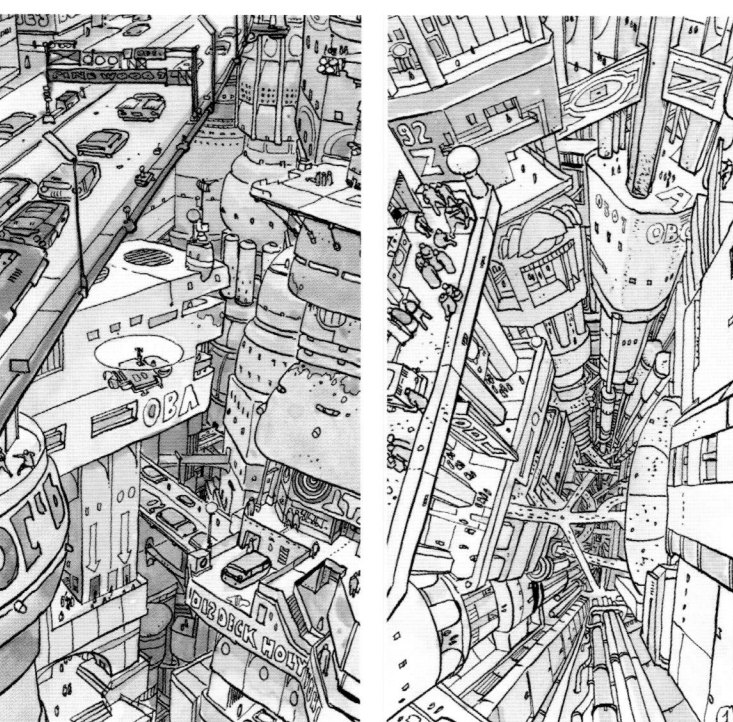

The Forgotten Page

And now for an amusing and paradoxical *Incal* anecdote: the page that is probably the most famous and emblematic of the entire series was initially...left out by Mœbius. The page in question, of course, is the second page of *The Black Incal*, which shows John Difool hurtling down the City-Shaft from the top of Suicide Alley in a headfirst, dizzying dive to the bottom. The tangled mess of levels, traffic lanes, bridges, and conapts, some of which provide glimpses of their occupants' personal lives, offers a striking view of *The Incal*'s unique universe. The vertical city Mœbius drew is much more impressive than the earlier one he'd sketched in *The Long Tomorrow*, the story written by Dan O'Bannon for a 1975 issue of *Métal Hurlant*, even though readers then had already been struck by the originality of the concept (see images below).

This time, the fineness of the line, the tiny, precise details in the way every part of the setting and background is rendered, the density of the human silhouettes that reflect the thriving, buzzing human activity of the City-Shaft, and the incongruous presence of odd white birds, the only hint of animal life in the otherwise suffocating concrete jungle, make this page (opposite) one of the most accomplished and spectacular pages in not just *The Incal*, but in Mœbius's entire oeuvre.

"Mœbius had left out the most important part!" Jodorowsky once exclaimed. "That page is the very essence of *The Incal*. Without that page, there is no *Incal*!" The fact that the page is numbered "1BIS"("bis" meaning "alternative" in French) in the bottom right corner is a testament to the oversight, which thankfully was corrected prior to its initial publication in *Métal Hurlant*. This small "glitch" can be attributed to the aforementioned vagaries of Mœbius and Jodorowsky's favored method of working in an oral tradition.

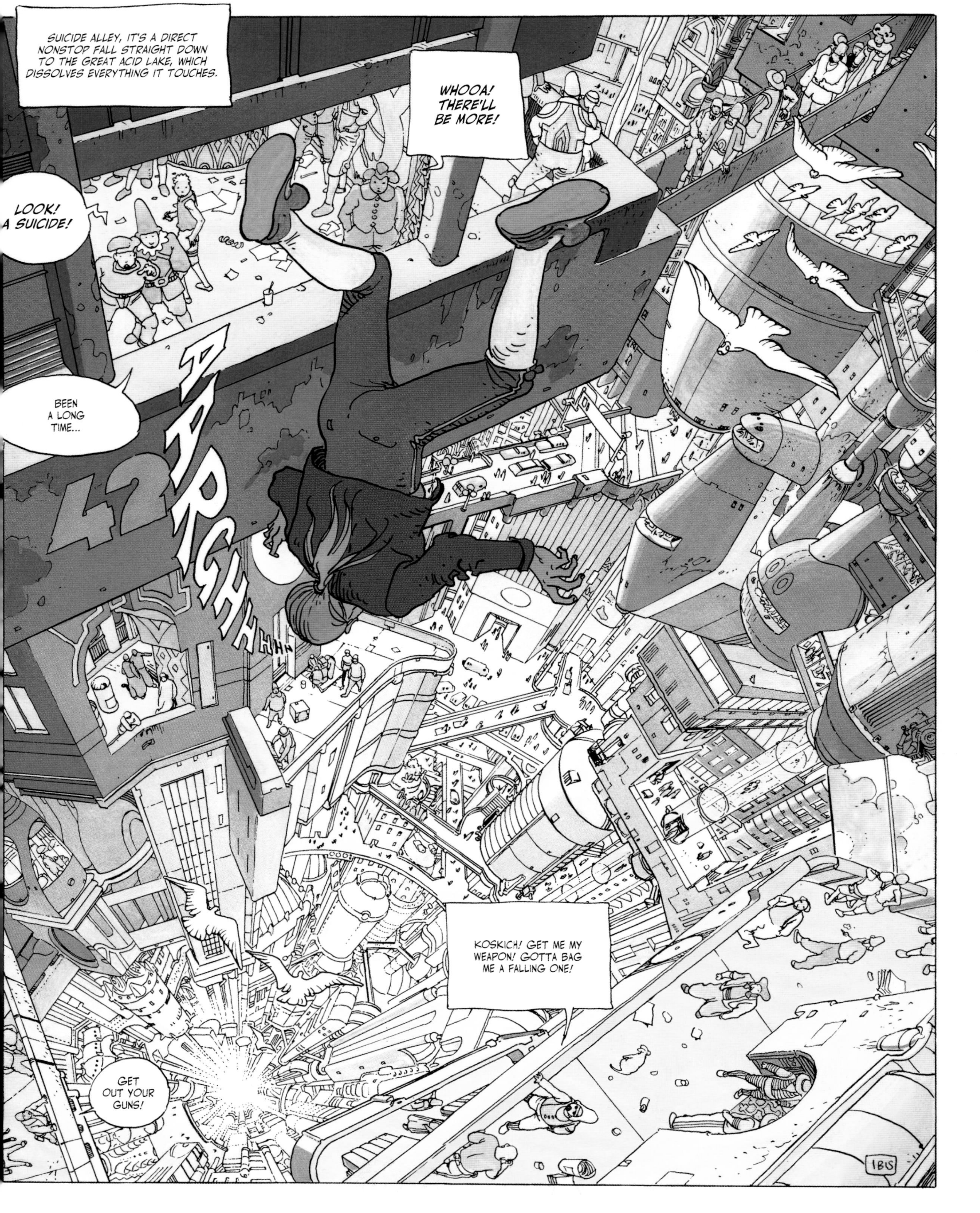
SUICIDE ALLEY, IT'S A DIRECT NONSTOP FALL STRAIGHT DOWN TO THE GREAT ACID LAKE, WHICH DISSOLVES EVERYTHING IT TOUCHES.
WHOOA! THERE'LL BE MORE!
LOOK! A SUICIDE!
BEEN A LONG TIME...
AARGHHHHHH
42
KOSKICH! GET ME MY WEAPON! GOTTA BAG ME A FALLING ONE!
GET OUT YOUR GUNS!
IBIS

Novel

Alejandro Jodorowsky: "When I met Mœbius, he was illustrating *Blueberry,* which, as everyone knows, is a story that never ends. I am against the notion of the ongoing series because it doesn't allow for a novelistic structure. It is a juxtaposition of fragments in which the characters don't change much and who ultimately turn out to have little depth. So what I proposed to Mœbius was a novel divided into five parts, the last of which itself would come in two parts. This allowed me to create a novelistic structure that can only really be understood in the final pages.

"The construction of *The Incal* is complex and comes entirely from me," Alejandro Jodorowsky continues. "The characters in the cycle come in pairs and together form a six-pointed star, just like the union of the two Incals—with the quintessence emanating from the center. Hence the need for six installments. The form reflects the content. In *The Incal,* there are seven main characters: Difool, Deepo, Animah, The Metabaron, Solune, Tanatah, and Kill Wolfhead. You could say that the androgyne is made up of the union of the other six. Similarly, the books come in pairs as well."

This structure was later to be complemented by the prequel *Before The Incal,* then by *After The Incal* and *Final Incal,* thus composing a sweeping novelistic saga divided into three big cycles, which in turn are divided into volumes that make up each of the books.

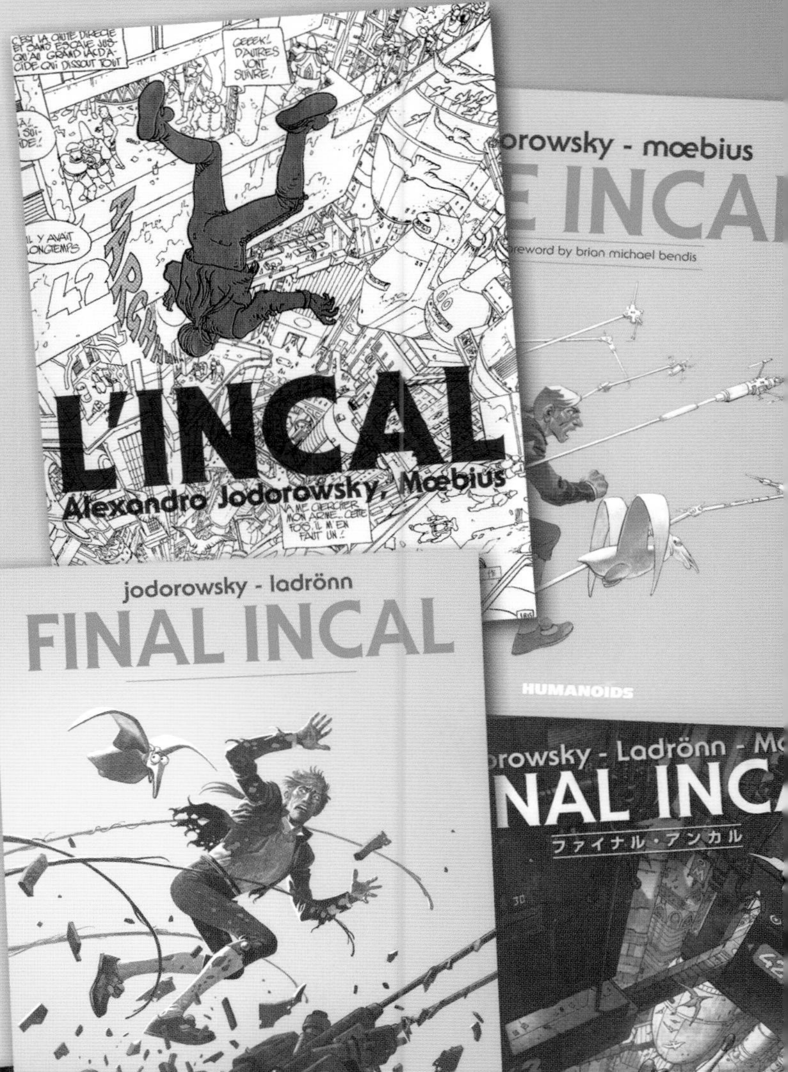
L'INCAL
Alexandro Jodorowsky, Mœbius
jodorowsky - mœbius
foreword by brian michael bendis
HUMANOIDS
jodorowsky - ladrönn
FINAL INCAL
ファイナル・アンカル

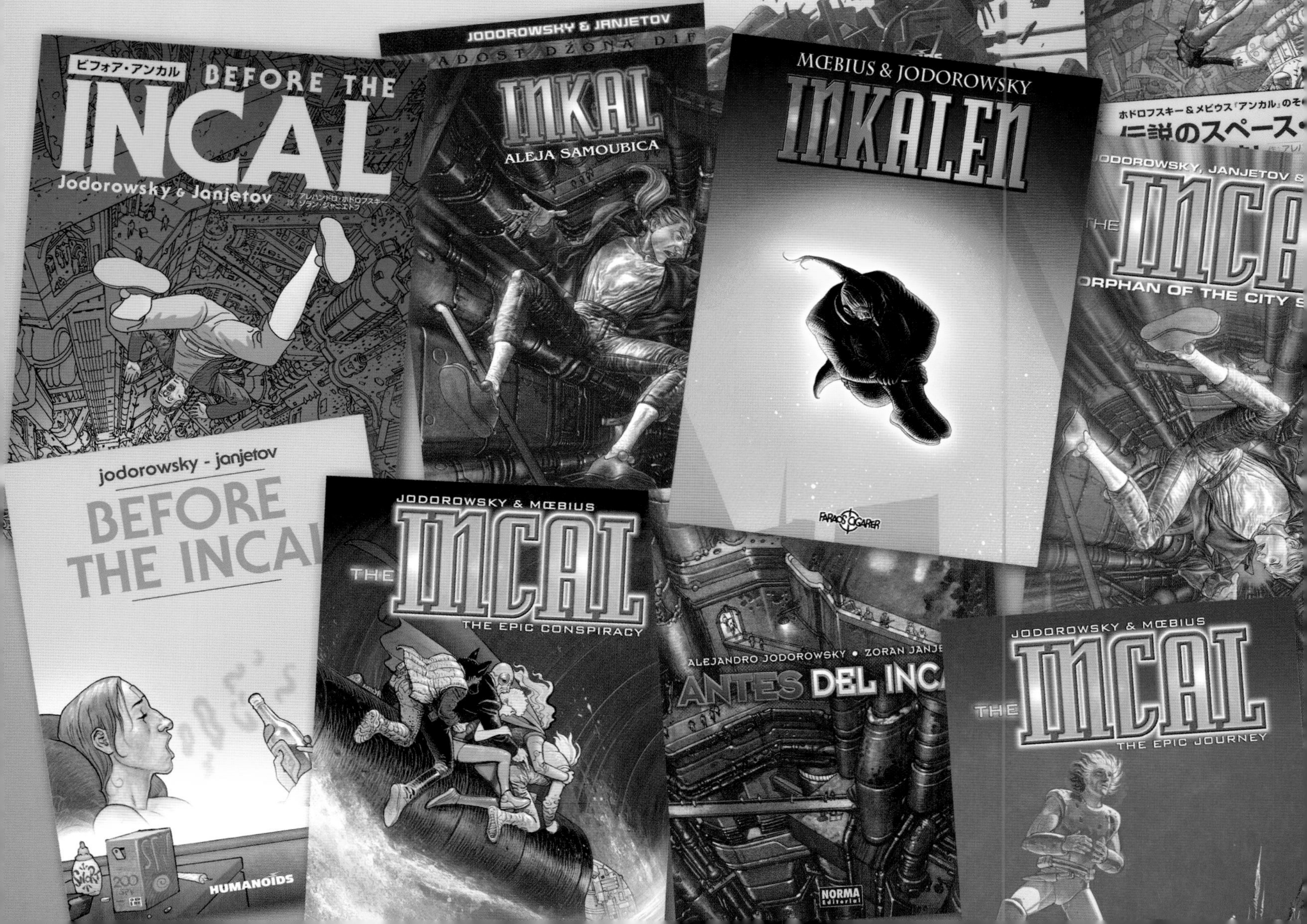
ビフォア・アンカル
BEFORE THE
INCAL
Jodorowsky & Janjetov
JODOROWSKY & JANJETOV
INKAL
ALEJA SAMOUBICA
MŒBIUS & JODOROWSKY
INKALEN
ORPHAN OF THE CITY
jodorowsky - janjetov
BEFORE
THE INCA
HUMANOIDS
JODOROWSKY & MŒBIUS
THE INCAL
THE EPIC CONSPIRACY
ALEJANDRO JODOROWSKY • ZORAN JANJE
ANTES DEL INC
NORMA
JODOROWSKY & MŒBIUS
THE INCAL
THE EPIC JOURNEY

3. The Black Incal vs. The Luminous Incal: Characters & Creatures

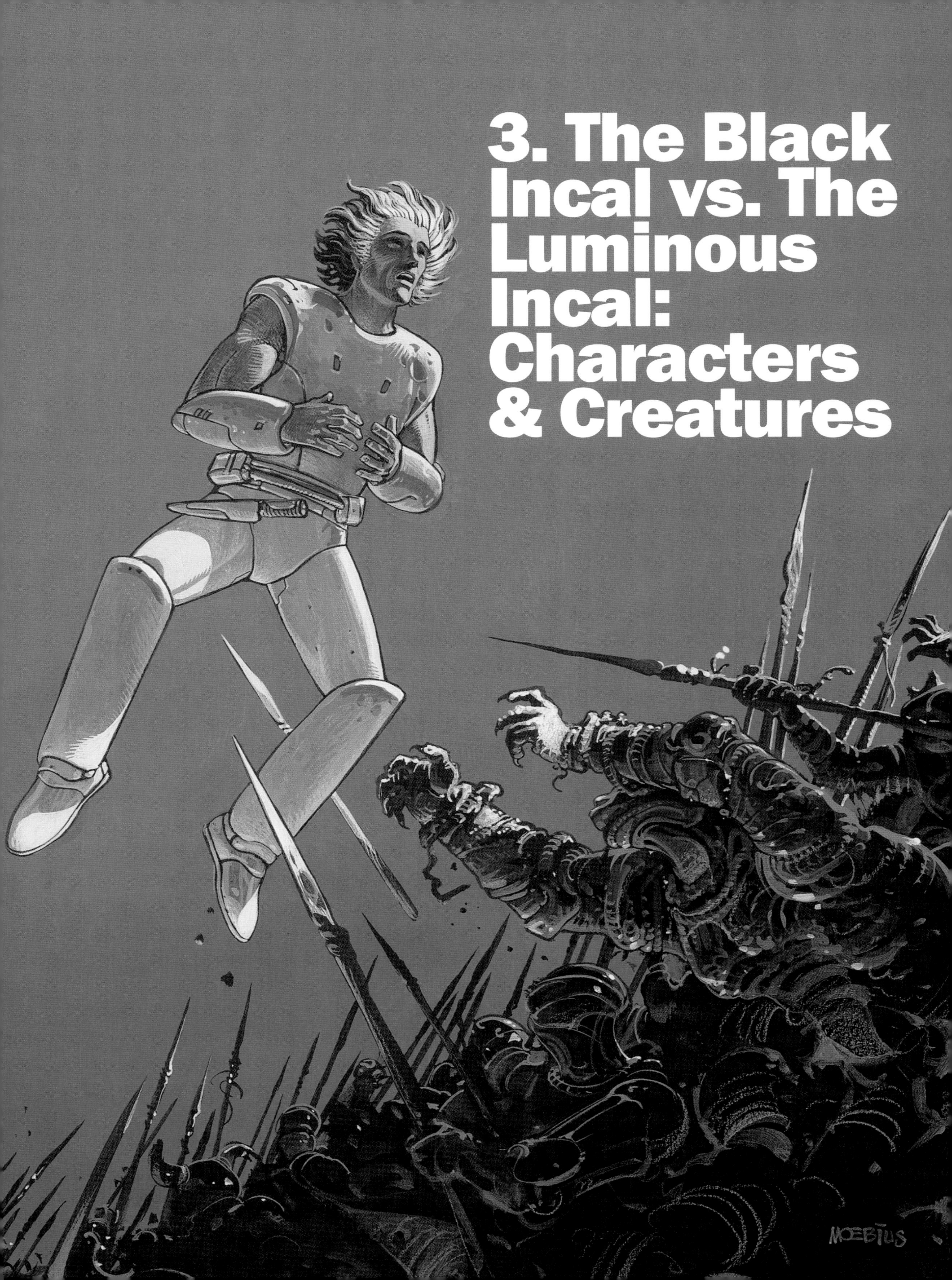
MOEBIUS

John Difool

Who is John Difool, really? A shabby loser, a Class "R" Private Detective? A guy who's misunderstood—the victim of the disastrous impression he makes, but who is so much more than that? The savior of the universe, who has a rendezvous with a destiny that's way too big for him, but who'll nevertheless fulfill the cosmic mission the Incal has entrusted to him—sometimes in spite of himself? Probably a little of all the above.

For Jodorowsky, the story of *The Incal*, "is the story of a character who has a very small ego and how he breaks that ego to become a truly cosmic character. The main character in [the series] is actually the universe." (*L'Année de la Bande Dessinée* 81–82).

John Difool is indeed not one entity, but multiple characters. We see this early on, in *The Black Incal*, when he's suddenly cut into four parts after the Incal challenges him; "For now, we must ask: 'Who is the real John Difool?' But first, we must know how many John Difools there are?" In the last volume of *The Incal*, Difool comes face to face with 78 billion individuals who all look exactly like him, whether they are men or women—which is understandably disturbing. "Don't you see? They're not people! They all look the same! They all look like me!!" In *Final Incal*, as in *The Black Incal* before it, a total of four John Difools cohabitate within the same character once again, but with a major difference this time around: in the last book, instead of seeing John's body cut into four, the reader is presented with four "whole" John Difools, who are simultaneously identical yet different, each endowed with a singular personality and a more or less "enlightened" ego.

Even before he ends up in those extreme situations, John Difool, like everyone else, and per Alejandro Jodorowsky's intent, is a human being who is constantly changing. In *Before the Incal*, young John is a sympathetic, naïve, honest, idealistic, and generous young man whose start in life is made difficult by the death of both his parents and by the toxic climate that prevails on Terra 2014. He is an altruistic individual who rejects injustice, who seeks to discover the hidden underbelly of the great city and to denounce the depravity of the ruling class, and who believes in love and friendship despite the disappointments and betrayals he keeps encountering on his life journey. Things start really taking a turn for the worst in *The Incal*, but in the meantime, John has undergone forced brain surgery of the kind one does not emerge from unscathed. Deprived of his memory, robbed of his past, bereft of his intelligence, and reduced to a caricature of himself, he is fated to live out a shabby life indeed: that of an individual absent of the slightest ambition, save for the small pleasures found in a bottle of liquor, a hit of SPV, and a roll in the hay with a homeo-whore. Probably not the best choices for a guy who's supposed to save the universe...

And yet, what a character he turns out to be in *The Incal*! Full of vitality, a relentless capacity to rebound, to be funny, and overall, an immensely sympathetic figure. It's hard to resist the appeal of John Difool, whose bandage-covered nose, at the beginning of *The Black Incal*, harks back to Jack Nicholson in Roman Polanski's *Chinatown*. In spite of his faults, his weaknesses, his selfishness, and his cowardice, we love John Difool. And perhaps we love the whiny, grumpy Difool even more than the evolved Difool whose refined face reflects the inner beauty and

nobility he demonstrates intermittently when he rises to the task of the cosmic mission entrusted to him. For what could be more amusing than seeing John Difool grumbling, dreaming only of taking off with Animah for a planet-paradise while around him everyone is busy frantically trying to save the universe?

As both superhero and anti-hero, unquestionable star and simple sidekick, the main character and the supporting role, superhuman and pathetic, endearing and pitiful, John Difool, in Jodorowsky's words, "represents all the energy and all the possibilities of the universe." And that's surely enough to make him a genuine hero.

Luz de Garra

Fickle and vain. Contemptuous and arrogant. In a word, detestable. That is how Luz de Garra comes across to John Difool in *Class "R" Detective*, the second installment in *Before The Incal*. Luz de Garra is the perfect, albeit extreme, embodiment of the Aristo social class, their arrogance, their cruelty, and their total lack of consideration for those who aren't part of that same world. John's first encounter with her is through a video message summoning him to meet with her so she can entrust him with a mission he is in no position to refuse. "Young Aristo ladies often use pre-detectives as chaperones... If you do a good job, you'll be able to apply for Official Detective!" Kolbo-5 reminds him.

Meeting her in person does little to spark any enthusiasm in Difool: she's not exactly easy on the eyes—"Yikes, she's twice as ugly in the flesh!" he notes—and her intentions are nothing short of monstrous: she's in the mood to have a little fun at the expense of the hapless bedridden patients of a lower level hospital who have contracted the Meropa virus. But even in the life of John Difool, reality sometimes turns into a fairy tale. All it takes is one kiss—a less than enchanting prospect, given the woman's challenging physical features—for Luz's face to reveal, as if by miracle—an unlikely concept on Terra 2014—its true beauty, when her holo-makeup wears off sooner than expected.

Entranced and instantly smitten—"You, Miss Luz, are simply... everything!"—John is nevertheless not about to be promised a bright future. One could even say that his problems are only just beginning. Luz de Garra gets her twisted kicks by playing with him, taking advantage of his amorous feelings (a notion entirely foreign to the young lady's psychological makeup) and treating him like a toy, cruelly reminding them of their difference in station: "I already told you I have a taste for the exotic...like you, an average guy from the lower levels... Now get your tongue in my mouth!" This stirs up in poor Difool a fierce, growing, and understandable hatred of the Aristos. "She'll always be an Aristo, and I'll always be a rat from the lower levels," he says woefully a few panels later, while Kolbo-5 tries to comfort him with words that soon prove quite relevant.

This hatred reaches full throttle after Luz tries to make him her Mandog, in other words her "pampered little puppy." From that moment on, John becomes obsessed by a single thought: to take revenge on this woman who has betrayed and toyed with him. "I hope those soulless Aristos rot in hell! I hope that hypocrite's face gets covered in boils... I never met a more detestable woman! I despise her!"

The frustration that comes from his clashing feelings about Luz in turn motivates John to solve the Big Secret and thus kill two birds with one stone: not only will he pierce the mystery behind the sociopolitical system, but that revelation will cause Luz to open her eyes and behold the ghastly nature of their society and earn his love. Once again, Kolbo-5 proves to have been prophetic: "Life is full of dramatic events, and constant surprises." By the same token, John is able to overcome his thirst for revenge and prevail over his own ego to use his determination and insight for the good of the community.

As for Luz, from then on, and thanks to John, she acquires and becomes driven by a political conscience, a notion hitherto unknown to her, and is finally touched by the grace of love—a love that refills the "tree of life" and reaches its eternal and cosmic dimension in the last pages of *Final Incal*. For the love between Luz and John goes far beyond a classic relationship. This love is capable of saving the entire universe, as Elohim tells John: "Of all living beings, only you and Luz know true love... The virus gathers its strength from a lack of emotion. Your love will be immune to it." They are thus called on to become a "universal antidote," the only ones capable of thwarting the schemes of the Benthacodon and the Prez. As Luz informs him, "Without us, the black meca-mutant will transform all life in the universe into soulless machine."

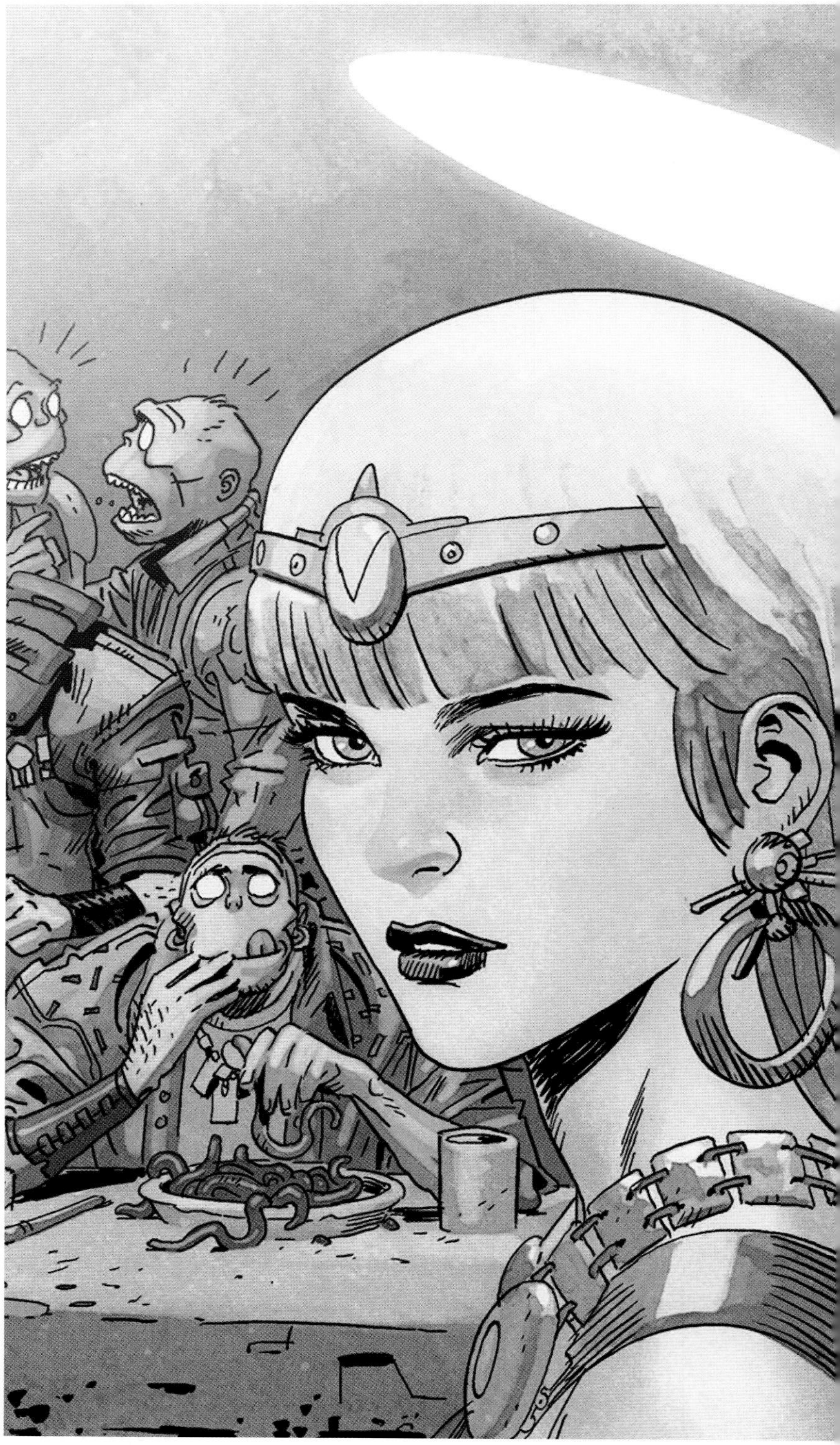

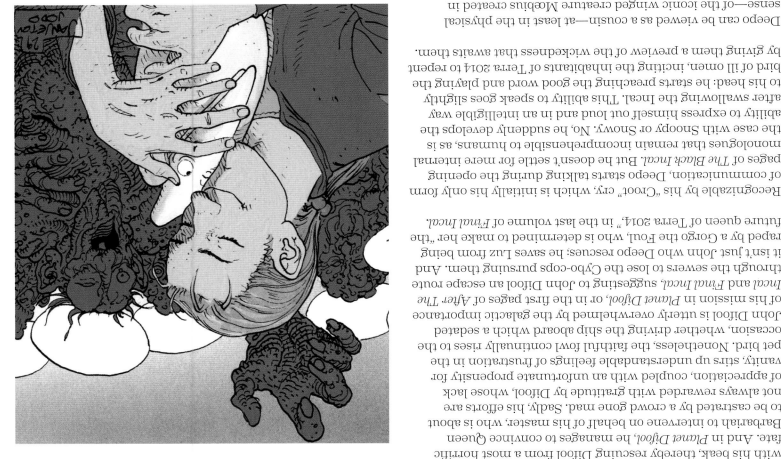

Deepo

Traditional Franco-Belgian comics are populated by countless heroes who are accompanied by an animal sidekick. It was therefore logical for Jodorowsky and Moebius, who wanted to follow in Hergé's footsteps, to give John Difool a pet as loyal and resourceful as Snowy in *Tintin*. But in the bleak, concrete universe of Terra 2014, animals aren't exactly in abundance and instead seem to have mostly been replaced by robots. Nonetheless, in *Before The Incal*, young John Difool does come across an actual animal: he saves the life of a baby concrete seagull, whose dying mother is no longer able to care for him, by adopting him and naming him Deepo.

While Deepo occasionally demonstrates regrettable clumsiness, he is a resourceful companion who saves John's hide in many difficult circumstances. He's the one who, in *The Luminous Incal*, shatters the Techno-Pope's shadow crown with his beak, thereby rescuing Difool from a most horrific fate. And in *Planet Difool*, he manages to convince Queen Barbariah to intervene on behalf of his master, who is about to be castrated by a crowd gone mad. Sadly, his efforts are not always rewarded with gratitude by Difool, whose lack of appreciation, coupled with an unfortunate propensity for vanity, stirs up understandable feelings of frustration in the pet bird. Nonetheless, the faithful fowl continually rises to the occasion, whether driving the ship aboard which a sedated John Difool is utterly overwhelmed by the galactic importance of his mission in *Planet Difool*, or in the first pages of *After The Incal* and *Final Incal*, suggesting to John Difool an escape route through the sewers to lose the Cybo-cops pursuing them. And it isn't just John who Deepo rescues: he saves Luz from being raped by a Gorgo the Foul, who is determined to make her "the future queen of Terra 2014," in the last volume of *Final Incal*.

Recognizable by his "Croot" cry, which is initially his only form of communication, Deepo starts talking during the opening pages of *The Black Incal*. But he doesn't settle for mere internal monologues that remain incomprehensible to humans, as is the case with Snoopy or Snowy. No, he suddenly develops the ability to express himself out loud and in an intelligible way after swallowing the Incal. This ability to speak goes slightly to his head: he starts preaching the good word and playing the bird of ill omen, inciting the inhabitants of Terra 2014 to repent by giving them a preview of the wickedness that awaits them.

Deepo can be viewed as a cousin—at least in the physical sense—of the iconic winged creature Moebius created in

Arzach. And in addition to being a lifesaver, Deepo has also been gifted with a good-natured personality, a winning combination that makes him the perfect sidekick—always there to help out his master when needed and to give an extra touch of humanity—so to speak—to the story.

Yet Deepo has to resolve to leave John to his fate in the penultimate page of *Final Incal*. As the latter prepares to dissolve "into the universe like a star" with Luz, Deepo remains on Terra 2014, perched on the shoulder of Kill Wolfhead, who remarks, "I don't know if we'll be seeing them again," in a tone tinged with nostalgia. Deepo simply responds with his usual, if somewhat plaintive, cry, as if he has returned to his original animal state, forever deprived of the human language he once acquired by absorbing the Incal. As if, at this time, things have finally returned to normal—well, normal for the Jodoverse.

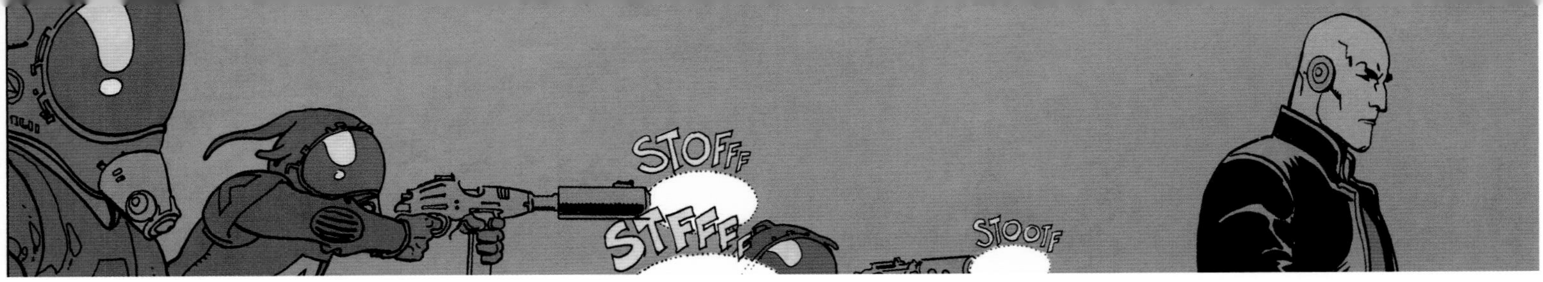
STOFFFF
STFFFF
STOOTF

The Metabaron

Mœbius: "The Metabaron is my grandfather. When Alejandro asked me to draw the character, that's the Metabaron that appeared before me: same face, same features. He had asked me to portray my vision of my mother and father. Not a psychological portrait or a caricature, but rather an impression of them, how I felt about them when I was a child. What could have come out of that was an abstract drawing or some doodles, but what came out were hurriedly drawn figurative representations. I would spend 15 seconds on each drawing and it would have been hard to see anything Mœbius or Giraud-like in them, but strangely enough, the Metabaron emerged very clearly. In *The Incal*, it's my grandfather who is wandering around. As a child, I was afraid of him, he scared me. I always felt he was either not listening to me or listening to me too closely. There was a disconnect between the way he perceived me and the way I wanted him to perceive me. When I drew a metal-capped ear on the Metabaron, as if he had a disability, or, just the opposite, a more functional, artificial ear, what I was expressing was childish rebellion."

The Metabaron makes his very first appearance in *The Black Incal,* decked out all in black, self-assured, head shaved, a prosthesis in lieu of a right ear, with a "don't mess with me" look about him. Such is how he comes across to the reader: a modern-day rock star. A few years after the creation of *The Incal,* this larger-than-life character proved to be entirely deserving of Jodorowsky's decision to make him the pivotal figure in an epic tale "full of noise and fury," as the author once described it.

The Metabaron, under the epithet No Name, would indeed later go on to become the main character in his own series, *The Metabarons,* the space opera saga written by Jodorowsky and illustrated by Juan Gimenez, and spun-off from the world of *The Incal.* After that, the character known as the galaxy's ultimate warrior went on to star in new adventures developed by Jerry Frissen and a new generation of artists such as Valentin Sécher, Niko Henrichon, and Esad Ribic, under the series title *The Metabaron.*

When the reader is introduced to him in *The Incal,* the Metabaron is on his way to the Amok headquarters. The comments that ricochet around him as he walks past speak volumes about the mix of respect and fear he inspires in those who have heard of him. "That's the Metabaron! It's him! The great killer! The greatest mercenary in the whole system! He's finally come out of his Meta-bunker. They say he once killed seven men in one second." For the Metabaron, we find out, is a hitman, a ruthless mercenary who offers his services to the highest bidder, a relentless killing machine. However, that doesn't mean he's altogether devoid of sentiment: if he's come to see visit the Queen of Amok, it's because she's holding his son, Solune, hostage, whom she is prepared to return to him unharmed on one condition: that the Metabaron bring her, "in 24 hours, dead or alive...!" a certain John Difool.

Over the course of *The Incal,* the Metabaron emerges as one of John Difool's travel companions, and as one of the key characters in the narrative. His physical appearance gradually evolves, as does Difool's. Without losing any of his arrogance or magnetism, he also gains some humanity and loses the darker side of his character, which made him so intimidating initially. We even catch him cracking a smile and injecting a little familiarity in the way he expresses himself: "This creature reminds me of my good old Meta-skiff," he says good-humoredly in *What Is Above*. His natural authority gradually becomes enhanced by a kind of benevolence, as in the scene where he trains John to compete in the Great Nuptial Games, like a big brother or a father taking care of his protégé.

And his human dimension fully manifests when he acts jealous of Difool, who he still sees as a "worthless bum" and "trivial detective" and who he never imagined could possibly win Animah's heart—he thinks their love is foolish. The Metabaron, jealous of John Difool...who would have thought? At the end of *The Black Incal,* the Metabaron returns to his Meta-skiff, where a household robot named Tonto (which means "idiot" in Spanish) is waiting for him. A few years later, Tonto would go on to become one of the main characters and the narrator of *The Metabarons.* Jodorowsky named him as a tribute to the Lone Ranger's Native American sidekick, who starred in one of the author's all-time favorite comic books as a kid.

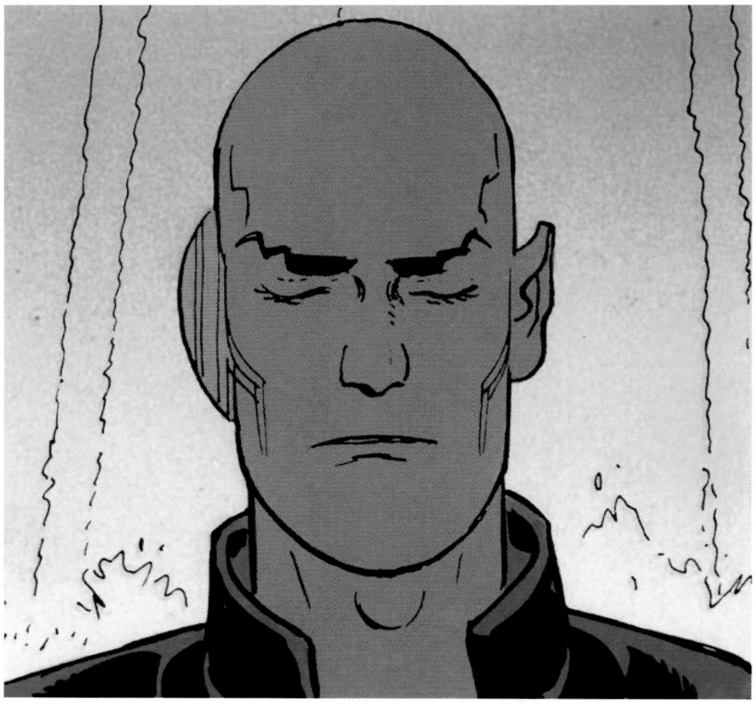

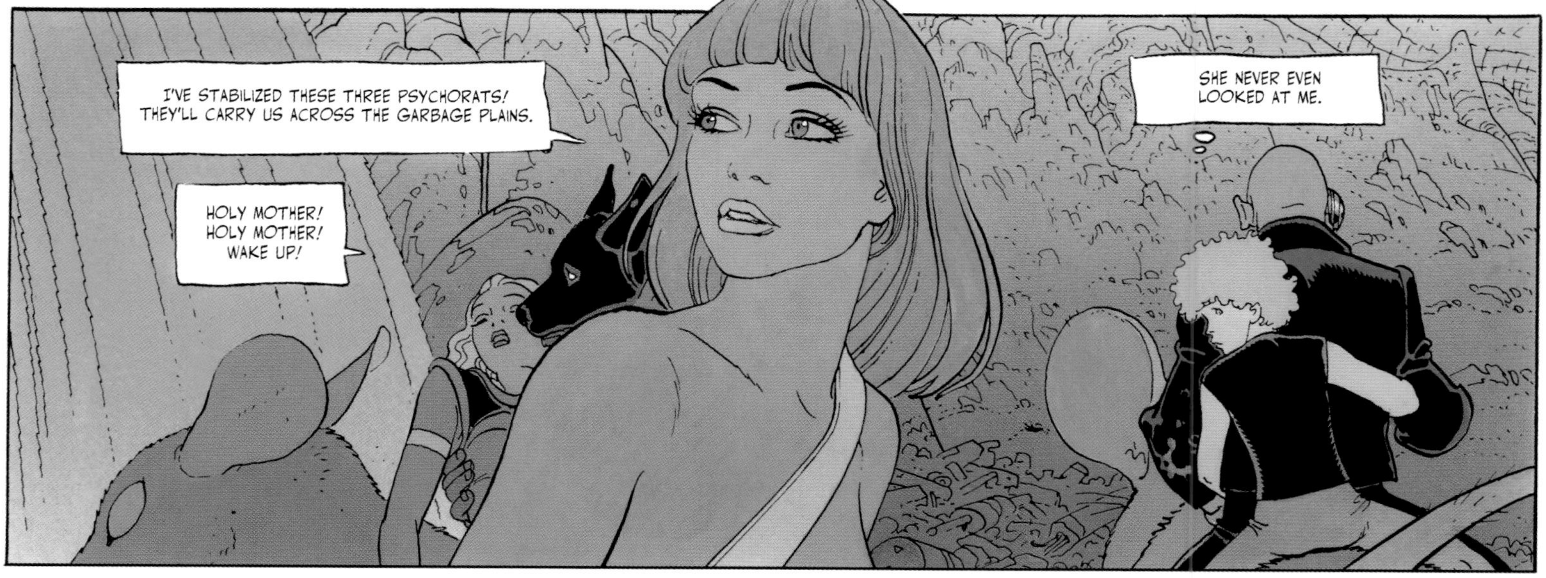
I'VE STABILIZED THESE THREE PSYCHORATS! THEY'LL CARRY US ACROSS THE GARBAGE PLAINS.
HOLY MOTHER! HOLY MOTHER! WAKE UP!
SHE NEVER EVEN LOOKED AT ME.

Animah & Tanatah

A key character in the *Incal* series, Animah is the sister of Tanatah and the guardian of the Luminous Incal. Her kingdom is Center Earth, across which she gallops on the back of giant Psychorats after the paradise turned into a giant garbage dump. According to Mœbius's notebooks, among the many names the creators considered for this character included: Hetna the beautiful, Any Mamundi (Anima Mundi), Arua (most likely a reference to *Ar-ruah*, which means "spirit" in Hebrew, but which is also derived from a pun in French obtained from "with rats"). The rats in her entourage read backwards as "star." As such, one can imagine her straddling the plane of the psyche represented by the Psychorats. Jodorowsky points out that "Animah is John Difool's mother," she's a reincarnation of his mother, hence the similar features between the two. It's no coincidence that Mœbius makes a connection between Animah and the Virgin Mary in his notebooks, "Virgin mother, daughter of your Son," as per Dante's definition of the Virgin Mary. Yet although John and Animah conceive Solune, his guardianship is entrusted to a ruthless killer: the Metabaron, thus converting "the one who sows death" into "the one who guards life."

Tanatah is the flip side of the coin. She kidnaps Solune to force the Metabaron into doing her a favor. As the Queen of Amok, she summons power to seize the City-Shaft. Her failure leads her to join the cause of the Incal and her true personality is then revealed: she is the guardian of the Black Incal, which she once gave to the Techno-Technos under the influence of the Darkness. The name "Tanatah" comes from *Thanatos*, the personification of death in Greek mythology.

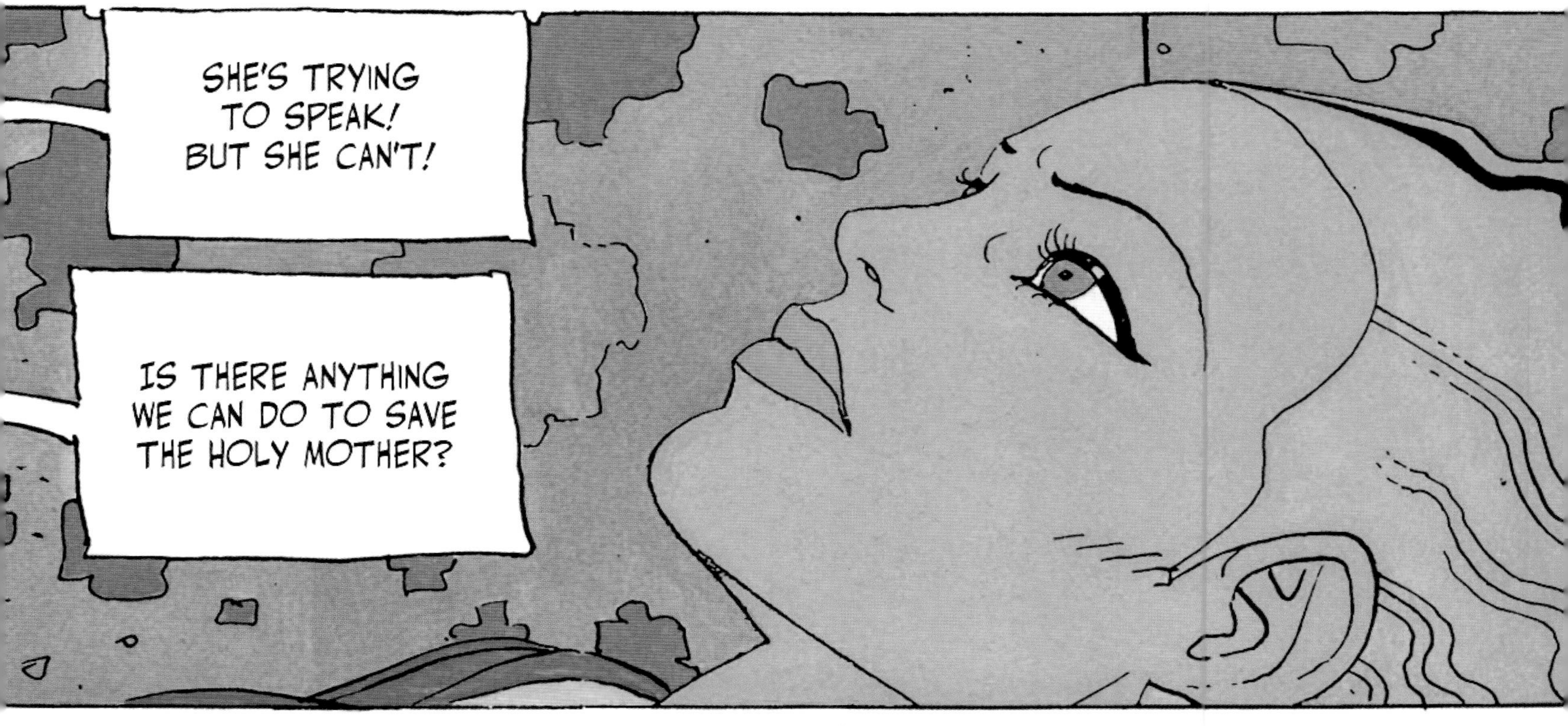
SHE'S TRYING TO SPEAK! BUT SHE CAN'T!
IS THERE ANYTHING WE CAN DO TO SAVE THE HOLY MOTHER?

Solune

Alejandro Jodorowsky: "Solune, John Difool's child, is the Sun and the Moon of the Tarot. The Emperoress—the Emperor and the Empress—is the original Hermaphrodite. Solune is also a hermaphrodite, but every symbol is essentially a hermaphrodite. Each of us has a masculine and feminine side. The Emperoress, i.e. the master of the galaxy, is not the true Androgyne: Solune will later take his/her place. It is for this reason that the Emperoress is in an egg; she/he is only the first step toward the true Androgyne. Why is Solune John Difool's child? Because each of us carries, however mediocre it may be, a divine seed deep in our mind, our soul, our subconscious. This seed is found in the alchemical result of Rebis (meaning 'dual'), or in the mythical avian Simurgh from *The Conference of the Birds* by the Persian poet Attar."

Solune becomes the perfect androgyne. As version or a representative of John, Solune becomes the living consciousness of the Starship created by the union of the two Incals, and then the Patmah that reigns over the Empire. In an early draft, he was named Parisis, then Erol 17. He was originally going to be the Metabaron's younger brother, a status that would have limited his role. Her/his symbolic significance is found in his/her name, which combines the words for Sun ("Soleil" in French) and Moon ("Lune" in French), once again mixing masculine and feminine.

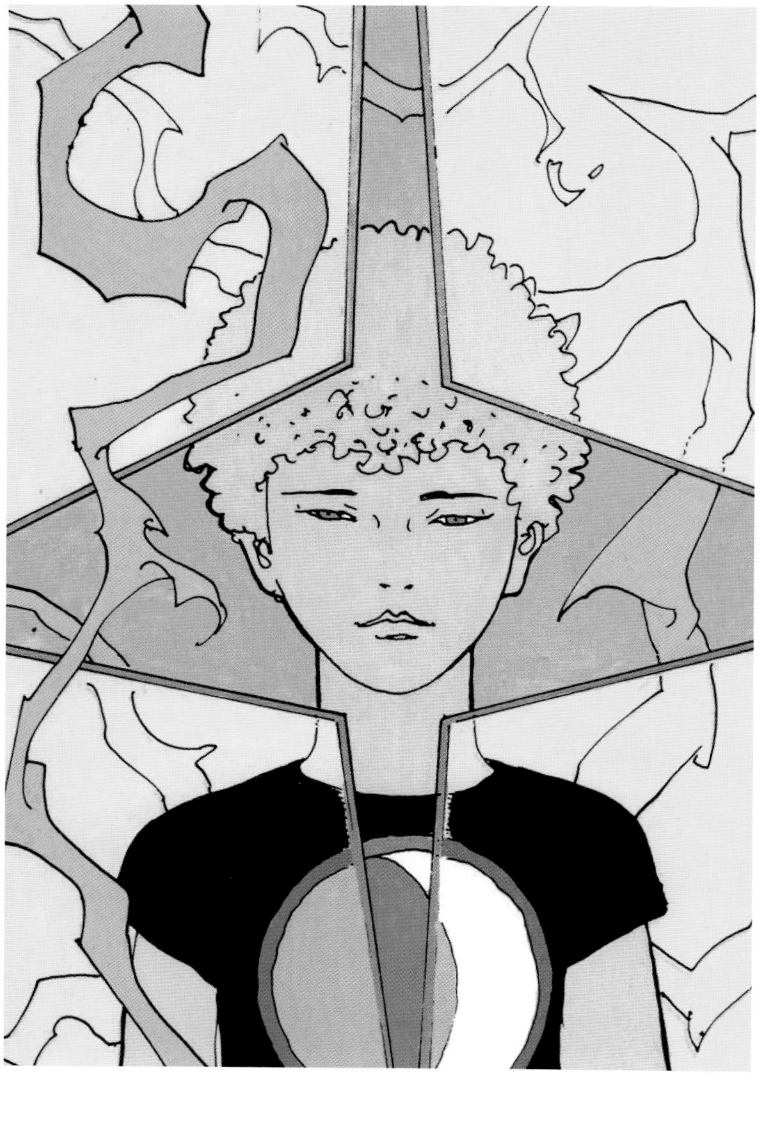

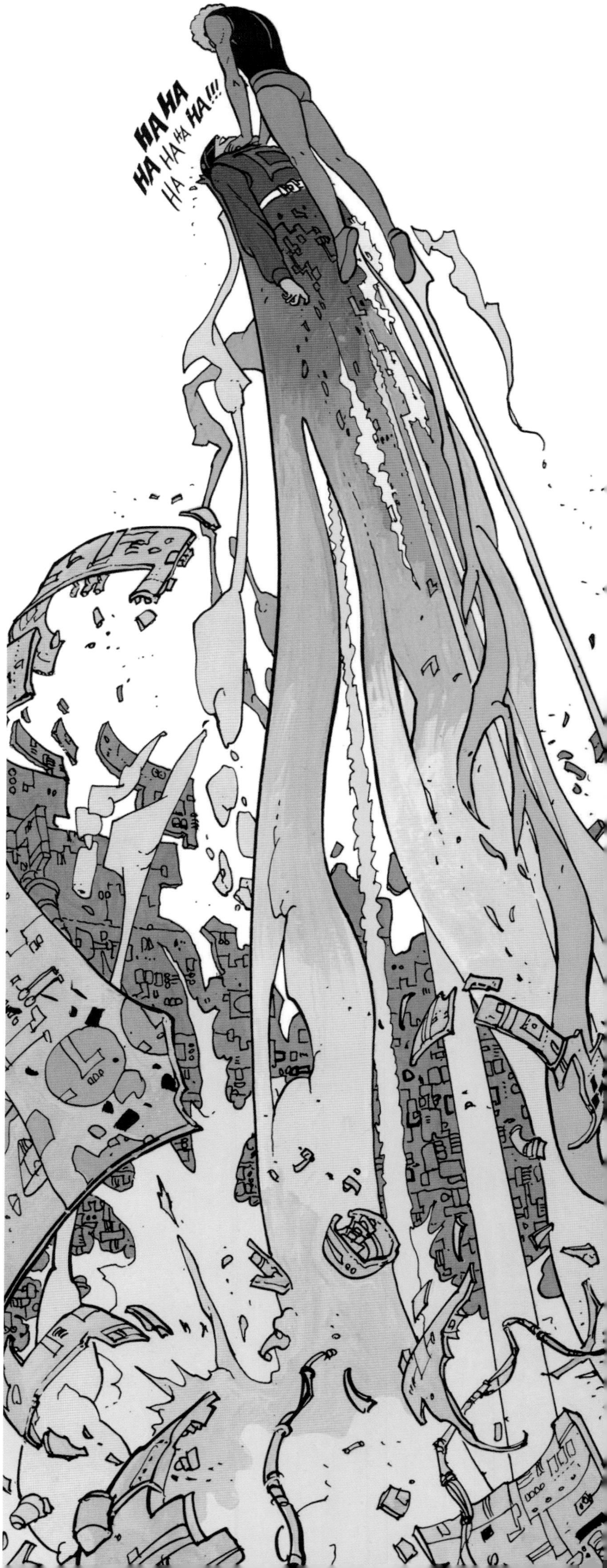
HA HA
HA HA HA HA!!!
HA

Kill Wolfhead

We first meet Kill Wolfhead in the opening pages of *The Incal*. He is just about to give an orgasm to Lady Nimbea Supra Qinq, an Aristo from the uppermost level who's come slumming at the Daredevil nightclub, when Difool, who's been hired to get the lady home before midnight, gets fidgety as the fateful hour approaches, shooting at Kill and bringing the passionate frolics to an abrupt end. "You little bastard! You shot a hole in my ear!" Kill cries out, while Difool tries to justify his act—"Let me explain, Kill! The lady and I have a contract"—as Nimbea expresses her own frustration, "That rotten bastard! I was finally about to have an orgasm! Tear him apart, Killy!"

The scene is filled with irresistible comedy worthy of a vaudeville act. As Kill prepares to beat the crap out of Difool, the Class "R" Detective manages to distract him by drawing his attention to Nimbea, who now finds herself sitting before them in her actual body, that of "an old woman, whose holo-mask wore off at midnight!" Following this revelation, things happen very fast, as John Difool later tells the Cybo-cops who arrest him. Kill goes crazy, convinced that the hapless Difool is responsible for Nimbea's transformation, and chases after him through the Daredevil, which forces Difool to escape through a ventilation shaft in which he has a pivotal encounter that sets the whole story in motion: an encounter with a monstrous mutant who hands him the Incal...

It would be reductive to see Kill as a simple thug, bullying the weak with his physical strength, a vulgar guard dog devoid of personality. He goes on to show that he possesses the qualities of a warlord capable of leading an insurrection as well as a certain technological know-how that enables him to repair the Necrodroid. Kill eventually joins Difool's group of companions, letting his burning desire for payback find almost childish expression on certain occasions, before he manages to eventually make peace with Difool. And, in a comical reversal of power, a transformed and self-confident Difool even manages to give Kill an order, "Can't you shut the damned thing up? I've had enough robots to last me a lifetime!" without provoking an angry reaction. With a hole in his ear that gives him a sense of fragility and humanity, Wolfhead emerges as a familiar and, in the end, appealing figure in the story, a loyal companion and a colorful character who's perfect in the role of sidekick, without which no good story is complete.

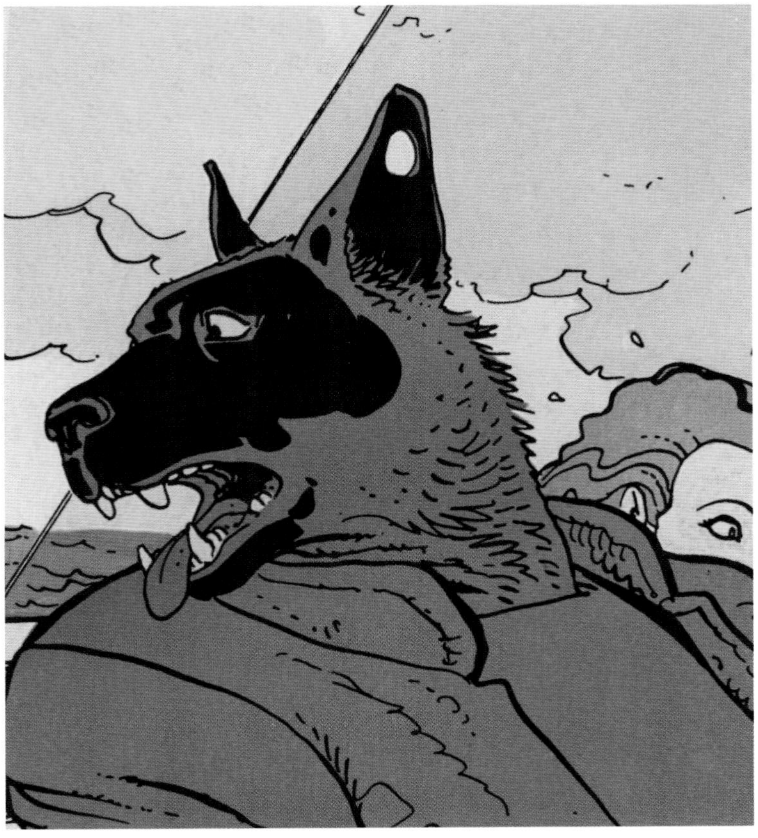

And in *Final Incal*, he acquires an even greater dimension. Kill becomes a genuine and charismatic leader, a great revolutionary figure that ranks among the most beautiful characters in the *Incal* universe. Fighting alongside the leaders of the Free Bio Army, he's become the general of the first rebel division, an uncontested and respected leader. His words of wisdom in the last pages of *Final Incal*, as he talks about the friends he's lost in combat and tells Luz he's just a soldier, are among the most moving in the whole series.

Arhats

With their white beards, body-length tunics, and their two hands joined together, the Arhats are the friendly 1,000-year-old guardians of legend. Twelve of them, like the apostles, welcome John Difool and his companions, whom they then help through the mirror, the "vibrating doorway that opens onto the miraculous forest of singing crystals."

The Arhats are good-natured sages whose message is not accessible to everyone: "Who's that old fart?" cries out an ignorant TV-addict upon seeing one of them on the screen. Spiritual guides whose advice is not only beneficial to the characters in *The Incal* with whom they are talking, but also to the reader: "Do not concern yourselves! Concentrate on making progress in your tasks!" They are like protective guardian angels moving through space by means of crystals—a recurring motif in Mœbius's work—holders of knowledge and experience that they seek to share after their world was destroyed.

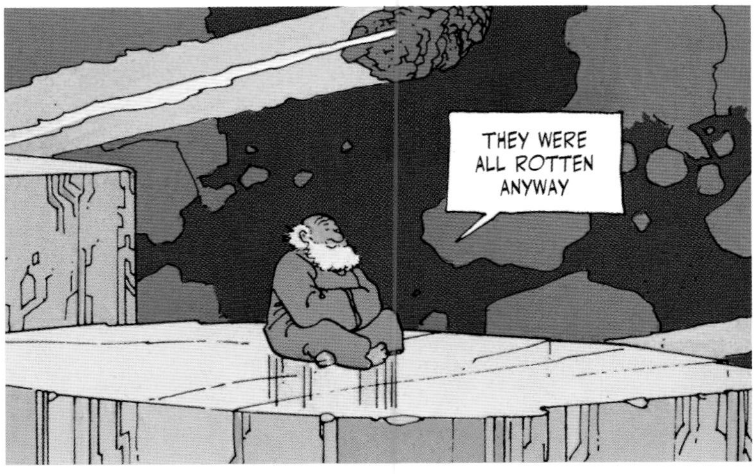
THEY WERE ALL ROTTEN ANYWAY

Protofather

It would be tempting to categorize John Difool as the typical confirmed bachelor, holed up in his conapt man-cave like a bear in his den, drowning his solitude in the arms of homeo-whores and reducing happiness on Terra to a good swig of the ol' whisky. But that would be neglecting to take into account the trials and tribulations of life as a Class "R" private dick who suddenly finds himself encountering the Incal. And thus John Difool becomes, in spite of himself, an honorable father and family man at the head of a household of 78 billion children, each of them blessed with his face. But he is more than just a father; he's actually the "Protofather," as he learns from the mouth (or rather beak) of a Berg. "Wait! You said your name was John Difool? John Difool! That was the name of the Protofather!"

Upon being ratted out to the local authorities by his nemesis Gorgo the Foul, who still holds a grudge for having been relegated to second place at the Great Nuptial Games ("I should have won, not him. There should have been 78 billion foul ones! It ain't fair!"), Difool figures he can escape the situation by claiming to be just another member of the local population and to lack any distinguishing features. "I'm a real Jondiff. I curse the Protofather. I spit on his DNA!" Alas, it's a lost cause: the presence of a navel on his stomach—helpfully pointed out by the aforementioned grudge-holding and sportsmanship-lacking Gorgo—is a dead giveaway that leads him straight before a court. There he is tried publicly for being single-handedly responsible for the hatred that their collective mother, Barbariah, harbors toward her children, which in turn has led to the misfortune of all 78 billion of them.

Barbariah

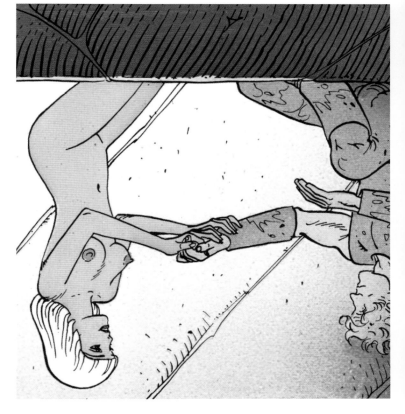

After winning the Nuptial Games, organized to decide who will have the honor of impregnating the Protoqueen, John Difool discovers to his great horror that the lady in question doesn't quite meet his criteria for feminine beauty, to put it mildly. "It's a nightmare!" he cries out, gazing down at a tub filled with a liquid of dubious composition, on whose surface floats a giant eye and a mouth meant to embody his betrothed. And yet it really is Barbariah, who urges him to come and join her—"Make love to me! Drown yourself in me, my love!"—and who then has the wisdom to take on a human appearance in order to awaken poor John's suddenly missing libido. For she understands the psychology of those she calls "short-lived mortals" and the fact that they require an image in order to be able to love. And so she transforms herself into Animah (whom she refers to as a "frigid bitch"), with whom Difool is hopelessly in love, and he doesn't have the strength to resist this perfect representation of the woman he adores, even going so far as agreeing to give up his life just to spend one moment of bliss with her. This action, however, will cause John to feel guilty after the fact for betraying the real Animah with her own image.

Of note is John's physical transformation on pages 202 and 203 in *What Is Above*, the fourth volume in *The Incal*, where this scene comes into play. His features become more refined, his face smoother, the crosshatching that made him look like Red Neck (a pal of Blueberry, the iconic character created by Jean-Michel Charlier and Jean Giraud/Gir) disappear to give way to streamlined facial features, as if the intimacy he is about to share with Barbariah/Animah were giving him a newfound purity. This is yet another sign of the constant evolution that Moebius imposes on his characters and his art in *The Incal*.

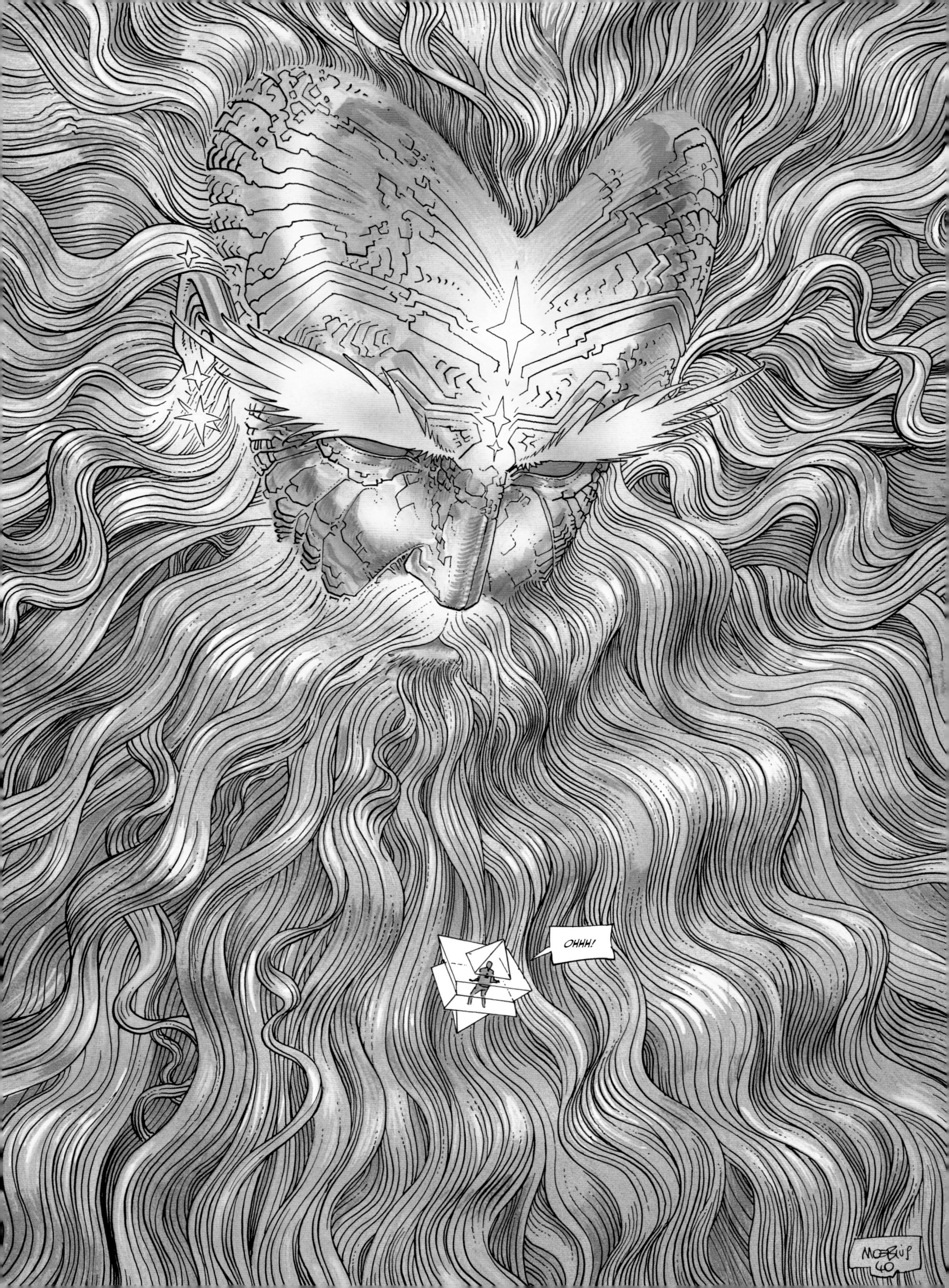
OHHH!
MOEBIUS
40

Orh

"I am ORH, the eternal light. I am the entity that was sent to create this time and this space." In the last pages of *The Incal*, a character appears who is someone we haven't seen before but who nevertheless looks familiar. The long golden beard that flows across the page, that regal forehead, the impression of omnipotence and serenity that emanates from his beautiful face... There is a divine quality about Orh, at least in terms of the classical representation of God in Western culture and art. The reader, however, has every right to ask the same question as John Difool—now reduced to the size of a tiny, frail creature who seems to drown in the hairs of Orh's flowing, undulating beard—does: "But, who are you?"

In the 1993 issue #27 of the fanzine *Sapristi*, Jean Giraud/ Mœbius offered up an analysis of the character: "Orh is definitely the ultimate possibility of representing a palpable and, above all, representable supraconsciousness. There are many other ideas behind it. Once you make the decision to show him, then you frame him into what has been conceived, what is human. What's interesting for the individual is having an area to which he doesn't have access but which he knows exists. It's in this area that there is another space of freedom and where you can draw from your intuition, otherwise you're only repeating and combining elements that are already known. When you say: 'God is dead,' the one who died is ORH (in French there is the added subtle linguistic similarity between ORH and 'dead' ('mort')). And this means that it's this image of the old god, with the features of a patriarch, that's dying, and that is also why, at the end of *The Incal*, we see a child appear. God is dead, long live God! But it's not the real, unfathomable god, it's the god that, each time we recreate ourselves individually or collectively, who ages with us and who's a projection of all our dreams, anxieties, fears, of our entire personal experience and of everything our parents taught us."

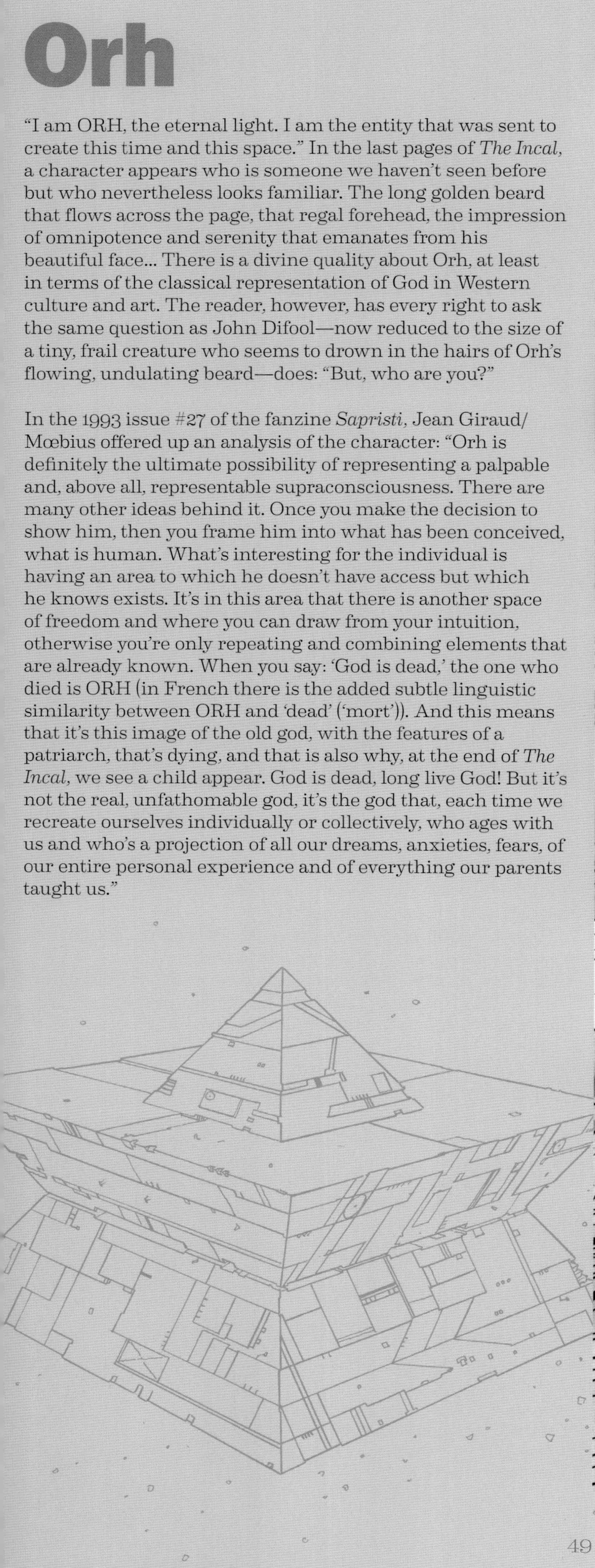

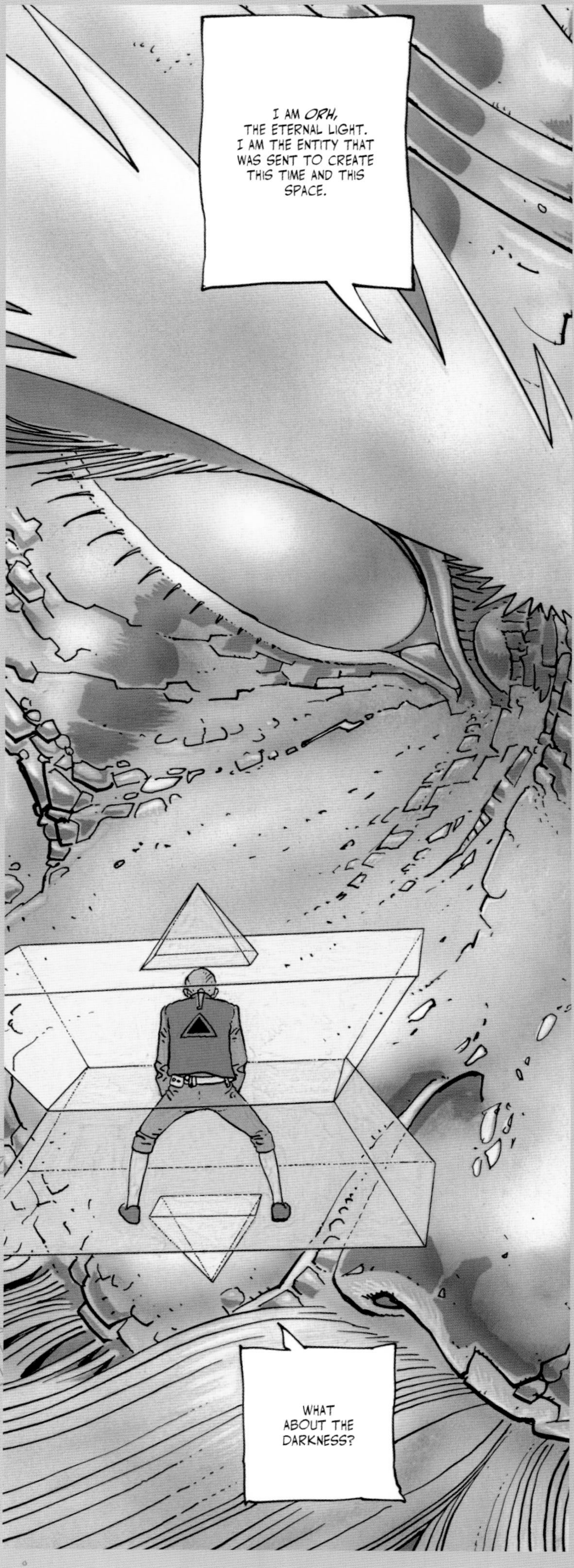
I AM ORH, THE ETERNAL LIGHT. I AM THE ENTITY THAT WAS SENT TO CREATE THIS TIME AND THIS SPACE.
WHAT ABOUT THE DARKNESS?

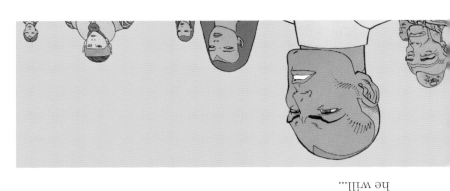

Raïmo

The comrade leading the united colonial Troglosocialiks.

"Raïmo was cast aside in the *Incal* series and we failed to realize how important he was as a character." Alejandro Jodorowsky says with regret. "In actuality, it's a family, a tribe. The hero as a complete family. It's the end of the individual hero, who cedes his place to a 'hero-family'. It's a collective character, something foreign to John Difool, whose big mistake was to never come out of his shell. The Raïmo family travel in a starship called *Hope*—the hope brought by a galactic family that represents the pure and ecological side of the galaxy. They come from an environmentally friendly planet, they are settlers, and they will fight against the artifice of the Techno civilization that has taken over the world. Their family has seven members—five adults and two children—just as there are seven members in the fellowship of the Incal. And there is another similarity between the two groups: they unite against the Darkness. Raïmo is undoubtedly one of the most positive characters in the series, the one with the least evidence of a dark side in him. Everything about him makes him the classic archetypal hero, whereas the Metabaron is a more modern hero and John Difool a perfect anti-hero."

In the planning stages of *The Incal*, Raïmo first went by the name Raïmon—similar to Raymond, which just so happened to be the name of Jean Giraud's father. Giraud said that he had made Raïmo—who, in his view, embodied the holier-than-thou, rigid, ridiculous rebel—in the image of his father: the slightly distant and absent image of a man who loved to lecture. But nothing is ever simple and clear-cut in the *Incal* universe: "Raïmo" is also the name of a Parisian ice cream shop located in the 12th arrondissement, where Jodorowsky enjoyed going when he lived in Vincennes... But regardless of his origins, Raïmo remains one of the outstanding figures in the *Incal* saga. He deserves to follow in the Metabaron's footsteps and star in his own spinoff series. Perhaps one day he will...

Kaïmann

Commander Kaïmann makes his first appearance in the last installment in *Before the Incal*, *Suicide Alley*. A man dressed entirely in black, he's at the head of a formidable armada of pirates lusting for conquests, planets, and women. But his dignity and calm demeanor contrast with the traditional imagery of a pirate prone to all the excesses of body and mind. Indifferent to the orgies his men indulge in following their victorious missions, Kaïmann is prey to permanent grief, which is grounded in his endless quest for the perfect woman, whom he dreams about but who always slips through his fingers. "You know that my tastes are not given to such excesses. While my men cavort with these whores, my solitude will be my only company," he tells his second-in-command, the loyal Olaf.

But then one day, Kaïmann finally crosses paths with his heart's desire, who is none other than Luz de Garra. From that moment forward, he does everything in his power to satisfy even her smallest desires and offer her the "treasures from across the galaxies" piled up on Tortuga Island, his fabulous estate—whose name is derived from the Caribbean island that 17th century pirates used as their lair. Alas:

"Though I admire you as I admire no other man, I cannot love you, for my heart is promised to another," Luz explains. But when Kaïmann takes her to Terra 2014 to confront John Difool, whose memory has been erased, she understands that her love for John is no more than a memory now.

Kaïmann returns in *Final Incal*, but he's lost some of his magnificence. The Gouna attack has turned him into a carnivorous mutant, a kind of unrecognizable giant lizard who "has almost no humanity left in him." But this doesn't keep him from unwittingly stirring up feelings of jealousy in John Difool, who gets annoyed when he hears Luz tell the pirate she's in love with him. The Techno-surgeons are able to reverse the commander's mutation, but he subsequently gives up his life for the cause of all those fighting the Prez, in a selfless gesture equal to his nobility.

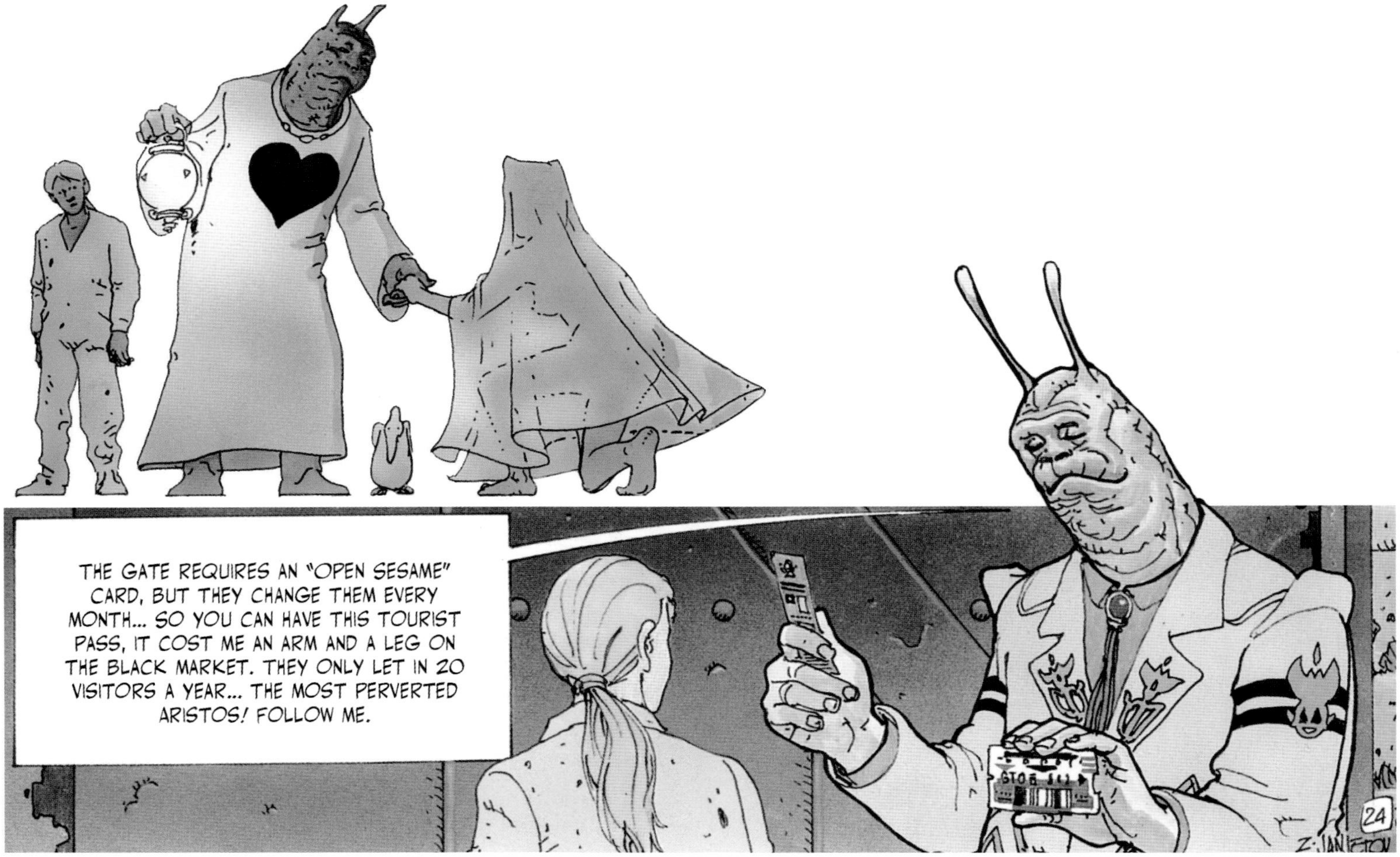
THE GATE REQUIRES AN "OPEN SESAME" CARD, BUT THEY CHANGE THEM EVERY MONTH... SO YOU CAN HAVE THIS TOURIST PASS, IT COST ME AN ARM AND A LEG ON THE BLACK MARKET. THEY ONLY LET IN 20 VISITORS A YEAR... THE MOST PERVERTED ARISTOS! FOLLOW ME.
24

Snailhead

Let's face it: Snailhead is anything but attractive, be it from a physical or a moral standpoint. This mutant we meet in *Before The Incal* initially appears under the twin guises of a pimp and a drug dealer. As the Amorine supplier of John Difool's mother (who calls him a "slimy mutant"), Snailhead keeps her in a state of dependency, making it possible for her to ply her trade as a prostitute on a daily basis.

But appearances can be deceiving: Snailhead actually saves young Difool's life a little later on, when, overcome with grief after the death of his parents, the latter tries to kill himself by jumping from the top of Suicide Alley. John soon learns that Snailhead, far from being responsible for his mother's death, was deeply in love with her and was only providing her with Amorine to help her stay alive as long as possible after she contracted the deadly and incurable Meropa virus. Difool also finds out that behind the dealer exterior is a real moral authority within the GTO compound, where mutants live and where Snailhead, a reverend with the Neuro-Emotional Church, offers John a place to live and helps him discover the healing power of Love.

John Difool and Snailhead meet up again in *Psycho Anarchists*, the fourth volume of *Before The Incal*. Having had his lower and upper limbs amputated for committing an unforgivable crime—"My only crime was believing in an emotion that had been unknown for thousands of years: love."—Snailhead is now the leader of a group of anarchists fighting against the corruption of Terra 2014 and for the triumph of unbridled love.

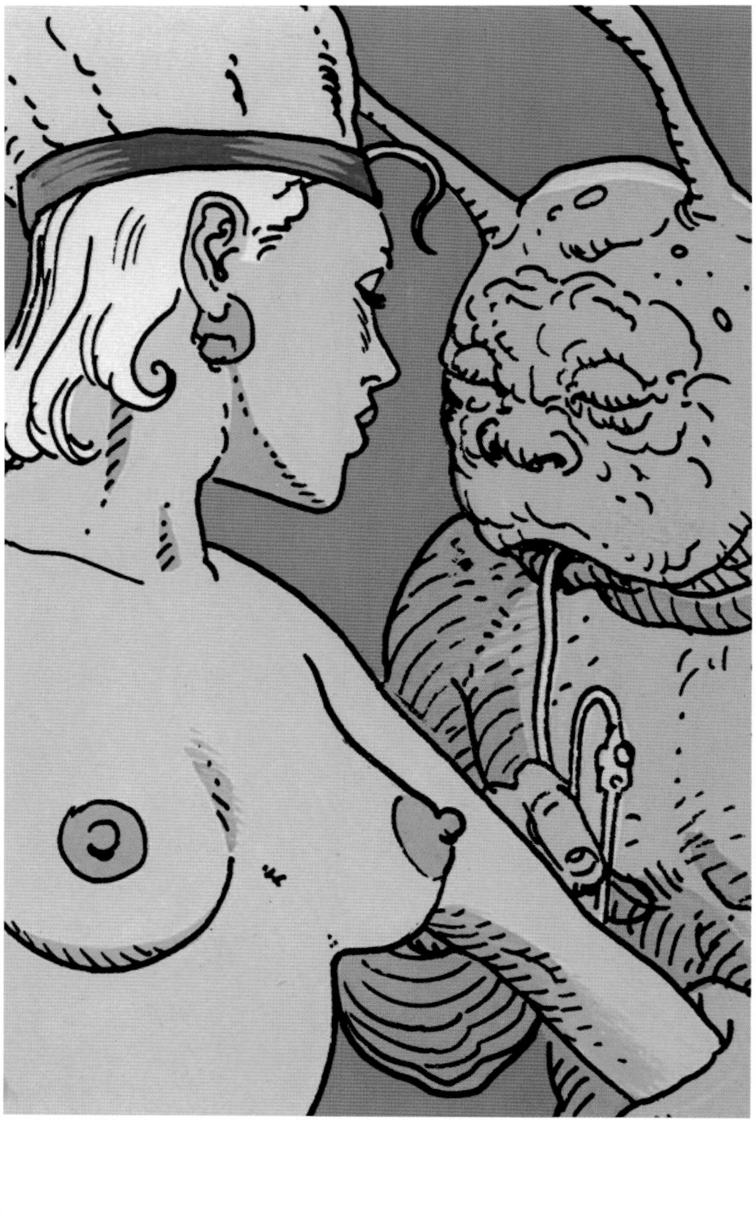

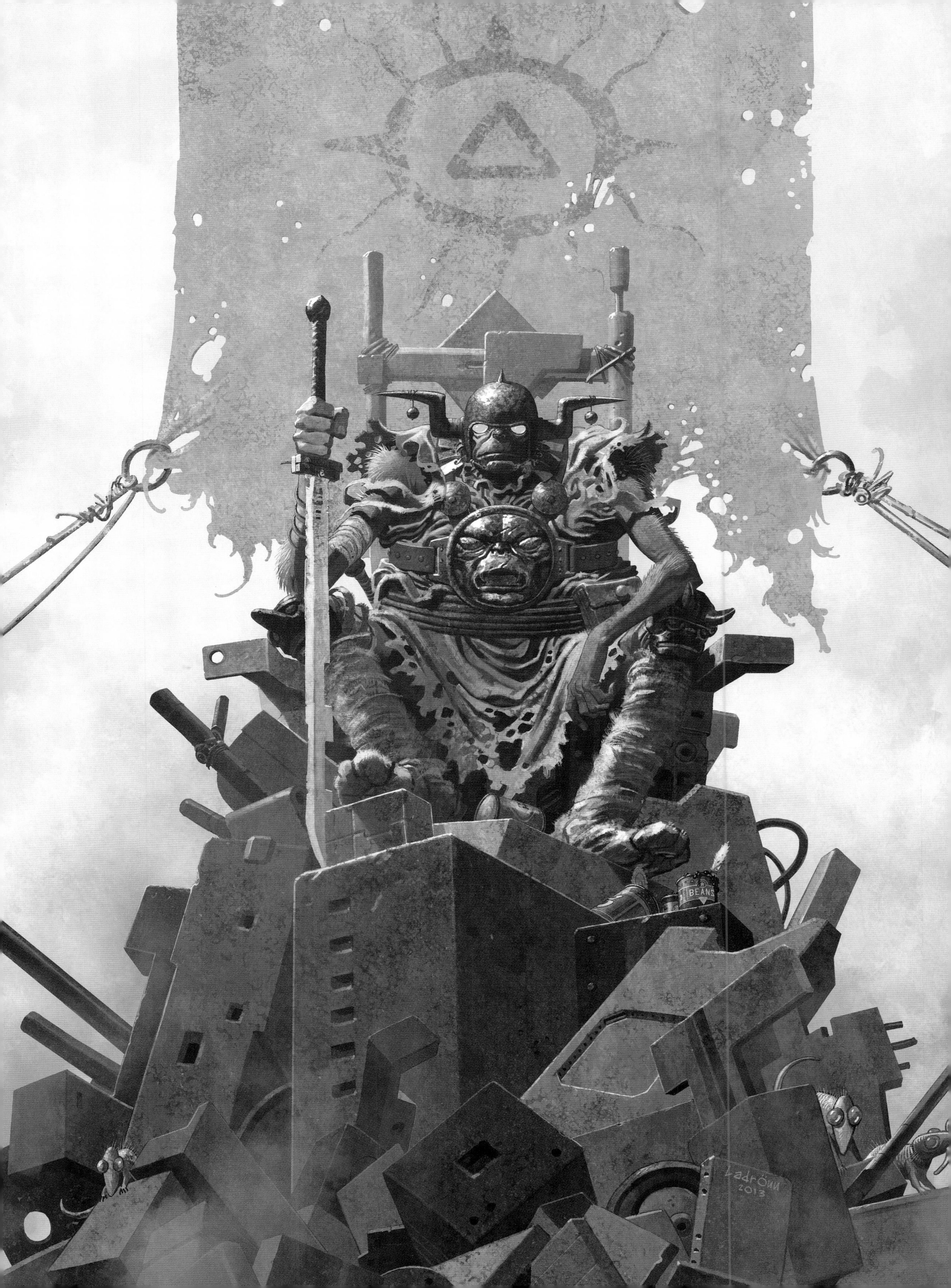
BEANS
Ladrönn
2013

Gorgo the Foul

Gorgo the Foul makes his debut appearance in *What Lies Beneath*, the third volume of *The Incal*, shortly after Difool and his friends land on the great pile of trash of Center Earth. Gorgo would have fit in perfectly with the cast of *Mad Max*, with an outfit made of rags and a head coiffed in a sort of jester's hat that makes him look both threatening and grotesque. The head of an army of trash-eating mutants with empty gazes, he rules as lord and master over the dump and uses a most dreaded weapon: nets of saliva. Hurling these slime vines, he and his troop launch an attack against the container in which Difool and company have sought shelter from a garbage storm.

He appears again in *What Is Above*, as one of the participants in the Five Thousand Year Nuptial Games, a competition created to designate the one who will have the honor of impregnating the Protoqueen. The contest involves fighting hundreds of opponents armed to the teeth, each more savage than the next, to try to make it to the top of the sacred nuptial cone. Just as he is about to be the first to reach the summit, poor Gorgo is overtaken at the last second by John Difool, who has gone through intense training and is now driven by a heretofore unseen furor—and assisted by the parapsychic powers that the Metabaron transmitted to him. Much to his great disappointment, Gorgo the Foul has no choice but to accept defeat, which is being served up with a hearty side dish of humiliation—because let's face it, getting beat by some "human wimp" is enough to make any mutant furious.

Years later, Gorgo returns as a guest star in *Final Incal*, even lending his name to a volume of the book. But it's a changed Gorgo, gone from the status of military brute at the head of an unruly mob, to that of true revolutionary, in love with Luz de Garra, whom he worships as a goddess, and ready to blindly follow in the fight against the Prez, a fight for freedom and the preservation of all bio-life. "We can't just sit around on our asses waiting to die," he shouts, to motivate his troops. "Let's fight for our survival! Destiny is in our hands. I'll unite all the tribes and we'll head to the surface and kill the Prez and that scrap metal army of his!" His legendary verve does wonders in the heated battles he leads his men into against the Cybo-cops. "I'll give them a lil' something that'll fry their memory cards," he says, after tossing a bomb at them. "Go to paleo-hell, you puppets!" he screams as he charges them head down, his swords his only weapons against the deadly Kogans of the Cybo-cops.

A colorful and engaging character, Gorgo is nonetheless a soldier with morals that can be rudimentary and muddled at times. Determined to take Luz as his wife and to plant in her "the seeds of the new generation" (a euphemistic expression Gorgo uses to describe what is nothing less than rape), it takes a last-second intervention by Deepo (assisted by the Incal) to rescue Luz and bring this crude warrior back to his senses. Jodorowsky was tempted more than once to write the solo adventures of Gorgo the Foul, undoubtedly because of his extreme—and often base—qualities.

Kolbo-5

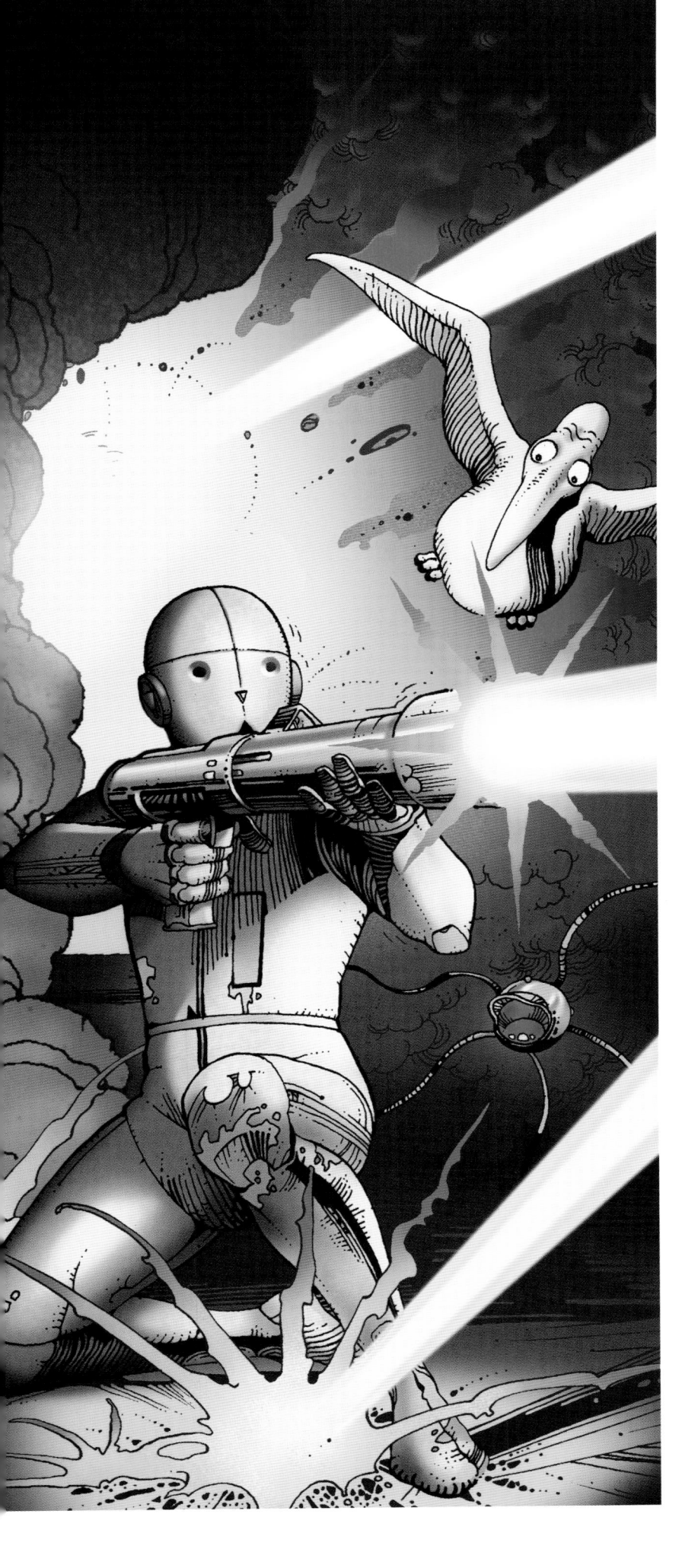

Kolbo-5 the robot enters the scene on the last page of the first volume of *Before The Incal*, when he saves the day for young John Difool, who finds himself in a delicate situation, surrounded by a gang of terrifying feminists who see him as a "dirty male." Yet his appearance is anything but heroic: he's missing an arm and a leg (both metallic, obviously), he hops instead of walks, and the rust on his carcass makes him like an old toy destined for the trashcan. It's been ages since he's had his nuts and bolts oiled, not since the tragic day he was thrown out with the trash, but Kolbo-5 proves still useful as he becomes a mentor, spiritual guide, and surrogate father for the newly orphaned John Difool, who finds it hard to fit into society. After John is invited to move into Kolbo-5's hideout, loneliness fades away for both of them, although in John's case, the loneliness is relative, since he can always count on his loyal Deepo to keep him company. As the affable Kolbo starts finding a new meaning to his existence, his protégé gradually reaches a higher level of consciousness thanks to the life lessons imparted to him by his new metallic friend. "Two is better than one, for if one falls, the other can come to his aid. What would become of one who fell without anyone to assist him?" the robot teaches him, introducing him to the wisdom of paleo-books from the pre-Techno-Techno era. And he doesn't hesitate to put Difool in his place when he descends into self-doubt: "Enough of your self-inflicted neuroses! A nice hot bath will bring you back to your senses!"

Kolbo-5 is a robot unlike any other. The spirit of religion fills this android who is decidedly too human and too sensitive to be just a mere chunk of metal casing. "Hear my prayer, Lord. Turn not a deaf ear to my sorrow," he implores when he has no news of John and Luz de Garra in *Vhisky, SPV, and Homeo-Whores*, the fifth volume of *Before The Incal*. His robotic circuits allow him to experience feelings and emotions, just as humans do, which is why the Techno industry, anxious to avoid mutual sympathy between robots and bio-beings, installed in the robots a self-destruction mechanism as a safeguard. If Kolbo-5 suppresses his feelings, it's not out of indifference, but rather that he knows that he will die if he allows himself to express empathy—a brutal death in the form of an explosion that will blow him into a thousand pieces. He's often forced to use reason to avoid getting emotional, even if that means taking a nice long shower to cool off when the heat of emotion is about to overwhelm him. "Stay calm, Kolbo-5! Keep those troublesome emotions out of you! Neutrality! Neutrality!" he tells himself. John listens to his advice and eventually comes to understand that the "poor pile of cold metal" is capable of love and that he is a true guru.

Kolbo-5 eventually explodes in the penultimate volume of *Before the Incal*, dying with the satisfaction of having experienced human emotions at last, in the form of what he poetically calls "the bitterness of despair," which surges through him when he discovers John Difool's memory has been surgically removed. Nevertheless, he returns in *After The Incal*, much to the great surprise of Difool, who saw him die—but "it was in another dimension: life has many layers," Kolbo-5 replies, ever the philosophical soul.

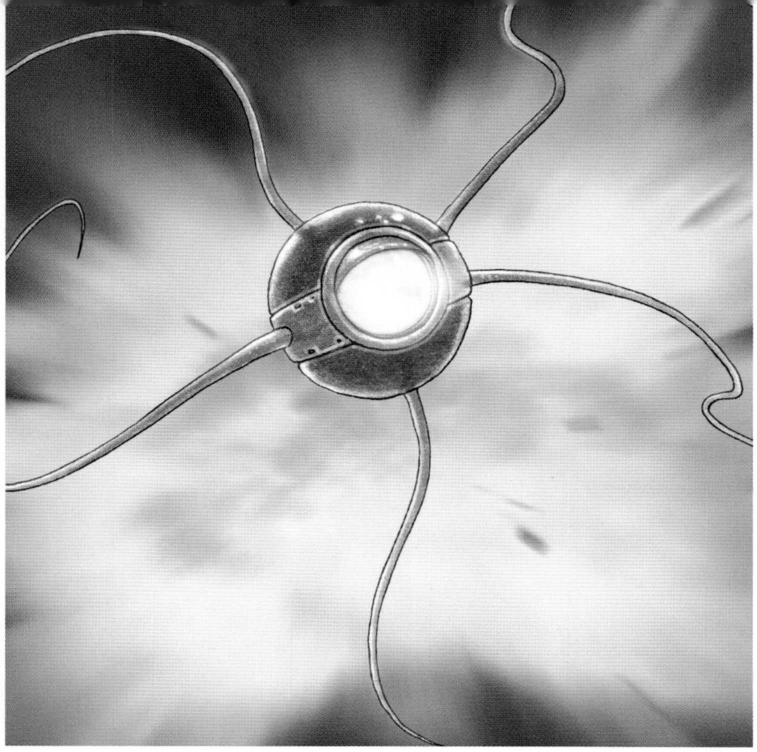

The Eyecop

Drones are an increasingly widespread reality nowadays, and whether the advantages of those strange machines outweigh the obvious disadvantages (killing from afar and the violation of privacy, among others) is still up for debate.

In *Before The Incal,* Alejandro Jodorowsky introduces a device inspired by drone technology: the Eyecop, a floating ball equipped with a camera and antenna that make it look like a flying insect. John Difool makes the acquaintance of one such "thing" as he's taking a bath and an Eyecop comes crashing without warning into his bathroom, breaking a window in the process—Steven Spielberg's 2002 film *The Minority Report* would go on to feature a nearly identical scene.

Though showing a blatant disregard of John's right to privacy, as well as any sense of propriety, the Eyecop nevertheless brings him good news and informs him of his appointment to the long coveted rank of Official Detective, Class "R." As events unfold, the device one might at first assume to be a detestable snitch proves to be a valuable ally endowed with consciousness: he refuses to allow Police Central the right to control his circuits and, in a beautiful gesture of self-sacrifice, asks John to remove his eye-camera before joining him and Kolbo-5 on their quest without so much as a moment's hesitation. "I'm just an honest Eyecop, after all," he says, in defense of his good intentions, as John smiles and thanks his "little spy." Proof once again that we should never completely give up on technology, and that even the worst situations have a way of turning themselves around...

Bergs

Who are the Bergs, and do they even actually exist? According to official propaganda, the Berg Empire—located in the Swan Constellation—intends to invade Terra 2014 to wipe it off the map. Difool encounters one of these mythical creatures in the first pages of *The Black Incal*. The mutant who hands him the Incal, the strange object on which "the fate of not only the planet but the fate of the whole universe" depends, decomposes under his very eyes to transform into a creature with the beak of a parrot, which is a distinctive feature of the Bergs. This freaky run-in inspires John's famous—and, as it turns out, prophetic—phrase: "I was involved in a mess of galactic proportions."

Incidentally, why do the Bergs all have a parrot's head? Jodorowsky and Mœbius provide the answer to that question in *Planet Difool,* the second part of *The Fifth Essence*. The responsibility lies with a parrot named Artrilys, who once won the Great Nuptial Games and with it the right to impregnate their queen, Barbariah, thus giving birth to children—called "Bergs" by the Terrans—who all inherited their father's face—that is, until a new generation of Bergs, born of the coitus between Barbariah and John Difool in *What Is Above,* all take after their new progenitor...

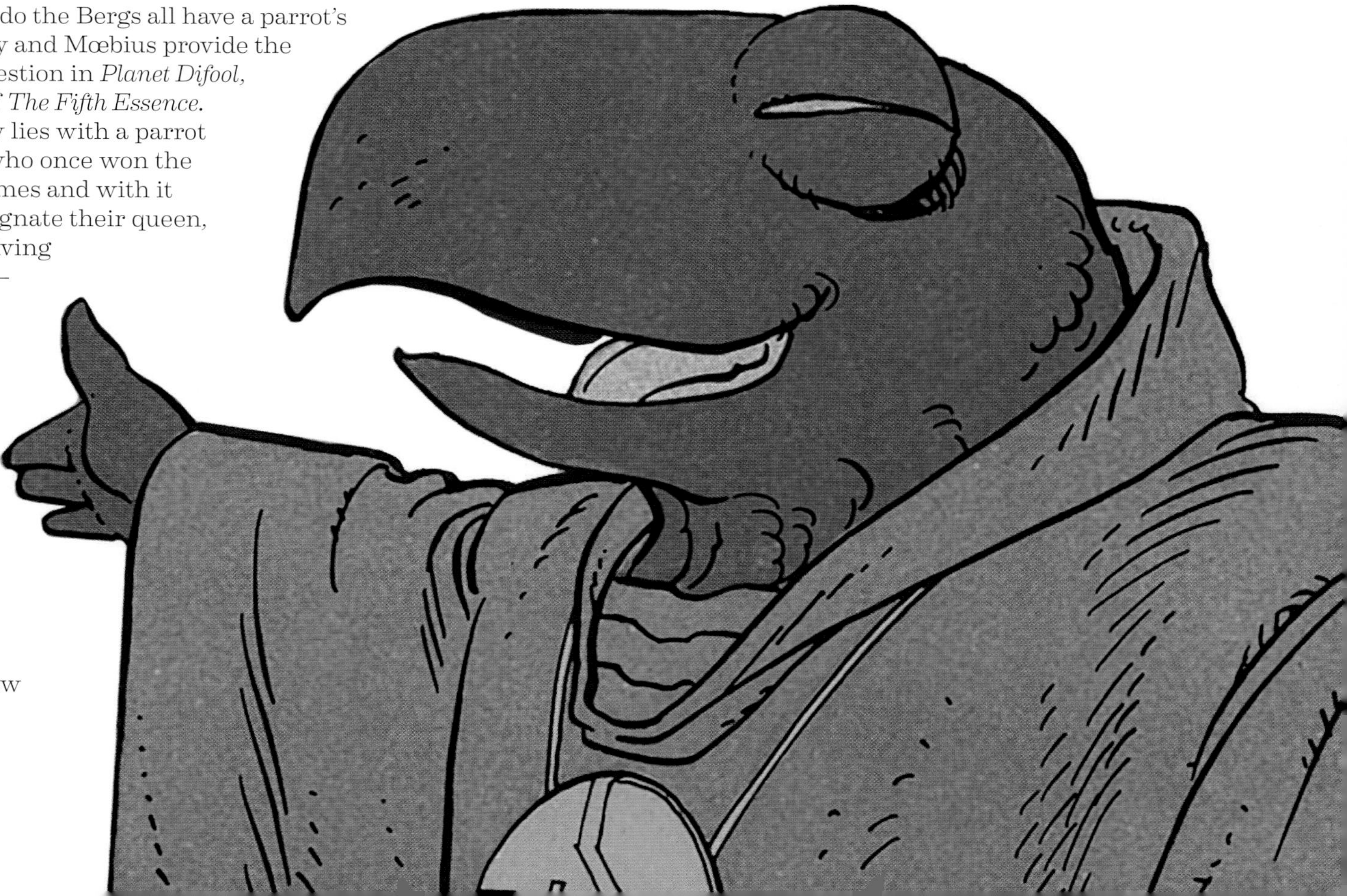

Archangels

Appearing in *Final Incal*, the White Archangels are "living, compassionate machines" that alone can overcome the black vampires, i.e. the supra-robots that pass "from one cosmos to another like the thread of a pearl necklace." These "celestial beings," as Luz calls them, which are like ectoplasm that illuminate space with their dazzling whiteness, function as both means of transport and weapons and have a highly distinctive sound: songs that produce "vibrations that affect the senses, making [people] more sensitive than usual." No wonder, then, that Luz can feel surging within her powerful, overwhelming feelings of love for John Difool. In this scene, one of the most beautiful and moving in *Final Incal,* Kill Wolfhead also opens up and reveals the nobility of the feelings buried deep inside his rough exterior shell as a man—or rather wolf—of war. "I have to overcome this pain and bury the past," he tells Luz. "The dead are no longer suffering and we must move forward."

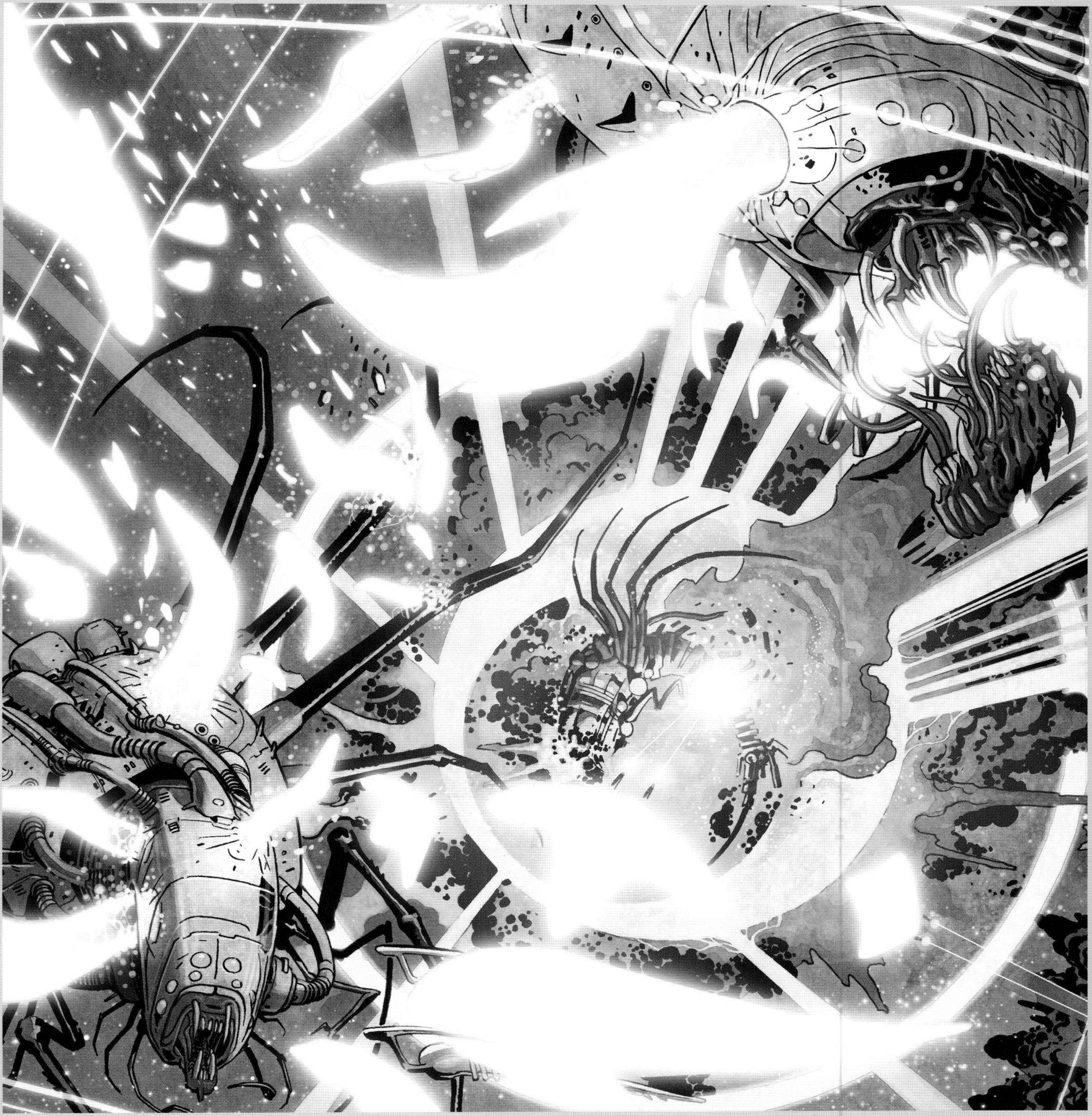

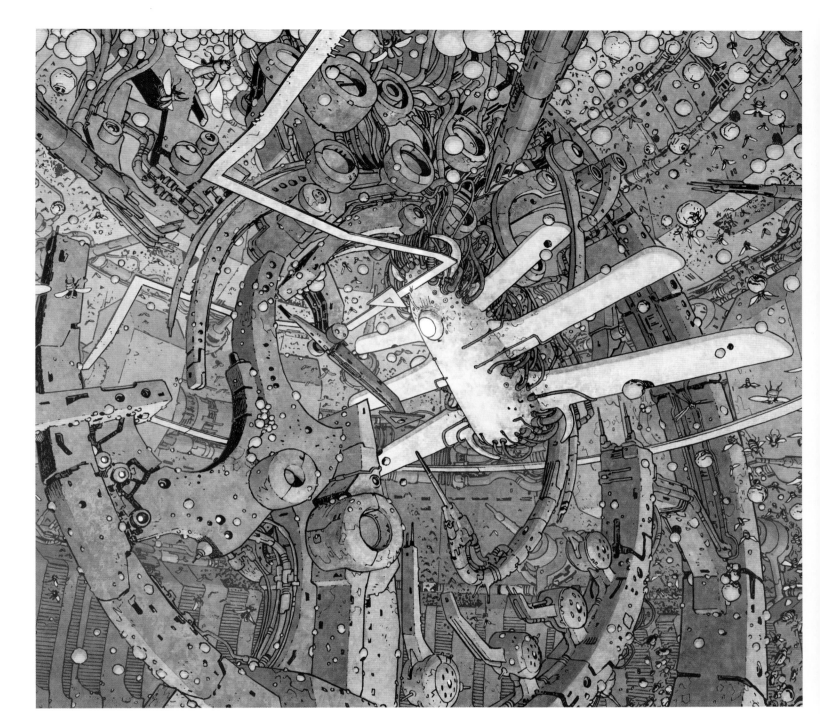

Elohim

Elohim is the counterpoint to the Benthacodon. One is white, the other black. One wants to return organic life to its central place again on Terra 2014, the other seeks to eradicate it once and for all. Elohim resembles a sort of immaculate insect, adorned with a cyclopean eye and whose wings have been cut off. These two meca-mutants engage in a merciless battle in *Final Incal*. "I am Elohim," the white meca-mutant, engaged in a war with the black meca-mutant, the Benthacodon...the monster who released the Biophage virus, not only on this planet, but throughout the entire cosmos. Organic life everywhere is in grave danger!" That's how he introduces himself to John Difool, who quickly realizes that he will once again have to play a role that is very possibly far beyond his abilities. Which is exactly what happens: Elohim informs John that he has "a mission and a destiny," before reactivating his memory and bringing forth the Incal. "Submit to the metamorphosis!" he tells him. "Become that which you truly are!"

But there's every reason to question Elohim's true identity. In *After The Incal*, he takes on the form of a blue-eyed, virginal-looking girl, who in turn takes on the form of an electronic insect aboard which John travels. Isn't it Elohim who, like a demiurge, appears again in the last pages of *Final Incal*, enshrouded in a dazzling and quasi-divine light to announce to John and Luz that it's up to them to "sow their love throughout the metallic universe" and that, thanks to them, "the universe will be saved"? Isn't he capable of "healing" the planet from its inside out, by connecting his arms to the earth? And doesn't his name simply mean "God" in the Hebrew Bible?

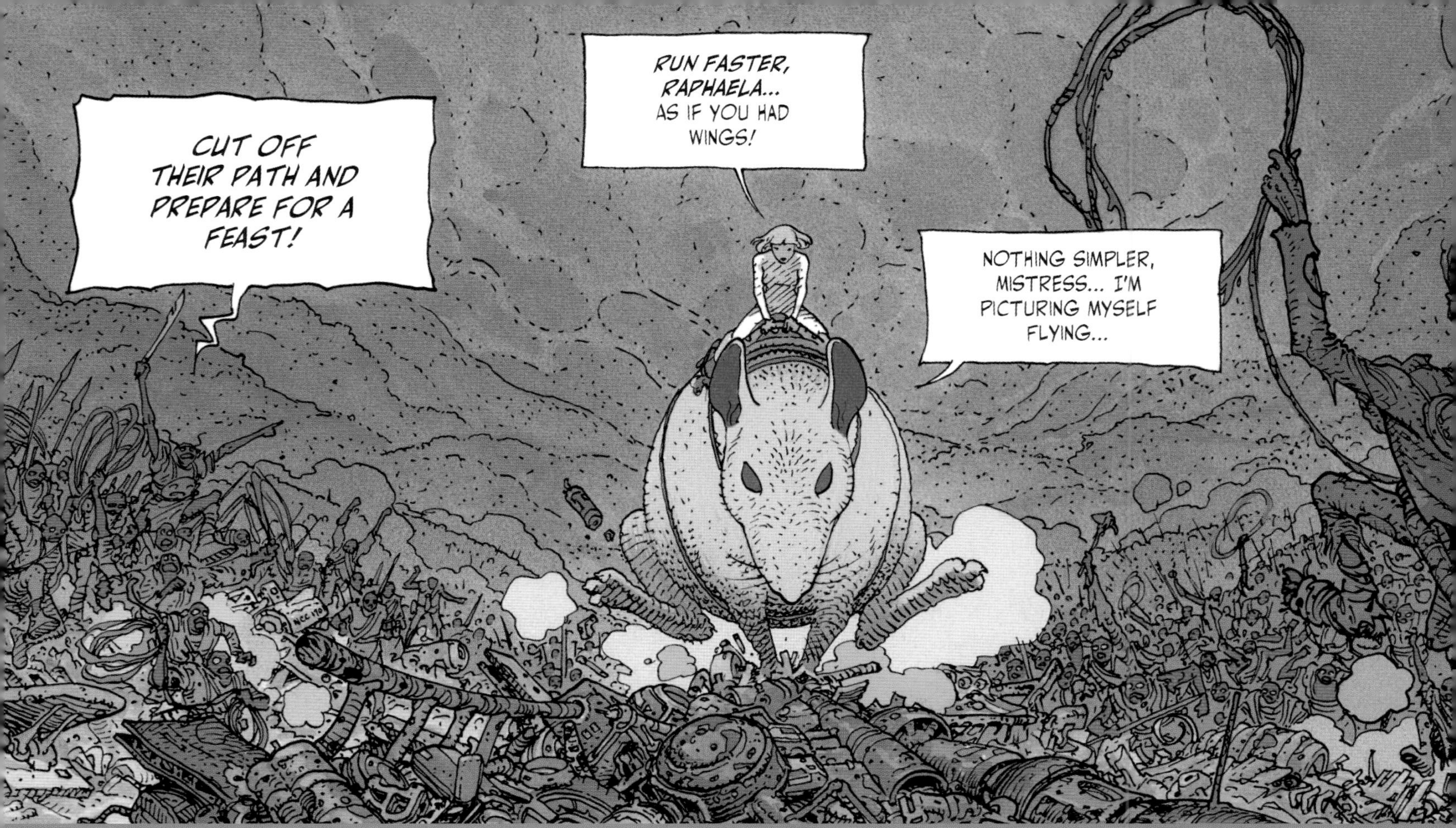
CUT OFF THEIR PATH AND PREPARE FOR A FEAST!
RUN FASTER, RAPHAELA... AS IF YOU HAD WINGS!
NOTHING SIMPLER, MISTRESS... I'M PICTURING MYSELF FLYING...

The Psychorats

Seeing rats running around a pile of garbage is not that surprising. Seeing enormous rats being ridden like horses by humans, on the other hand, is slightly more unexpected—although nothing should surprise us, really, in a story by Mœbius and Jodorowsky. The Psychorats, whose gray coats are spruced up with a lovely blue hue on their tails, ears, and noses, serve Animah, the queen of the rats. Their special trick is to grow larger under the effect of the fear they inspire in humans, as Difool, Kill Wolfhead, and others in Garbageland are quick to find out at their own expense, until Animah provides an explanation and a solution: "These are Psychorats! The more you fear them, the more they grow and multiply. Empty your minds! Let go of your fear and violence!"

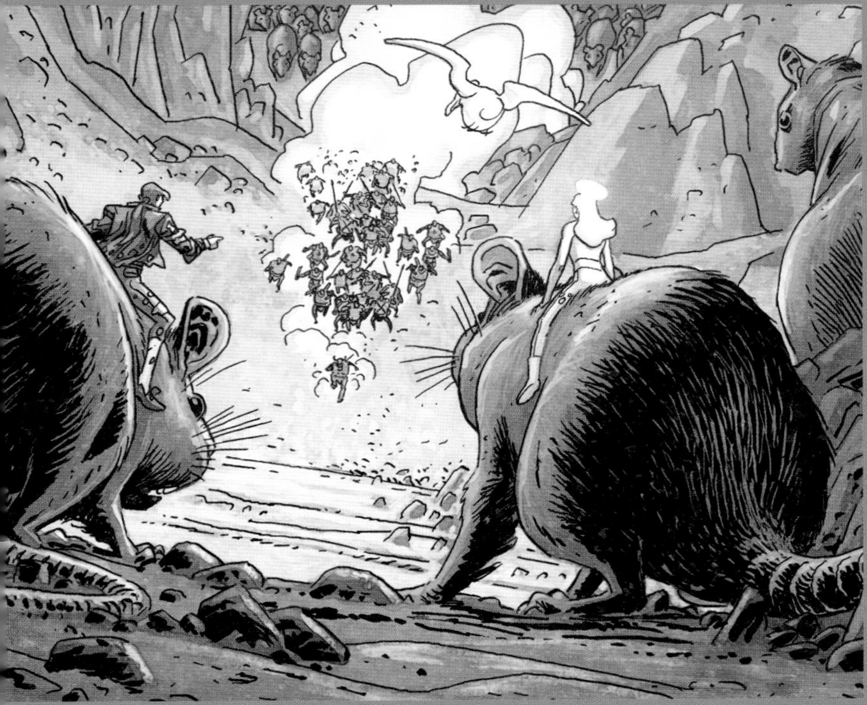

Danger feeds on fear. It is sometimes nothing more than a simple projection of our mind: it's enough to face a threat for it to vanish. Jodorowsky did the same thing with the nightmares that haunted him for a good part of his life. The terror of death plagued him until he was in his forties and decided one day to stare it in the face, causing it to disappear for good. The Psychorats are reminiscent of the giant white wolves in *Princess Mononoke*, the animated film directed by Hayao Miyazaki. And the scene in which Difool, Kill Wolfhead, and the others are trapped by millions of Psychorats brings to mind *L'Homme est-il Bon? (Is Man Good?)*, a short comic Mœbius created about a space traveler stranded on a hostile planet who's held captive by a horde of revolting creatures about as appealing as Animah's rodents.

The Psychorats make a comeback in *Final Incal*. After being hurled into the heart of Center Earth, John Difool and Luz de Garra come face to muzzle with a menacing horde of the creatures, who seem impervious to John's attempt to invoke the powers the Incal has given him. Fortunately, like Animah in *The Incal*, Luz—whose physical resemblance to the rat queen is striking—can hear their primitive thoughts and thus communicate with them, which then leads the animals to offer their help and take the pair to the headquarters of the rebels under the command of Kill Wolfhead.

UGH, IT STINKS!
PHEW! WHA-AAAH!
A RAT! A GODDAMNED FILTHY RAT!
CROUiii
??
UGH!
OOH NOOOO!
HOLY SHIT!

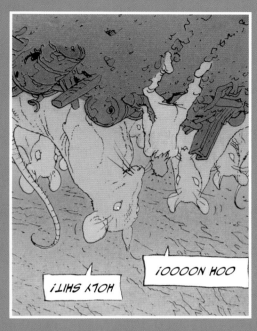

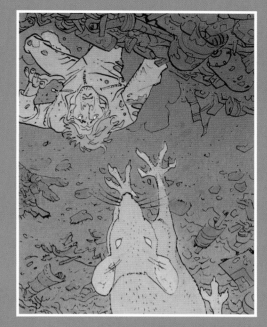

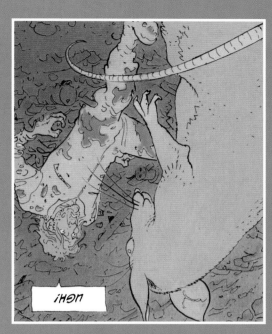

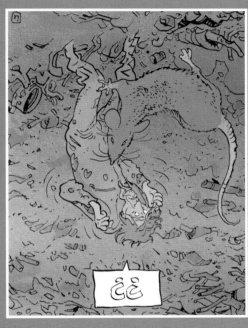

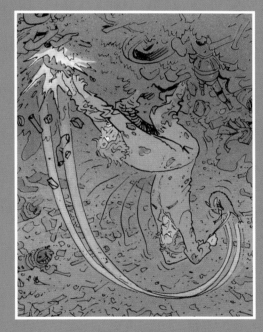

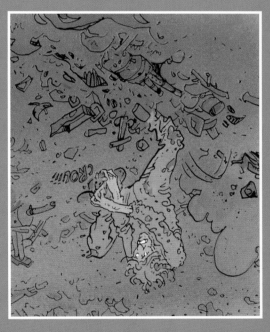

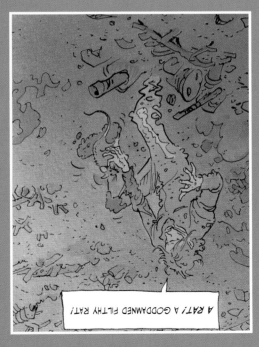

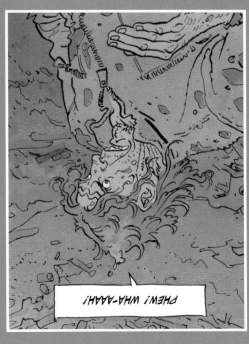

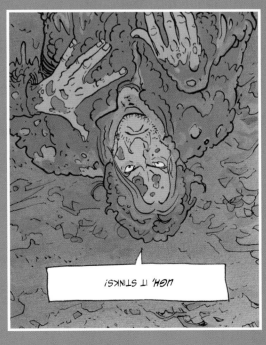

Anarchists

"Up with Psycho Anarchy!" Just after they manage to escape from the Aristo-maternity ward, where they discovered the horrible secret behind the Aristo halos, John Difool and Luz de Garra are rounded up by a group of Psycho Anarchists, in the fourth volume of *Before The Incal*, aptly titled *Psycho Anarchists*. These terrorists—who hide out in the lower levels—are mentally ill people suffering from a psychotic delirium, and their leader is none other than Snailhead, the mutant who once supplied Amorine to John's mother. His antennae and his two legs now amputated, he owes his life to his fellow combatants, whom he has converted to the anarchist cause. "This city is corrupt to the very bone in a way that cannot be cured. We fight to put it into a state of total dementia... so its citizens can discover unbridled love!" Snailhead explains to John and Luz.

Alert readers who have studied history may notice that the names of these Psychotic Anarchist comrades are derived from famous historical figures. While one of them is simply called Max Stirner, as an homage to the 19th century German philosopher considered one of the forerunners of anarchism, the names of other members of the group are more tongue in cheek, like Trosqui (Trotsky), who requires no introduction), Furiosso (Charles Fourier, inventor of *phalansteres*, self-contained residential buildings designed for a type of utopian community), and Borizvian, a reference to the French writer and musician Boris Vian.

The Necrodroid

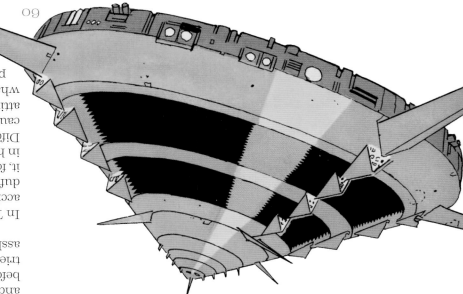

The newest marvel of presidential cloning, the Necrodroid is a conical-shaped robot-killer with impressive firepower. "The... the Necrodroid! The legendary, invincible killing machine! So, this is the ultimate presidential clone! Hide in your conapts, dear telefriends, if you want to stay alive!" This is what City-Shaft viewers see on their screens while the fury of this president-robot assassin wreaks havoc among the rioters attacking the city. "Kill! Kill! I've already exterminated over a hundred thousand! Soon every rebel will be dead! Ha ha ha! Then I'll take care of the Incal. I can feel it moving down there. Ha ha ha! This new body doesn't lack sensuality after all!"

But as it hunts down John Difool and his companions, the Necrodroid nonetheless suffers a series of setbacks as it goes through various stages of transformation: it first turns into a state-of-the-art robot, then into a Necro-Panzer assault tank that plows through the Crystal Forest, yanking Difool and the others from their hypnosis-induced sleep in the process. The whole cat-and-mouse game, of course, comes with witty comments delivered live to the masses of telefriends watching these events unfold from the cozy comfort of their conapts and giving the Prez's adventures the same undivided and rapturous attention they would to any other reality show promising the brutal demise of living, sentient beings.

It's last mutation resembles a kind of giant spider, armed with seven metal legs and a round head. This ridiculous and pitiful avatar is all the more grotesque given that pontificating sound bites continue to be broadcast all across the City-Shaft, interspersed with strange noises due to transmission difficulties. "There's nothing left but a walking holo-camera!" notes Animah, laconically—an observation that doesn't fall on deaf ears: John Difool decides to send a message to all viewers and incite them to leave their conapts to "go towards the light," before taking off with the Presidential head, who desperately tries to assert his severely diminished authority: "Put me down, asshole! I'm your Prez! Do you hear me?!"

In *The Dreaming Galaxy*, the last volume in *The Incal*, John accidentally finds the President's head at the bottom of his duffle bag. An unfortunate plight, when you really think about it, for the one who once thought he held the fate of the City in his hands. "What? The President's head? I forgot about it!" Difool says indifferently before throwing it on the floor. This causes the camera-Prez to turn on again—but with a new attitude, this time around. Unaccustomed to bowing to power, whatever form that power may take, the now humbled Prez puts forth his docile side, for authority has changed hands and now lies with John and his friends...

The Prezident's Hunchbacks

They are hideous, both physically and morally. The Prezident's Hunchbacks initially appear in *The Black Incal*, when they grab John Difool as he emerges from the ventilation shaft through which he was able to escape Kill Wolfhead. They are thugs on the payroll of the "Prez," the dictator who exercises power over Terra 2014. These unscrupulous henchmen are led by the fearsome Kabos, and are recognizable by the hump that deforms their backs and the shaved head that makes them look like skinheads, ready to pound anyone who doesn't pledge allegiance to their paymaster. Their savagery is on full display in *Before The Incal*, when they invade the GTO, the dilapidated ghetto the mutant outcasts call home, before wreaking death and destruction and murdering Bantih, John Difool's first love.

However, their brutality does not make them morons. They are loyal servants to the social order at work on Terra 2014, but their devotion to the Prezident's cause doesn't prevent them from demonstrating an ability to analyze a situation and the political forces involved, as in the scene in *The Black Incal* where Kabos orders his men to let the Metabaron escape, aware that the latter could turn out to be useful in a troubled political context. And the so-called halo disease that strikes one of them leads him to speak the truth in very candid terms—"Move your fat ass, pig..."—as he directs a Prezident incapable of assuming his responsibilities to inform the Emperoress of the gravity of the situation. An isolated case, certainly, and one that doesn't affect the complete obedience of the Hunchbacks, who are the last line of defense against the disintegration of a City-Shaft in the throes of a popular uprising, calling into question the iniquitous social order. The Prezident's Hunchbacks resurface in *Final Incal*, where they appear even more impressive at the hands of Ladrönn, whose drawing style accentuates their coldness and cruelty.

34
JANJETOV

The Cardioclaw

A repulsive monster with powerful metal clamps, the Cardioclaw is the guardian of the Inside/Outside, an uncertain place in which John Difool and Deepo take refuge after the concrete seagull helps him escape the Technopope at the beginning of *The Luminous Incal*. "Oh, it's probably just a techno-illusion. It'll pop if you prick it with your beak!" Difool figures, before heeding Deepo's urgent advice and resolving to seek the Incal's help. In a somewhat surprising act of bravery, John launches an attack against the Cardioclaw, which soon disintegrates into a flower in whose center sits the Black Incal. This victory—brought about by the Incal's intervention—causes the Technocity to explode. The Prezident, exasperated at having his decadent festivities interrupted, cries out: "How am I supposed to enjoy myself with one crisis after another? What a pain in the ass! Riots! Plots! Berg assaults! Spies! The Technocity destroyed!"

INCAL! INCAL! PLEASE! ANSWER ME! QUICK!

Diavaloo

The show must go on, even during riots! That would be a good motto for Diavaloo, the host of the cult show on Channel 79831 (the channel number changes, depending on the series) whose principle mission is the zombification of the masses. And indeed, his mediagenic verve and his insatiable appetite for blood never take a day off. We could even go as far as to say: during the riots that ravage the streets of Terra 2014, the show not only goes on, it feeds off the scenes of violence, stoking unhealthy excitement among the viewers and escalating cruelty in its celebrity host.

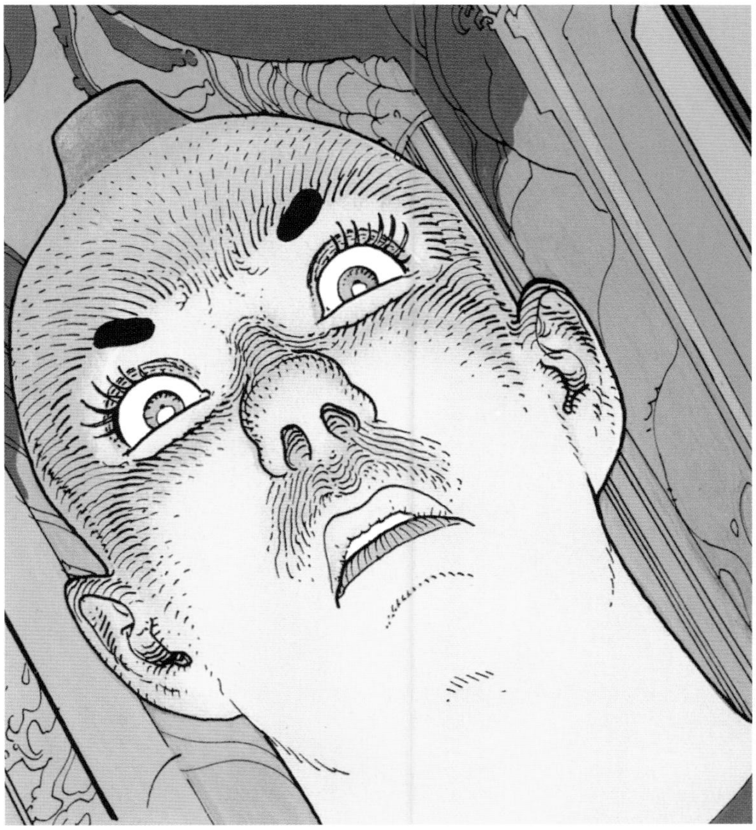

His mohawk makes him look like a punk, but his blissful, artificial smile counteracts this impression and makes him perfect for the job, even more cynical than some of our own contemporary television hosts. Diavaloo is both a real and virtual star. When he's not appearing in the flesh on a TV set, he remains visible thanks to his giant 3D effigy, which is displayed at the entrance of the studios and addresses the mass of TV addicts that hurry to attend the live recording of his show. But Diavaloo is more than just a screen icon. While he is introduced early on in the series, i.e. in *The Black Incal* (where his presence is hinted at rather than actually shown: everything suggests that the voice of the off-screen narrator taking great joy in the Prezident's successful cloning is his), it isn't until *Before The Incal* that he is placed center stage. In *Vhisky, SPV, and Homeo-Whores*, the fifth volume of *Before The Incal*, he reveals his true self. Endowed with political acumen and a lack of scruples that make him one of the mighty elite, he obeys the orders of the Supra Divinoid and thwarts Luz de Garra's plan to reveal the terrible secret behind the Aristo halo, which is the basis for the system's entire political organization and the power of the oligarchs. The show must go on, and it must do so continuously. Yet Diavaloo knows his place: under no circumstance can he threaten the foundations of society, even while giving off an impression of independence *vis-à-vis* the ruling classes. In one particularly over-the-top moment, in a scene dripping with hypocrisy and cheap melodrama, Luz declares on live TV her love for Diavaloo, plunging John Difool into unfathomable sadness.

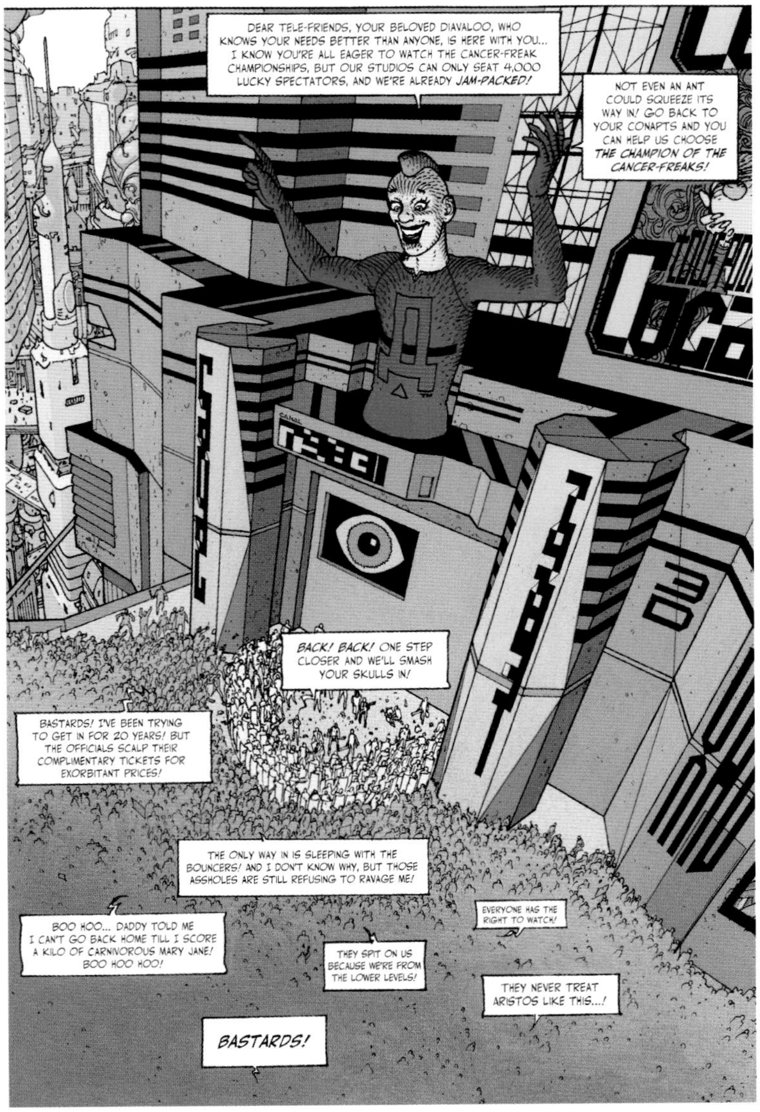
DEAR TELE-FRIENDS, YOUR BELOVED DIAVALOO, WHO KNOWS YOUR NEEDS BETTER THAN ANYONE, IS HERE WITH YOU... I KNOW YOU'RE ALL EAGER TO WATCH THE CANCER-FREAK CHAMPIONSHIPS, BUT OUR STUDIOS CAN ONLY SEAT 4,000 LUCKY SPECTATORS, AND WE'RE ALREADY JAM-PACKED!
NOT EVEN AN ANT COULD SQUEEZE ITS WAY IN! GO BACK TO YOUR CONAPTS AND YOU CAN HELP US CHOOSE THE CHAMPION OF THE CANCER-FREAKS!
BACK! BACK! ONE STEP CLOSER AND WE'LL SMASH YOUR SKULLS IN!
BASTARDS! I'VE BEEN TRYING TO GET IN FOR 20 YEARS! BUT THE OFFICIALS SCALP THEIR COMPLIMENTARY TICKETS FOR EXORBITANT PRICES!
THE ONLY WAY IN IS SLEEPING WITH THE BOUNCERS! AND I DON'T KNOW WHY, BUT THOSE ASSHOLES ARE STILL REFUSING TO RAVAGE ME!
EVERYONE HAS THE RIGHT TO WATCH!
BOO HOO... DADDY TOLD ME I CAN'T GO BACK HOME TILL I SCORE A KILO OF CARNIVOROUS MARY JANE! BOO HOO HOO!
THEY SPIT ON US BECAUSE WE'RE FROM THE LOWER LEVELS!
THEY NEVER TREAT ARISTOS LIKE THIS...!
BASTARDS!

Then, the two fake lovebirds, who become legal cohabitants to the rapturous acclaim of the billions of "tele-friends" duped by the hoax, treat themselves to a honeymoon aboard Diavaloo's harem-satellite, whose shape reflects the very features of the TV host's face. Diavaloo, free from the obligation of his public persona, can now reveal yet another side of his true nature: that of a cruel and sadistic individual, a megalomaniac and a cynic, who only gets off when one of his clones is murdered during sexual intercourse. True to his nature, Diavaloo soldiers on in *After The Incal* and in *Final Incal*. He praises the merits of the new Prezidential cloning, in a tone that is still as playful as ever but even more shocking given that the Biophage 13-X virus has already begun to infect the population. He's back on the air after submitting to the Prezidential injunction to get cloned, which now guarantees him "a magnificent metallic body," thereby forcing on viewers the slick and artificial version of a television icon that seems to promise happiness to the people even as they are in the throes of disease and suffering. Sound familiar...?

The Supra-Divinoid (aka The Central Cranium)

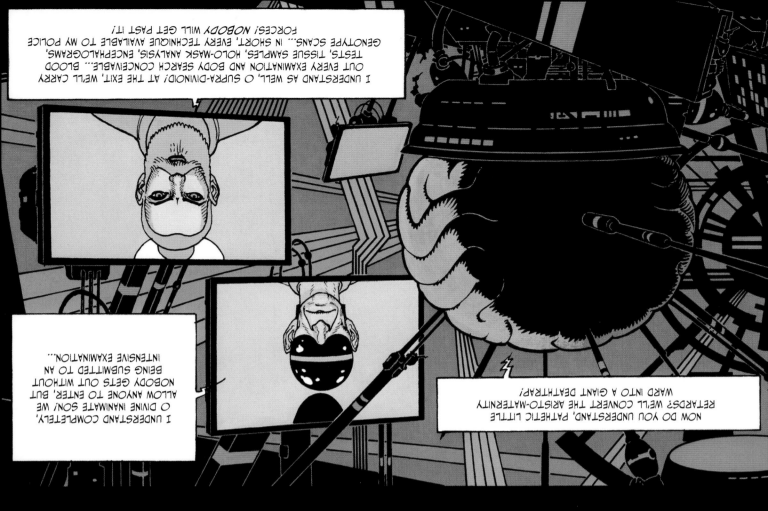

This is the master of the City-Shaft. The Supra-Divinoid (also known as The Central Cranium) oversees the various channels of communication that flow through the City and dispenses instructions to the various authorities, from the Prezident—whom he despises—to the Cybo-cops and the television network. This nightmarish entity is anything but glamorous. The Supra-Divinoid comes in the shape of an enormous cervical mass encased in a sophisticated structure, like the product of some unlikely biological/mechanical crossbreeding experiment. This monstrous creature, fully alive but devoid of the slightest shred of humanity, seems to have sprung directly from the twisted imagination of an irresponsible divine creator.

Both the Prez and the Technopope—who equally can't stand each other—report to him on their activities while exchanging insults and blaming one another for their personal failures. But all that does is draw his contempt, which he is fond of expressing in elegant language punctuated with colorful insults. Never one to run out of imagination or explicit metaphors, he describes them in turn as "pathetic little retards" (on a good day), or "scraps of zoological waste," "worthless feces-making bodies, destined to rot" and "degenerate humanoids" (on a bad day). There's no hiding anything from him: the Supra-Divinoid sees all, hears all, knows all. "I know everything! My non-biotic synapses are always aware of everything!"

A true underground authority who holds all the power, he can't always count on the efficiency of those under his command and who do his bidding, which sometimes fuels his frustration, again often articulated in a highly graphic manner, such as "By a thousand megatons of bio-shit!" And he will do everything he can to prevent the disclosure of the Big Secret, which could give rise to "a scandal of galactic proportions."

The Supra-Divinoid eventually meets an unhappy end in the last book of the series. He refuses to put himself at the service of the Benthacodon and is no match for the will of the Prez, who now holds absolute power in the form of a metal entity who is determined to establish the reign of metallic life. The super computer's arrogance and vanity come off as rather ridiculous as he faces a virus attack from the Prez, who embodies the Benthacodon's ideology. "The future is not metallic," says the Supra-Divinoid with confidence in *After The Incal*. "Primordial intelligence resides in the cell! Bio-techno is supreme!!" he cries out in *Final Incal* in one last burst of lyricism. But it's no use: the hour of the Supra-Divinoid's defeat has come. "I'm freezing... I'm... burning! Red...alert...Glouff...Hrrghh..." illustrates well the scene in which the Supra-Divinoid's brain is dissolved by the Prez, who then orders the power to be transferred to his palace. It's the end of an era...

NOW DO YOU UNDERSTAND, PATHETIC LITTLE RETARDS? WE'LL CONVERT THE ARISTO-MATERNITY WARD INTO A GIANT DEATHTRAP!
I UNDERSTAND COMPLETELY, O DIVINE INANIMATE SON! WE ALLOW ANYONE TO ENTER, BUT NOBODY GETS OUT WITHOUT BEING SUBMITTED TO AN INTENSIVE EXAMINATION...
I UNDERSTAND AS WELL, O SUPRA-DIVINOID! AT THE EXIT, WE'LL CARRY OUT EVERY EXAMINATION AND BODY SEARCH CONCEIVABLE... BLOOD TESTS, TISSUE SAMPLES, HOLO-MASK ANALYSIS, ENCEPHALOGRAMS, GENOTYPE SCANS... IN SHORT, EVERY TECHNIQUE AVAILABLE TO MY POLICE FORCES! NOBODY WILL GET PAST IT!

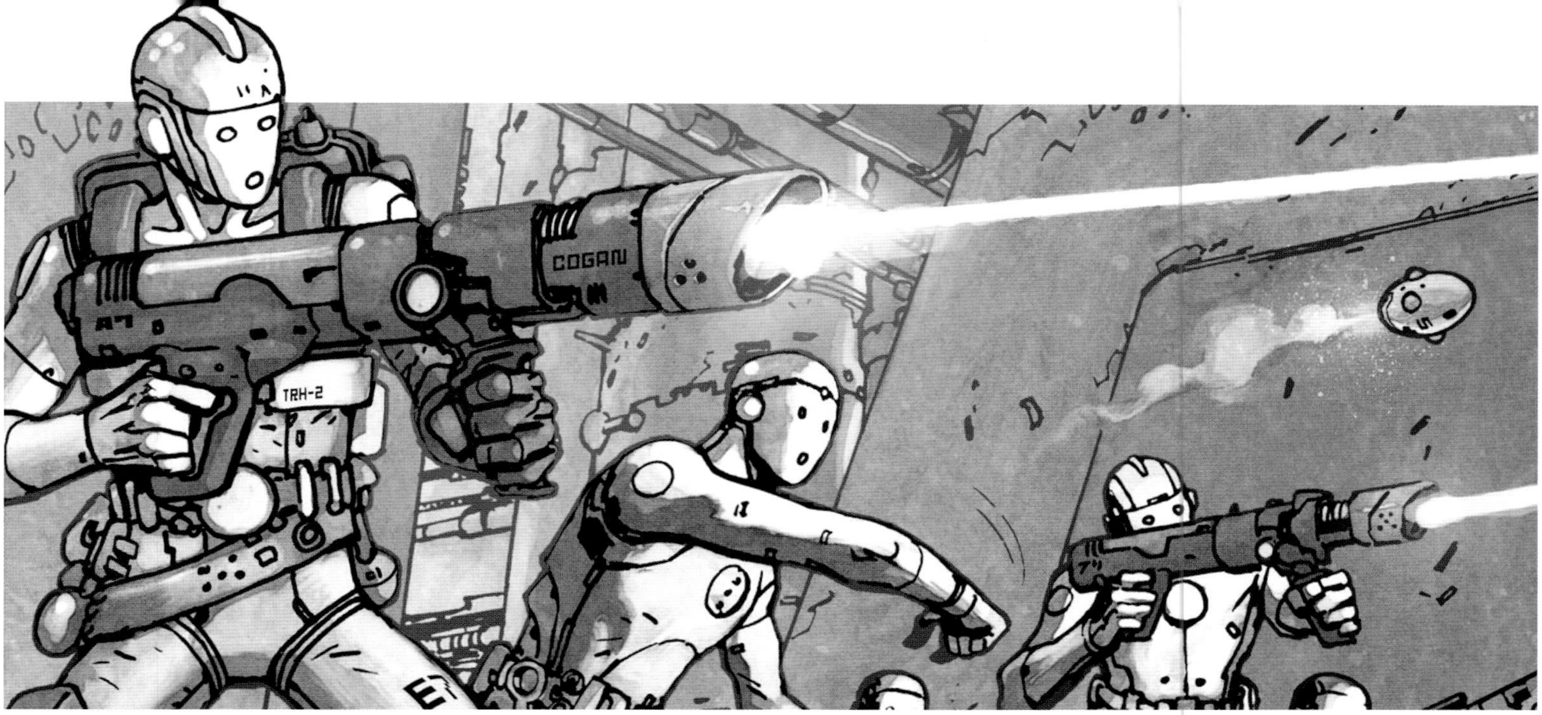
COGAN
TRH-2

Cybo-cops

In charge of maintaining law and order on Terra 2014, these robotic policemen are a prelude to the ones starring in Paul Verhoeven's 1987 film *Robocop*. There's no way of knowing whether the director or his screenwriters had read *The Incal*, but his protagonist's metallic exoskeleton is definitely reminiscent of the metal body of Cybo-cops. But there's one distinction: the feeling of coldness and insensitivity that Robocop initially portrays has nothing to do with the good-natured feeling that emanates from the Cybo-cops, especially P-Y, who interrogates Difool at the beginning of *The Black Incal*, and even less, of course, with the kind of paradoxical humanity that makes the unforgettable Kolbo-5 so appealing.

The tone shifts in *Final Incal*, however, as Ladrönn's Cybo-cops seem to have lost their empathy for the human race and instead become cold killing machines blindly devoted to their superiors and their missions. Whereas one of them, in *After The Incal*, is concerned about the potential consequences of the use of "tantrin gas" ordered by the Central Cranium to stop Difool from escaping through the sewage system—"But... couldn't it seep down to the 27th level? And kill the citizens there?"—in *Final Incal* the Cybo-cops come across as obedient and disembodied robotic creatures who would never challenge orders, docile servants of The Central Cranium, on whom they lavish honorifics such as "Your Divine Superiority," "Your Magnificence," or "Your Divine Magnanimousness."

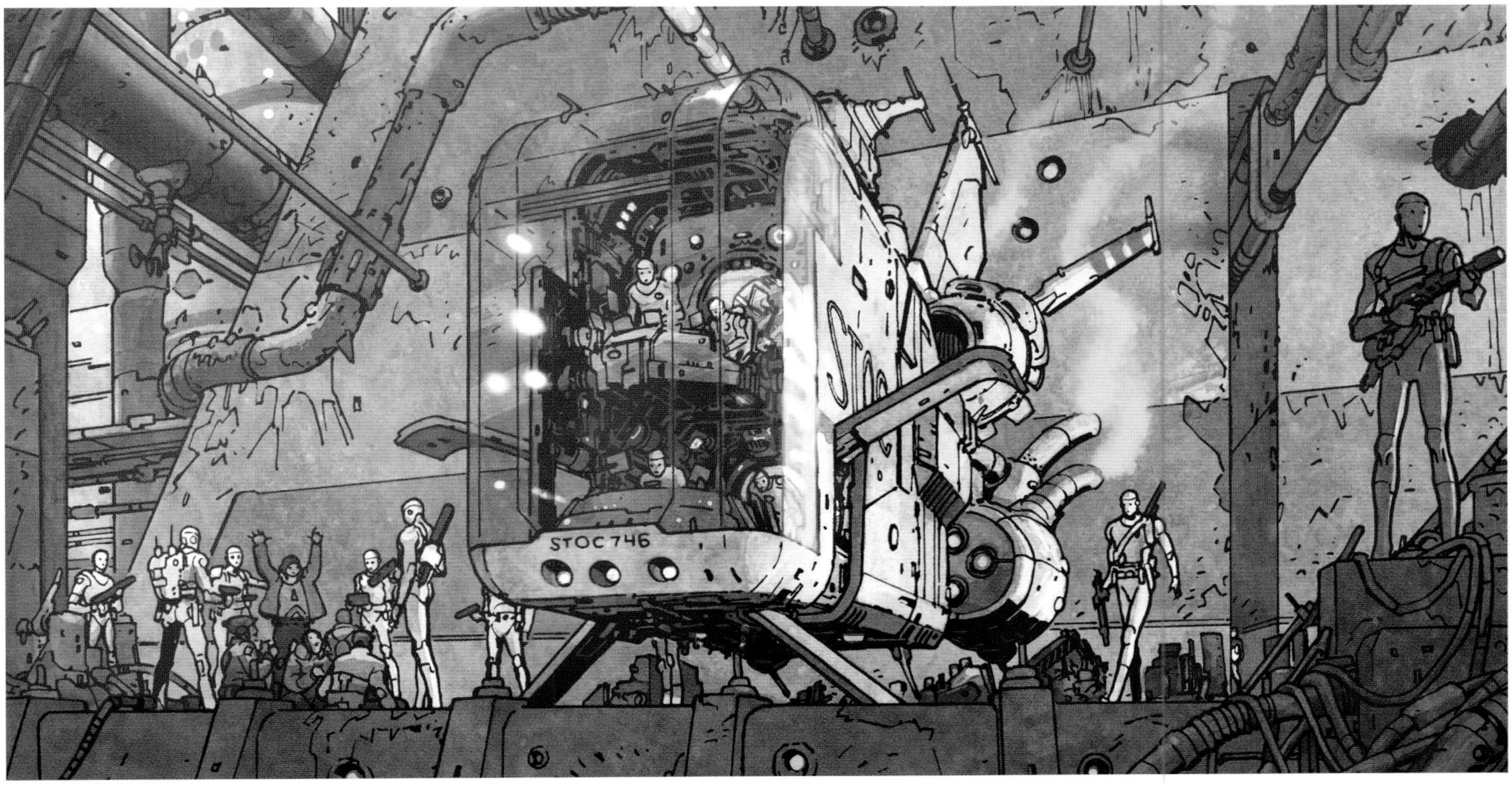
STOC 746

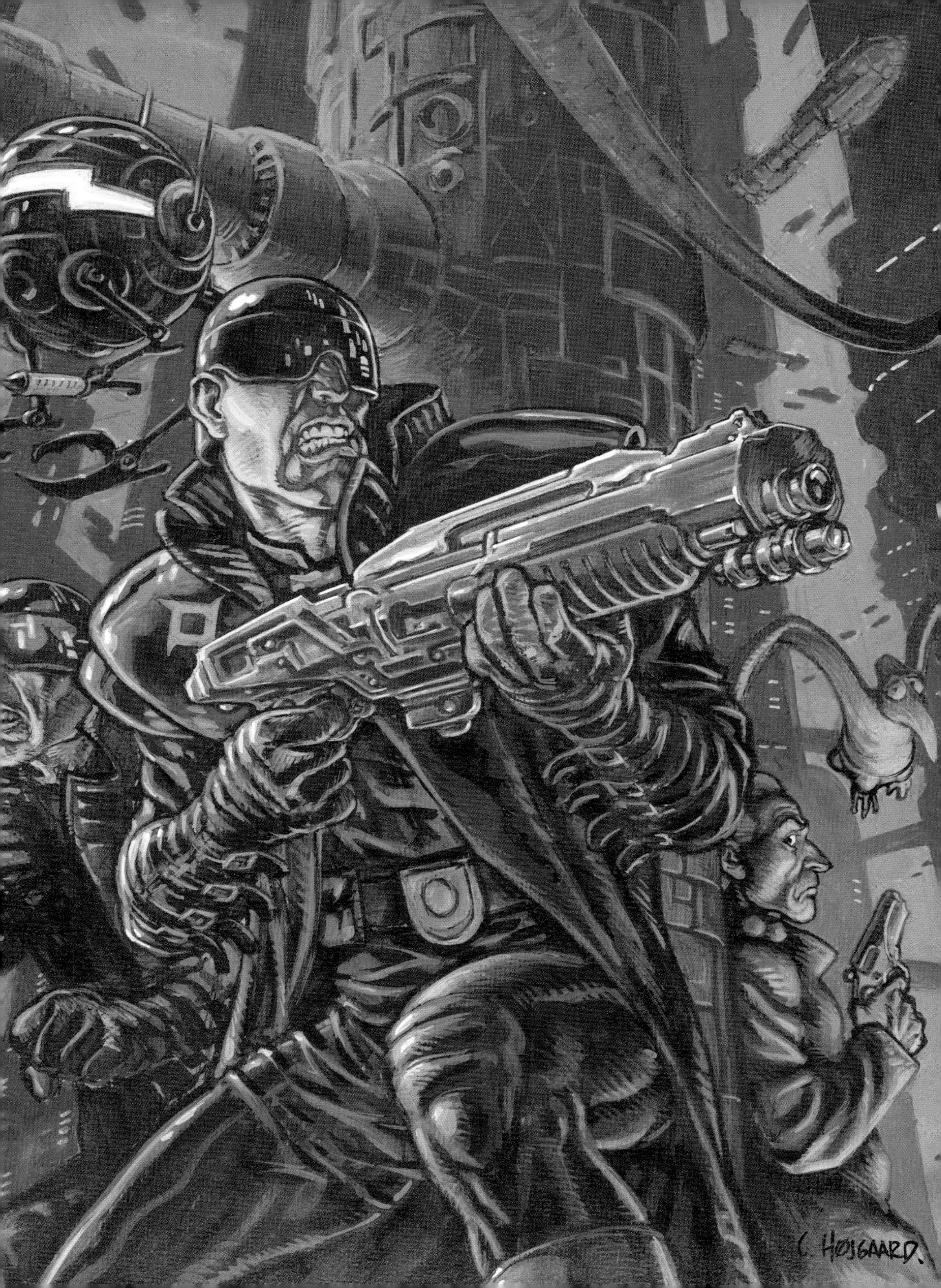
C. HØJGAARD.

His Supreme Highness

The theatrical, over-the-top Prezident of Terra 2014, who cares little about anything but his appearance, is not cut out for the responsibilities that come with his job. Instead, this incorrigible hedonist is primarily concerned with his physical appearance, which he upgrades on a regular basis via the miracle of "Prezidential cloning"—surgical procedures conceived and performed by Techno-Technos and broadcast live for audiences glued to their TV screens. Surrounded by a multitude of courtiers worthy of King Louis XIV (whose political vision and understanding of the common good our Prez is far from possessing), he likes to parade around in his various bodies and have people address him as "Your Supreme Highness." When necessary, his faithful Hunchbacks are there to remind visitors of the rules of proper etiquette, as John Difool can attest to. When the Prezident, who covets the Incal, orders his Hunchbacks to bring Difool to him, they make no bones about dragging him in by force and slapping him upside the head when he neglects to utter those three all-important ceremonial words.

A big fan of decadent parties where guests can consume "sublime" dragonfly soufflé while watching "absolutely divine" killings on their holovids, the full implication of the riots ravaging the City-Shaft doesn't seem to register with His Supreme Highness. "If riots didn't exist, we'd have to invent them!" he cries out gleefully while helping himself to a piece of cake. He has only one fear in life: to be summoned by the Emperoress. Good for little else than groveling before him/her, His Supreme Highness—"Lowness" would probably be more fitting—is the weak link in the Empire's chain, utterly incapable of thwarting conspiracies or dealing with uprisings. "You fool!" the Emperoress roars. "This miserable sector of the galaxy has always been the shame of the Empire! And now, because of you, you pig, it's turned into a door! A wide open door for the dark horrors, the intracosmic forces of putrefaction and destruction! What do you have to say for yourself?" He has nothing to offer up in response, except to recognize his faults and weaknesses while prostrate on all fours like an "impotent worm."

In After The Incal, and especially in Final Incal, everything changes. The man metamorphosizes, both physically and morally. The Prez takes on the central role of the main bad guy, a must-have ingredient if the hero (or anti-hero, in John Difool's case) is to have both a worthy opponent and a reason for existing. The Prez's latest cloning operation turns him into a cold and formidable being made of metal, the polar opposite of the often ridiculous image he projected in his previous incarnations. He has now acquired the taste for power—real power this time, and not just the appearance of power that he previously had to make do with.

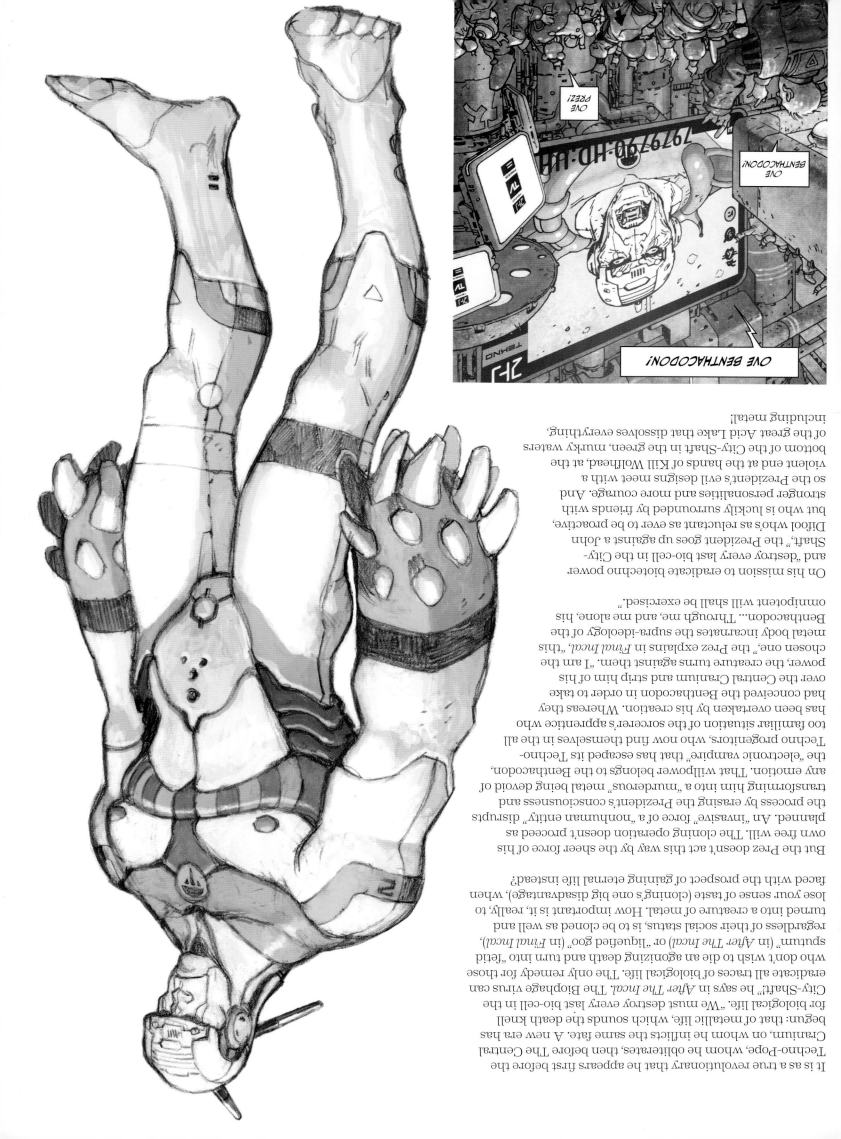

It is as a true revolutionary that he appears first before the Techno-Pope, whom he obliterates, then before The Central Cranium, on whom he inflicts the same fate. A new era has begun: that of metallic life, which sounds the death knell for biological life. "We must destroy every last bio-cell in the City-Shaft!" he says in *After The Incal*. The Biophage virus can eradicate all traces of biological life. The only remedy for those who don't wish to die an agonizing death and turn into "fetid sputum" (in *After The Incal*) or "liquefied goo" (in *Final Incal*), regardless of their social status, is to be cloned as well and turned into a creature of metal. How important is it, really, to lose your sense of taste (cloning's one big disadvantage), when faced with the prospect of gaining eternal life instead?

But the Prez doesn't act this way by the sheer force of his own free will. The cloning operation doesn't proceed as planned. An "invasive" force of a "nonhuman entity" disrupts the process by erasing the Prezident's consciousness and transforming him into a "murderous" metal being devoid of any emotion. That willpower belongs to the Benthacodon, the "electronic vampire" that has escaped its Techno-Techno progenitors, who now find themselves in the all too familiar situation of the sorcerer's apprentice who has been overtaken by his creation. Whereas they had conceived the Benthacodon in order to take over the Central Cranium and strip him of his power, the creature turns against them. "I am the chosen one," the Prez explains in *Final Incal*, "this metal body incarnates the supra-ideology of the Benthacodon... Through me, and me alone, his omnipotent will shall be exercised."

On his mission to eradicate biotechno power and "destroy every last bio-cell in the City-Shaft," the Prezident goes up against a John Difool who's as reluctant as ever to be proactive, but who is luckily surrounded by friends with stronger personalities and more courage. And so the Prezident's evil designs meet with a violent end at the hands of Kill Wolfhead, at the bottom of the City-Shaft in the green, murky waters of the great Acid Lake that dissolves everything, including metal!

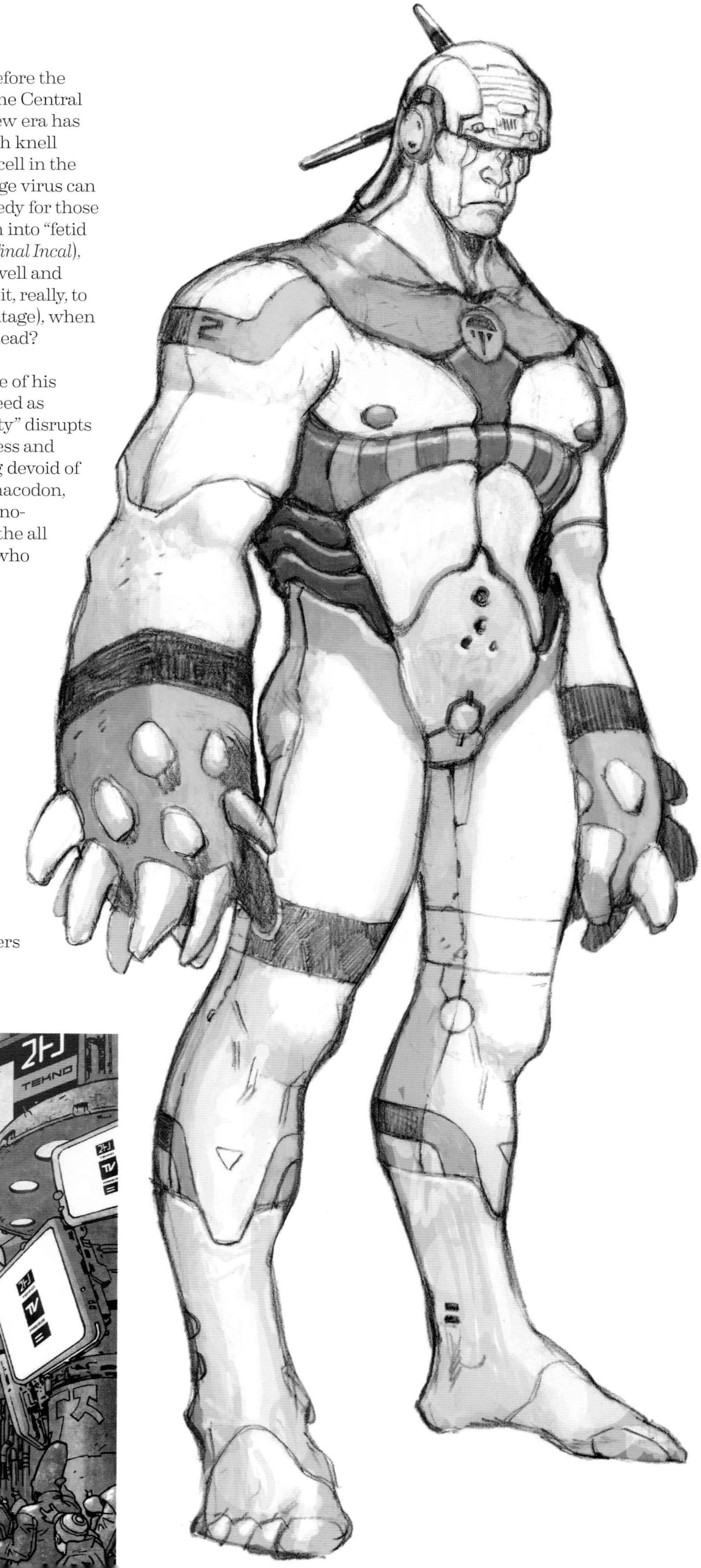

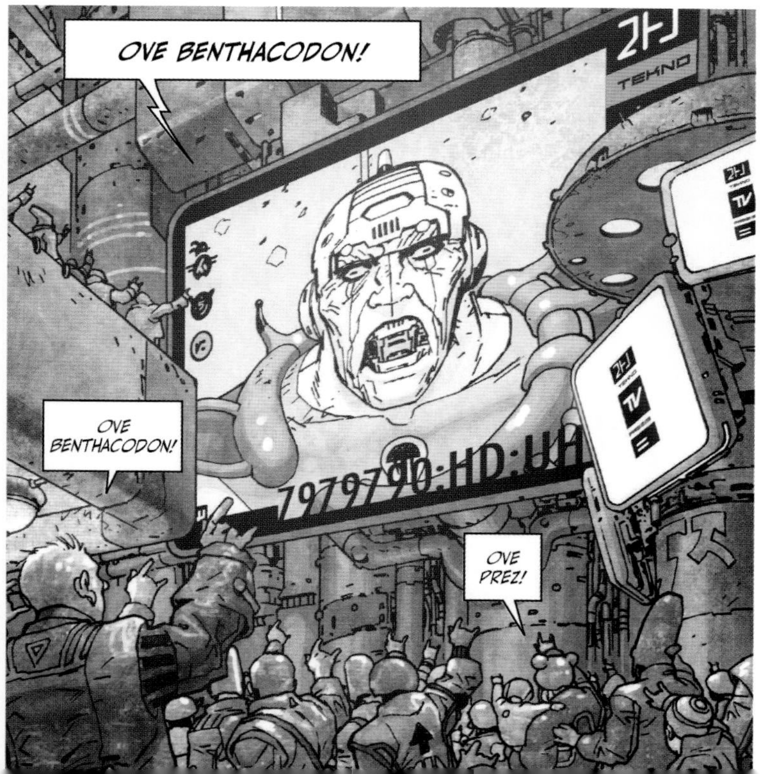
OVE BENTHACODON!
OVE BENTHACODON!
OVE PREZ!

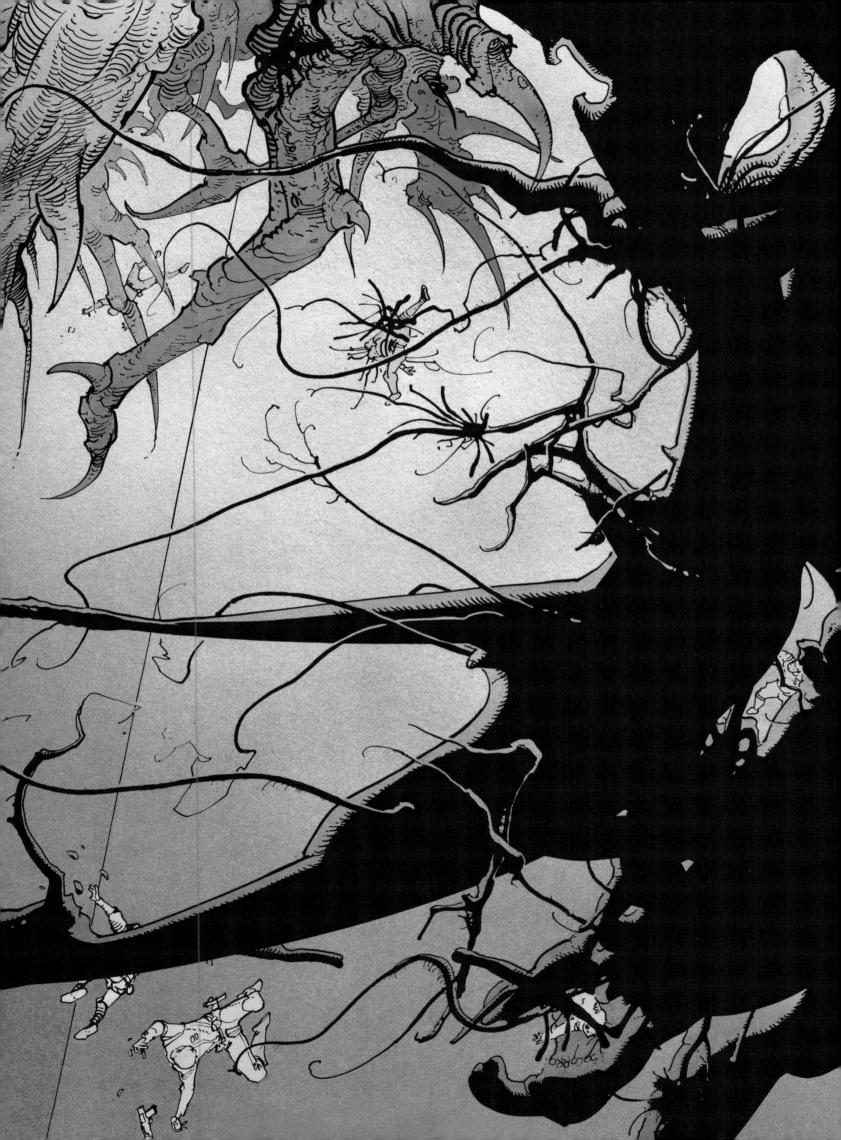

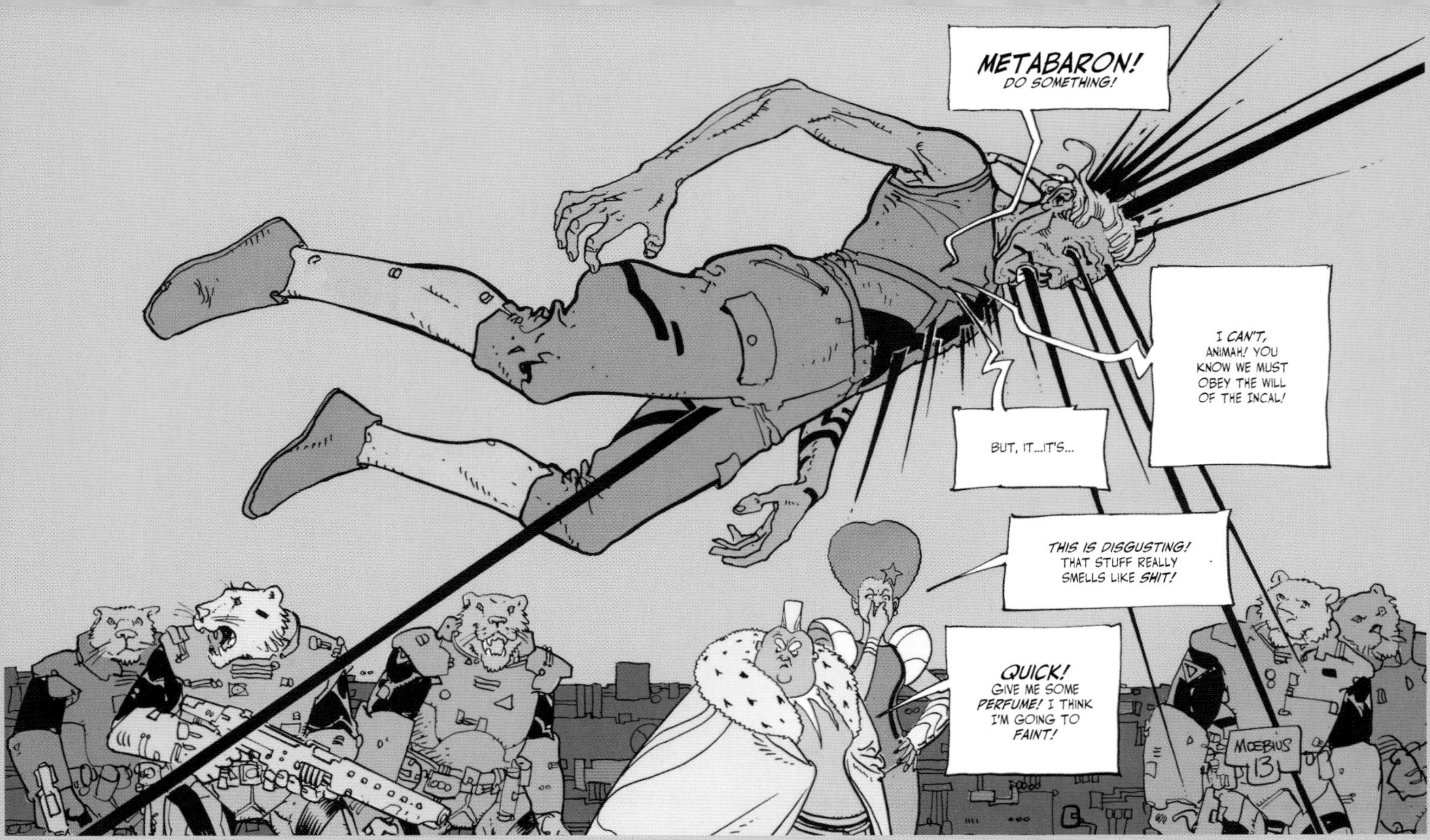
METABARON! DO SOMETHING!
I CAN'T, ANIMAH! YOU KNOW WE MUST OBEY THE WILL OF THE INCAL!
BUT, IT...IT'S...
THIS IS DISGUSTING! THAT STUFF REALLY SMELLS LIKE SHIT!
QUICK! GIVE ME SOME PERFUME! I THINK I'M GOING TO FAINT!
MOEBIUS 13

The Darkness

"It's hopeless! Our real enemy is the Great Darkness, but it appears invincible!" A multiform creature, the enemy of light, the incarnation of Evil and the darkest part of the *Incal* universe, the Great Darkness emerges as a titanic black mass that covers the entire surface of the panel in which it appears, as if it were going to leap off the page and spread to the reader, ready to absorb them. Then it pierces John Difool, suspending him in the air, before wrapping around his entire body, all the way "to the tips of his fingernails," much like a slick of black gold swallowing up an unfortunate bird trapped in an oil spill. But the Incal will be saved, thanks once again to Deepo, who discovers that a single hair on John's head has escaped the Darkness's grip. "The Darkness is the opposite of the Incal," Jodorowsky explains. "It's like night and day: day exists, it comes from the sun, but night does not exist, it is a shadow. It has no consistency, it's the sun that is hidden."

The Darkness has the ability to mutate into a monster with

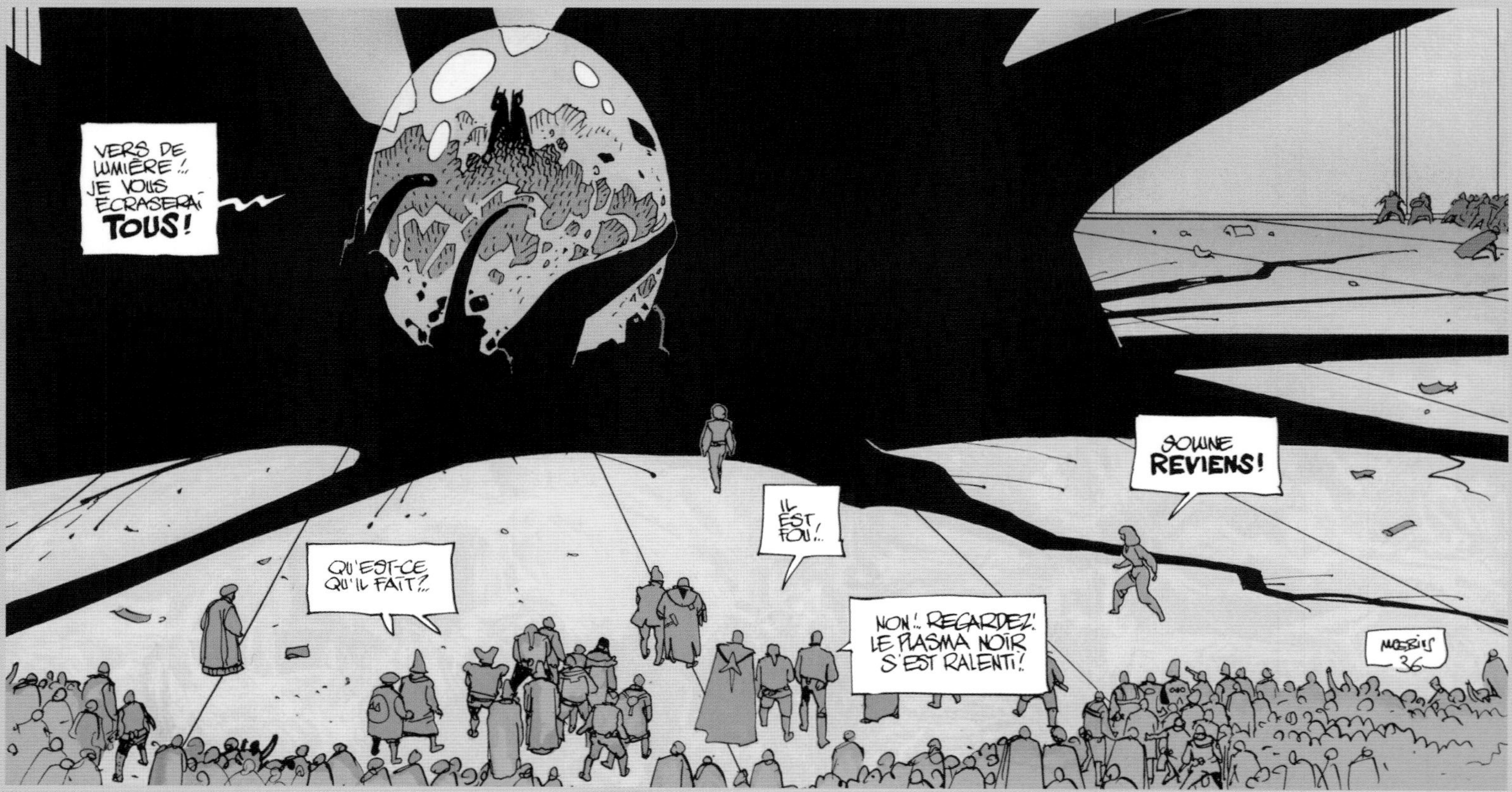
VERS DE LUMIÈRE !.. JE VOUS ÉCRASERAI TOUS!
SOLUNE REVIENS!
IL EST FOU !..
QU'EST-CE QU'IL FAIT ?..
NON !.. REGARDEZ ! LE PLASMA NOIR S'EST RALENTI !
MOEBIUS 36

sharp claws, its two red eyes making it look like a creature from Philippe Druillet's (one of Humanoids' co-founders) work, then into a kind of cosmic octopus with endless tentacles that would undoubtedly have been right at home in Ridley Scott's *Alien*. A veritable living nightmare and a symbol of our ancestral fears and most deep-seated terrors, the Darkness seeks to "strengthen your inner monsters to better feed on your terror," as it proves by turning the members of John Difool's group against each other and bringing out their inner demons, their most deeply buried instincts of violence, and the bloodthirsty monsters lurking deep inside them—and perhaps in the reader, as well...

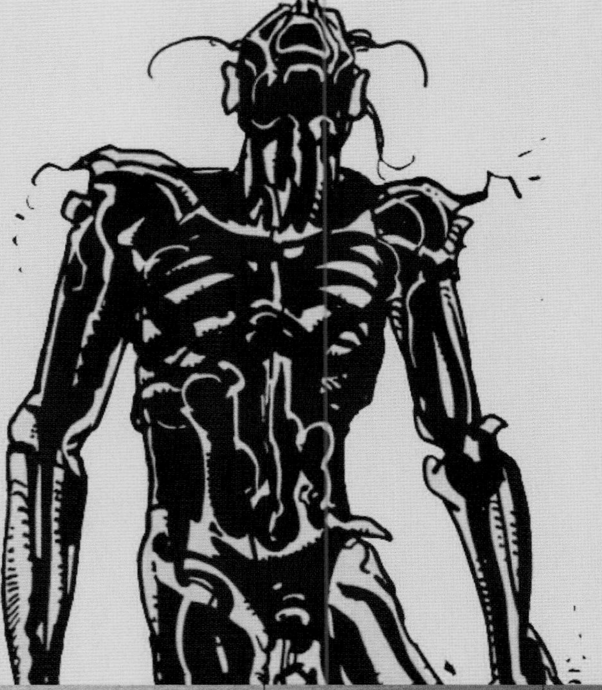

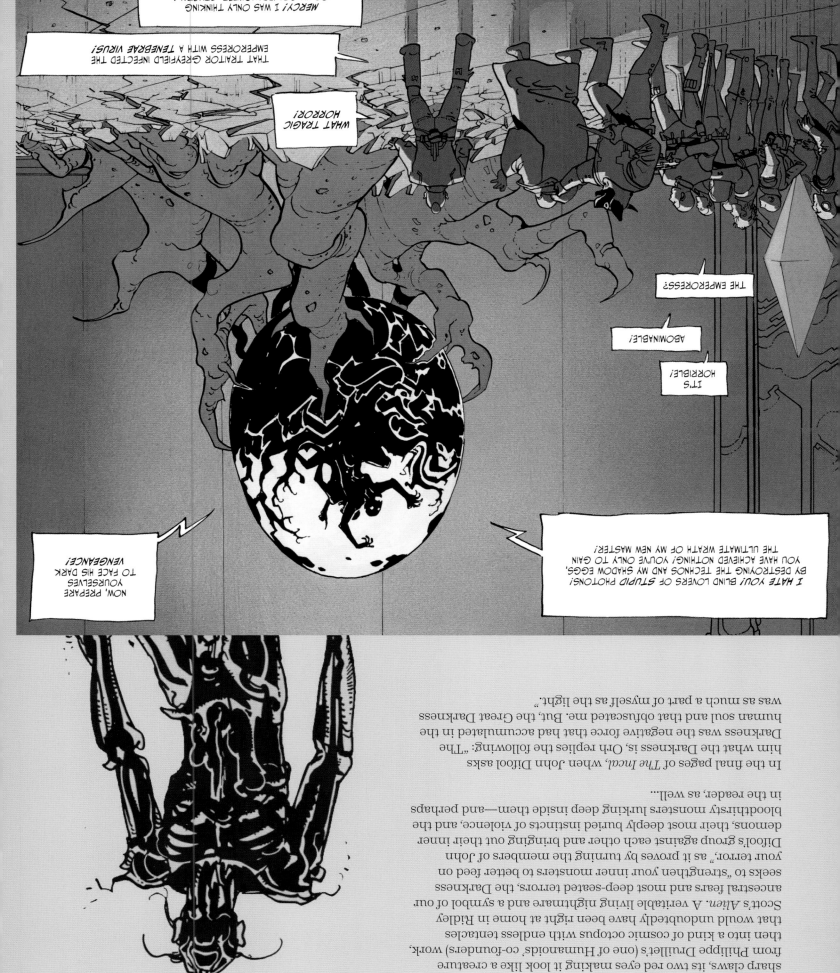

In the final pages of *The Incal*, when John Difool asks him what the Darkness is, Orh replies the following: "The Darkness was the negative force that had accumulated in the human soul and that obfuscated me. But, the Great Darkness was as much a part of myself as the light."

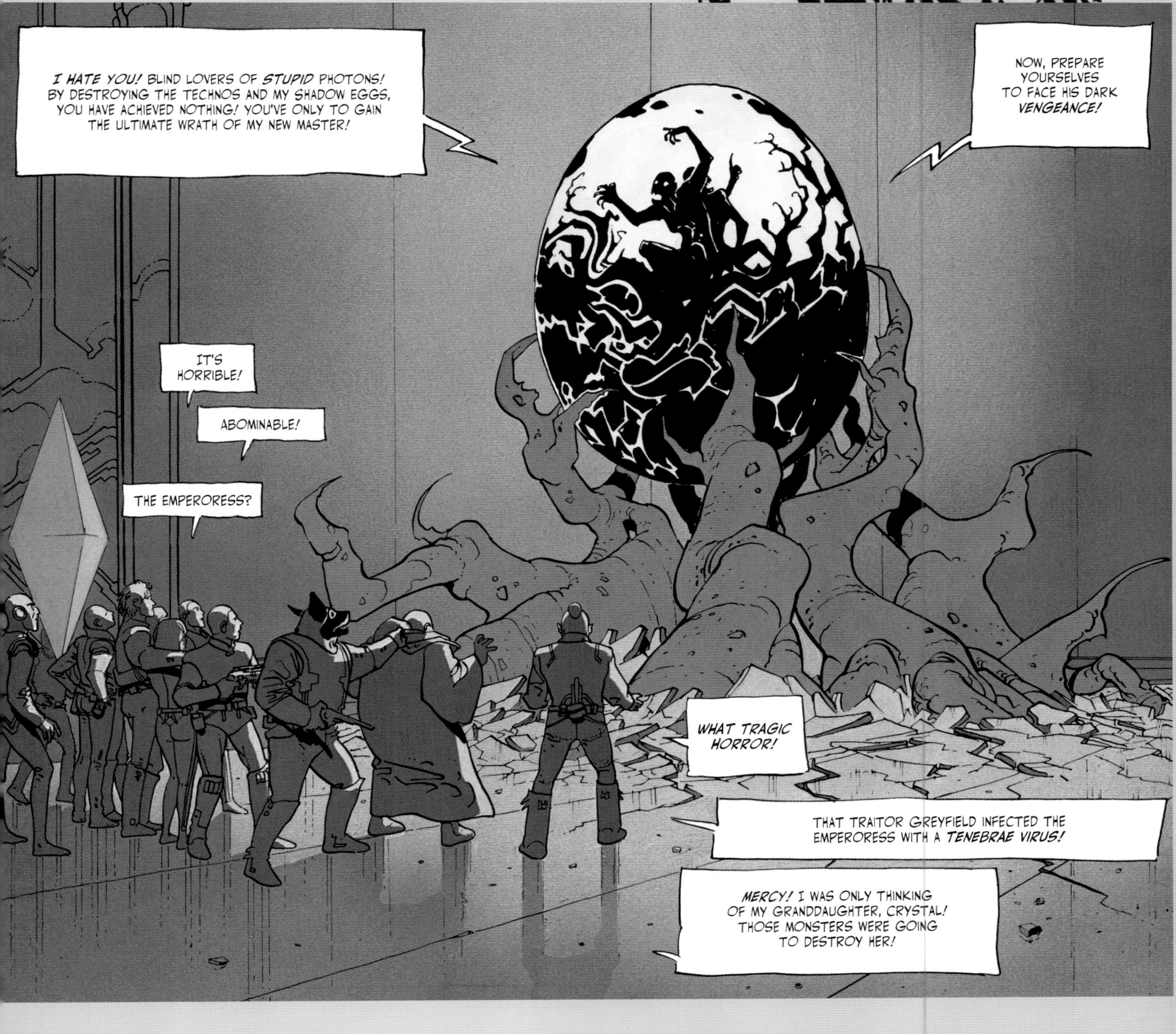
I HATE YOU! BLIND LOVERS OF STUPID PHOTONS! BY DESTROYING THE TECHNOS AND MY SHADOW EGGS, YOU HAVE ACHIEVED NOTHING! YOU'VE ONLY TO GAIN THE ULTIMATE WRATH OF MY NEW MASTER!
NOW, PREPARE YOURSELVES TO FACE HIS DARK VENGEANCE!
IT'S HORRIBLE!
ABOMINABLE!
THE EMPERORESS?
WHAT TRAGIC HORROR!
THAT TRAITOR GREYFIELD INFECTED THE EMPERORESS WITH A TENEBRAE VIRUS!
MERCY! I WAS ONLY THINKING OF MY GRANDDAUGHTER, CRYSTAL! THOSE MONSTERS WERE GOING TO DESTROY HER!

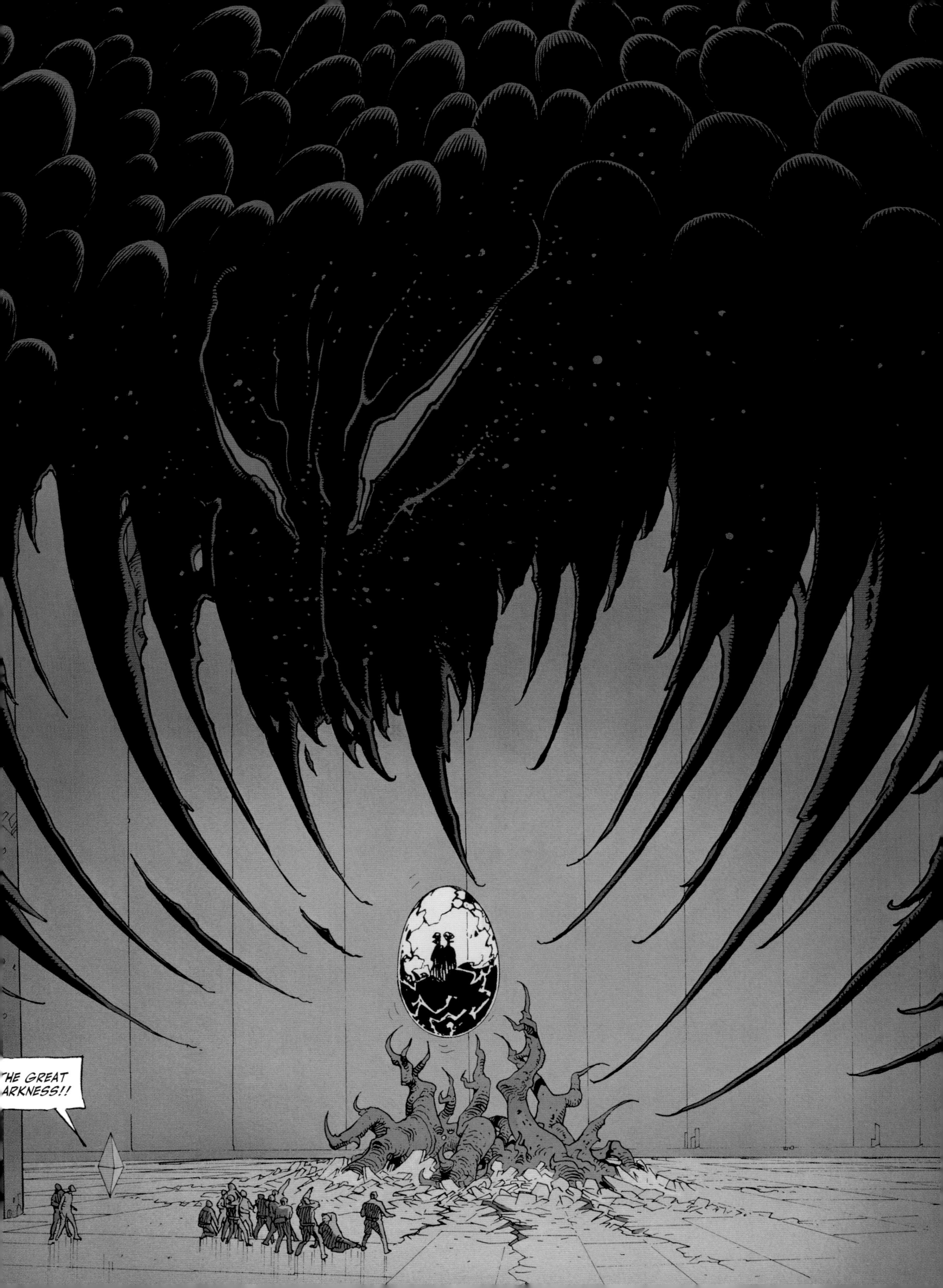
HE GREAT
ARKNESS!!

Gounas

Final Incal features an astounding and varied bestiary. While the khabra is a kind of distant cousin of the sheep, recognizable by its bleating and its horns, it's harmless in spite of its annoying tendency to bite. Not so with the Gounas, though, those biomechanical space spiders, veritable mythical creatures that no one had ever seen except in "the blood-curdling mythological tales of ancient paleo-books." As incredible as it may seem, even the 30,000 ships and 100,000 pirates deployed to push back the sinister creatures are defeated. Only one of them succeeds in escaping them: the ship of Commander Kaimann, aboard which are his faithful companions and the love of his life, Luz de Garra.

But the respite is short lived. Dozens and dozens of nightmarish creatures then emerge from the three Gounas, sowing death and destruction, impregnating the women on the ship who are then "disemboweled by the birth of these unthinkable half-metal, half-cellular aberrations" bursting out of their bellies, condemning them to an agonizing death. The few pirates that survive owe their salvation to Luz—or rather to her halo, which makes her a deity in the eyes of the Gounas, who take her with them as they leave. It is following this vicious attack, and now deprived of female company, that the surviving pirates go on to become farmers and shepherds...

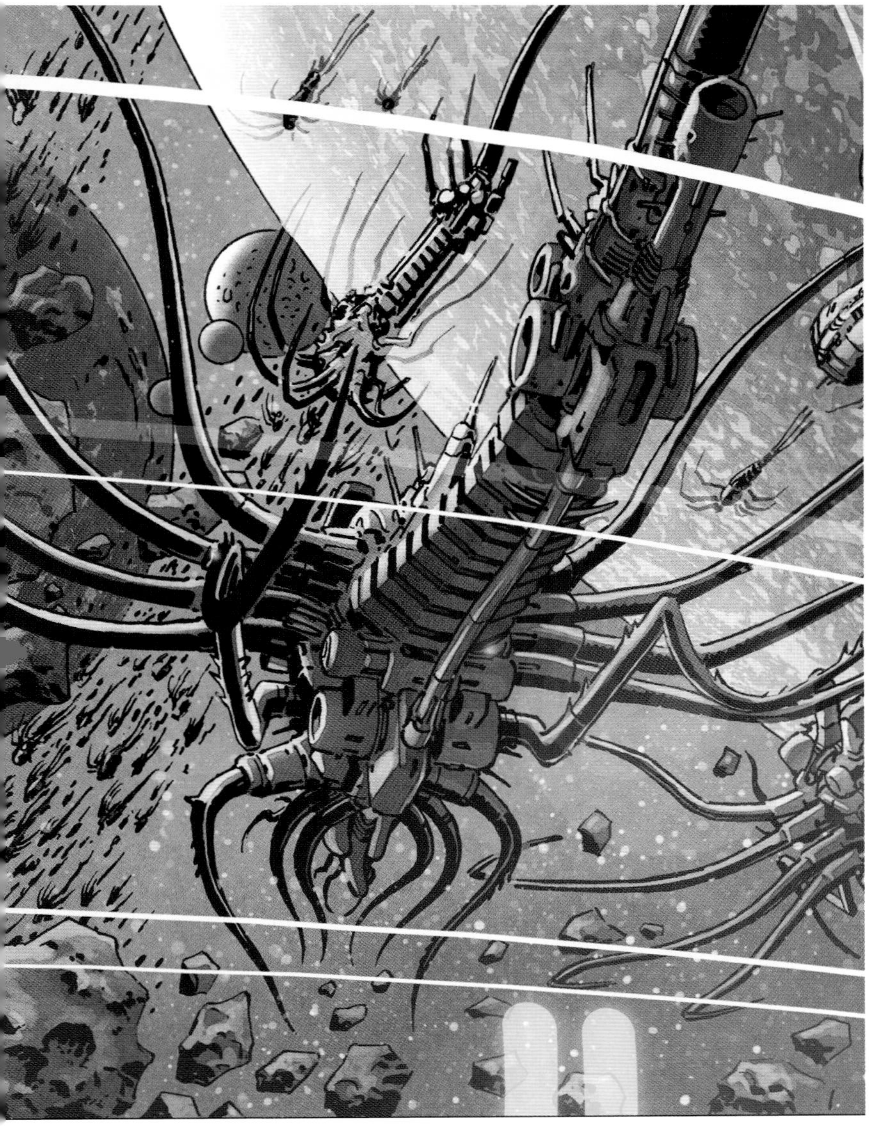

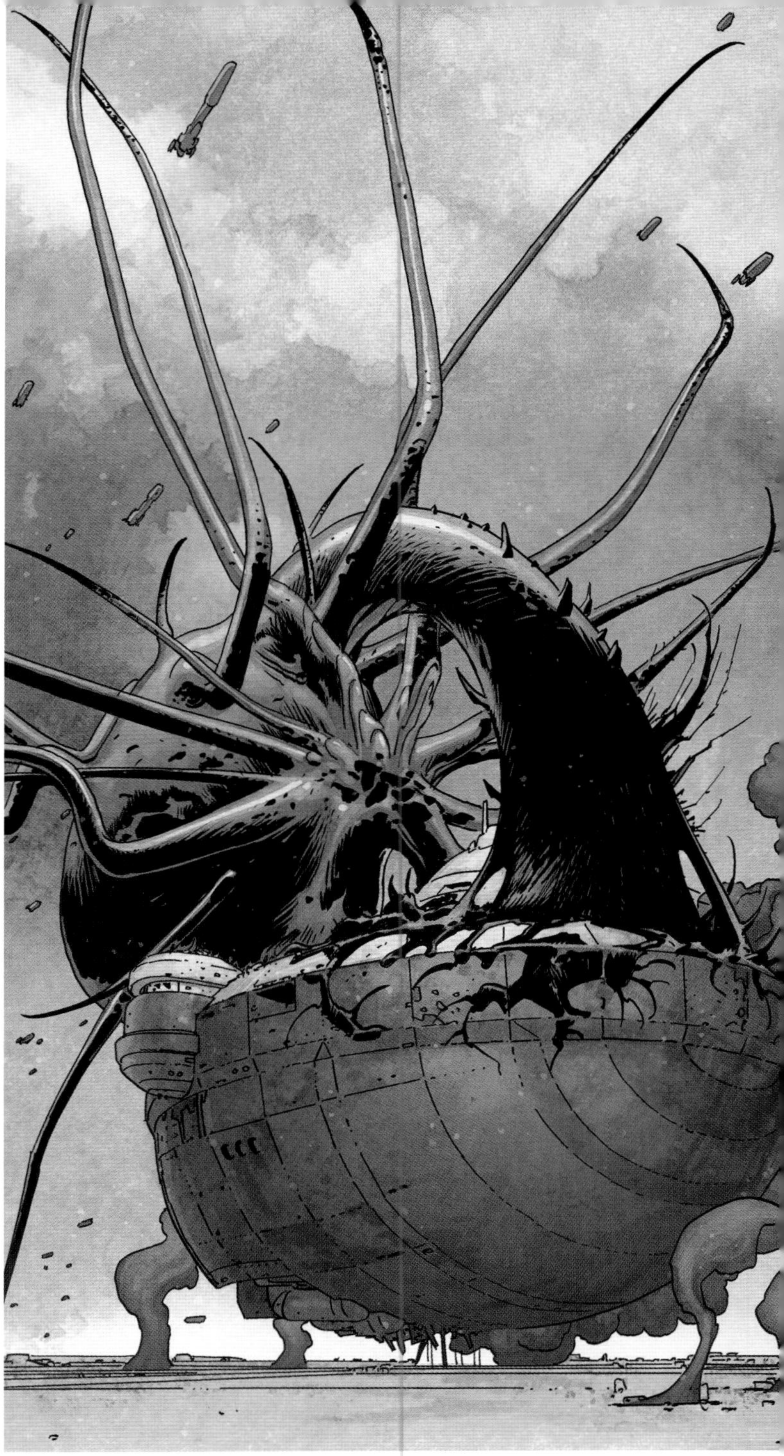

The Benthacodon

Like a spider hanging from the Prez's palace, the Benthacodon emerges as a kind of alternative version of the Darkness that filled the panels of *The Incal* with its Stygian blackness. As the pages of *Final Incal* unfold, this new peril, which Techno-Science created and then lost control of, keeps growing bigger, extending its monstrous tentacles like a giant octopus. It's unclear if Jodorowsky was inspired by an actual, dome-shaped jellyfish called Benthocodon to create this veritable "cancer of negative plasma," or "black golem of Techno-Thought" as referred to in *After The Incal*. The Benthacodon is the black soul of the Prezident, who is now subject to its will, and their pernicious common goal is to eradicate all biological life from the universe and to promote "metallic consciousness's ultimate triumph."

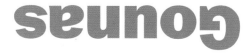

4. Across The Incal: Timeless Worlds & Infinite Ephemera

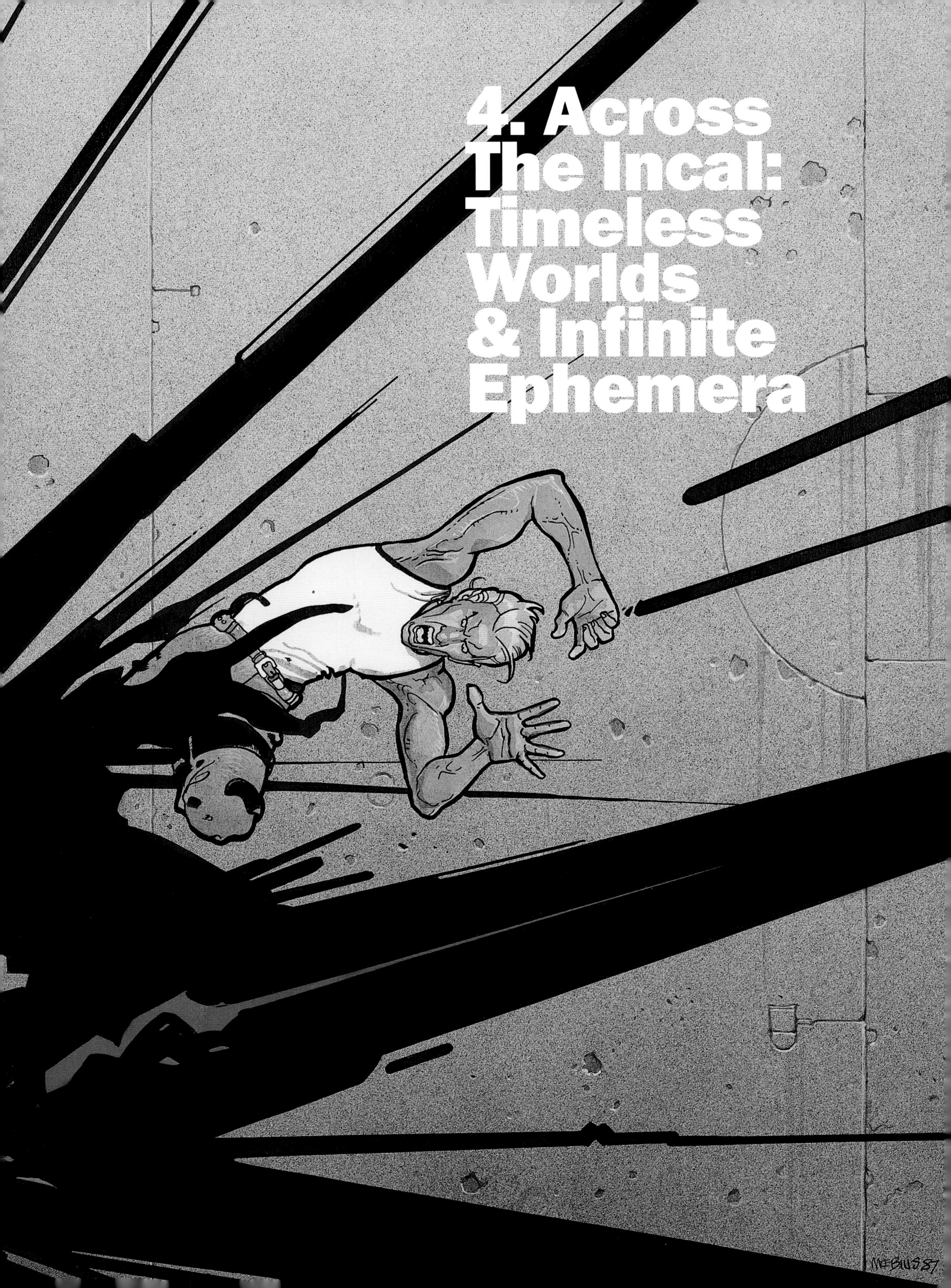
MŒBIUS 87

Galaxies

The Incal saga takes place in several galaxies set in a distant future—or, at least, in an undefined time period. The narrative unfolds on two of them: the Human Galaxy and the Berg Galaxy. The latter is called Attrili. The Berg home planet is Orgargan and is located in a "tri-solar system" near the core. "There," "at the center of the desert system stands the huge mass of Ooror, the three commandments... 120 thousand years old, seat of the original motherhill, primordial ovulation and den of the beloved Protoqueen [Barbariah]." The Berg Galaxy counts a population of 78 billion, all of them physically identical, born of the same father (of whom they are the spitting image) and of the same mother, the Protoqueen.

The Human Galaxy is made up of 22,000 major planets spread out over many systems, which, of course, don't all have names. The story does however mention planets Demos, "a colonial planet in the Phydar system," Alyx III, Badmek, Barnab, Del Ray III, and Laylin. The action takes place on four main planets: Terra 2014 (sometimes referred to as Ter 21), where the story begins and where John Difool comes from: the Golden Planet; Aquaend, and Technogea.

The Golden Planet is the imperial planet, from where the supreme authorities rule over the Empire in a political, religious, and military capacity. It houses the palace of the Emperoress; it oozes luxury and opulence and, as its name suggests, is made entirely of gold.

Aquaend is a penitentiary prison," "a water world, a planet without land... Battered by an endless stream of hurricanes, cyclones, downpours, and storms." It's said to be the most dreaded prison planet in the Empire. It's a world from which there is no escape, the end of the road for the hapless souls sentenced to imprisonment there, as suggested by its name. This is the world where the Imperial Assembly send Kamar Raïmo, spokesman for the colonial planets, and his fellow rebels. Under the surface of the raging waves, what awaits the prisoners is perhaps even worse: "According to the Galactic Guide, the sea is full of poisonous algae, acid-based plankton, carnivorous fish, and all that."

Technogea is the Techno planet. Just like the imperial planet is made of gold and Aquaend is made of liquid, the seat of Techno power is completely mechanical and metallic. It is an artificial planet protected by a psychic shield that only the Bergs, who are endowed with a molecular structure different from that of humans, can breach. When they are driven from their planet, the Technos find refuge on a floating fortress named War Star, which "can atomize an entire solar system in a matter of seconds! It's filled to the brim with murderous super-soldiers!" as Difool explains to Animah in The Fifth Essence, before adding, "It's the most dangerous place in the whole galaxy," and I'm being conservative."

Terra 2014 is undoubtedly the planet described in the most intricate detail in The Incal. "The terraformed planet of Ter 21 belongs to sector 669 of the Exofringe," according to the terminology used in any good galactic guide worthy of its name. The journey John Difool embarks on in the first three installments of The Incal provides a cross-sectional view of Terra 2014, from the City-Shaft to the Portal of Transfiguration—in other words, from the physical world to the spiritual world. But in Final Incal, Terra 2014 finds itself in an unfortunate position. Threatened by the alliance between the Berthacodon and the Prezident, which aims to erase all biological life from its surface, the planet is in danger of becoming a "metallic sphere...inhabited by heartless robots" because of the disappearance of the Mother Tree, the creator of all organic life...

It would be unthinkable to finish this planetary overview without mentioning a celestial body equally extraordinary, but very real: while the Human Galaxy featured in the Incal saga contains 22,000 major planets, at the time they were creating their series, Alejandro Jodorowsky and Moebius were unaware of an asteroid named...**261690 Jodorowsky.** And for good reason: this minor celestial body wasn't discovered until December 24, 2005, by a French amateur astronomer named Jean-Claude Merlin, thanks to a telescope located in Arizona, which he used online from the comfort of his home. Merlin's discovery was made official in 2013 and thus the writer of The Incal joined the illustrious group of comic creators and characters who have had an asteroid named after them by Merlin, from Mandryka, Bilal, Marsupilami, and Claire Bretécher, to Marjane Satrapi, Cabu, and Wolinski.

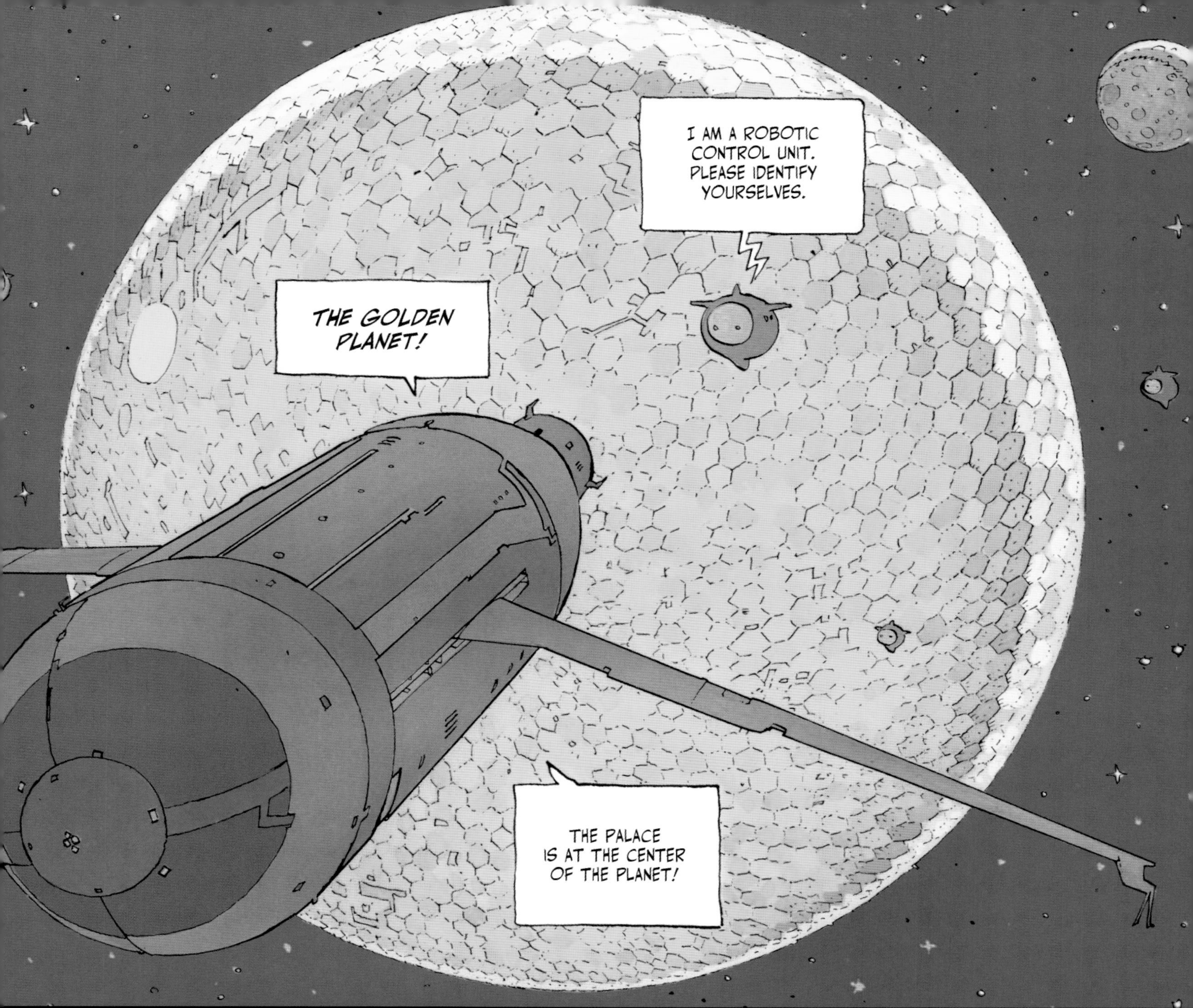
I AM A ROBOTIC CONTROL UNIT. PLEASE IDENTIFY YOURSELVES.
THE GOLDEN PLANET!
THE PALACE IS AT THE CENTER OF THE PLANET!

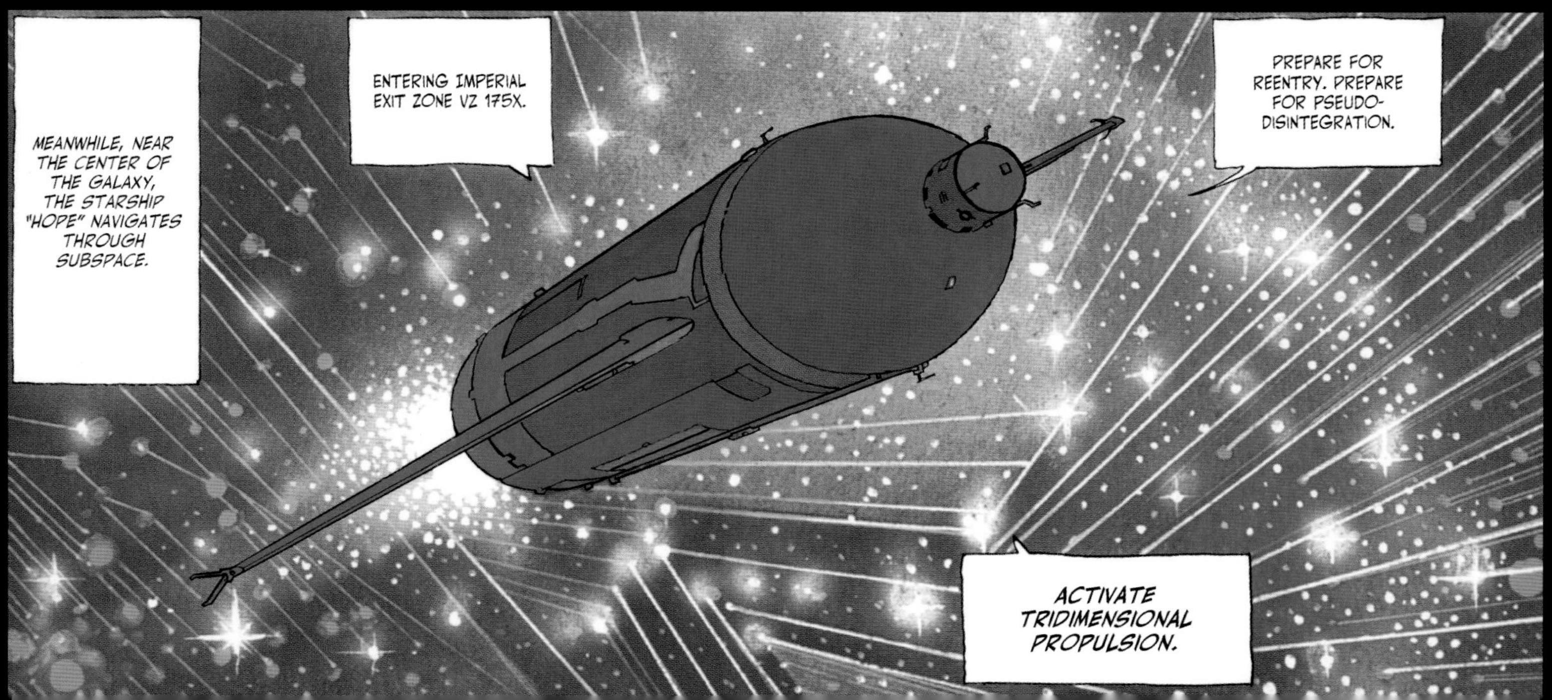
MEANWHILE, NEAR THE CENTER OF THE GALAXY, THE STARSHIP "HOPE" NAVIGATES THROUGH SUBSPACE.
ENTERING IMPERIAL EXIT ZONE VZ 175X.
PREPARE FOR REENTRY. PREPARE FOR PSEUDO-DISINTEGRATION.
ACTIVATE TRIDIMENSIONAL PROPULSION.

The City-Shaft

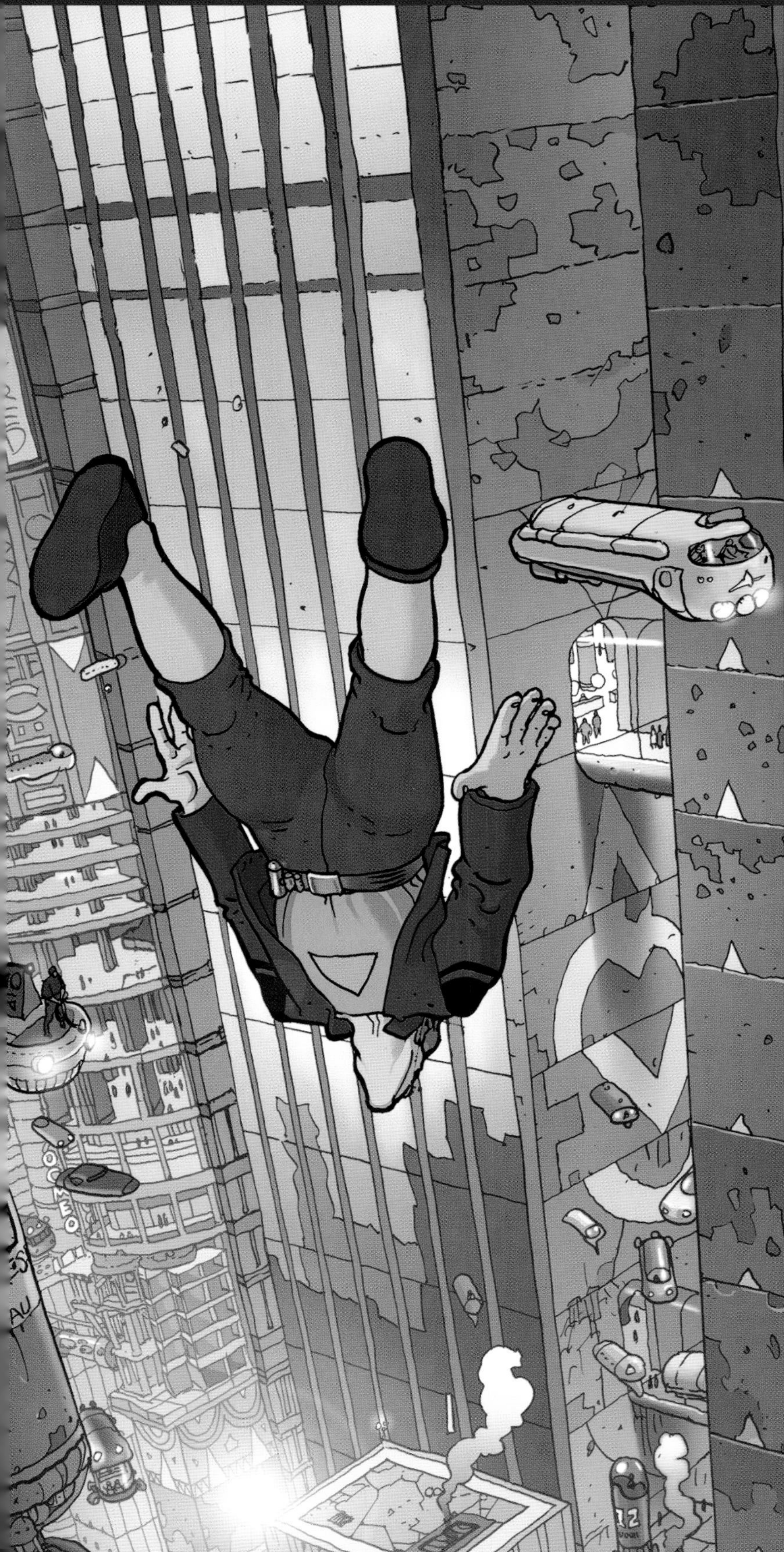

Carved into the ground and located on the surface of the desert planet Terra 2014, this vertical, spiral-shaped city is organized into levels, which are assigned to residents based on their social status. The privileged, for instance, take up the upper levels, while the lower levels are home to those members of the population deemed of a dodgier reputation. At the very bottom of the city lies the Acid Lake, an expanse of puke-colored liquid that serves as a dumping ground, and whose corrosive waters dissolve the bodies of the hapless souls leaping to their deaths from the top of Suicide Alley.

The spectacular set piece of the City-Shaft, on the second page of *The Black Incal*, has made a strong impact on countless readers. The way Mœbius renders the scene in a dizzying high-angle shot is captivating indeed. Perhaps we should see the City-Shaft as the blueprint for what the cities of the future will be like, and as the flipside of the current model for our modern cities, which currently are busy breaking vertical records by erecting skyscrapers that stretch to ever more elevated heights.

While the opening of *The Incal* shows John Difool falling from the top of Suicide Alley, the whole story then transforms this fall into an ascension, which follows a ring structure Mœbius created to evoke reversal. The characters fall only to rise up again and the entire symbol itself is reversible. "A fall takes place from one ring to the next, until the end of the fall, which is the center," says Jodorowsky. "Until one has reached the lowest depth of the descent, one cannot go back up. It is a theme that is found in different traditions. In the Gospel, after He is taken down from the cross, Christ descends into the depths for three days. According to the Gnostics, there He encounters His older brother Lucifer, whom he then merges with to ascend as a being of light. Christ makes his ascension after being put in the tomb. Lucifer himself is a light bearer, a fallen Angel, a receptacle of divine essence, the Incal in each of us."

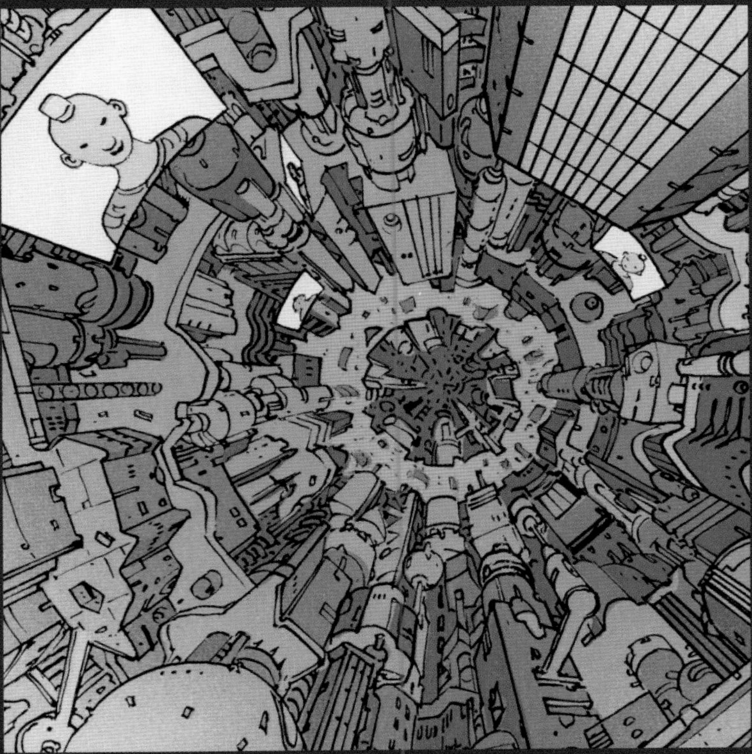

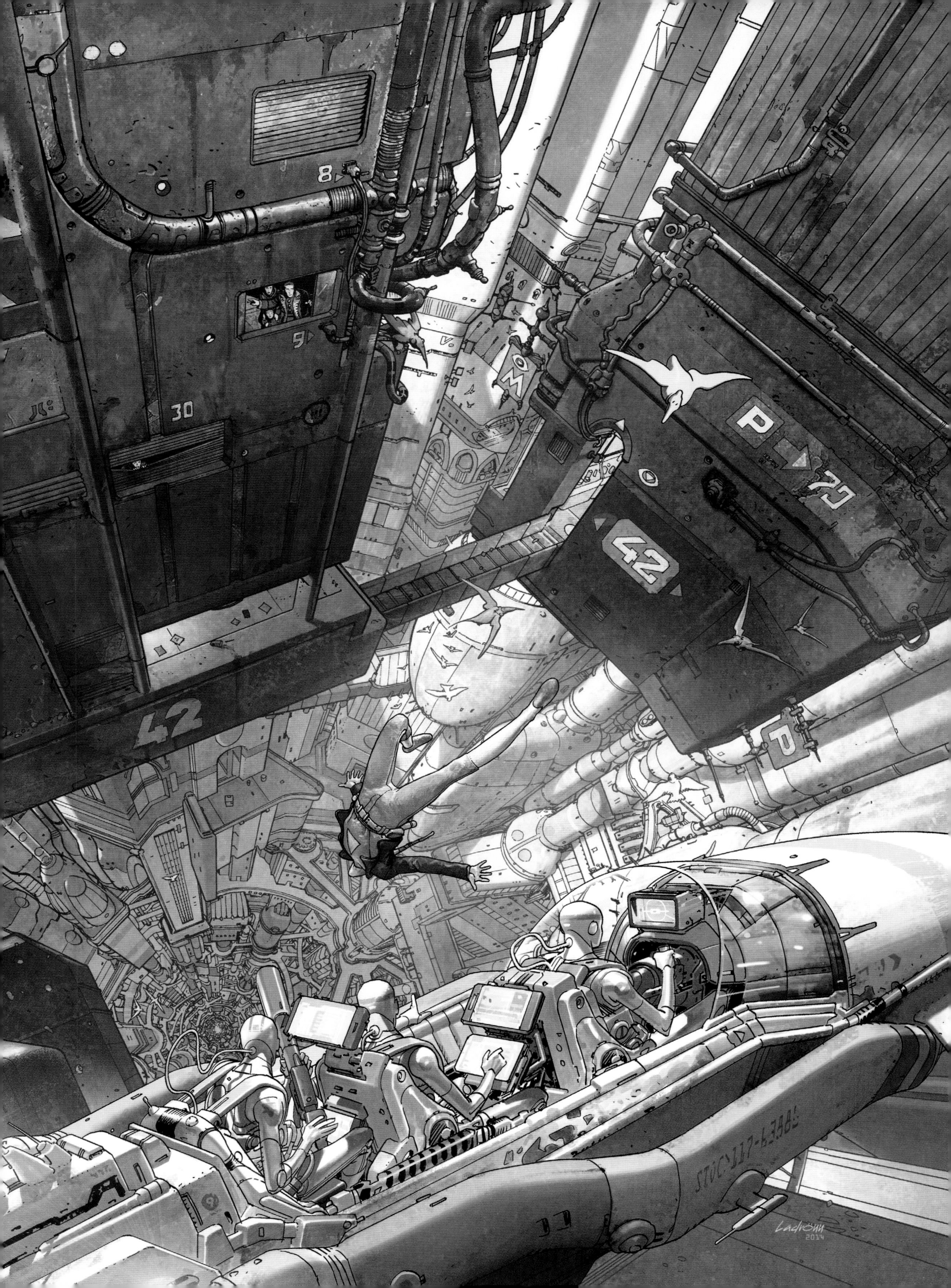
8
9
30
P
42
42
P
Ladrönn
2014

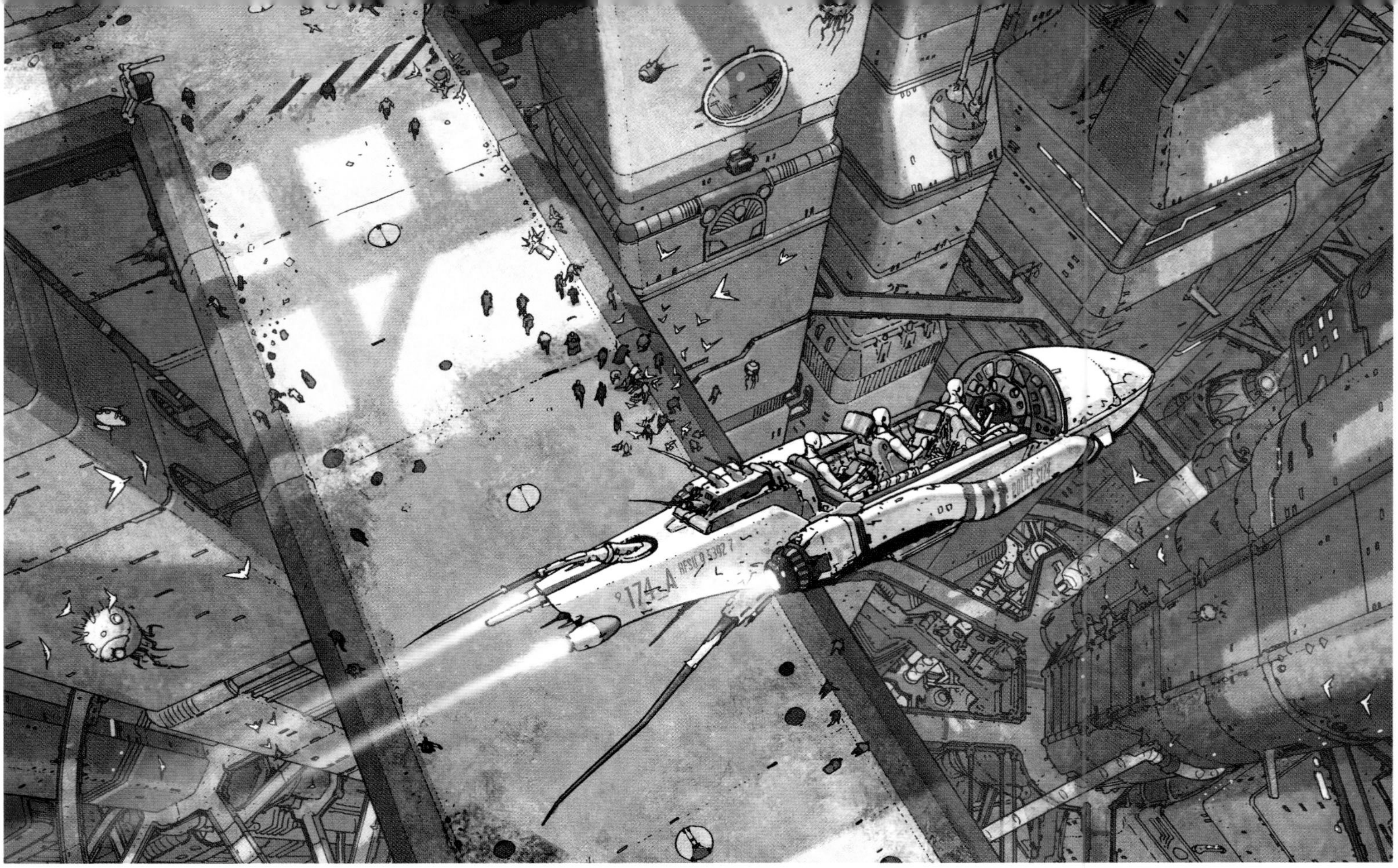

Suicide Alley

Paris has its Champs-Elysées, Los Angeles has Sunset Boulevard, New York has Broadway. Terra 2014's "pride and joy" (if one can use the term) is Suicide Alley. This is where people come to take a stroll, stop to watch a street fight or, best of all—in terms of entertainment value—witness people commit suicide by jumping over the guardrail for "a direct nonstop fall straight down to the great Acid Lake."

A long, wide, concrete avenue that cuts through the City-Shaft, Suicide Alley doesn't discriminate between social classes, and for the space of a walk through town, brings together people from all the different levels. The show is free, available to everyone, and always comes with encores: one suicide begets another, as if throwing oneself head first toward death triggers in some people a morbid copycat effect and an irresistible desire to end their life. Lower level residents love to sit at their window and watch the dance of falling bodies. Or, even more twisted and perverse: they get their rifles and try take out the poor souls, who've been turned into human clay pigeons in one macabre game of target practice. In any case, the rules are set in stone: no leapers allowed before 6 a.m., so as to give the maintenance crews time to proceed with the great clean-up of Suicide Alley.

The first pages of *Before The Incal* are full of sordid scenes featuring Aristos who've come all the way from the upper levels to treat themselves, aboard a flying barge, to the sight—and torment of—all those poor souls who've chosen to take their own lives. Let us hope that Suicide Alley will remain nothing more than a wacky whimsy concocted by storytellers, and that it won't one day become the ultimate reality of an entertainment-driven society, in which death becomes nothing more that amusement, designed to arouse excitement among the most jaded, and collective enjoyment among the privileged classes who've seen it all.

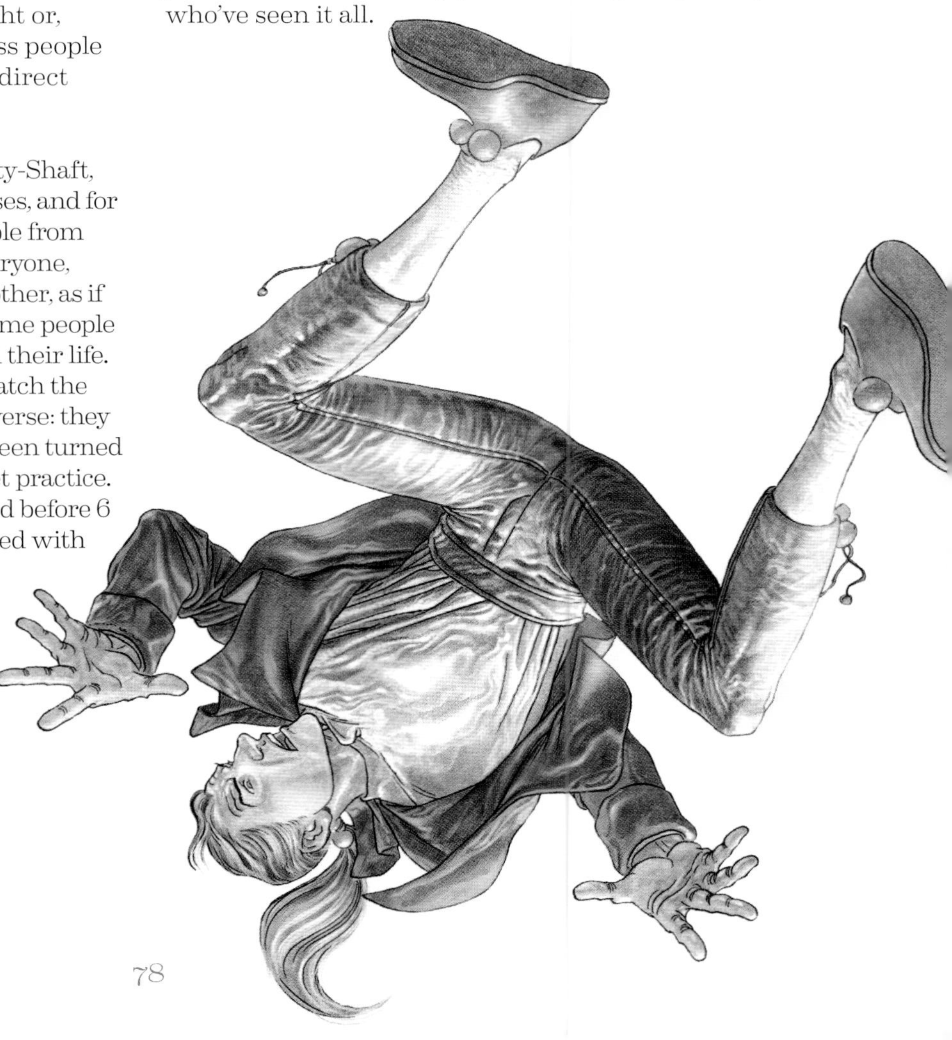

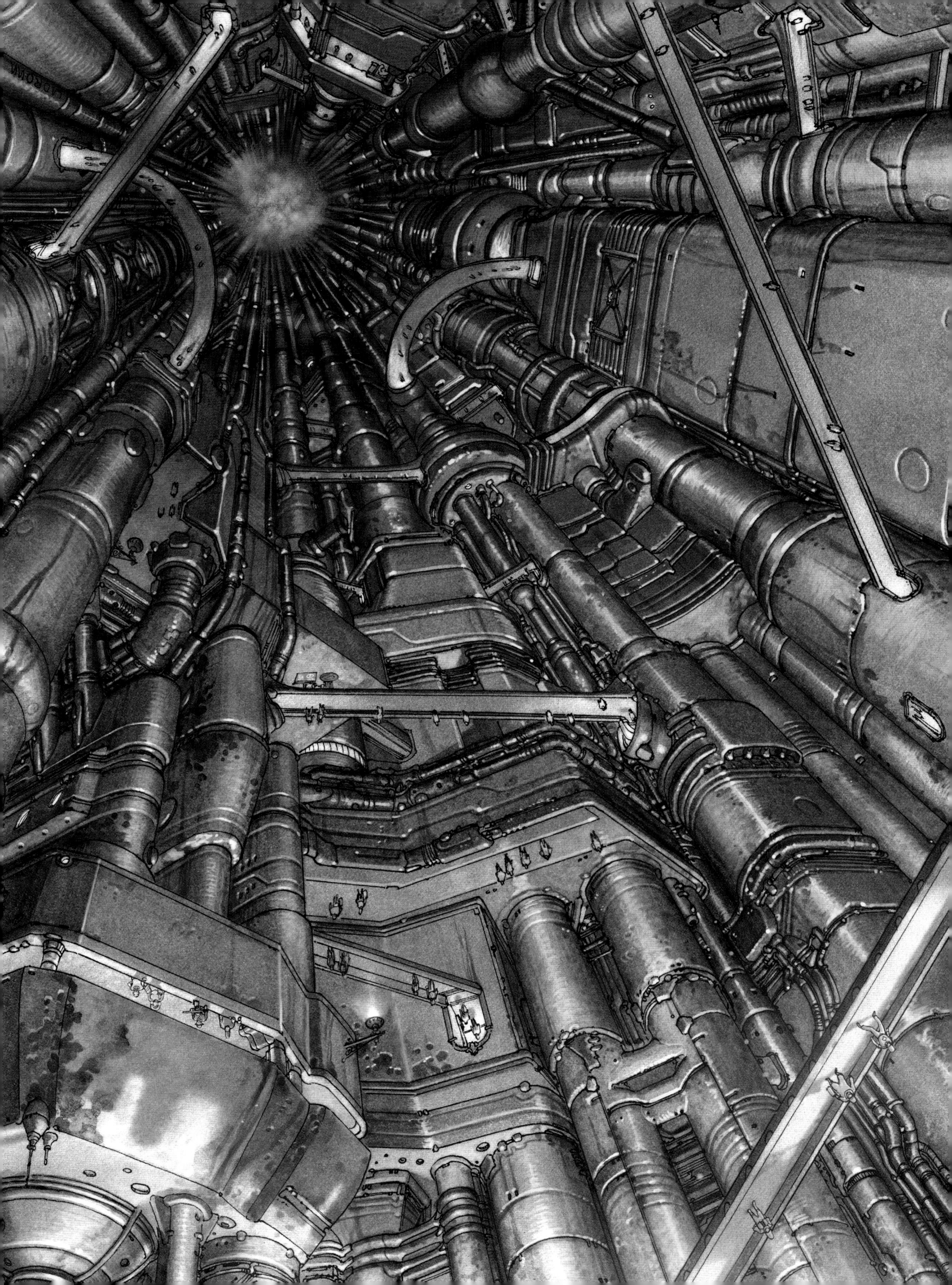

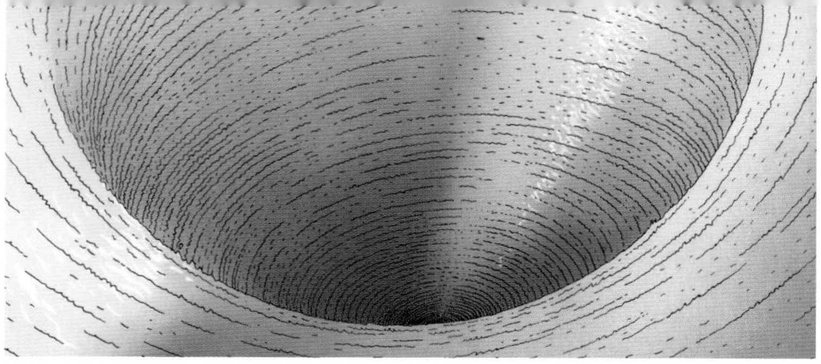

The Acid Lake

Woe to those who fall into the Acid Lake! Just ask any of the many suicide candidates leaping to their deaths from the top of Suicide Alley to plunge head first into this vast expanse of acid. The liquid's greenish color and the gas fumes emanating from its surface leave no doubt as to the leapers' fates: the hapless souls will meet their end as their flesh is eaten away by the "great Acid Lake, which dissolves everything it touches." John Difool nearly comes close to meeting with the same tragic fate after being pushed off the top of Suicide Alley by masked assailants determined to get him to talk. Located at the very base of the City-Shaft, this large dumping ground serves as a machine that destroys bodies and trash. Its purpose is to purify the city by ridding it of all the elements likely to defile it. But its other purpose is to conceal a secret and to ban access to the underground world of Center Earth.

"But there's nothing this deep except the Acid Lake!" says the Metabaron to Tanatah, as she drags Difool and his entourage down into the bowels of the City-Shaft. "So everyone believes," she replies. "In truth, there is a vast world at the center of the planet, beneath the Acid Lake. The great Crystal Caverns... Pyramid Island... Animah and I came from this secret world." After being sucked into the great whirlpool of the Acid Lake, they arrive at a subterranean river that leads them straight to Garbageland, a veritable lava flow of garbage that seems to extend to infinity and which Difool describes in a few concise and well-chosen words: "Ugh, it stinks!"

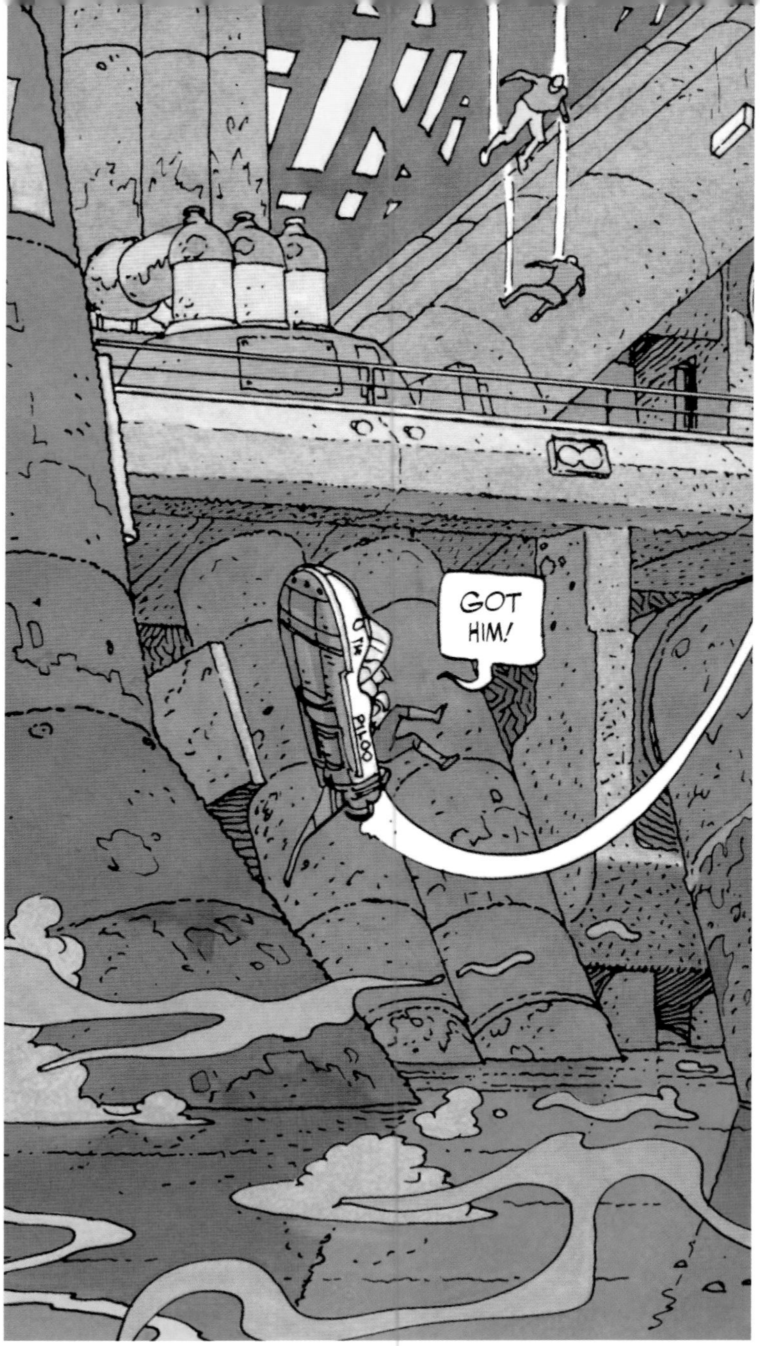
GOT HIM!

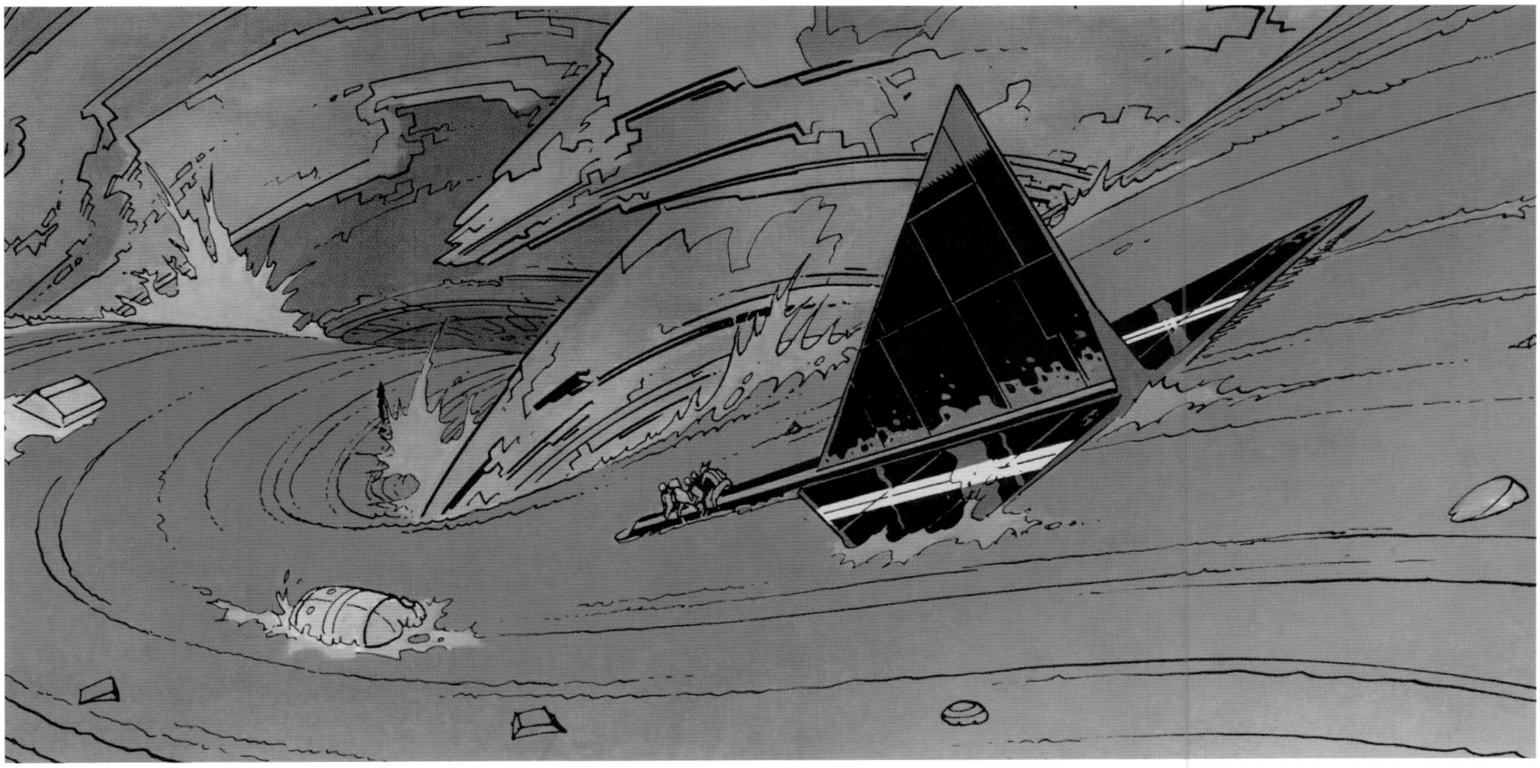

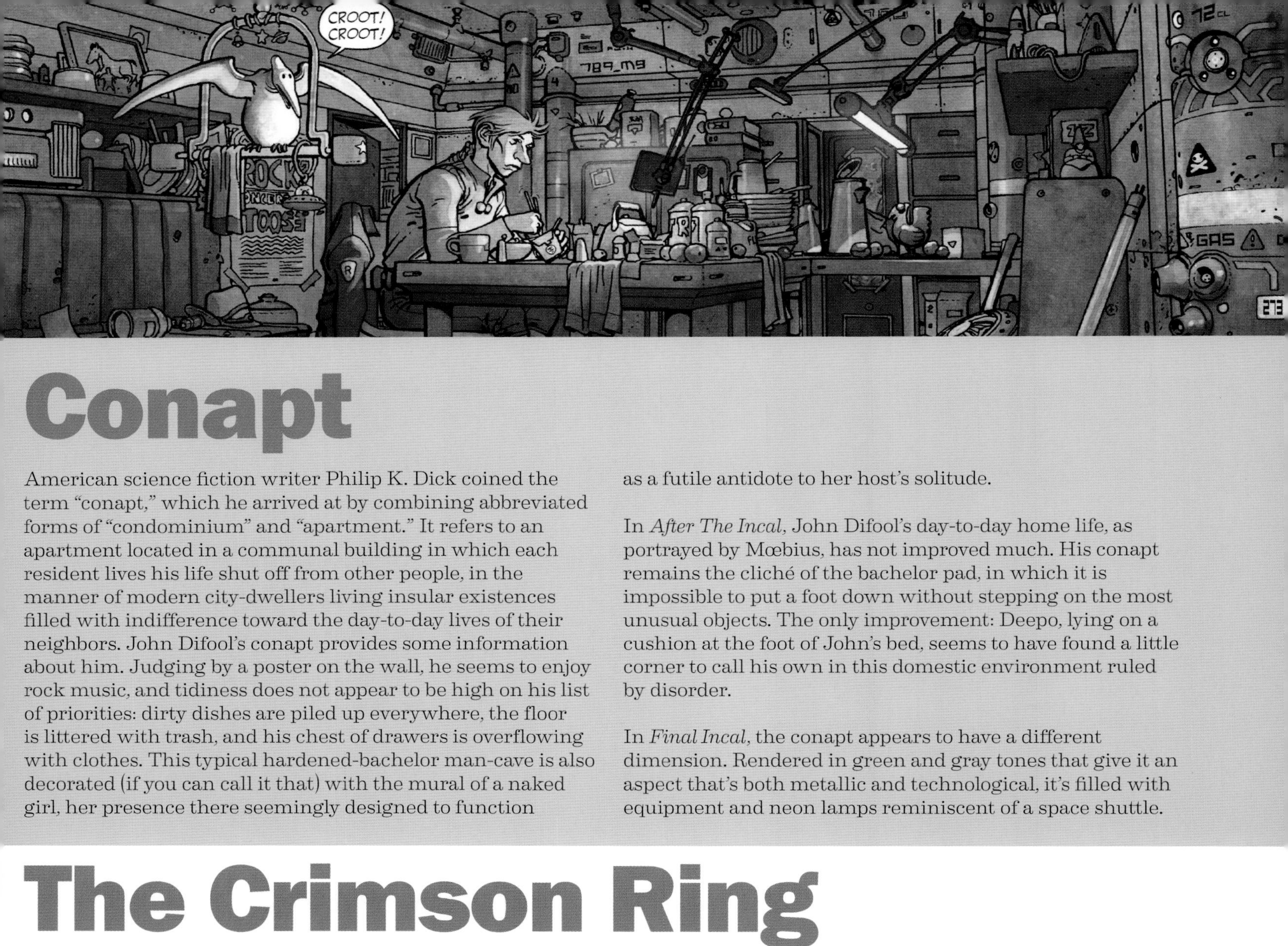
CROOT! CROOT!

Conapt

American science fiction writer Philip K. Dick coined the term "conapt," which he arrived at by combining abbreviated forms of "condominium" and "apartment." It refers to an apartment located in a communal building in which each resident lives his life shut off from other people, in the manner of modern city-dwellers living insular existences filled with indifference toward the day-to-day lives of their neighbors. John Difool's conapt provides some information about him. Judging by a poster on the wall, he seems to enjoy rock music, and tidiness does not appear to be high on his list of priorities: dirty dishes are piled up everywhere, the floor is littered with trash, and his chest of drawers is overflowing with clothes. This typical hardened-bachelor man-cave is also decorated (if you can call it that) with the mural of a naked girl, her presence there seemingly designed to function as a futile antidote to her host's solitude.

In *After The Incal*, John Difool's day-to-day home life, as portrayed by Mœbius, has not improved much. His conapt remains the cliché of the bachelor pad, in which it is impossible to put a foot down without stepping on the most unusual objects. The only improvement: Deepo, lying on a cushion at the foot of John's bed, seems to have found a little corner to call his own in this domestic environment ruled by disorder.

In *Final Incal*, the conapt appears to have a different dimension. Rendered in green and gray tones that give it an aspect that's both metallic and technological, it's filled with equipment and neon lamps reminiscent of a space shuttle.

The Crimson Ring

Welcome to the Crimson Ring (also referred to as "the Red Ring"), its guilty pleasures and its abominable mutants! It's here, in the heart of these lower levels giving off a whiff of danger, perversion, and sensuality, that the Aristotourists from the luxurious higher levels come to let loose. "I want to party till my halo drops!" says one such character on the first page of *Before The Incal*. "I just installed a new kitbox, and it's already dripping wet!" replies another. "I'm dying to find someone who's got the virus!" adds a third. In the Crimson Ring, everything goes, nothing is taboo. All one needs to do is pay and respect the safety guidelines of the Prezident's Hunchbacks, who turn into tourist guides for the occasion. "Stay together! The area's crawling with Psycho Anarchists!" one of them warns. The Crimson Ring is to Terra 2014 what Pigalle, 42nd Street, or Soho once were to the buses of tourists visiting the dodgy neighborhoods of Paris, New York, or London. Except for one major difference: beyond the lurid depiction of well-known and improved fantasies—"Homeo-whores à la carte! Build your own fantasy!" reads the storefront touting the advantages of "digital sex"—it highlights the social divide that is at the heart of the City-Shaft, with the various residential levels reflecting the sociological diversity of the residents. This divide is carved in stone and insurmountable: in the City-Shaft, the social elevator is out of service. There is no climbing the social ladder. The only way to go is down, to the sound and beat of the desperate souls throwing themselves from the top of Suicide Alley...
It is in one of the hellish establishments in the Crimson Ring that young John Difool loses his virginity, dragged there by older friends who choose a woman for him entrusted with the task of making him a man, by virtue of a somewhat clichéd tradition. "Good job, Johnny! You were fantastic! How does it feel to be a man?" his friends cry out as they applaud his performance. The only consolation following this initiation ritual is that he runs into Deepo, the concrete seagull, and saves him from the gratuitous cruelty of a group of horrible kids, taking the orphaned chick home with him.

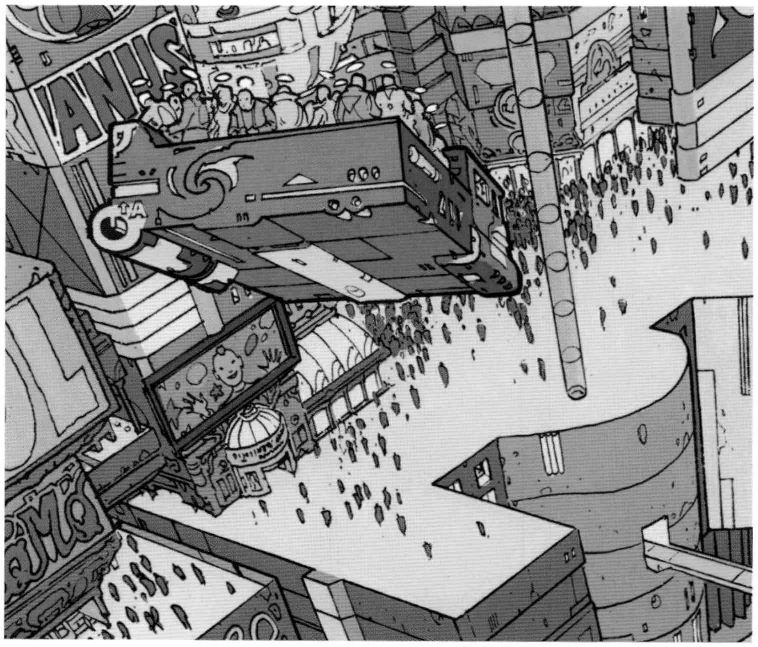

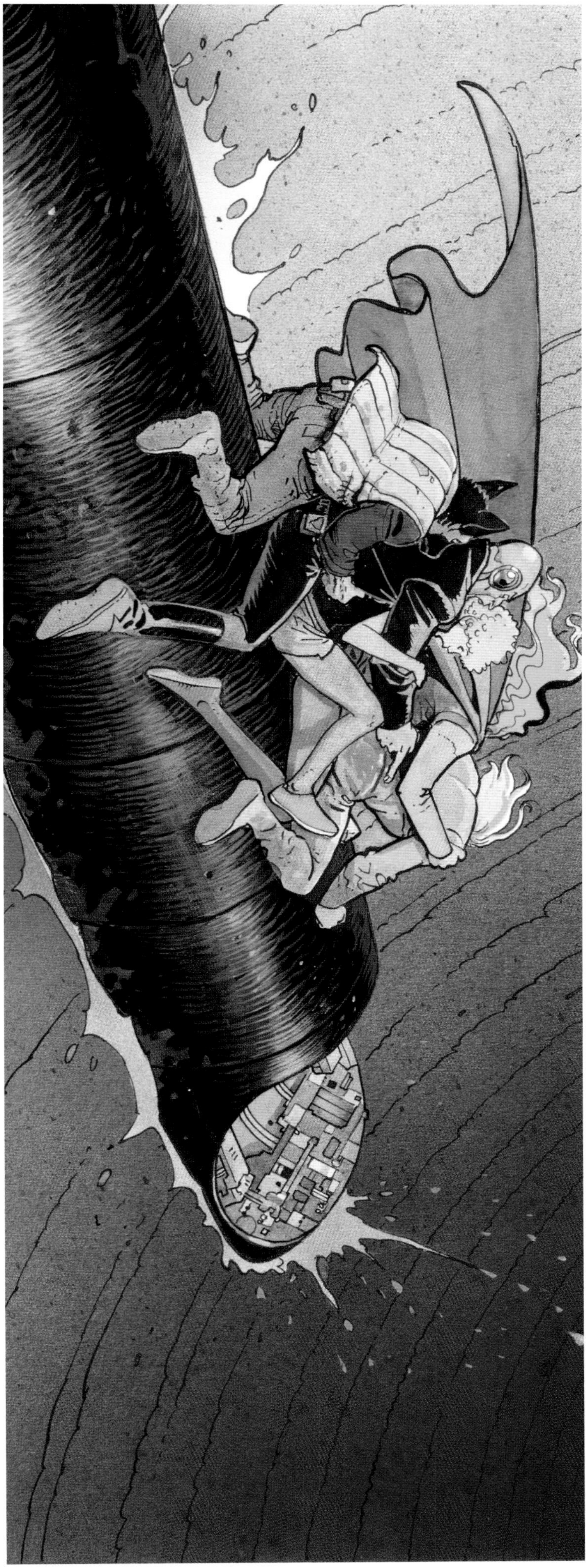

Center Earth

This putrid land, located beneath the Acid Lake, is where the aggressive mutants led by Gorgo the Foul dwell, among the mountains of garbage they feed off. This is where John Difool and his companions end up in *What Lies Beneath*, the third volume of *The Incal*, after traveling aboard the metacraft and following Tanatah's directions. The landscape is anything but delightful. "What a sight!" The Metabaron cries out. "Garbage, as far as the eye can see!" Kill Wolfhead replies. "Yes, but it's the only way to get to the true heart of the planet!" Animah reassures them.

But the next stage of the journey is a complete reversal: the light of Center Earth comes from the Interior Sun. To get to it, they must first reach a tower in the middle of the garbage dump, then cross the labyrinth that leads to the ray of light produced by the Interior Sun. In essence, Garbageland is a no-man's land that separates the physical world from the spiritual world. When climbing the first ladder, they move from the corrosive acid to crime and poverty, then to the middle classes addicted to 3D TV, then to the city that recycles corpses, to the Aristos, and finally to the Prezident's palace. At that point, they have to launch into space, toward the sun and the stars, to find supreme power over the physical world, along with the Emperoress, who's back to being a psychic entity and a spiritual symbol.

In the other direction, when one climbs down the second ladder, one passes through the symbolic architectures of the spiritual world: the tower, the ray, the forest of singing crystals guarded by the Arhat sages, then the crystal tower inside of which is the Portal of Transfiguration. Beyond that point, a traveler must have the purity of heart that enables them to transform into energy so they can then plunge into another space and time: the interdimensional Pyramid Island, a sacred and interior place, a "metaphysical" world, but one which nonetheless brings us back to the material dimension with the creation of the Starship.

In short, "what lies beneath is like what is above," according to the principle of traditional symbolism as defined by *The Emerald Tablet*, the foundation of alchemical thought, and from which volumes 3 and 4 of *The Incal* borrow their title.

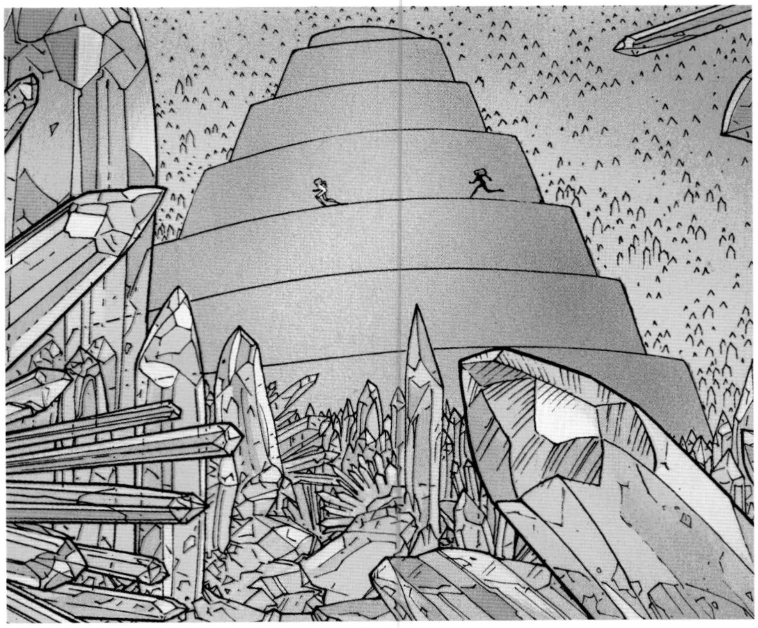

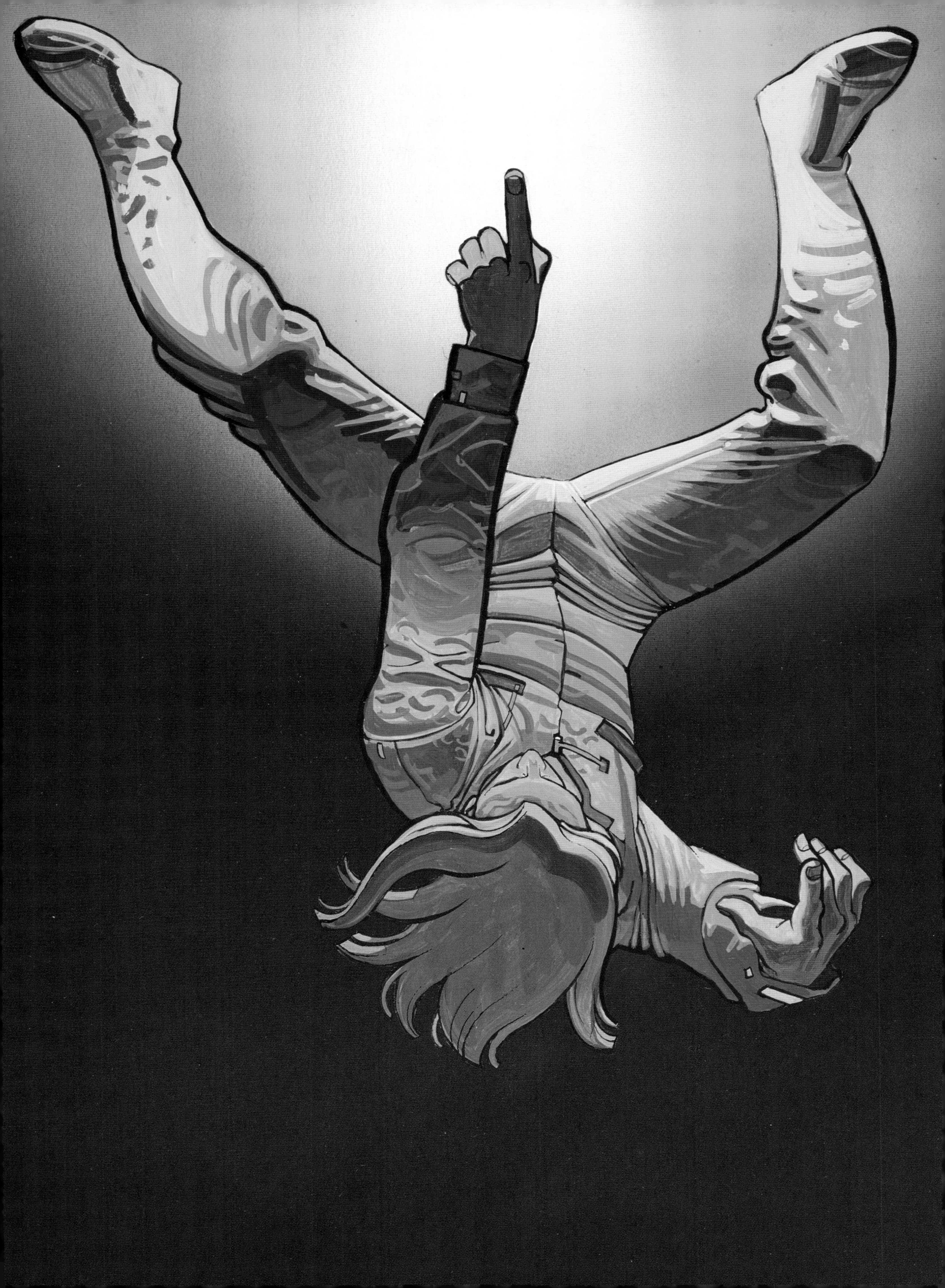

The Starship

Separating the two Incals makes it possible for the Great Darkness, to which the Black Incal is connected, to emerge. The subsequent fusion of the two Incals produces the Starship, which is not a physical vessel but rather, according to Jodorowsky, "the manifestation of the celestial consciousness, for everything is mixed together in a kind of cosmic game. Everything is alive. Not 'alive' as in normal life, but filled with consciousness. Everything lives on consciousness, everything feeds on consciousness."

The consciousness of this Starship, in which John Difool travels, is the perfect androgyne, Solune. She/he only achieves true transparence through the gift of self, the death of the ego, and release of individuality that alone makes it possible to pierce the Darkness, whose nucleus is ultimately light. The Great Darkness is only the "negative force accumulated in the human heart," which obstructs the ancient light. Orb, of whom "The Great Darkness was as much a part as the Light." But John Difool doesn't sacrifice his ego to the creation of the Incal's world via fusion, and the subsequent dawn of a new time. He retains his individual consciousness, as he cannot give the gift of self, or perhaps simply he is the dreamer of the Incal's world. "The adventure is not over, because John Difool is coming back," Jodorowsky says, "He must remember. But he didn't do the work, whereas his friends were dissolved so that he could do the work. The next process would be the dissolution of Difool. It would be the acceptance of death because, in the Incal cycle, John Difool doesn't accept the prospect of dying."

The Great Nuptial Games

This Berg religious tradition is categorical: every five years, the Great Nuptial Games take place on Orgargan, the Berg home world (it should be noted that one year on this planet equals 1,000 days on Earth). Whoever among the smorgasbord of different races and species survives the no-holds-barred contest wins the right to impregnate the Protoqueen. Legend has it that after 24,000 such impregnations, the Berg race will finally reach its great golden age.... The rules couldn't be simpler: energy or ballistic weapons are banned, only "physical strength, skill, endurance, and knowledge of combat" are permitted.

The scene preceding the big contest, drawn by Moebius in *What Is Above*, is as spectacular as the sprawling image of Teutonic Knights lined up as far as the eye can see in *Alexander Nevsky*, Sergei Eisenstein's 1938 film. The sheer compact mass of the crowd of participants is overwhelming, but the artist's pen strokes manage to give a sense of collective power, while at the same time making it possible to distinguish the first few rows, before a later panel zooms in on them in a hieratic posture. Even John Difool is almost impressive—which is saying a lot.

The site of the Great Nuptial Games—a gigantic cone about to be charged by a horde of fighters, some of whom are humorously sketched by Moebius—resembles a Dante-esque vision of Ancient Roman gladiatorial battles. As for the fight scenes, as epic as they are comical, they're worth their weight in kublars. "These humans are really funny," laughs one of the Bergs in the audience. "Look at that fat one that just fell! I want to eat that one!" another cries out giddily. All those competitors, fully determined to reach the summit, bring to mind the seven candidates for eternal life in search of wisdom who climb a sacred hill in *The Holy Mountain*, the 1973 film directed by Jodorowsky—albeit with additional violence and savagery thrown in.

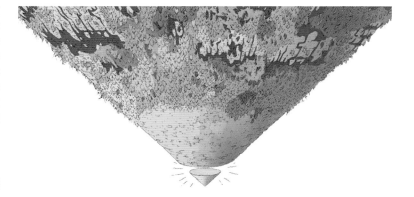

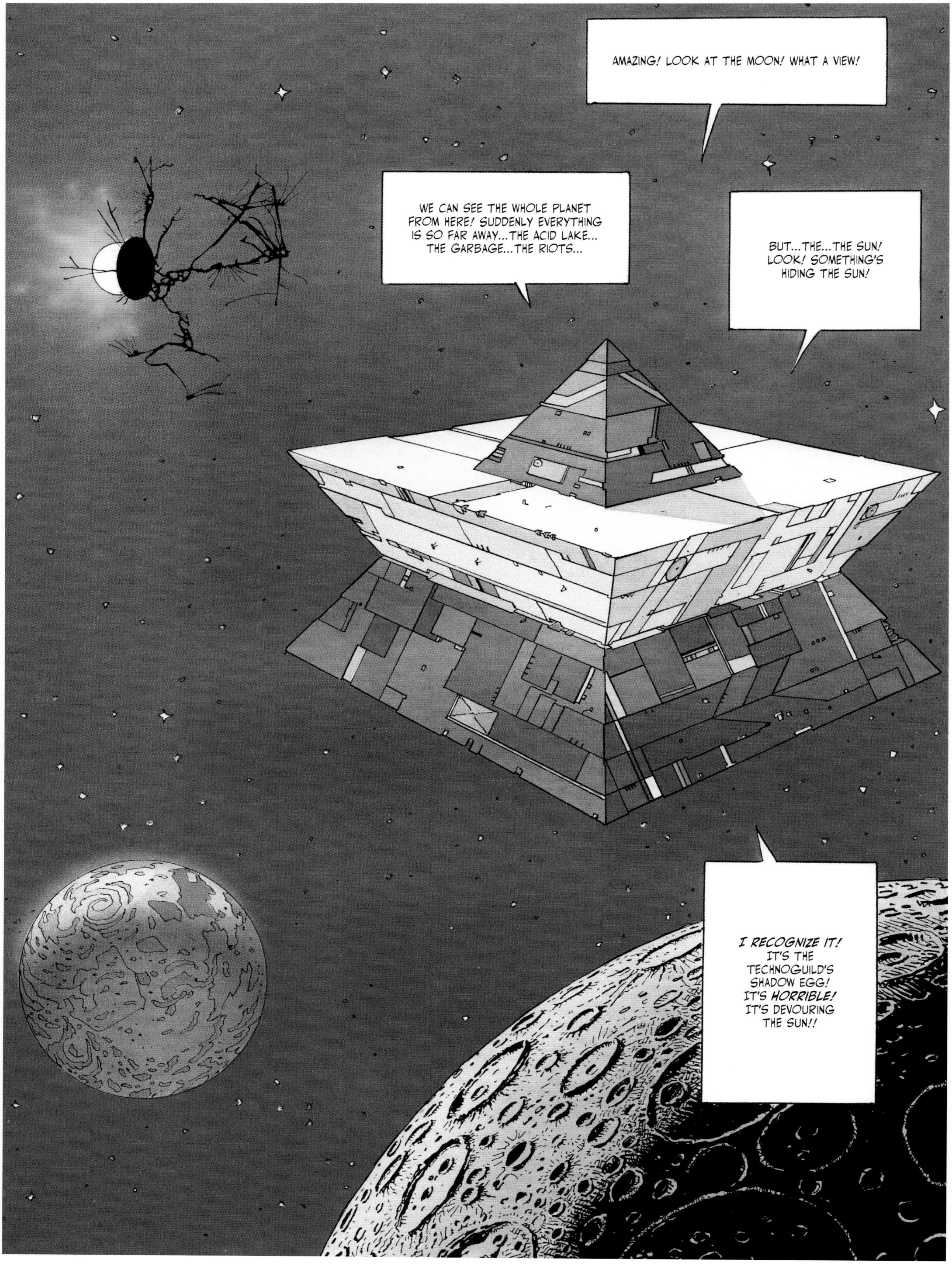
AMAZING! LOOK AT THE MOON! WHAT A VIEW!
WE CAN SEE THE WHOLE PLANET FROM HERE! SUDDENLY EVERYTHING IS SO FAR AWAY...THE ACID LAKE... THE GARBAGE...THE RIOTS...
BUT...THE...THE SUN! LOOK! SOMETHING'S HIDING THE SUN!
I RECOGNIZE IT! IT'S THE TECHNOGUILD'S SHADOW EGG! IT'S ***HORRIBLE!*** IT'S DEVOURING THE SUN!!

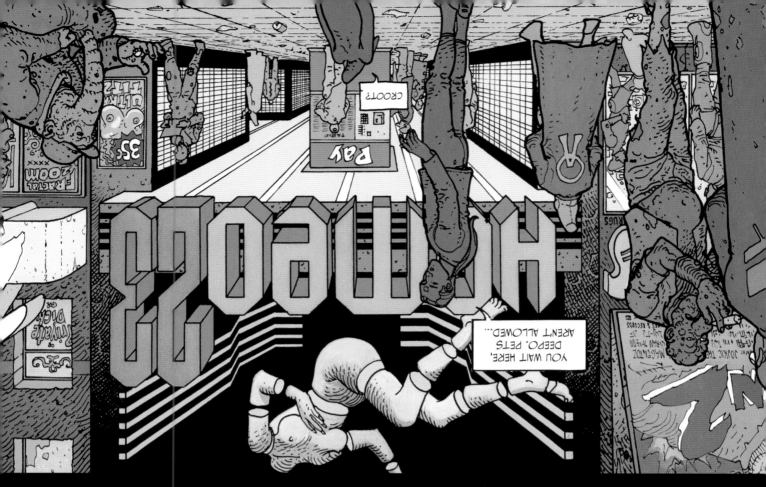

Vhisky, SPV, and Homeo-Whores

This isn't just the title of the fifth volume of *Before The Incal,* it's also the combination of John Difool's three favorite indulgences, and he couldn't begin to imagine life without the regular surrender to these vices of his. Just as the Technopope prepares to cut into him, poor John—convinced the end is nigh—silently begs the Incal to get him out of this jam and send him "back in time to [his] good old conapt. With a nice full bottle of wiskey and [his] faithful box of first class SPV!" Alert readers will have noticed the variations in the spelling of his favorite libation, which varies from "vhisky" in *Before The Incal* to "wiskey" and "whisky" in *The Incal.*

In the second chapter of *The Black Incal,* we see John relaxing in a bath and taking a swig of whisky, as if he had found the way to true happiness. But perhaps it's just the artificial pleasure of SPV, which, as a footnote informs us, is a "light hallucinogen for mainstream consumption" (any similarity to the marijuana that Jean Giraud/Mœbius consumed on a regular basis might be more than mere coincidence...). "Ahh... A bottle of whisky, a box of SPV, a cigar and a hot bath... What more could I wish for?"

A homeo-whore, perhaps? And who should make an appearance in the very next panel? One such homeo-whore, as a matter of fact, ordered by Difool, who, we are led to infer, is a regular client of the "Paris Level Sexual Credit Union"—a place described by John himself as an "upper-class establishment," an expression that—depending on interpretation—could have sarcastic undertones.

In the dystopian future in which *The Incal* is set, prostitution has made "progress." Now, all the client has to do is click on a few icons to custom design a lady endowed with his favorite physical attributes and guaranteed to make his wildest fantasies come true. John's deflowering scene in *Before The Incal* offers up a caricatured example of the process. His party buddies, who take him to go "blow money on homeo-whores," design a "really special" creature for him, a monstrosity with orange skin next to whom poor hapless John looks like a scared little boy.

The reader discovers, in *What Lies Beneath,* that the homeo-whore—whose vocabulary, like that of all her fellow working girls, is reduced to a friendly but limited "cootchie cootchie coo"—is not just anyone. She is none other than Animah, who obeyed the will of the Incal by choosing John Difool to be Solune's father. "You had to be the father. And for that I had to transform myself into a homeo-whore. When you went for one of your frequent visits to the Red Ring, I met you in that den of iniquity!"

In a nod to the original, Ladrönn reproduces the same scene in *Final Incal.* Lying in a bathtub, holding a bottle of whisky, his stash of SPV within reach, Difool is enjoying the delights of a bubble bath and smoking a nice cigar as images of homeo-whores having sex with zoo creatures unfold across his video screens. The whole panel has the same rose-tinted and somewhat supernatural atmosphere that Mœbius had already used in *The Incal.* A few pages later, riding a Psychorat through the devastated landscape of Center Earth, Difool gives into his natural tendency to whine by explaining to Luz that he would much prefer "a nice hot bath and a tall glass of whisky..."

YOU WAIT HERE, DEEPO. PETS AREN'T ALLOWED...
HOMEO23
Pay
TARIF
CROOT?
FRACTAL ZOOM
XXXX
35¢
ULTRA TITZ
Private Dick
RUGS

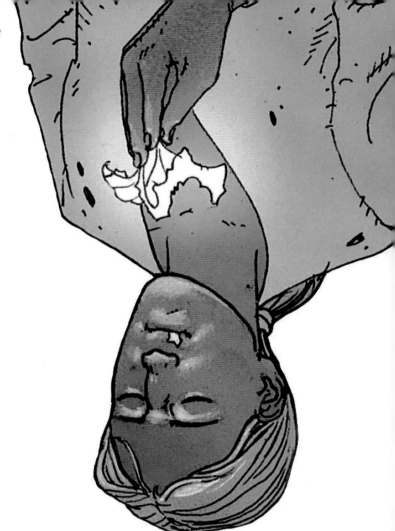

Amorine

Amorine can be thought of in two different ways. At first glance it's a toxic and pernicious drug that creates dependence in the consumer. Such is the case for John Difool's mother, who is introduced in the early pages of *Before the Incal*, like a prostitute demanding her fix, like a junkie hooked on heroin. "My God, this life sucks! Wake up, Snailhead. I need another dose of Amorine!" she says to her pimp (although a little later in the story, we discover that his role goes beyond just that of a small-time dealer). In the next panel, she is seen shaking, with dark circles under her eyes and deep, sunken eye sockets, indicators of a state of health which, to put it mildly, is less than glowing. She has just learned that she will have to do without Amorine due to a Cybo-cop raid of the underground lab that manufactures it. Even in front of her son, she can't hide her addiction: "Quiet, Johnny, I couldn't cope without Amorine!"

In reality, Amorine is "not a drug, it's a fragment of the divine," she explains to John in a holovideo message she left for him before she died. It turns out that she had contracted the Meropa virus and was taking the drug to fight the incurable disease in order to stay alive as long as she could. "Saint-Amorine" is extracted from the flowers of the Amarax, explains Snailhead, who, in the meantime, has gone from dealer to High Priest of the Neuro-Emotional Church. For love has disappeared from the bioperfect civilization, but "this flower that grows in our hearts will transform the world." And "Thanks to Amorine, humans will become whole again, by tasting the forgotten and sacred emotion..."

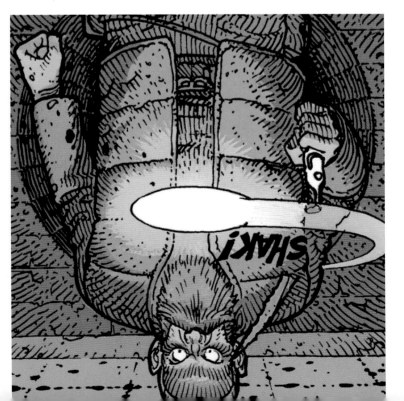

Halo

How do you recognize an Aristo? By the white halo that hovers above their head, like an ectoplasmic extension of their physical being. But the Aristos are no saints—they're quite the opposite, in fact. There's nothing they love more than to go slumming in the lower levels of Terra 2014, shamelessly abusing their position of dominance without a care for the consequences their actions will have on the poor, hapless souls they exploit with impunity. Their halo is, first and foremost, a distinctive sign of social membership that immediately identifies them as belonging to the upper class. A sort of totem or VIP pass that entitles them to everything, without having to be burdened by any moral constraints—which aren't much of an issue in the *Incal* universe to begin with.

It should come as no surprise, then, that Oliver, John Difool's father—as well as the inventor of many clever apparatuses that unfortunately often malfunction—makes fake halos that allow him and his son to crash Aristo parties in order to strip the wealthy of their jewels. But a true Aristo halo is also a weapon. When handled with dexterity, it can sever an opponent's limb or slit a throat.

It will take all the shrewdness John Difool and Luz de Garra possess to uncover the hidden reality behind the Aristo halos. Far from being an appendage that attests to natural social superiority, it turns out to be just a vulgar implant "grafted on" in secret operations carried out in Aristo-maternity wards by corrupt doctors. In the end, perhaps the only halo worthy of respect is the one that a smitten Luz draws in chalk on the bedroom wall above John's head. "Take a look! You've got your halo, and now we're equals! Turn off the light and come here!" she tells him, proud of her clever resourcefulness.

Her halo ends up saving her life in *Final Incal*. As she prepares to try to negotiate with the Gounas, Luz realizes that her halo makes her a true deity in the eyes of those horrific metal spiders, which wreaked havoc among Kaimann's pirates.

Cocaloco

Any resemblance to an American brand of soft drink that is consumed throughout the world and that sponsors major sporting events such as the World Cup or the Olympics cannot, of course, be anything but sheer coincidence. Readers are free to make the association of their choosing between "coca" and "loco." The resulting portmanteau may lead one to assume that the consumption of this beverage causes a kind of madness in anyone who drinks it, or even addiction. Indeed, the population of Terra 2014 is relentlessly bombarded with aggressive advertising and has literally gone crazy for Cocaloco.

According to research conducted by Kolbo-5, Cocaloco is indeed ubiquitous. The brand is present on the streets in the form of classic advertising slogans: "Cocaloco for all—All for Cocaloco" or propaganda: "Don't you dare look elsewhere 'cuz we've got the BEST!" A quick look at Luz de Garra's apartment reveals that the overreaching marketing campaign orchestrated by the brand has also managed to sink its tentacles into the most unexpected everyday objects, from an air conditioner to a duvet cover, or plastered as "art" on the walls.

But Cocaloco is more than just a simple drink, as TV host Diavaloo acknowledges on an episode of his reality entertainment show: "Cocaloco, the only fluid more precious than blood!" Founding and subsidizing educational establishments akin to "correctional colleges" is not enough for the mega-corporation; behind its façade as a thirst-quenching (and thirst-making!) machine it seems to also be involved in shady goings on which John Difool, with the invaluable help of Kolbo-5, will be all too happy to elucidate.

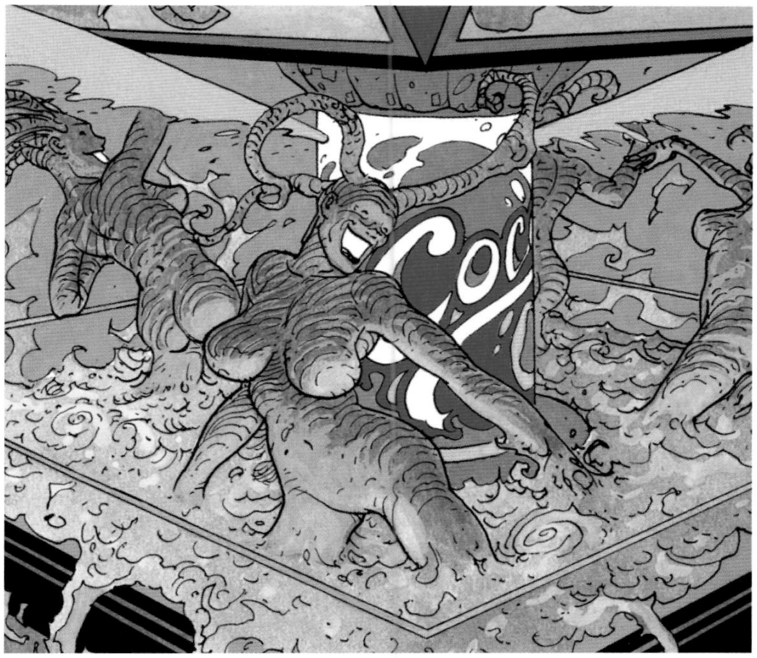

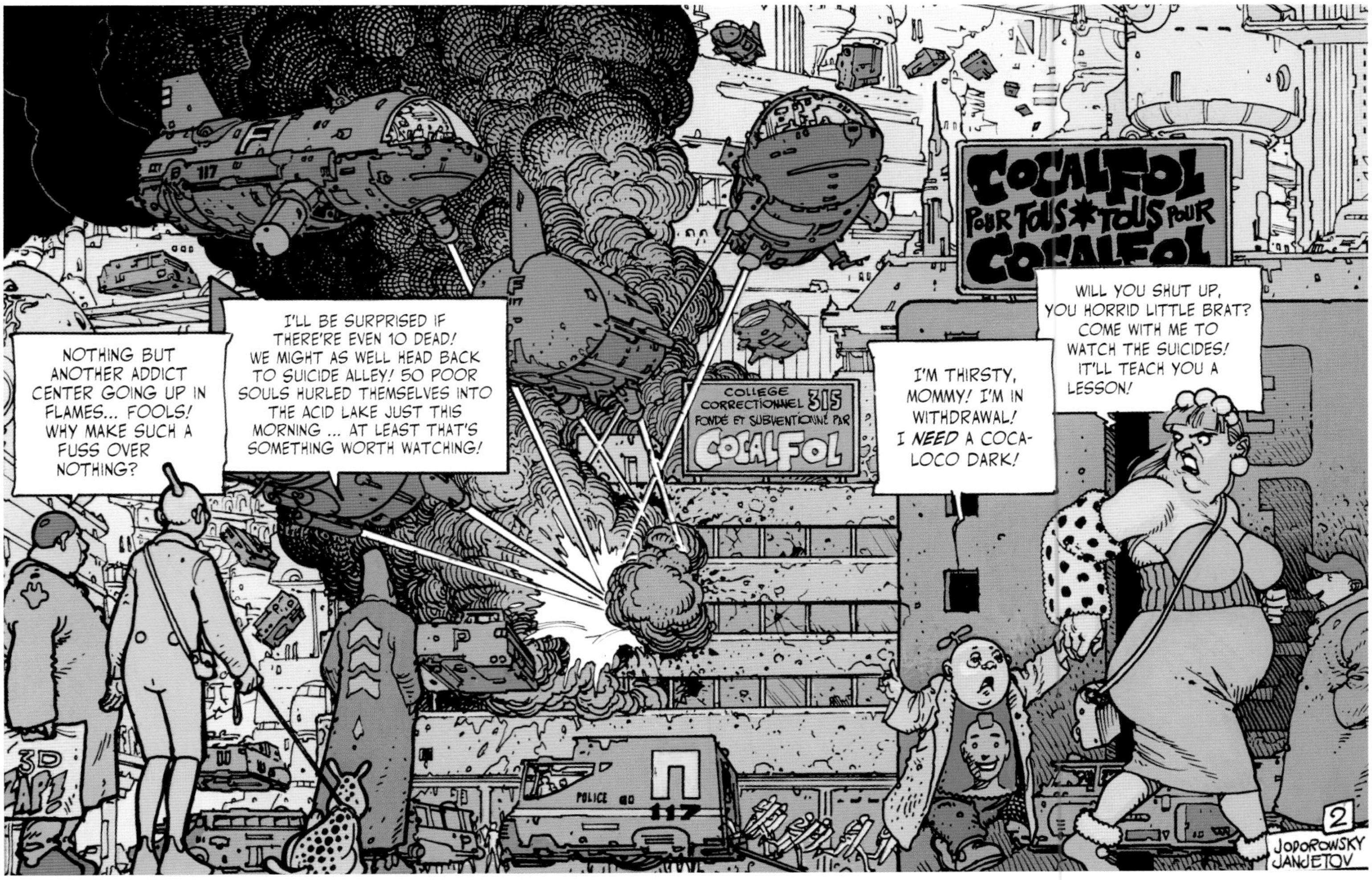
COCALFOL
POUR TOUS ✱ TOUS POUR
COCALFOL
NOTHING BUT ANOTHER ADDICT CENTER GOING UP IN FLAMES... FOOLS! WHY MAKE SUCH A FUSS OVER NOTHING?
I'LL BE SURPRISED IF THERE'RE EVEN 10 DEAD! WE MIGHT AS WELL HEAD BACK TO SUICIDE ALLEY! 50 POOR SOULS HURLED THEMSELVES INTO THE ACID LAKE JUST THIS MORNING ... AT LEAST THAT'S SOMETHING WORTH WATCHING!
COLLEGE CORRECTIONNEL 315 FONDÉ ET SUBVENTIONNÉ PAR COCALFOL
I'M THIRSTY, MOMMY! I'M IN WITHDRAWAL! I NEED A COCA-LOCO DARK!
WILL YOU SHUT UP, YOU HORRID LITTLE BRAT? COME WITH ME TO WATCH THE SUICIDES! IT'LL TEACH YOU A LESSON!
POLICE
117
2
JODOROWSKY
JANJETOV

5. Beneath The Incal: Themes & Influences

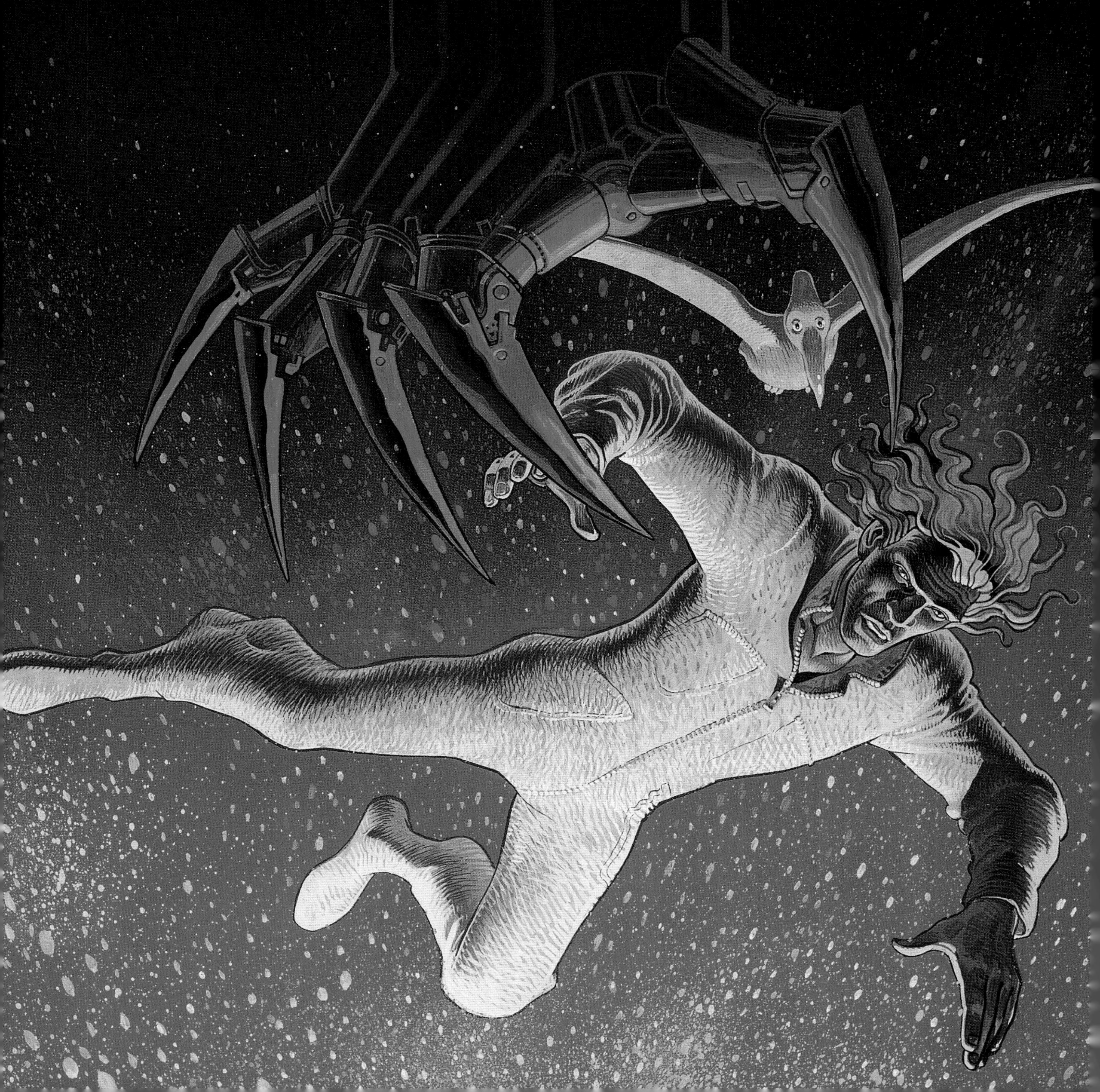

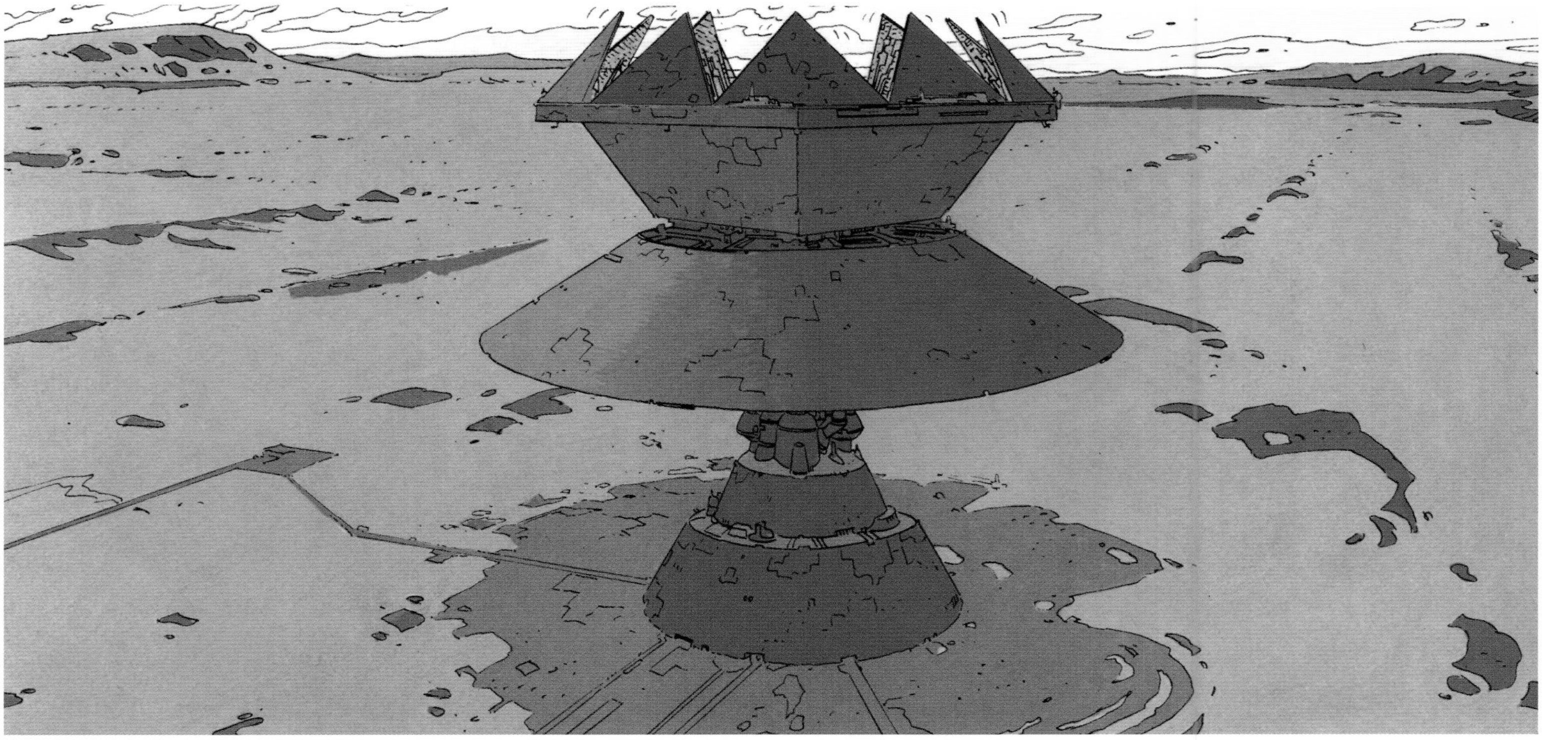

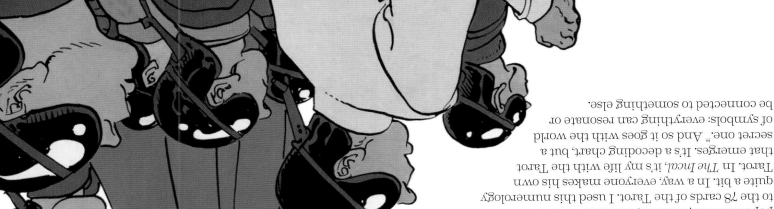

The Tarot

Alejandro Jodorowsky used all his "esoteric" knowledge to enrich, if not give birth to, *The Incal.* There are close connections to the Tarot in the work. John Difool represents the Tarot Fool who's always accompanied by a pet dog. "This companion who follows the hero represents the animal nature that remains part of us all," the writer explains. "Mythological heroes are but the developments of this ancient wisdom. In *The Incal,* the hero's animal nature is represented by a bird, Deepo. Difool is the one who leaves and doesn't know where he's going. He reaches the highest level of knowledge but must constantly start over."

Some of the locations in *The Incal* also feature references to the Tarot. "The Techno Tower, which is destroyed, is a negative interpretation of Card 16, the Lightning-Struck Tower or the House of God," continues Jodorowsky. "Similarly, the Crimson Ring corresponds to the belt of the Tarot's Devil, which is red. It might be of interest to note that I spent my early childhood in a desert village in Chile called Tocopilla. At the time, I didn't know what that name meant. I later found out, much to my surprise, that 'Toco' means double square—the sacred rectangle—and that 'Pilla' means the devil. I landed smack in the middle of my own theories! The devil on one side and the sacred rectangle on the other, the Black Incal and the Luminous Incal. In addition, Tocopilla is located on the 22nd parallel, which corresponds to the 22 major arcana of the Tarot. The Berg Planet, which eventually becomes Planet Difool, has a population of 78 billion, a number that is not unrelated to the 78 cards of the Tarot. I used this numerology quite a bit. In a way, everyone makes his own Tarot. In *The Incal,* it's my life with the Tarot that emerges. It's a decoding chart, but a secret one." And so it goes with the world of symbols: everything can resonate or be connected to something else.

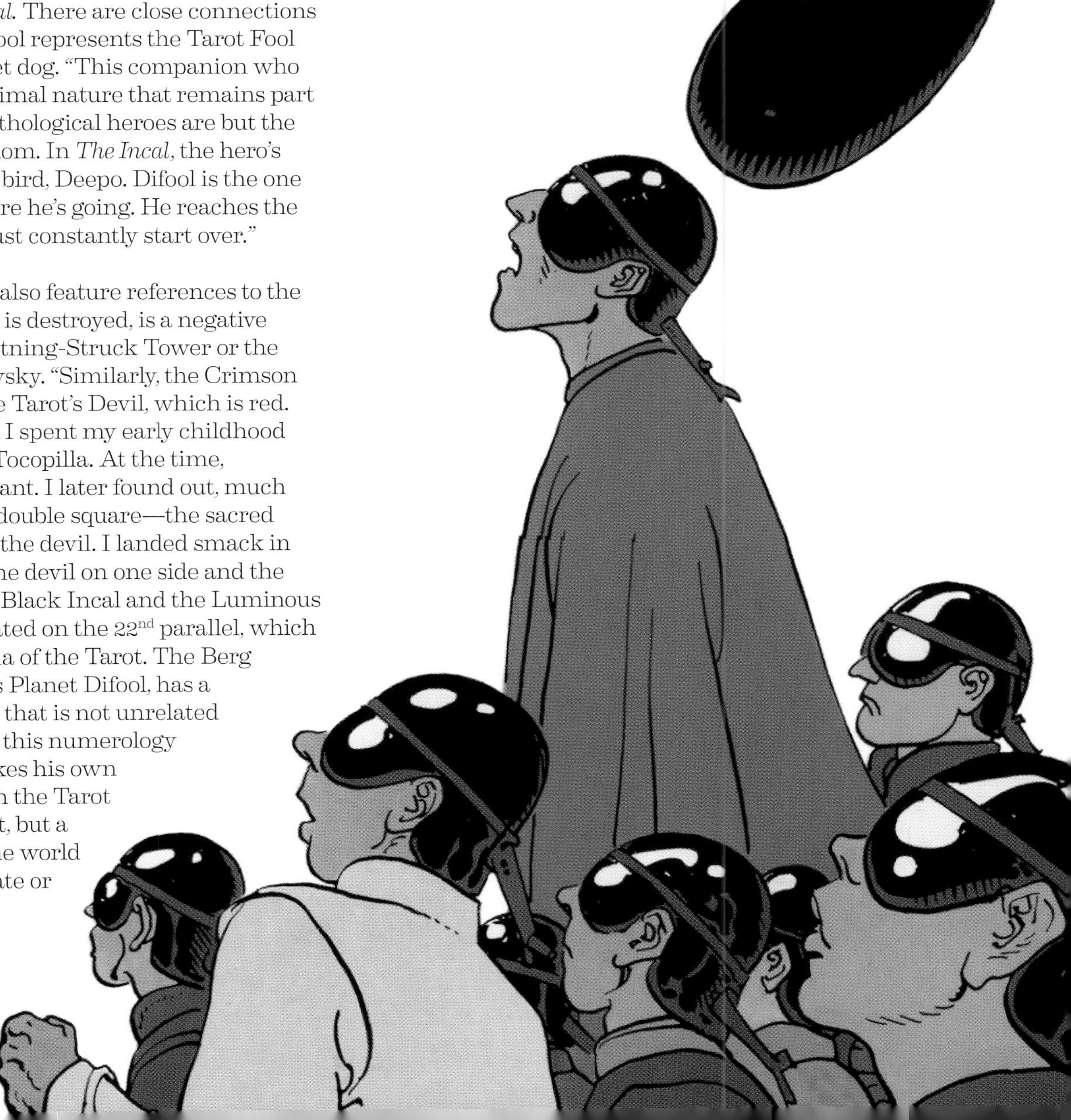

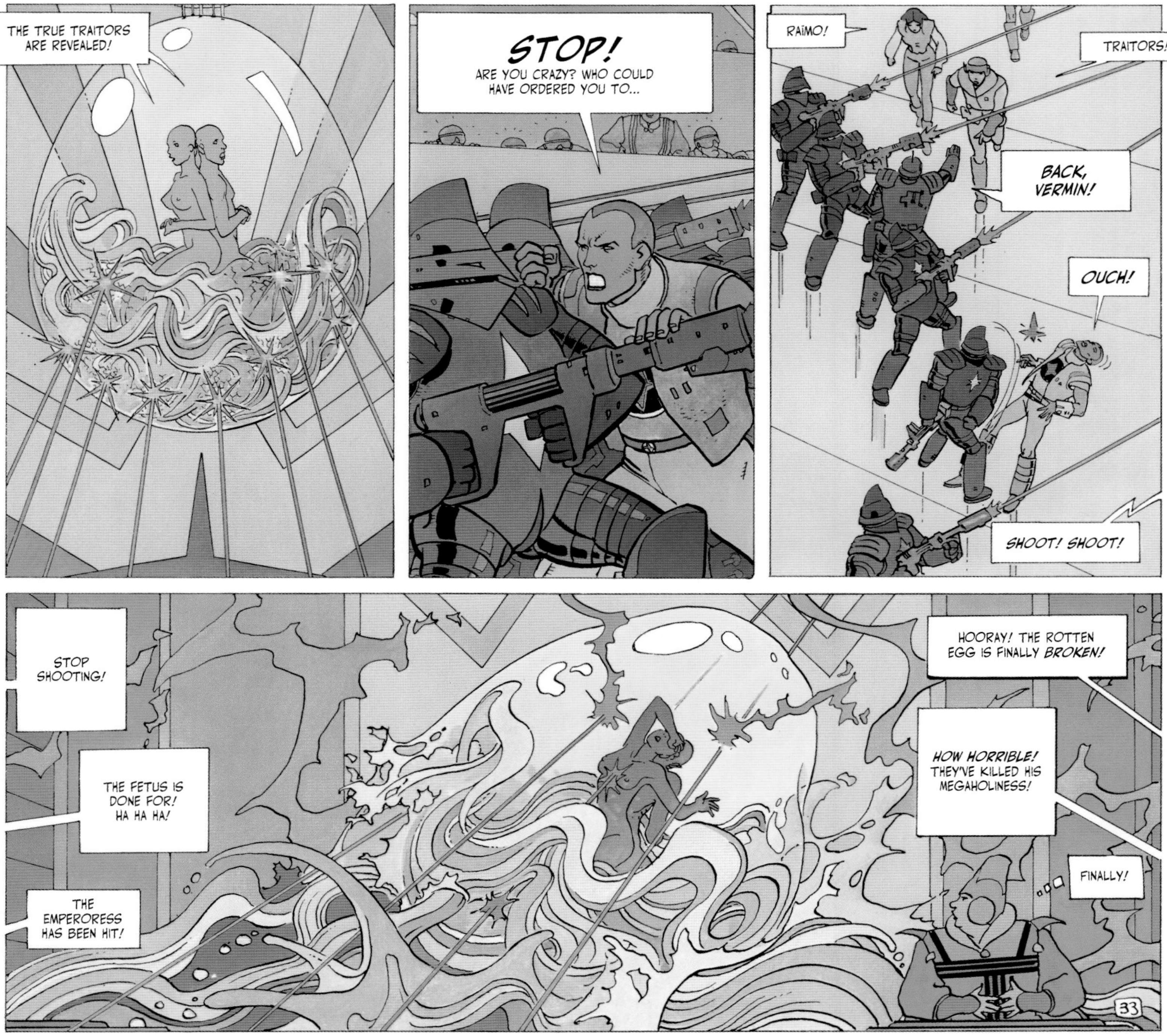
THE TRUE TRAITORS ARE REVEALED!
STOP!
ARE YOU CRAZY? WHO COULD HAVE ORDERED YOU TO...
RAÏMO!
TRAITORS!
BACK, VERMIN!
OUCH!
SHOOT! SHOOT!
STOP SHOOTING!
THE FETUS IS DONE FOR! HA HA HA!
THE EMPERORESS HAS BEEN HIT!
HOORAY! THE ROTTEN EGG IS FINALLY BROKEN!
HOW HORRIBLE! THEY'VE KILLED HIS MEGAHOLINESS!
FINALLY!
33

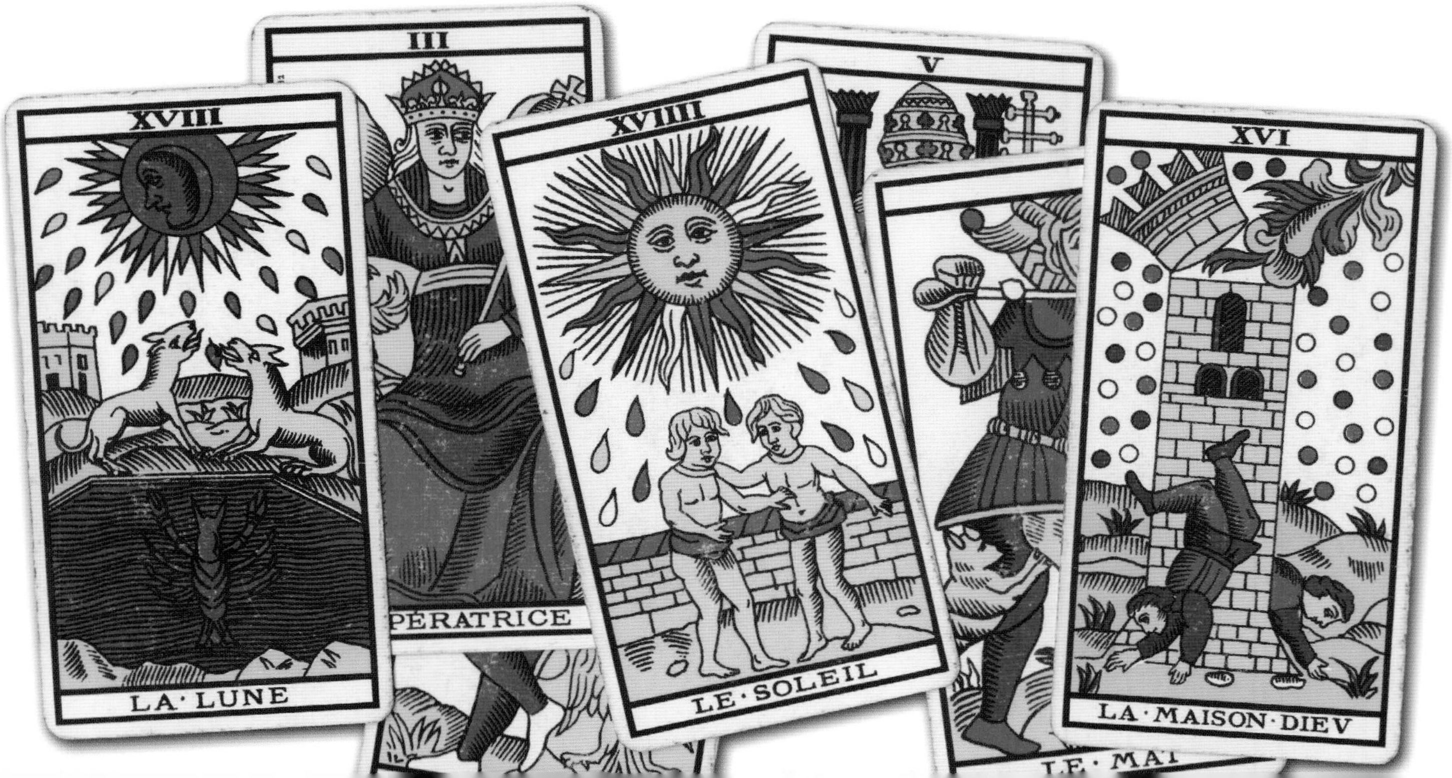
III
V
XVIII
XVIIII
XVI
LA·LUNE
PÉRATRICE
LE·SOLEIL
LA·MAISON·DIEV
LE·MAT

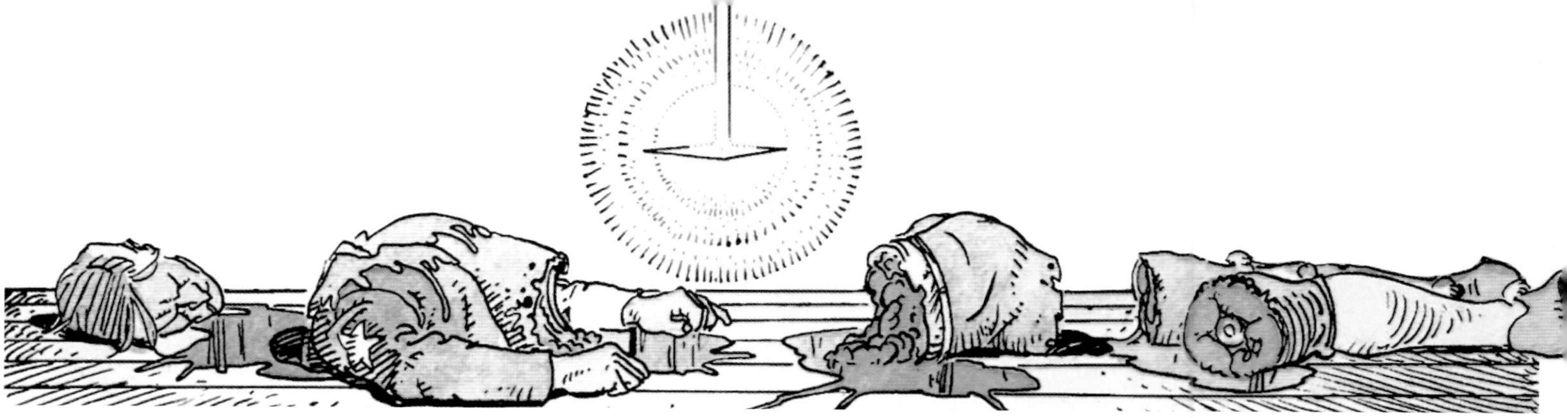

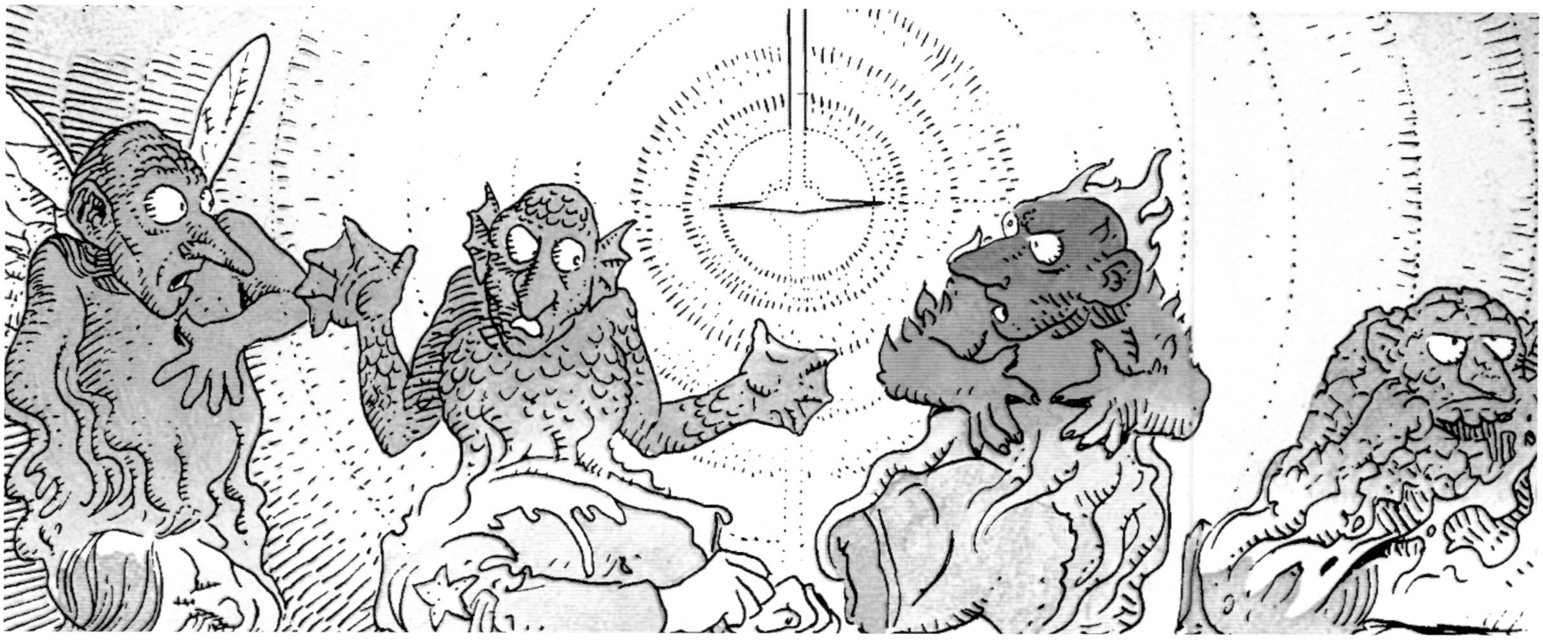

Alchemy

"Each of us carries, however mediocre it may be, a divine seed deep in our mind, our soul, our subconscious. This seed is found in what alchemists call the rebis, or the dual matter," Alejandro Jodorowsky once said, prior to the release of the French softcover edition of *The Black Incal*. Alchemy is one of the various esoteric sources that run through the *Incal* saga, beginning with the titles of the different books. Indeed, *The Black Incal* and *The Luminous Incal* refer to the work of black and the work of white, the first two stages of the "Great Work," i.e. the making of the Philosopher's Stone. According to alchemists, this substance is capable of changing valueless metals into precious ones, as well as curing diseases and prolonging human life.

What Lies Beneath and *What Is Above*, the third and fourth volumes in the *Incal* series, refer to a formula found in *The Emerald Tablet*, a famous text of alchemical literature, according to which "That which is below is like that which is above and that which is above is like that which is below." As for *The Fifth Essence*, the final, two-part installment in the saga, it refers to the notion of quintessence, which complements the four elements of earth, water, air, and fire. In fact, John Difool divides himself into four elements in *The Black Incal* after getting acquainted with the Incal itself. Lastly, one can't help regarding the character of Orh at the end of *The Fifth Essence*, as an allusion to gold—the last stage in the allegorical transmutation of metals so dear to alchemists.

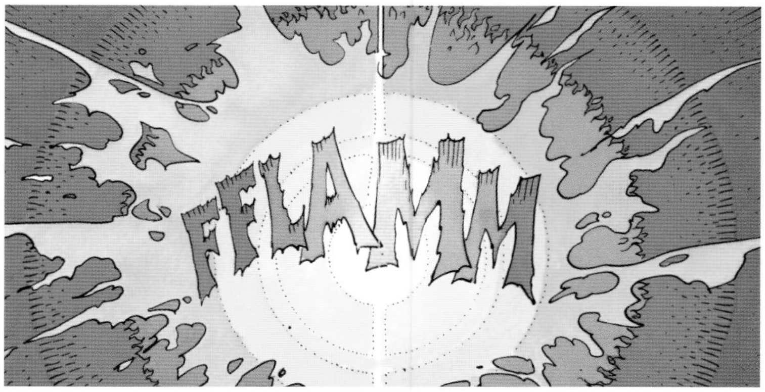
FFLAMM

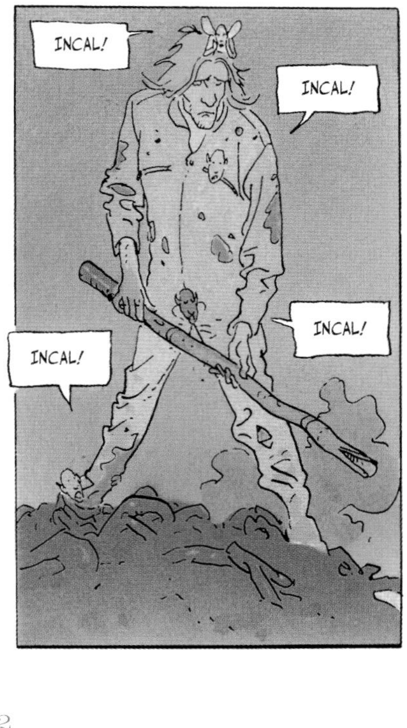
INCAL!
INCAL!
INCAL!
INCAL!

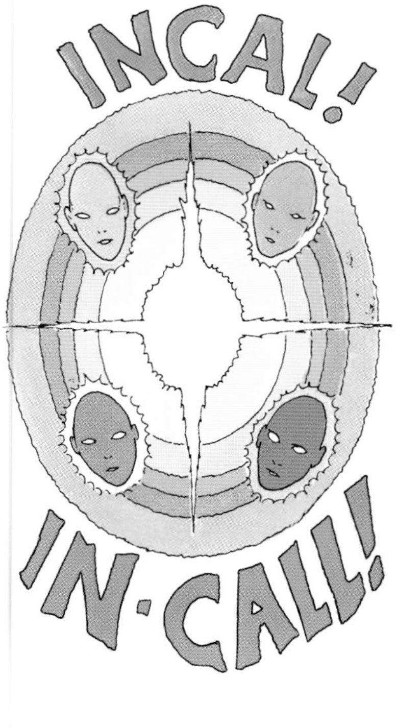
INCAL!
IN-CALL!

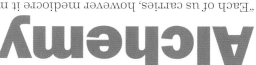

Metamorphoses

The Incal was not illustrated in a set and immutable style, as per the traditional process of developing a comic book. Mœbius used a variety of drawing techniques, captions, and layouts. They borrow from the whole visual culture of the "Ninth Art," from Europe to the United States. This graphic form, which is in constant evolution, goes hand in hand with the transformations in the narrative. This mode of production stems from the seemingly paradoxical "formal freedom." Mœbius made his own: the time constrictions he imposed on himself—to finish one page per day and one book in six weeks—left his hand free to take full advantage of the immense capital of drawing know-how he had accumulated. The aim was threefold: spontaneity, expressiveness, and readability. The idea was to give *The Incal* a spirited style that wasn't academic. Using all the tools unique to the art of drawing emerged as being more important than playing by the rules.

This method meant reducing the sketches to their most basic. The ink hits the blank page directly and as a result, some of the characters have physical features that change. Speaking about John Difool, Mœbius said he's endowed with a head with three speeds. "I have a hard time staying with one specific form, and it's practically congenital," he once explained. "Depending on my mood at the time, I tend to lean toward a square, a triangular, or a rectangular shape. I go from one type of anamorphosis to another, in a perfectly intangible way. I have no idea what kind of pressure or trigger sets off this phenomenon. But I had to make do with this defect and turn it into quality. It was my only way out: having several different styles at my disposal."

At first glance, this approach would seem to produce pages that are less aesthetic and perhaps less original. But then you realize that they stem from an art that's specific to comic books and that the energy they release is the energy of the universe portrayed in *The Incal*. Mœbius the playwright thus overrides Mœbius the illustrator. "Mœbius has reached such a technical level that he no longer needs to think to draw," said Jodorowsky. "In a metaphysical way, his drawing does the thinking. If he started controlling it, it wouldn't work as well."

The Incal incorporates a wealth of different sources and elements, even various references that go from the baroque language of Philippe Druillet to the "clear line" technique characteristic of Hergé or Joost Swarte. This was more than a conscious and deliberate choice that Mœbius made on his own: it would appear that these forms forced themselves upon him. "Suddenly, I could see my hand doing [Edgar P.] Jacobs!" the artist said. "Because there was no other solution. Which leads me to think that with *The Incal*, I'm doing something that's not overly calculated, not overly intellectual and which, as such, is likely to be right," said Mœbius in the *Mœbius Transe Forme* exhibition catalog. "The theme of transfiguration and transmutation as a function of the spiritual impulse can be found throughout *The Incal*."

Alejandro Jodorowsky: "Throughout the series, practically every character undergoes constant transformations. I didn't want characters that remained identical unto themselves, from the beginning to the end of the story. We ourselves are constantly changing, throughout life: perpetual evolution and perpetual change. Generally speaking, I find cartoon characters very static. And even those you find in Shakespeare: Hamlet, for example, remains Hamlet from beginning to end. I think that's inaccurate, and that one can change, halfway there, internally AND externally.

"That's all John Difool does: he metamorphosizes, makes progress, and sometimes even regresses. In the third installment, he's become handsome. In the fourth, he loses his looks at the same time he loses the Incal. But something of that remains: he'll never be the same again. From the beginning, John Difool's been introduced as someone who's a bit simple, a little foolish, someone who will gain self-awareness only gradually. So he's a pathetic, total loser who is going to grow and then retain the memory of the wisdom he acquired while the Incal was within him."

Mœbius: "We are constantly changing, and it is generally in response to various stimuli, visible or invisible, internal or external, but which lead us to action in our life, a physical and psychic change. For me, the visual metamorphosis present in my drawings is not a fetish or a graphic discovery, it's a metaphor for what is constantly happening inside of us."

(Catalog of the exhibition *Mœbius Transe Forme*, Ed. Cartier Fondation Cartier pour l'art contemporain/Actes Sud, 2010.)

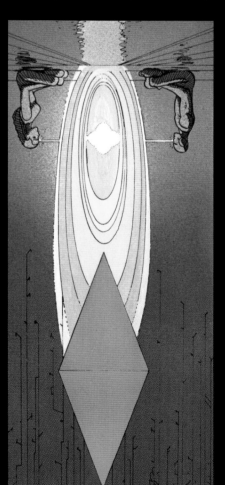

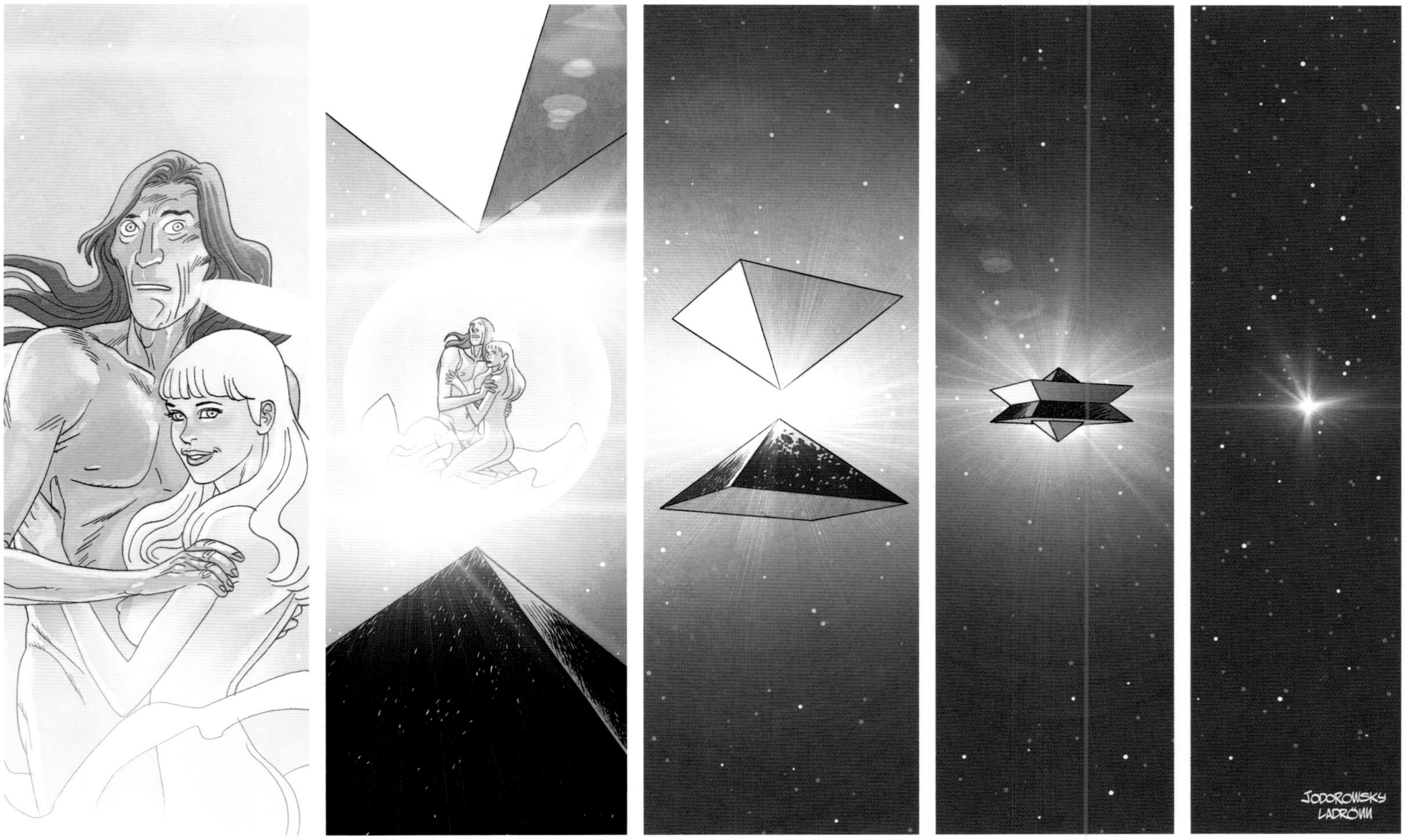
JODOROWSKY
LADRÖNN

Esotericism

Alejandro Jodorowsky: "A mystery is something that can't be processed by the intellect. And the universe of *The Incal* cannot be understood via the intellect. Why? Because it constantly discriminates. It makes distinctions between what is small and what is great, what is beautiful and what is ugly. But the universe is an absolute totality, there is no discrimination! The whole universe can fit into a single grain of sand. And the grain of sand positions itself to be penetrated by the universe. Try to wrap your head around that one! *The Incal* is an inconceivable story that I wrote using something other than my intellect. And it is an inconceivable story because it was completely improvised. First, I dictated part one, *The Black Incal*, to Mœbius. Six months later, I invited him to dinner. Then I took him to a Barbara concert (a popular 1960–70s French singer of mostly melancholy songs), because I knew how much he loved that singer. He was won over and he continued to draw *The Incal*. But I had no idea where I was going with it! The story constructed itself, one step at a time. I have books on Kabbalah, alchemy, Buddhism, and all the religions of the world in my library. In *The Incal*, there are also many things but we must not try to define them. When I dictated the story to Mœbius, I had read all these books. But we must not try to explain *The Incal*! It must be received as an adventure that goes directly into the subconscious."

John Difool's initiation, his rise toward the divine, and the messianic parable he embodies don't take away from the humor typical of a comic book hero. "I didn't write *The Incal* to convey any message but to tell an adventure story," said Jodorowsky. "When you write, you use everything. History, for example. Illustrators enrich their comic books by both using history and distorting it at the same time, and nobody finds fault with that. So why shouldn't I be able to use esotericism to enrich a story? Nothing prohibits it; it too is part of history. I wanted to bring out a narrative that preexists in our subconscious, with humility and unpretentiousness. And I came up with a cosmic comic. And a comical one. Just for the fun of it, and for the pleasure of collaborating with someone... I applied my knowledge of Chinese culture and the I Ching, which talks about the square of Earth and the square of Heaven, to *The Incal*. In *The Incal*, on the one hand there's the square of Earth, the descent toward Earth, the bottom, what is below, the crossing of the galaxy, the entry into the subconscious. And, on the other hand, the rise toward the supra-conscious, that which is above, the square of Heaven. The Chinese use the double square to explain this."

Nevertheless, this use of esotericism doesn't necessarily imply full and complete adherence on the part of the writer. "I do not really believe in esotericism, but I use it as an element of great beauty," says Jodorowsky. "In the same way that we use the Middle Ages, the costumes of the armies or the samurai. Why should it be taboo to introduce elements of esoteric doctrine into a story, which correspond to the language of dream? Esotericism is all one big dream. The subconscious manifests itself by seeking consolation to deal with life. We try to find comfort in order to process this horror. We need consolation. For me, *The Incal* is a great consolation, like everything else I do, generally speaking."

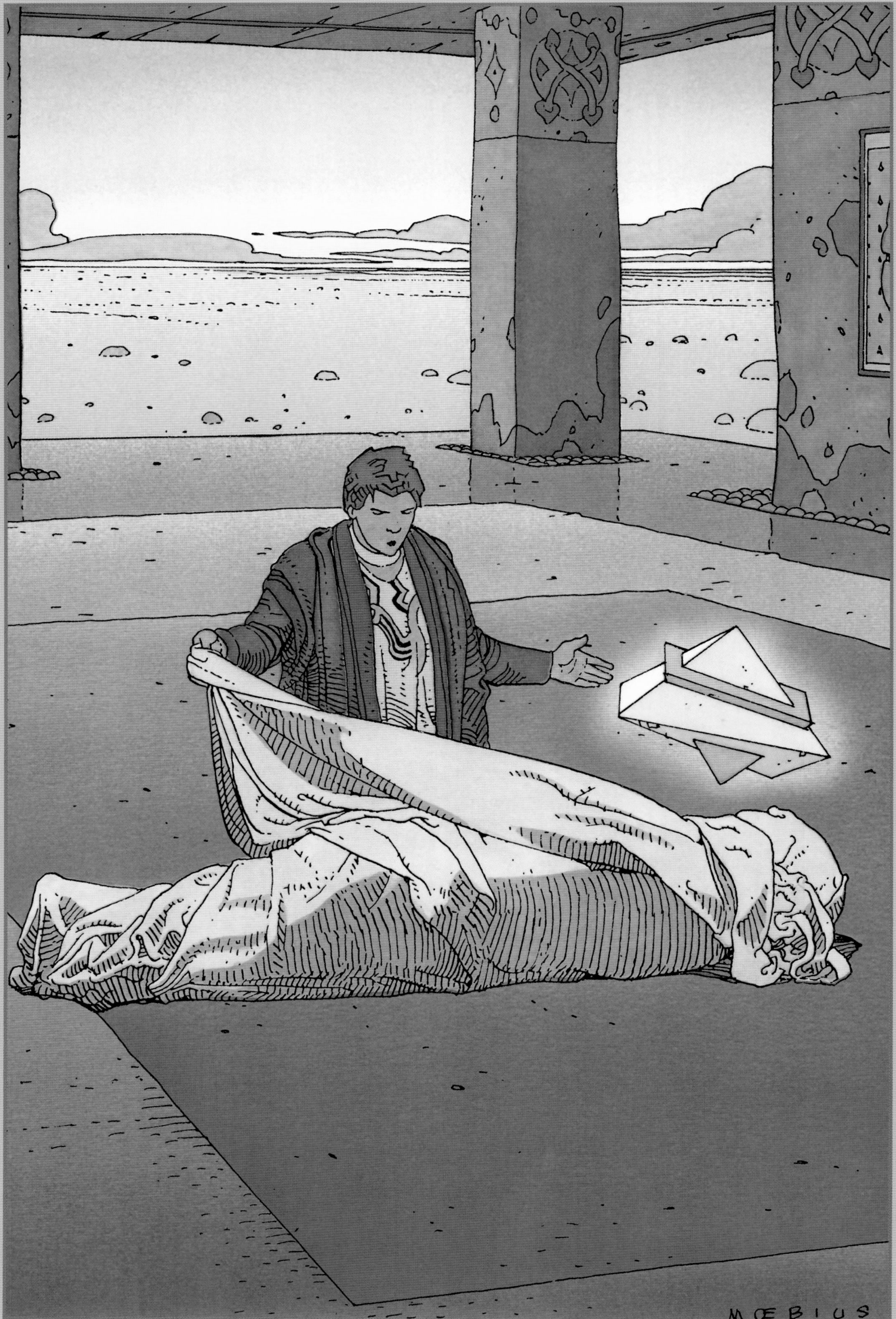
MŒBIUS

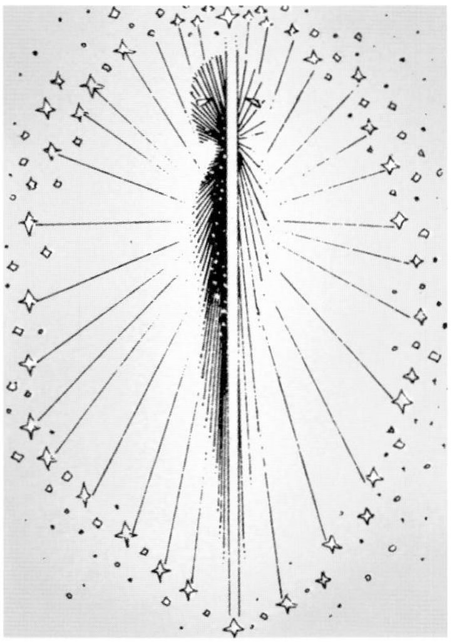

Duplication

In *The Incal*, the story progresses and is constructed via duplication and repetition. Each character becomes or has his own double, based on the principle of symmetry, with each character having either a twin or an opposite, and duality, with two values or roles coexisting within a single character.

John Difool is first literally cut into four, then he puts himself back together and physically transforms himself. He has incorporated the Incal (two entities in one) but has to temporarily delegate his role as carrier of the Incal to his child Solune, and finally he ends up fathering 78 billion facsimiles of himself. Starting out as a shabby detective, then becoming the catalyst and genetic cog in the predetermined plans of the Incal, he ends up the Eternal Witness, leading to the repetition of the entire story. Animah has an opposite double in the form of Tanatah, and a counterfeit in the form of Barbariah. Raised by an adoptive father, i.e. a duplicate of the father (the Metabaron), Solune (the perfect androgyne) succeeds the imperial androgyne who was preyed on by the Darkness. John Difool's group of seven has its own mirror group: Kaimo's group, also made up of seven members. And so on and so forth...

Moebius: "When John Difool is driven by his authentically eternal nature and lets the energy of the universe flow through him, he is transfigured, he undergoes a physical transformation: his hair cascades down like the mane of an angel and his face exudes strength and beauty. But as soon as that comes to an end, he goes back to being the same ordinary, almost abject man he really is, deep down." (Exhibition catalog for *Moebius Transe Forme*, ed. Fondation Cartier pour l'art contemporain/Actes Sud, 2010.)

In symmetry and duality, everything is therefore double: a duplicate, a reflection, an inversion. These structures are free, evolutive, and interactive: the entire narrative shows how they are made and unmade, interacting from one character to another. A logical and linear construction, which is traditional with the adventure genre, is replaced here with an approach that uses random and shifting associations. It is the very logic found in dreams that drives the narrative, which draws directly from the authors' personal worlds—both their subconscious (the resurgence of the family story, as well as Jodorowsky's common themes and obsessions) and the experiences they shared together (the failed film project *Dune*). In the story, mankind is saved by sleep. For this universe is perhaps actually the dream universe. To preserve it is to dream it over and over again, in the authors' stead...

In *The Incal*, Difool is divided into four. In *Final Incal*, he is multiplied into four entities, who all end up on a barge together, lost in the meandering flow of time. But the question remains the same as the one the Incal first asked: "Who is the real John Difool?" Only one of them will remain in play: the ugliest one, the one who defines himself as the "paleo-toad" who opened up his mouth hoping to swallow the moon!"

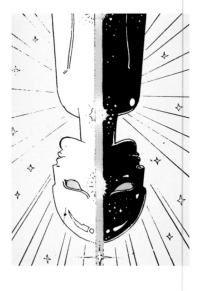

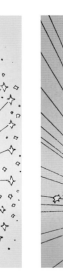

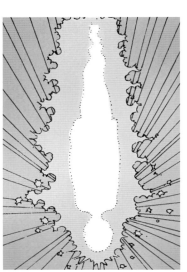

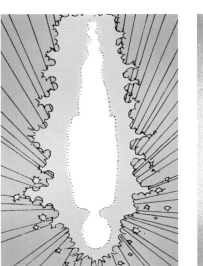

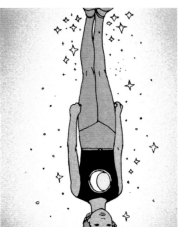

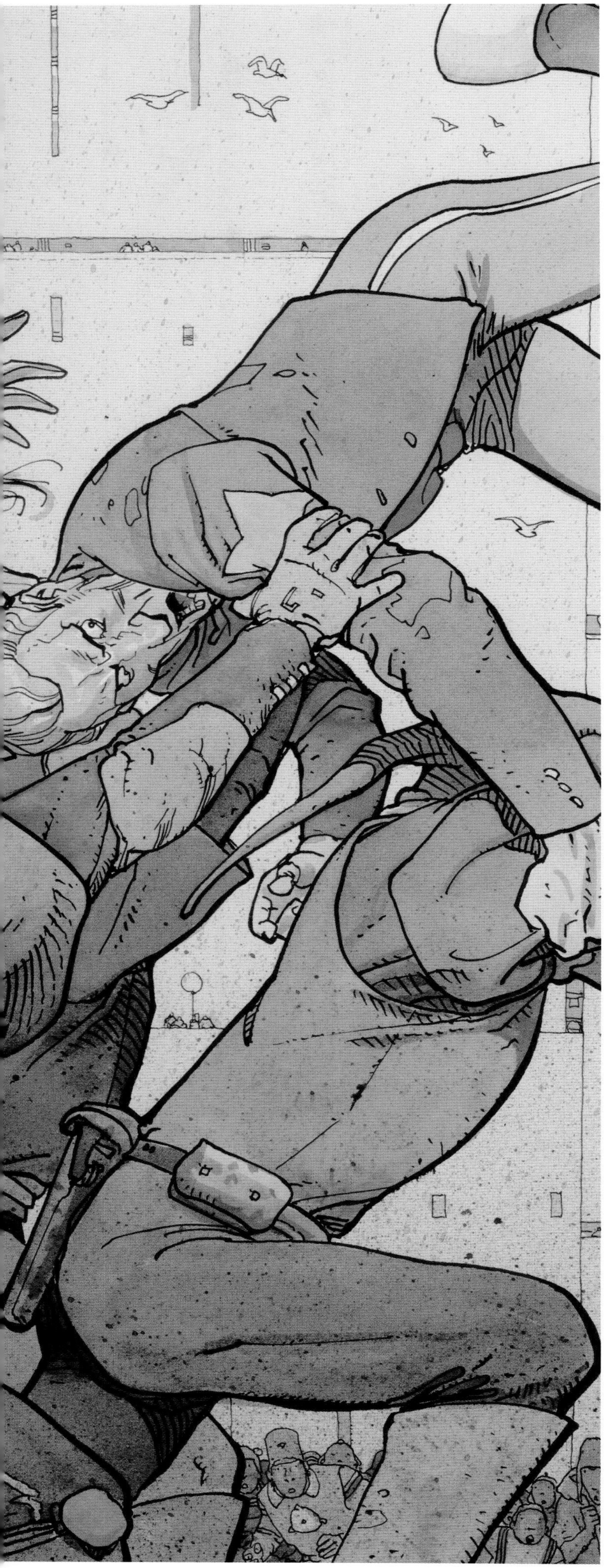

The Subconscious

Mœbius: "There are parallels between Animah and Tanatah, the two sisters, and my mother. They represent the two sides of her. Similarly, I found personal elements in John Difool, certain traits of my father, but also traits of another man, with whom my mother lived for some time and who, physically, bears a strange resemblance to Difool. Or rather, John Difool bears a strange resemblance to him! This was done involuntarily. I always wondered why I chose this face, which was not theoretically a very marketable face, or a very friendly face, or very pleasant to look at, or even pleasant or easy to draw. In any case, it is through drawing that my family relationships emerged. Perhaps that's because it's connected to the most subconscious level in me. My drawings are not always the ones I wanted to do: they are what I managed to do despite the obstacles I encountered. For example, I could have drawn Kill Wolfhead as some random bastard, but out of the blue I said to myself: 'I'm going to do a wolfdog.' That's exactly the dog my grandfather had. Kill also has a hole in his ear: he always has a problem listening to others... This work of the subconscious is sort of like what Carlos Castaneda called 'being in agreement with the intention.' The world is constantly sending us signs of recognition."

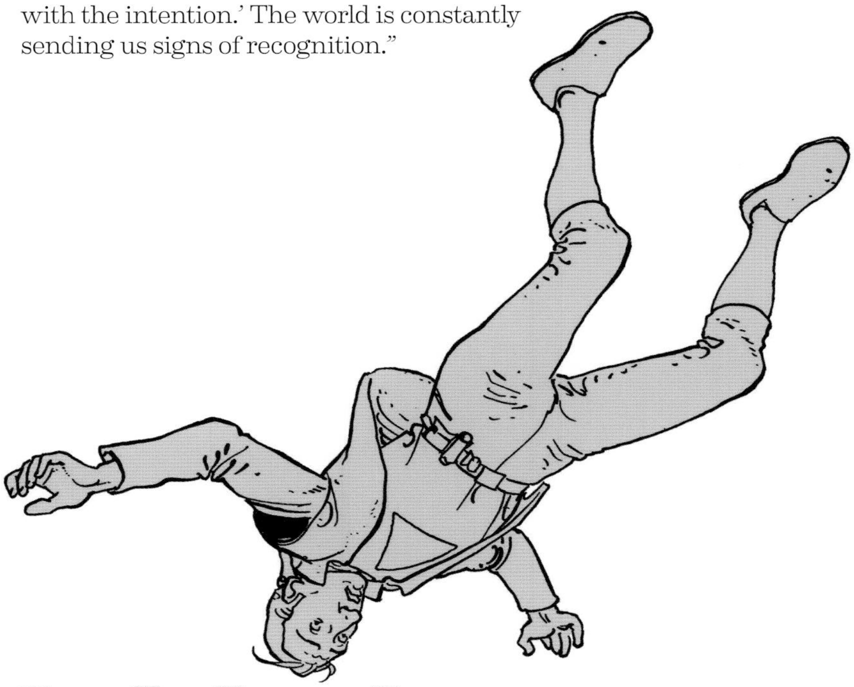

Initiation

Alejandro Jodorowsky: "With *The Incal,* I gave birth to a tale of initiation. John Difool finds within himself what he was looking for on the outside. In my film *El Topo,* the hero starts out as a criminal and ends up a Buddhist monk. In the same way, Difool is constantly evolving. Initially, he's ignorant. He starts out from nothing and he arrives at the whole: he ends up being the witness to the entire cosmos. In *Final Incal,* he attains love, with the woman he loves but also with everything! For love is the fluid that gives birth to the cosmos. It's a creative act; Creation is the result of the great Love. *The Incal* is a total cosmic dance: everything is love around a static point. Everything moves except the center. And the center is John Difool."

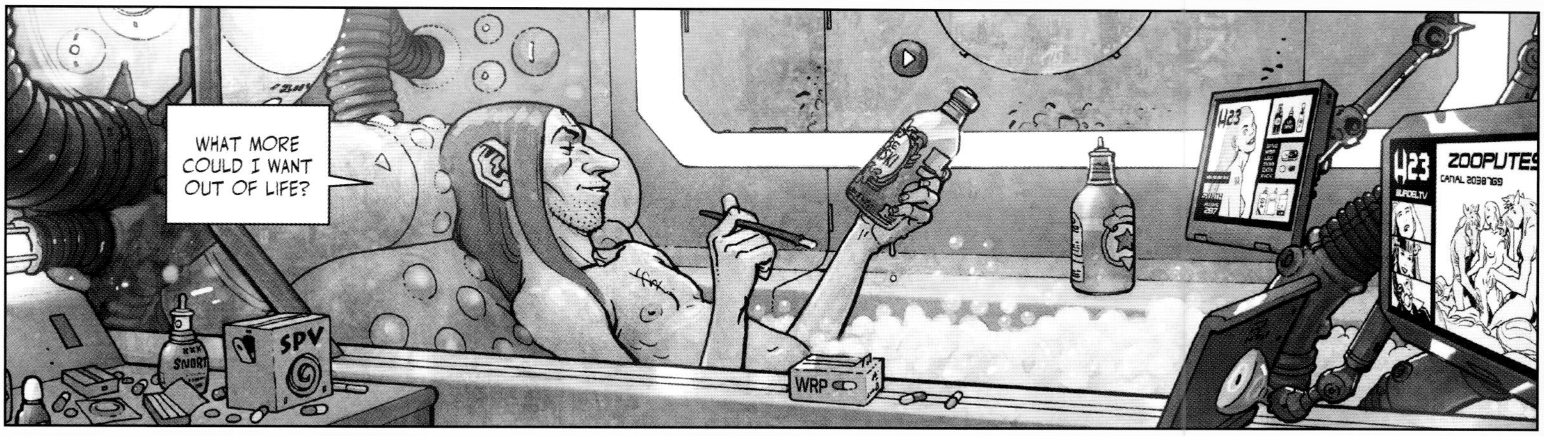
WHAT MORE COULD I WANT OUT OF LIFE?
ZOOPUTES

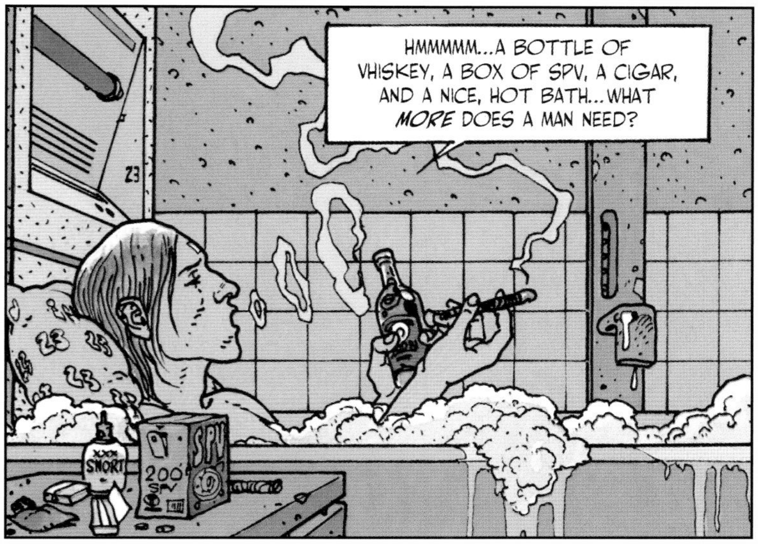
HMMMMM...A BOTTLE OF VHISKEY, A BOX OF SPV, A CIGAR, AND A NICE, HOT BATH...WHAT MORE DOES A MAN NEED?
SPV
SNORT

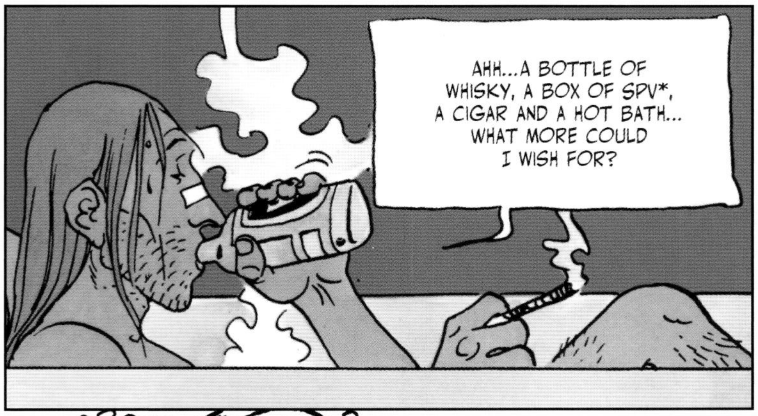
AHH...A BOTTLE OF WHISKY, A BOX OF SPV*, A CIGAR AND A HOT BATH... WHAT MORE COULD I WISH FOR?

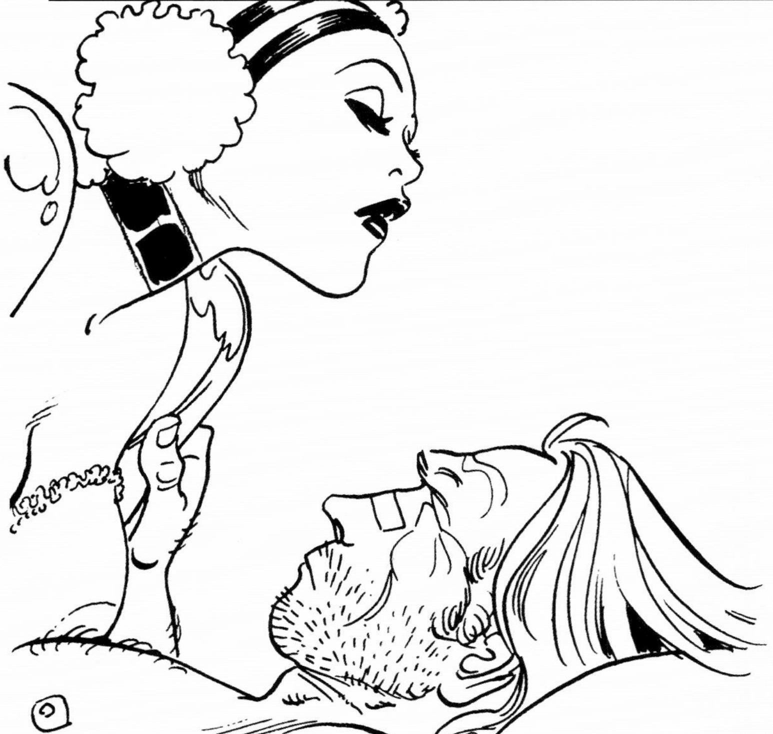

Genealogy

Alejandro Jodorowsky: "The individual is not merely an individual, but a family tree. The forces of our parents remain alive within us. If we come from a strain of generations made up of single children, there are at least 14 entities at work within us: two parents, four grandparents, and eight great-grandparents. They are both positive and negative forces in our lives. These people come together to form a ship, and it is this ship that carries each being toward infinity. I tested this with Mœbius. I brought together 21 students and I had Mœbius play family with these 21 people, each of whom was meant to be a specific member of his family. We were the 'spaceship' aboard which Mœbius sailed!"

Mœbius: "While writing the script for *The Incal,* Alejandro entered into a state of trance and telepathic communication with my psyche. I was going through a personal crisis at the time, and he told me he would be willing to help me study my family tree. For years, he's been organizing therapy sessions that use the Tarot as a starting point and that he combines with massages—which are linked to emotion—energy, and a systematic exploration of the family tree, meaning each person's family history. What emerges from this process is the link between family relationships and our own actions, some of which we endlessly repeat. This can help understand the origin of certain compulsions, which makes it easier to find the way to free oneself of them or to avoid self-destruction. In an almost magical way, *The Incal* transposes elements of my personal background as Alejandro was able to capture it—in other words, my personal background seen through his own lens. For we always need someone to send back to us a reflection of ourselves, which is often more complete than what we can perceive on our own. That was a major moment in my life. I wasn't really expecting much, and certainly not something that powerful, that accurate, and that extraordinary. The connection with *The Incal* emerged with great force."

If one wanted to draw a poetic conclusion, one could say that this marvelous vessel known as the *Incal* saga was enriched by two new "pilots," in the guise of Zoran Janjetov and Ladrönn, who joined forces with Mœbius in order to take readers on a journey to discover the boundless and constantly renewed imagination of Alejandro Jodorowsky... And the forces of all these creators will hopefully remain alive in the memory of every reader for years—and generations—to come!

KILL... ME...

DIE, DIRTY POISONER! LONG LIVE THE PREZ!

CAN'T DO IT, DAD!

SORRY, DAD!

Patricide

In *Before the Incal*, while still a teenager, young John Difool faces a painful but inevitable decision: killing his father. The latter was sent to Cybo-prison, where he underwent "remodeling," having his memory progressively erased. He is now one of the Prezident's Hunchbacks—a security detail made up of thugs easily recognizable by their enormous humped backs, brutes ready to carry out all the dirty, violent work required of them.

During a violent scuffle in the GTO, John is captured by the Hunchbacks before being rescued by one of their own, who turns out to be none other than John's father, Oliver. The remodeling process he underwent is just about to be complete, meaning that within a few short minutes, his memory will be permanently erased. "I'll be just another Hunchback! A ruthless murderer! Now run, before I kill you!"

To avoid being killed by his father, who soon won't be able to recognize him anymore, John has no choice but to shoot him, metaphorically "killing" his father. Before he runs off, he cries out, "Farewell, father!"

This scene foreshadows what will be one of the fundamental motifs of *The Metabarons*, a series written by Jodorowsky and illustrated by Juan Gimenez, whose first volume was released in 1992. Before a son can aspire to the noble title of Metabaron, the heir must first kill his father, the current Metabaron, in hand-to-hand combat.

Tintin

The authors of *The Incal* had fun inserting little nods to the universe of Hergé's *Tintin* here and there. "I remember that we had talked about doing a story that would contain the action of *Tintin*... I always felt we needed to return to *Tintin*," Jodorowsky said in a 1981 interview in *L'Année de la BD*.

Perhaps unsurprisingly, neither Tintin nor John Difool wear traditional, contemporary pants, despite the fact that these are more practical for a life fraught with dangerous situations. While the former opted for golf pants, the latter, like many other Terra 2014 residents, walks around in the same type of trousers favored by nobles and members of France's 18th century bourgeoisie.

Also of note is that they both demonstrate a certain flair for unusual hairstyles: a tuft for one and a ponytail for the other. But instead, we should view John Difool as a kind of polar opposite of the famous reporter: one character's homebody temperament (seriously compromised by the incidents in *The Incal*) and grumpy pessimism, to the other character's spirit of adventure and irrepressible optimism.

Alert readers (and Tintinophiles) will surely notice the unexpected presence of Philippulus the prophet, straight out of the *Tintin* volume *The Shooting Star*, crying "Repent!" on page 31 in *Before The Incal*. As for the statuette "made completely from non-synthetic gold," which young John Difool and his friends plan to steal on page 68 of the same book, it would probably not have been out of place in another *Tintin* classic, *Prisoners of the Sun*.

HERE'S THE PRIDE OF THE MUSEUM: A STATUETTE OF AN ANCIENT GOD MADE COMPLETELY FROM NON-SYNTHETIC GOLD... THAT'S RIGHT, DEAR TELE-FRIENDS...*NA-TU-RAL* GOLD...OF IMMENSE VALUE... *FOUR THOUSAND MILLION KUBLARS* AT THE VERY LEAST...

LET ME THROUGH, I'M PREGNANT! THE METABARON'S GOING TO KILL US ALL!

HELP! I DON'T WANT TO DIE!

REPENT!

TRAMPLE THE BITCH!

I JUST SHAT MYSELF!

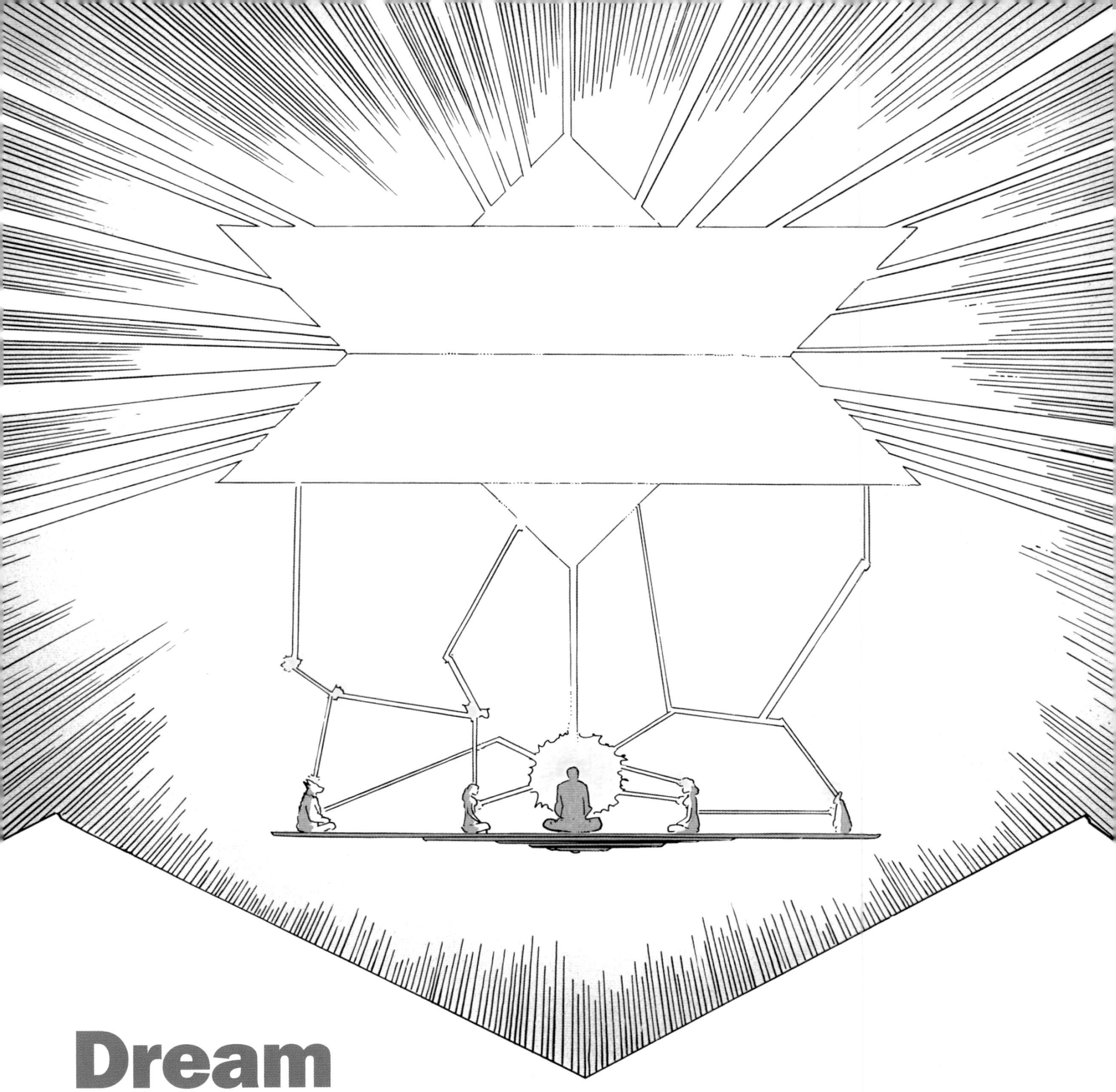

Dream

"*The Incal* started with a dream," recalls Alejandro Jodorowsky. "One of those lucid dreams where you're conscious of the fact that you're dreaming. I was sitting in space and asking to see my inner being." When he woke up, the writer jotted down the following lines in his dream journal:

> *I see two triangles interconnected like a Star of David. They become two pyramids interconnected in a single shape. They are facing me. In the dream, I tell myself that I must become the pyramids. I enter the pyramids. I am in the pyramids. I explode in the center like a universe of fire.*

"At that moment, in my dream, my brain burst into light and I woke up. That's how *The Incal* started," says Jodorowsky.

"I didn't invent it, it came to me in a dream. Immediately afterwards, I began to create the characters for a story in which I wanted to tell about how someone became the Incal... To write that story, I tried to let go of all logic and reasoning. I put myself in a state of receptivity in order to receive the story from my subconscious. I woke up with a revelation: true magical art is to receive something that is your inner heaven."

And so, Alejandro Jodorowsky's dream went on to become a now seminal comic book illustrated by Mœbius and, by the same token, John Difool's dream, as well as a source of inspiration and great pleasure to creators and readers the world over.

Truth

The Incal loop is a reference to the deceptive nature of truth. It denies the work the power to convey any message. The purpose of *The Incal* is none other than to make people dream. Because "to dream is to survive," according to the only definitive slogan of the series—a slogan that only has value for those who would pay heed to it.

At the end of *The Holy Mountain*, Jodorowsky's cult film, the camera pulls back from the scene and the characters, and the viewer discovers that the Immortals of the mountain and the landscape are just part of a soundstage.

The whole plot is turned upside down: the sages whose quest was at the very core of the film turn out to be nothing more than artifice and make-believe.

That finale seems a fitting summary for Jodorowsky's feelings about the truth of art. His life and work are fueled by research and the study of traditional truths and esotericism, but that quest rejects his ultimate goal: transcendence. And yet while transcendence may be nothing more than a dream, it is a dream so strong and so beautiful that it has the power to transform our existence.

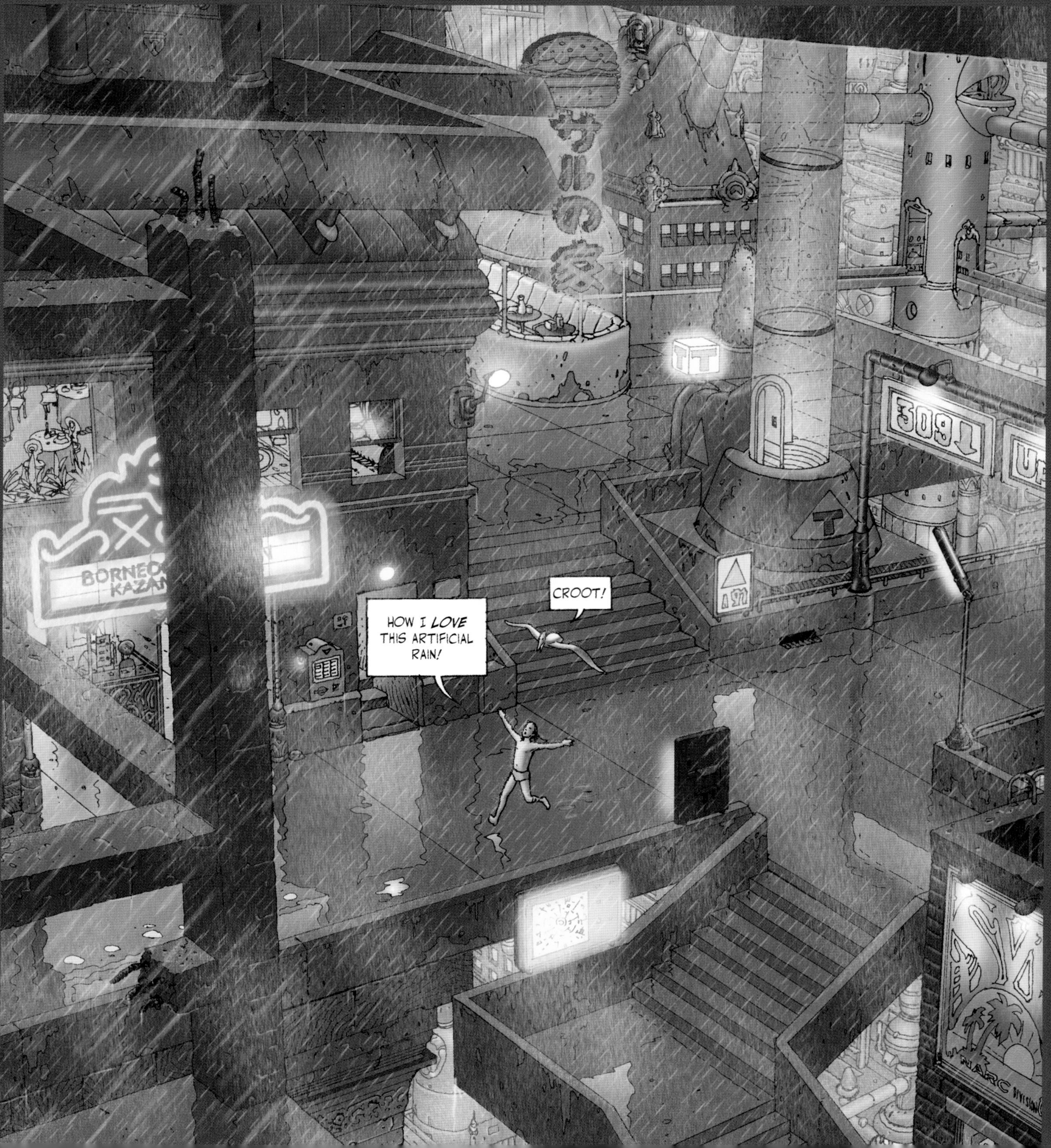
HOW I LOVE THIS ARTIFICIAL RAIN!
CROOT!
3091
BORNEO
KAZAN

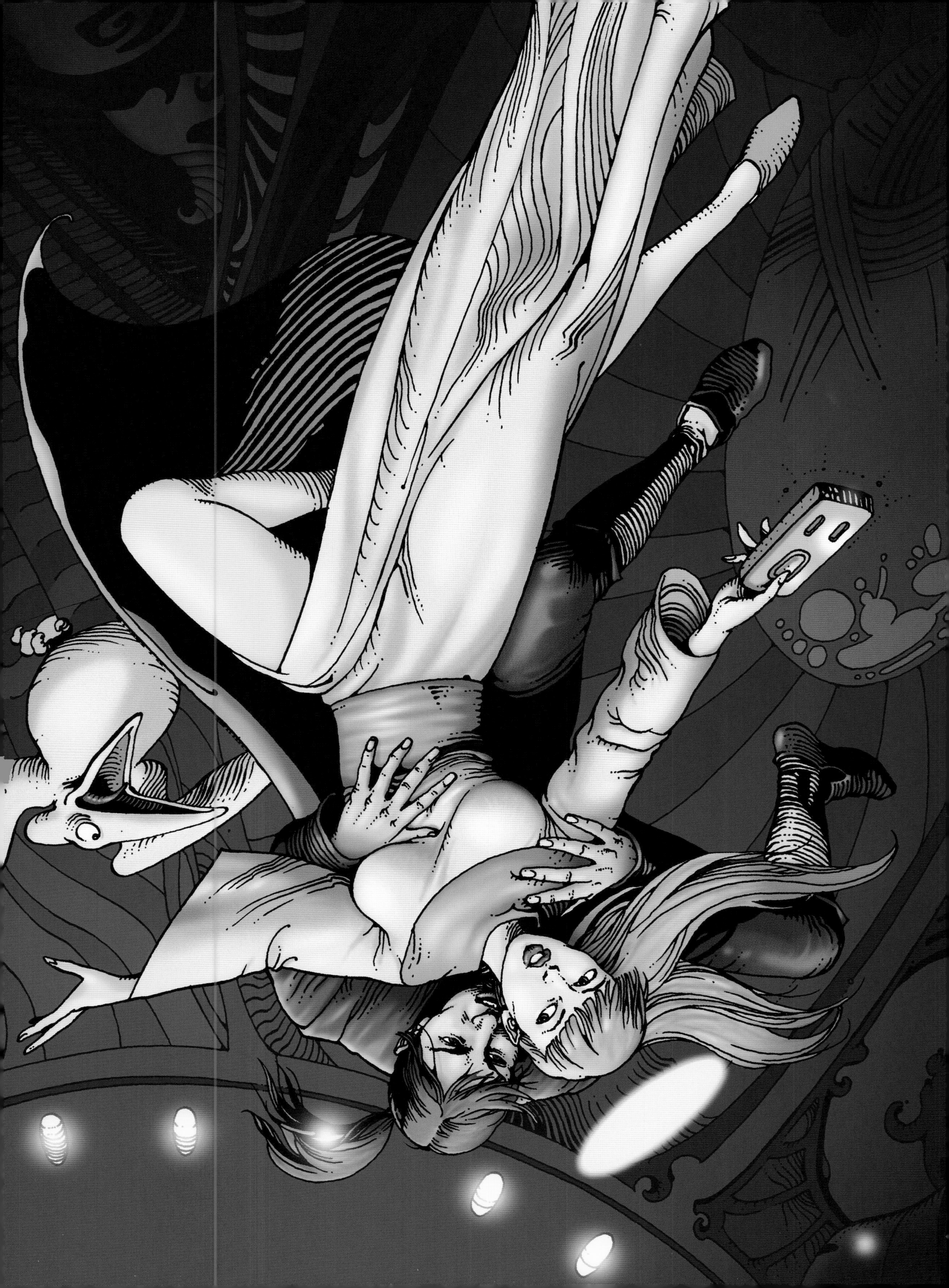

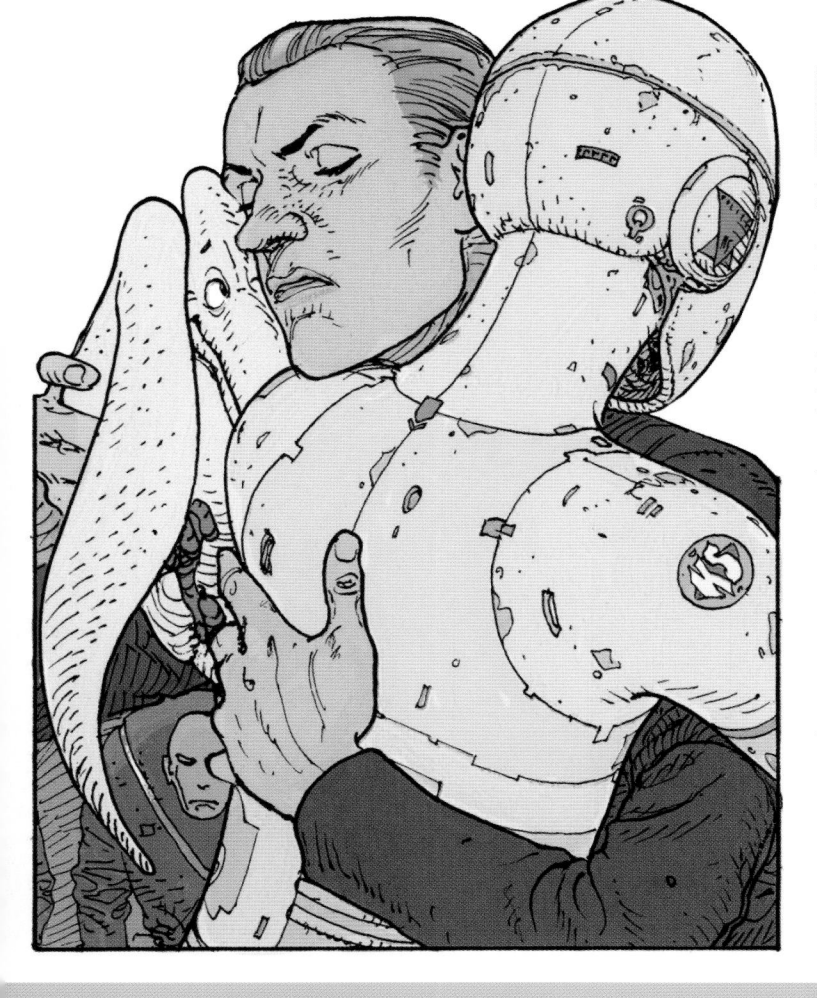

Friendship

Fortunately, even in the dehumanizing context of the City-Shaft, feelings haven't completely disappeared. When John Difool seems to have given up all hope as he's laid out on an operating table and is about to have his free will removed thanks to Luz de Garra's betrayal, the sudden and unexpected arrival of Kolbo-5, Deepo, and the Eyecop, come to rescue him—"My friends, my *real* friends!"—reconciles him with the notion of friendship. As for the relationships, which, over the course of the different *Incal* books, bring together the members of the group that forms around Difool, they are definitely dictated by mutual interest and the need to defeat a common adversary. However, they nevertheless give way to a bond that resembles a form of friendship, which even Kill Wolfhead eventually subscribes to: "Thank you, Deepo! You saved my skin!" he says to John's concrete seagull. "Bah, I just love the [bullet] hole in your ear!" Deepo answers.

Final Incal gives rise to relationships between some of the characters who, although they aren't friends in the strictest sense of the term, are nonetheless noble, like the form of camaraderie that brings Kill Wolfhead and Gorgo the Foul closer together, united as they are by the same destiny and goal: their fight to the death against the Prezident and the Benthacodon, and the subsequent continuation of bio-life in the galaxy.

The Big Secret

While *The Incal* is a world replete with mysteries and secrets, there is one in particular that piques John Difool's curiosity in *Before the Incal*. Why don't the prostitutes from the Crimson Ring—whom Difool had been intimately familiar with and whose names intend to trigger burning flames of desire, such as XB-34 the Beautiful, the Whale of Aldebaran, Hot Connie, and the TechnoDominatrix—ever give birth to children? Was this to mean that none of them ever procreated? Or were they hiding the fruit of their mating, be it for business or love? Could it be that he, John Difool, son of a prostitute for whom he found it perfectly normal to rope in clients, was an exception to the rule?

John, who is supposed to conduct an investigation and solve a police case if he ever hopes to obtain his private detective license, decides to seek out the answer to this question. "That's my investigation! The case of the whores' missing children! How is it possible that more than 20,000 prostitutes never bring babies into the world?" From then on, he goes on a quest to hunt down what he calls "the Big Secret." He also plans to take the opportunity to get revenge on Luz de Garra, the young woman who betrayed his love by getting him to sign a contract in which he agreed to become her Mandog—in other words, to abdicate his intelligence and free will.

With the help of Kolbo-5, who intervenes in the nick of time and keeps him from being reduced to a state of mental retardation, John goes on to uncover a terrifying secret, code-named "Taboo #MK-3507" and involving the entire socio-political system, from the Prez to the Cybo-cops to the Techno-Technos and even the Cocaloco beverage. It's a secret

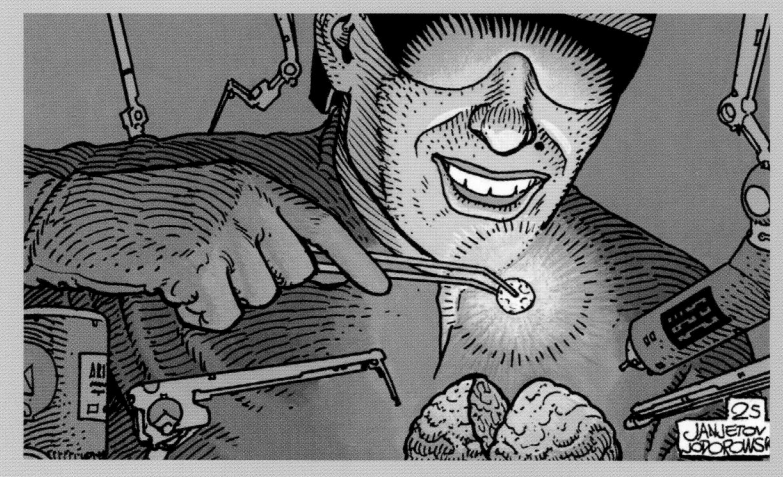

likely to set off "a scandal of galactic proportions": the babies of Crimson Ring prostitutes are injected with a "disgusting liquid" called Top-33, before being frozen and transferred to the Aristo-Maternity ward. What he discovers there, accompanied by Luz with whom he is once again in love, is that the social hierarchy is only a sham, and that the so-called superiority of the Aristos is based on a process of adoption and that each aura hovering over the head of an Aristo implies the death of a poor child. "Our grand aristocracy is built on the spawn of lower-level whorehouses! It's horrible! We must alert the entire galaxy to this scandal!" cries out a transfigured Luz, now endowed with a social consciousness and the political lucidity she had lacked before, while John, bolder than he has ever been, demonstrates an eagerness to get involved that was previously unseen in him.

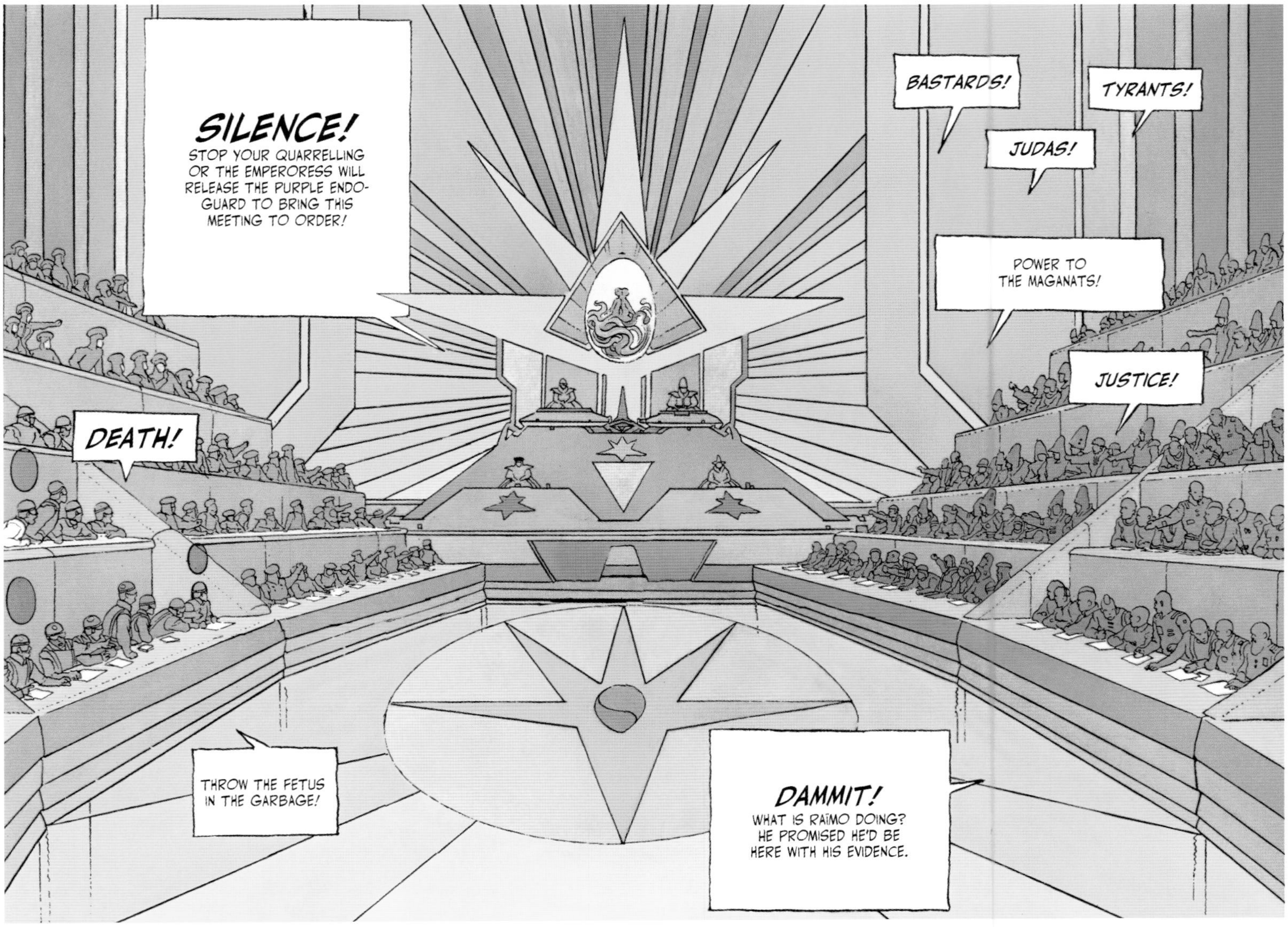
SILENCE! STOP YOUR QUARRELLING OR THE EMPERORESS WILL RELEASE THE PURPLE ENDO-GUARD TO BRING THIS MEETING TO ORDER!
BASTARDS!
TYRANTS!
JUDAS!
POWER TO THE MAGANATS!
JUSTICE!
DEATH!
THROW THE FETUS IN THE GARBAGE!
DAMMIT! WHAT IS RAÏMO DOING? HE PROMISED HE'D BE HERE WITH HIS EVIDENCE.

Social Organization

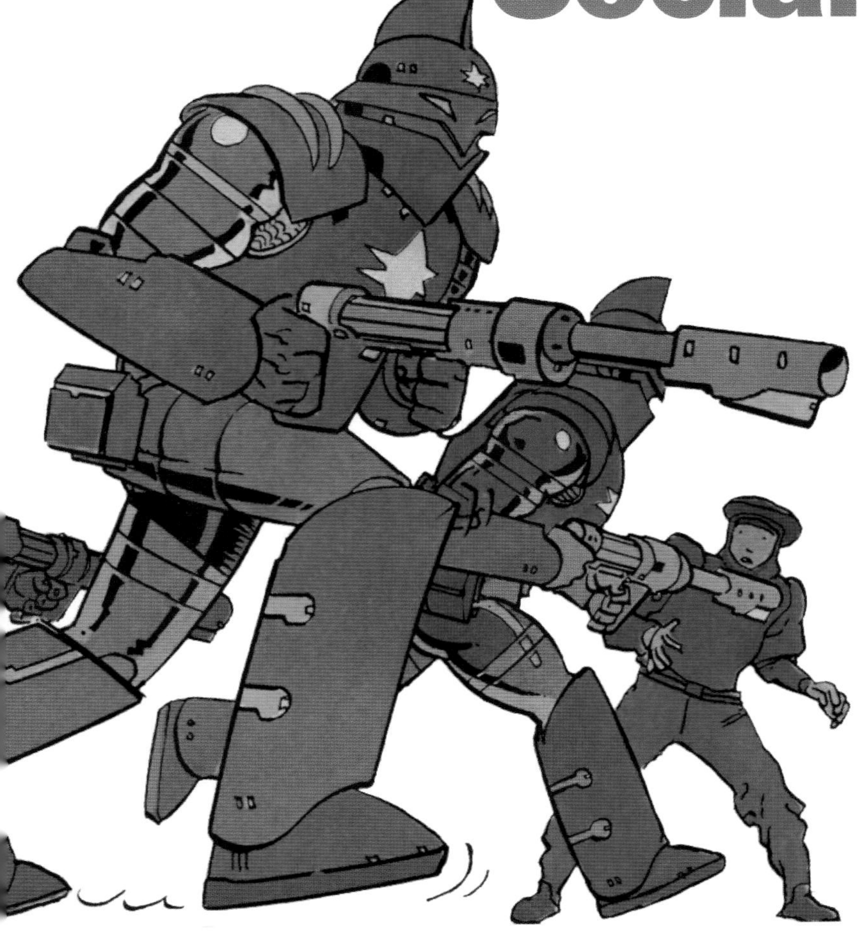

The social hierarchy here is conceived as satire. *The Incal* suggests that humans are in a state of complete degeneration, cut off from the interior principles that should guide them. They are alienated by 3D TV and they are slaves to meaningless pleasures. At the start of the series, John Difool himself is a perfect embodiment of the kind of materialism and individualism characteristic of people living in large urban complexes. In reality, humanity is no longer in harmony with the inner figure of the Incal, which is the symbol of the interconnectedness of the heavenly world and the terrestrial world, a token of cosmic harmony. In the social organization, however, there remains a trace of the ancient state, of the distant past in which the Earth was a paradise before men destroyed the planet, before the endless expanse of garbage known as Center Earth, in a time when the Interior Sun wasn't hidden and when the Myth was alive.

Remnants of this golden age can be seen, for instance, in the figure of the Emperoress who reigns over the Human Empire, an androgyne encased in an active egg, a symbol of the time when opposites came together. As such, the organization of the Empire combines a spiritual or religious hierarchy with modern social classes.

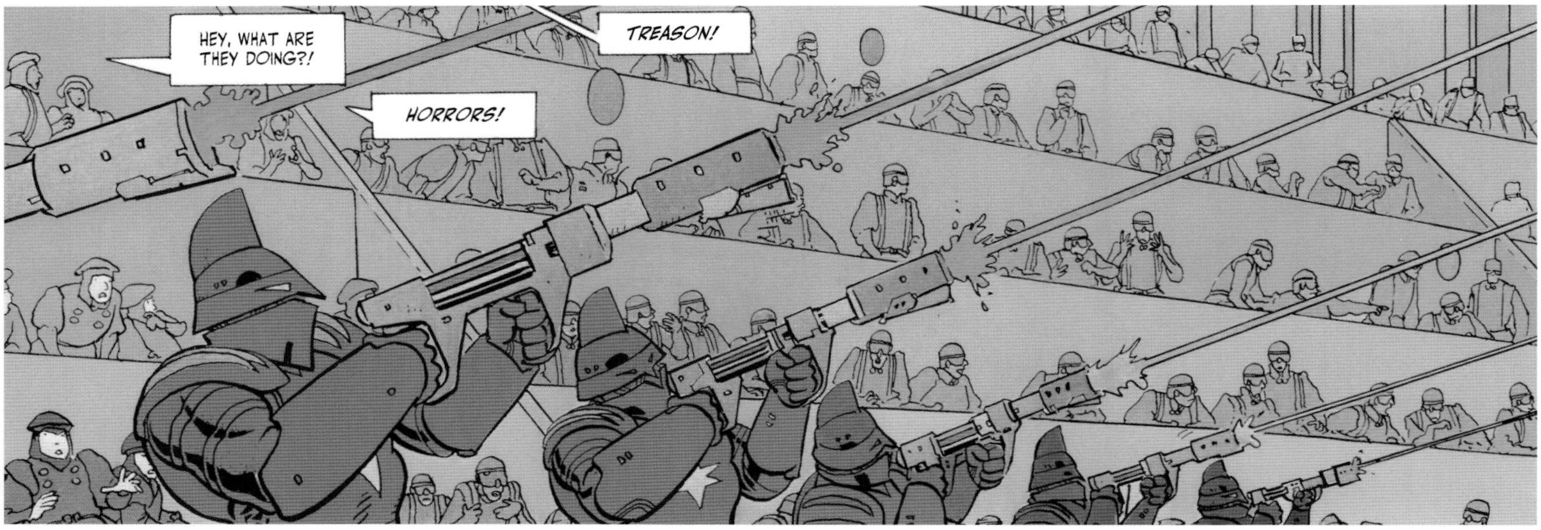
HEY, WHAT ARE THEY DOING?!
TREASON!
HORRORS!

Directly under the Emperoress are the Mentreks, while watching over Him/Her is the Purple Endoguard: they represent spiritual authority and temporal power. The merchant class is represented by the Maganats. The Iimans are corrupt priests associated with the Maganats. The Ekonomat world is made up of administrators and economists. The Technoguild are a combination of scientists and power-hungry technocrats in the service of the Darkness. The Aristos are a pseudo-class of privileged people mandated by the Empire who have clearly been ruined by excess and depravity.

Among this vast collection of players that mixes corporations, castes, classes, and committees of experts, only the united Troglosocialik colonial forces seem to be concerned with the wellbeing of humanity and not just their own powers and privileges. Their name and uniform brings to mind the Soviet Union, represented by Raïmo of Kamar.

What about the lower classes? In the City-Shaft, the upper circles are occupied by the Aristos as well as the Cybo-cops, automated policemen manufactured by the Technos who, as such, indirectly control repression and justice. The resistance, led by the people of Amok, are hiding out in a bunker at the Acid Lake level and therefore on the plane of maximum dissolution. Between the two are the middle and alienated classes, the poor, and the unemployed.

Corruption, insanity, repressive technology, decay, and waste-eating acid: the universe of urban metal is synonymous with death and repetition. It is only fitting that the Technos use the corpses of Aristos to make the machines and the Cybo-cops. What we have here is the ruthless caricature of a society of overconsumption that has reached the ultimate stage, where it feeds on its own waste. It's the negation of the living and the natural. The Prezident himself is but an entity without an actual body, changing his appearance from one incarnation to the next, as his latest cloned organism invariably succumbs to decay. Each cloning operation provides the occasion for a massively popular live TV broadcast and, once again, it is fitting that, over the course of the story, the Prez will transform into a Necrodroid wreaking terror and death, only to end as a vulgar holo-camera on legs.

What *The Incal* denounces, of course, is power that is no longer linked to any spiritual values. The antithesis of this totalitarian materialism is portrayed in the figure of the Patmah Solune, the Incal's avatar, who achieves inner and mental androgyny—rather than outward and physical one, like the Emperoress.

This symbolically leads to his/her retroversion through the Darkness, whereas Solune offers salvation from it. And in fact, he is immediately voted into power and becomes leader of the Empire.

The positive social structure suggested here is similar to that of the power of an enlightened king-pontiff, who would govern via clairvoyance in order to spread peace and equality in a world that would regain its ecological and spiritual equilibrium. It's reminiscent of the traditional role of the Wang, the sovereign pontiff of ancient China, who regulated the harmony of the kingdom by becoming the bridge between Heaven and Earth in the Middle Chamber (or Ming-Tang), the Sacred Imperial Palace.

But let's not forget that *The Incal* is a fable, of course... A narrative filled with images that are sometimes funny, sometimes magical. It would be presumptuous to read in these images any political opinions whatsoever on the part of the authors!

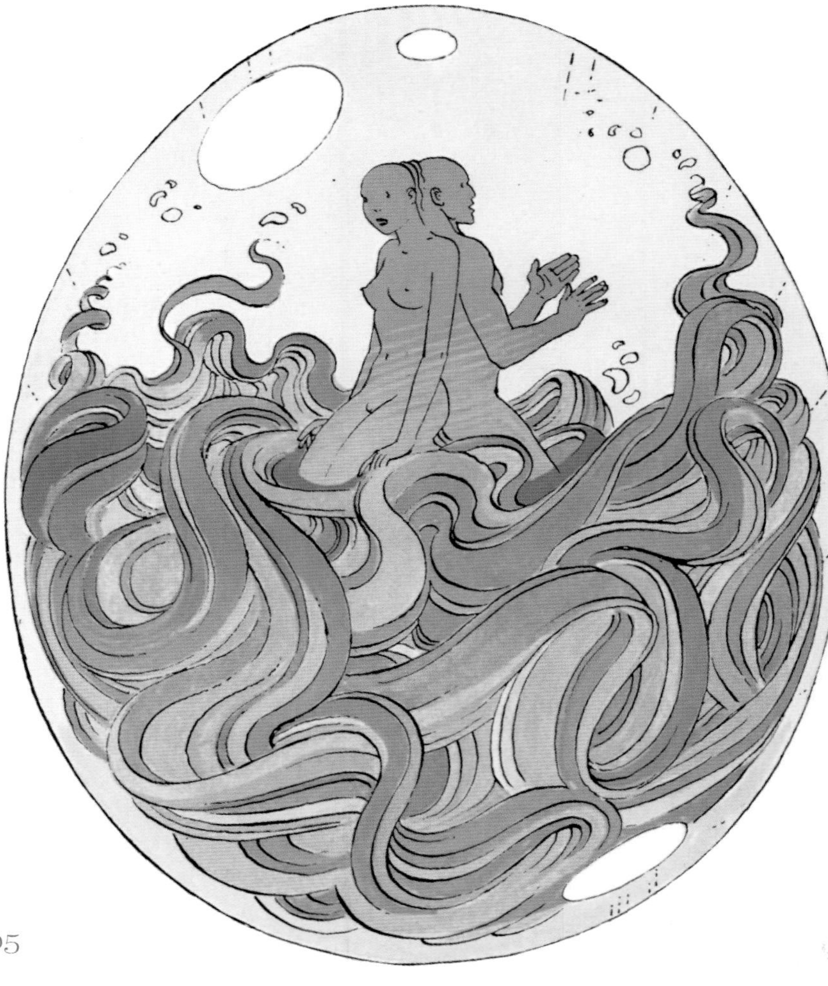

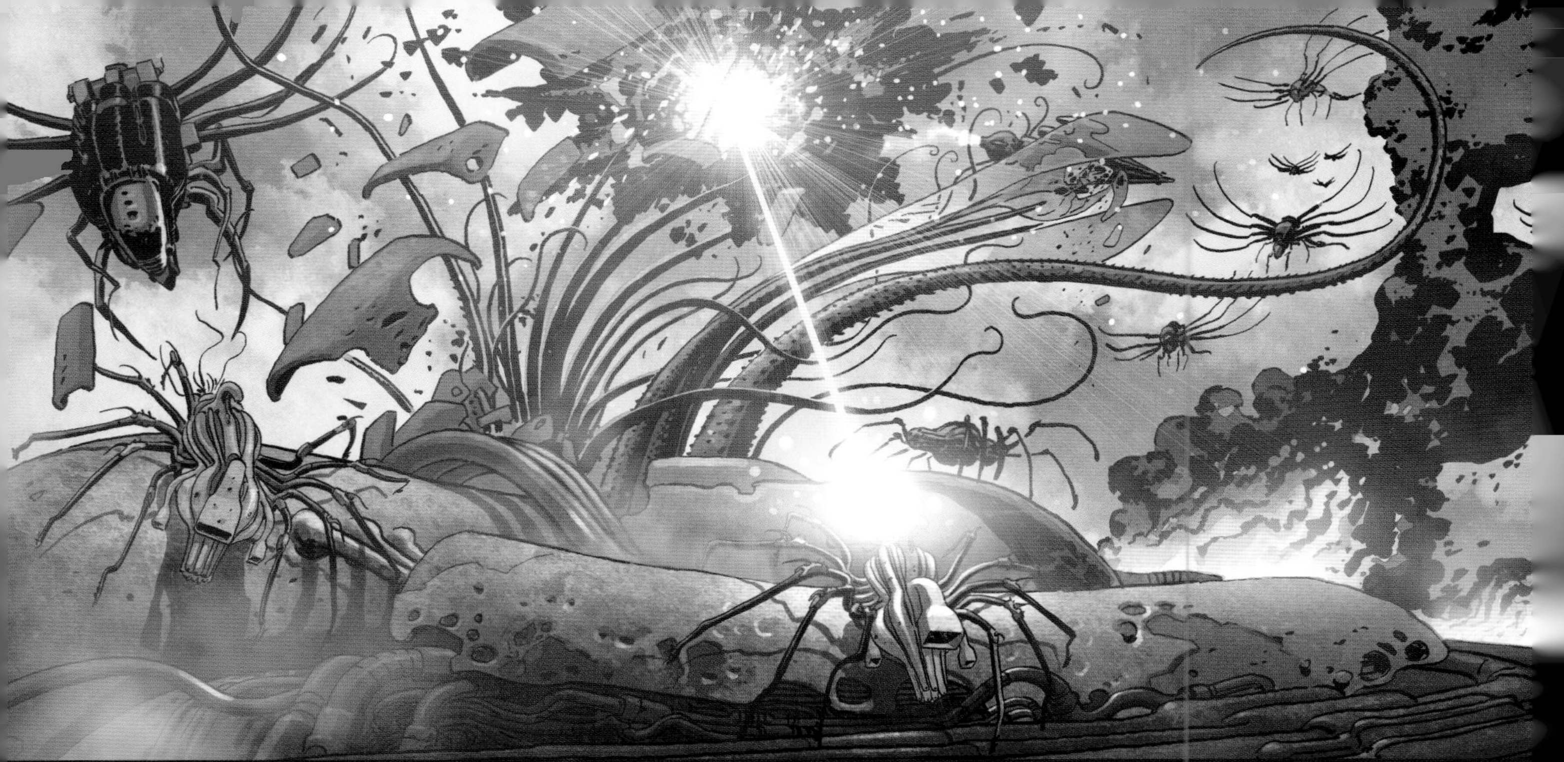

War

True to form, with *The Incal,* Jodorowsky brings us an epic tale that borrows from various genres, ranging from science fiction to mysticism and from adventure to romance (and what a love story it is, between John and Luz!). Among the genres covered in the third cycle of the *Incal* saga, *Final Incal,* there is one with particular scope: the war narrative. By deciding to end all bio-life and bio-techno power to establish the dictatorship of metal, the Prez unleashes a conflict of monstrous and unprecedented scale. His war against organic life gives birth to a resistance made up of a motley coalition of insects, White Archangels, Elohim, Aristos, Technos, Gorgo the Foul's men, and the comrades led by Kill Wolfhead, who all unite to rise up against the tyranny of the Meca-Prez who now serves the Benthacodon. There, in the role of leader-in-spite-of-himself, is our old friend John Difool, oscillating between his chronic defeatism, his usual cowardice, and his occasional, spontaneous bouts of courage (punctuated with his eternal rants, without which Difool wouldn't really be Difool). If it weren't for Luz, *Final Incal* could very well fall into a "guy story" kind of category, filled with blood, sweat, manly camaraderie, and testosterone. But her presence lends a much-needed feminine touch to the story, like an oasis of sweetness in a world of brutes in the throes of violence, savagery, and destruction.

At the end of the book, in a scene full of tenderness and poetry, John and Luz finally come together in the flesh, in the middle of an idyllic pastoral setting, while lovely insects buzz and flit around them. Then, swarms of thousands of them appear and scatter a shiny layer of dust over the inhabitants of Terra 2014, regenerative pollen that enables the metallic citizens to recover their former bodies. "I'll never crush an insect again as long as I live!" one of them cries out, suddenly touched by grace and intoxicated by the happiness of being returned to his original flesh. "Soon the rivers and seas will be full of fish and the fields will be covered in plants and animals," Kill Wolfhead predicts. Terra 2014 has now regenerated and been restored to its original state: biological life has triumphed over metallic life. The war has been won... for now.

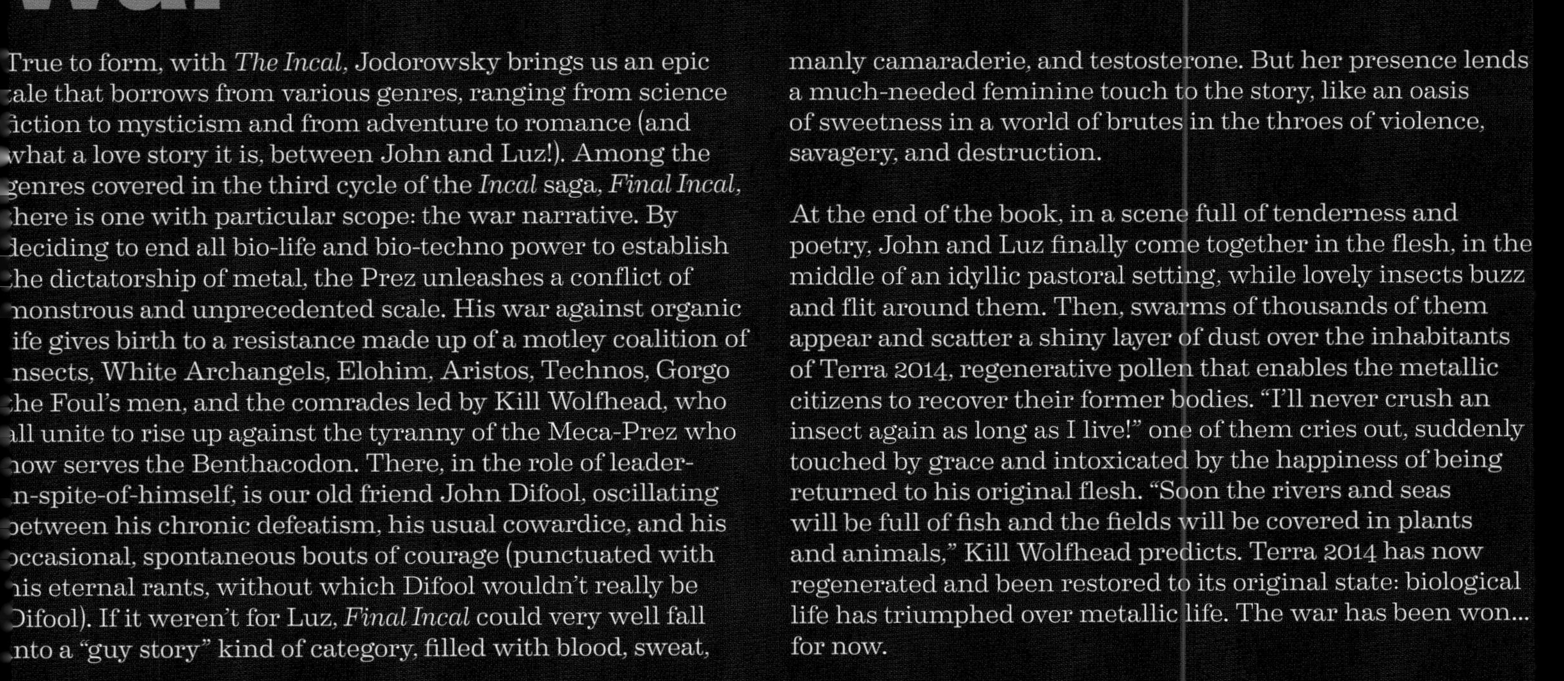

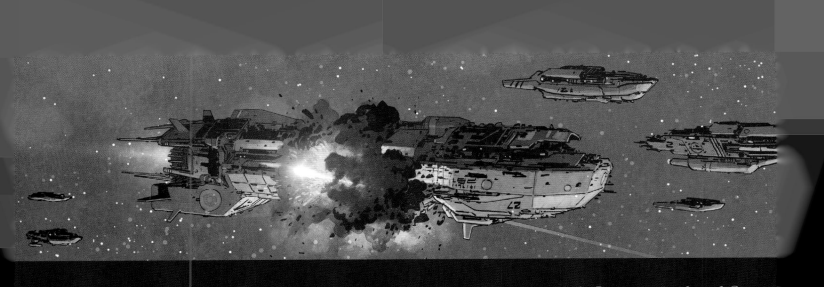

Revolution

Urban riots take up many panels in *The Incal*. They constitute a banal, nearly daily aspect of life on Terra 2014. In *Final Incal*, however, what's at work is a real revolution, carried out from the depths of Center Earth under the leadership of General Kill Wolfhead and his men. They gather in a secret base dubbed "the dumping ground," a veritable underground fortress in the shape of a troglodyte city, which Ladrönn renders with stunning realism. "My comrades and I traveled far and wide to find help in our fight against the tyranny of the Meca-Prez and the Benthacodon," the revolutionary explains to Difool and Luz, who have just been taken to him by the Psychorats.

These soldiers' credo fits in a few short sentences whose familiar echoes evoke the past combats of crude, earthly paleo-revolutionaries of the 19th and 20th centuries. "Consciousness gives life to our lives!" proclaims Lieutenant-General Hipo-San. "No love without freedom!" Commander Avicene cries out passionately. "No freedom without consciousness!" Colonel Don Poulpo concludes.

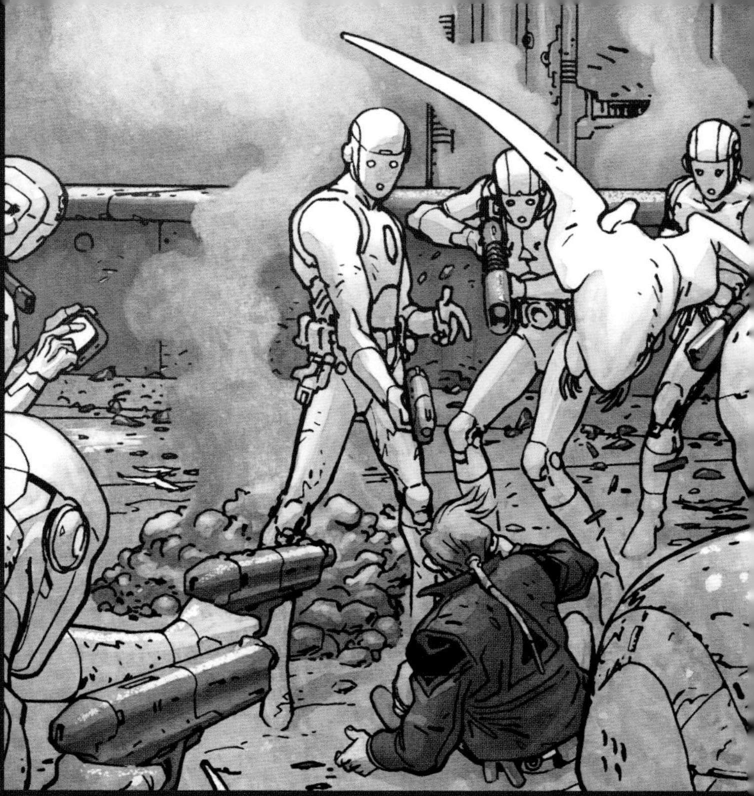

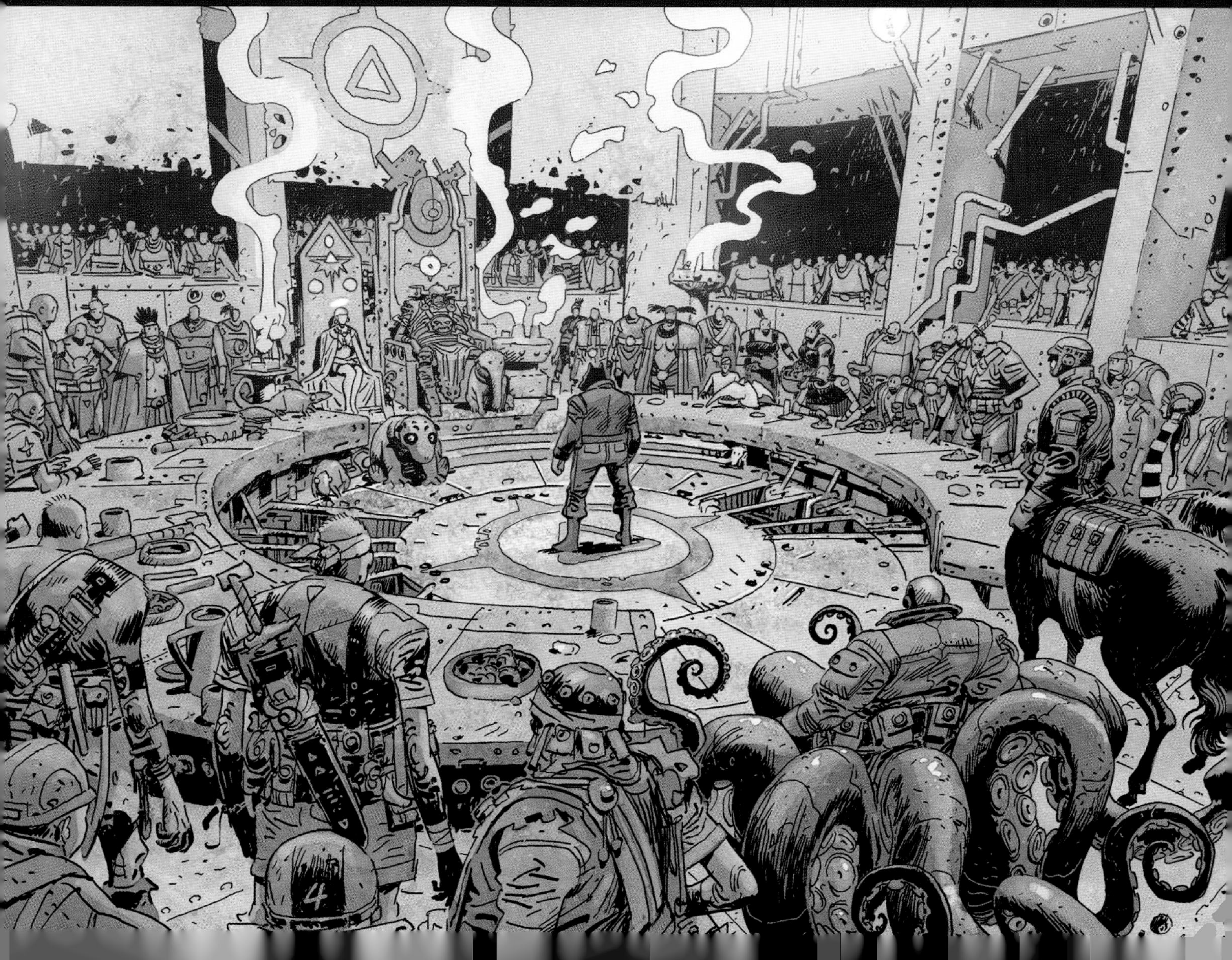
4

Crime Fiction

"*The Incal* is a crime novel with an ultra-cosmic plot," according to Jodorowsky. "A crime novel *à la* Philip K. Dick that reaches extreme circumstances: the disappearance and complete metamorphosis of the universe. Danger, in *The Incal*, is constantly growing bigger and more menacing, throughout the book. At first, it only threatens one individual, then one social group, then all of humanity and, ultimately, the entire universe! The Darkness threatens to swallow up everything... But the story doesn't end there: it's all just beginning."

You could even say that *The Incal* starts out like a James Bond film, with a pre-opening-credits scene of pure action that then backtracks to explain how the story reached that point. The world of our pathetic little Class "R" Detective is a sci-fi version of tropes found in the American crime novel genre, complete with tough-talking Cybo-cops, a beaten-up hero, and alluring homeo-whores plying their trade in smoke-filled cabarets. Before starting *The Incal*, Jodorowsky read the entire oeuvre of Mickey Spillane, a master of hardboiled crime fiction. "What I wanted was Spillane's rhythm," the writer once said. "*Kiss Me Deadly*, Robert Aldrich's film adapted from Spillane's novel, was also a huge influence. It opens with the discovery of a sort of Pandora's box with an atom bomb in it, and ends with the apocalypse. But *The Incal* is an inverted Pandora's box and its apocalypse is ultimately positive. It leads not to the destruction, but rather to the recreation of the universe. Moebius is the one who brought a little peacefulness to it. He said to me: 'Give the reader a break, let him catch his breath!' But I kept telling him: 'Start with a punch in the face!' And that's how *The Incal* starts: 'with a punch in the face.'"

The investigation element is also present, namely in *Before The Incal* via young Difool's quest to find an explanation for the 'Big Secret' gnawing at him: why don't the Crimson Ring prostitutes ever give birth? Subsequently, as the story progresses in *After The Incal* and *Final Incal*, this investigation element, characteristic of a certain type of classical crime fiction, eventually disappears to give way to a quest that extends far beyond the often trivial stakes around which many crime novels are constructed, and instead brings into play cosmic and planetary stakes of a whole other magnitude.

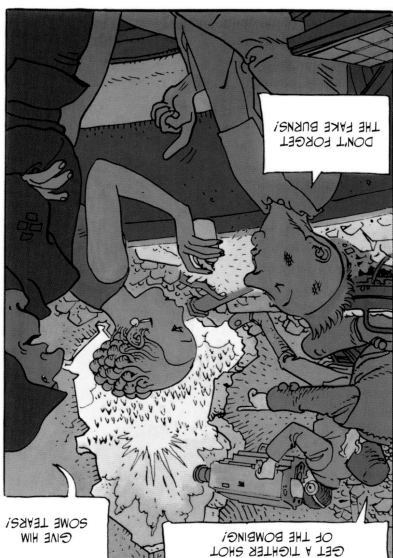

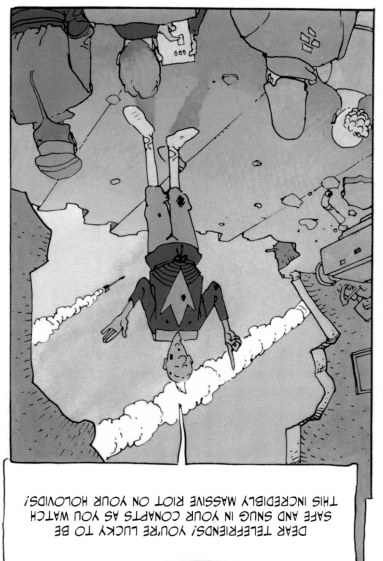

Reality TV

Jodorowsky and Mœbius did not invent reality TV. This type of television program consists of following the everyday life—albeit largely scripted and staged—of people who are typically either completely anonymous or minor celebrities of some sort. Inspired by documentaries, plays, and fiction all at once, it first made its appearance on the American television landscape in the early 1970s, before becoming a genre in its own right; it is now familiar and widespread regardless of the amount of criticism and controversy it has attracted.

But while the authors of *The Incal* can't claim to have given birth to this genre, they were the first to integrate it in a comic book and to push the notion to such extremes, perhaps foreshadowing what tomorrow's reality TV will look like—unless, even more disturbing but quite plausible, it has already become part of our daily environment and we are too used to its excesses to realize it.

In *The Incal,* from the comfort of their cozy little conapts, residents of Terra 2014 have the great "privilege" of being able to watch live broadcasts of the many prezidential clonings—surgical procedures that come to them via a media frenzy as artificial as it is obscene. But they can't seem to get enough of it, as evidenced by the way they sit all nice and attentive on their couches, enraptured by the saccharine propaganda oozing out of their super high-tech, ultra-modern 3D TVs. Clearly, any resemblance to the viewers that we are now is nothing but pure coincidence designed to serve the needs of the narrative. For we television viewers of the 21st century are too informed, too lucid, and too rational to let ourselves be caught in such traps set by the political-media establishment. Right...?

In *Before The Incal,* Jodorowsky and Janjetov go all out with the concept, cranking the scenes of reality TV up quite a few notches. The "addicts," hopped up on Cocaloco and various other substances, look downright dazed, as if their universe were reduced to the space of their TV screen. They revel as much in the report of an umpteenth Prezidential cloning as they do in scenes of riots wreaking violent, bloody chaos across the city. It gets to the point where it's hard to tell whether such spectacles are real or staged anymore. "We're hovering right above this great show of military might. Make your predictions, Tele-friends! What will the death toll be? Who will be the final victor? Place your bets with 79831, the oldest channel in the galaxy!" enthuses Diavaloo, the celebrity TV host in charge of keeping a viewership hungry for thrills, tragedies, and scandals captive, and above all, tuned in.

GET A TIGHTER SHOT OF THE BOMBING!
GIVE HIM SOME TEARS!
DON'T FORGET THE FAKE BURNS!

DEAR TELEFRIENDS! YOU'RE LUCKY TO BE SAFE AND SNUG IN YOUR CONAPTS AS YOU WATCH THIS INCREDIBLY MASSIVE RIOT ON YOUR HOLOVIDS!

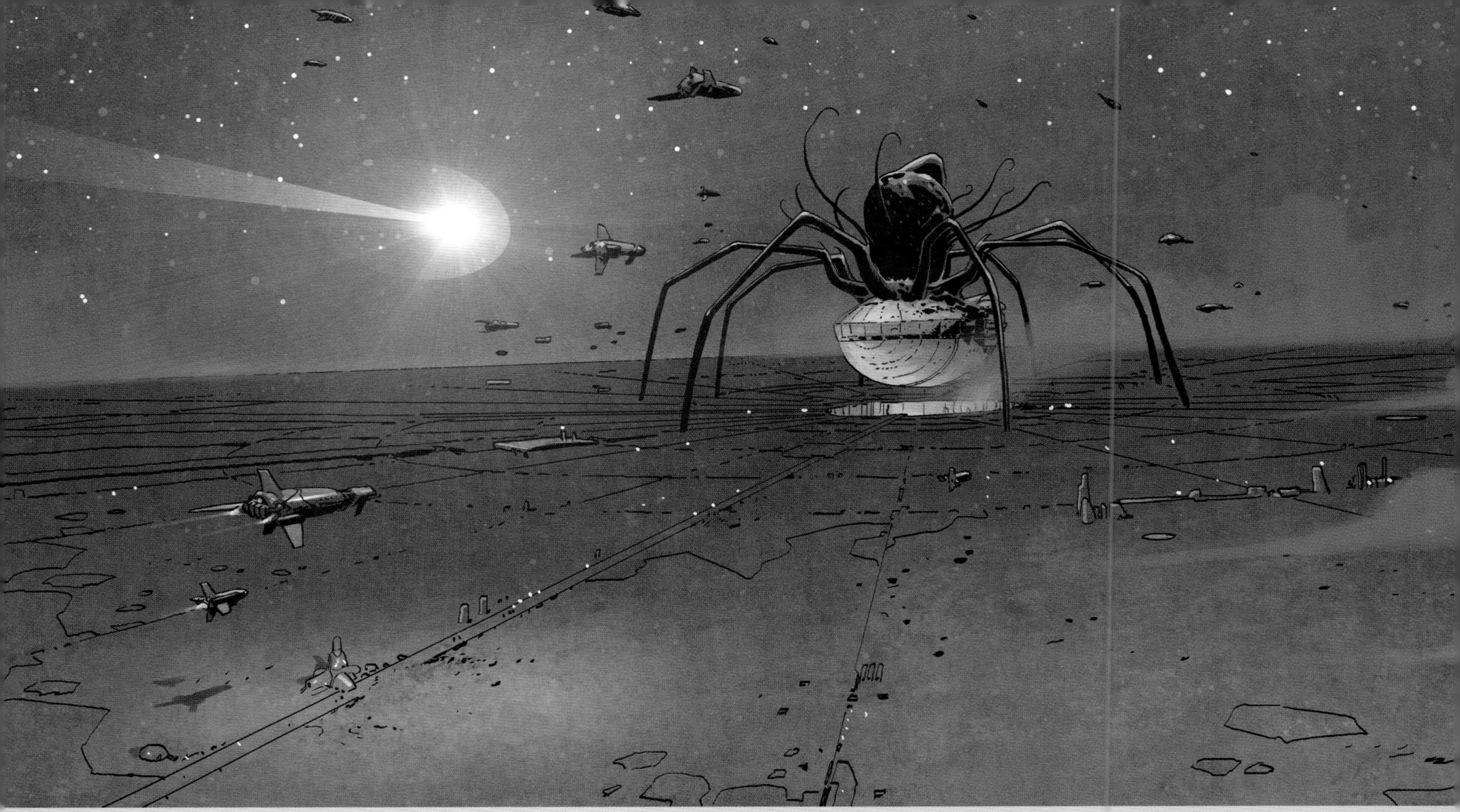

Science Fiction

This, of course, is the genre to which *The Incal* belongs first and foremost, combining various characteristic tropes, especially at the thematic level. In the great pantheon of sci-fi, *The Incal* can be viewed as the tale of a parallel universe. As such, the reference to American writer Philip K. Dick automatically comes to mind, because of the use of realities that are traps, multi-faceted, or that require transformation, and which open up onto other worlds, possibly of a divine nature (this was an obsession of Dick's later work). But the similarities stop there. Instead, *The Incal* is more in step with an overall evolution of science fiction that began in the 1960s, when, under the influence of counterculture and Eastern philosophies, the genre grew wary of the notion of objective reality and began to address the issue with more literary approaches.

The Incal was created by lovers of sci-fi who gleefully dove into brilliant set pieces worthy of the best space operas (ranging from battles between intergalactic spaceships to empires of extraterrestrial races), who didn't hesitate to reshape physical or astrophysical laws while being mindful of projecting apparent rationality—in the manner of the big names in hard sci-fi—and who fill the narrative with multiple nods to other works of the genre. They do this via a certain propensity for colorful and imaginative linguistic detail, showing Difool forced to withdraw five "kublars" from his account to pay the "homeo-whore" and having to return to his "level" (where he lives in a "conapt"), while on giant screens across the city, the ninth Prezidential "cloning" is being broadcast live. More poetic are the wonders of distant planets where masses

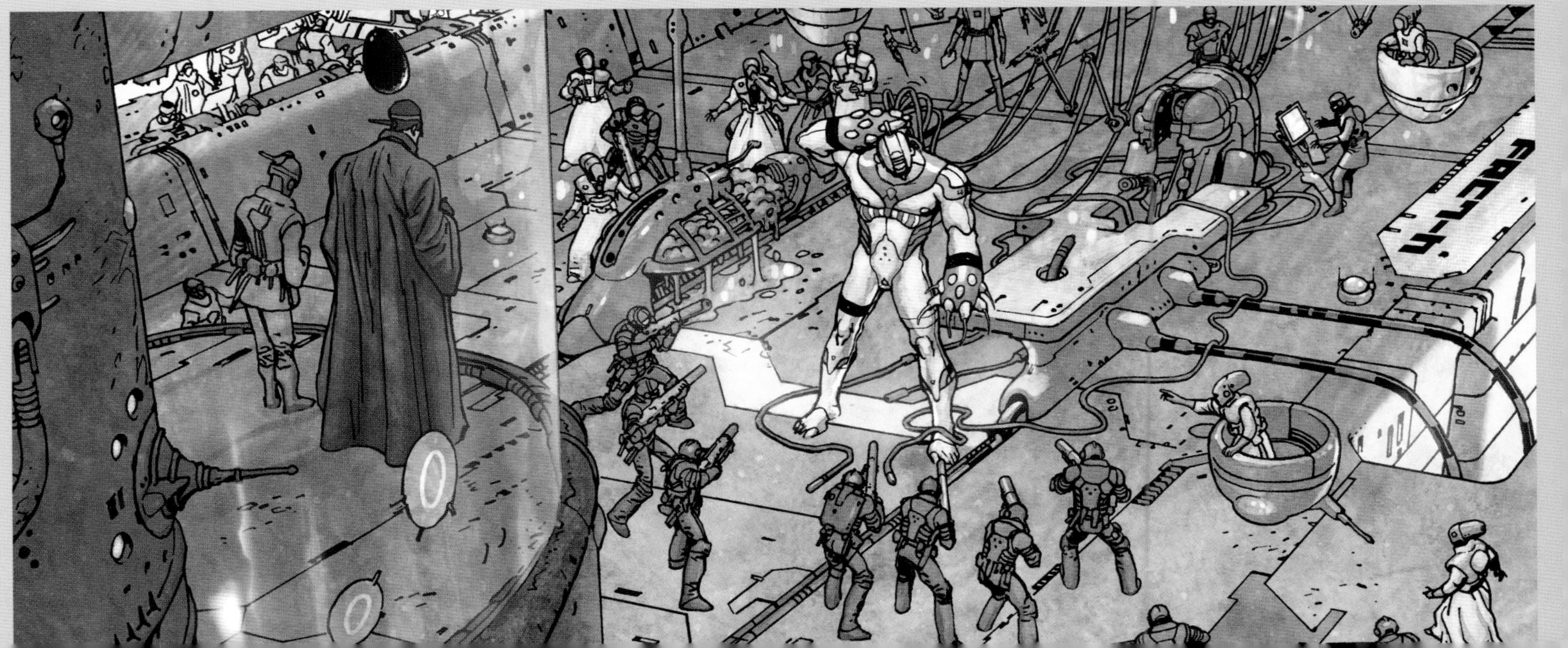

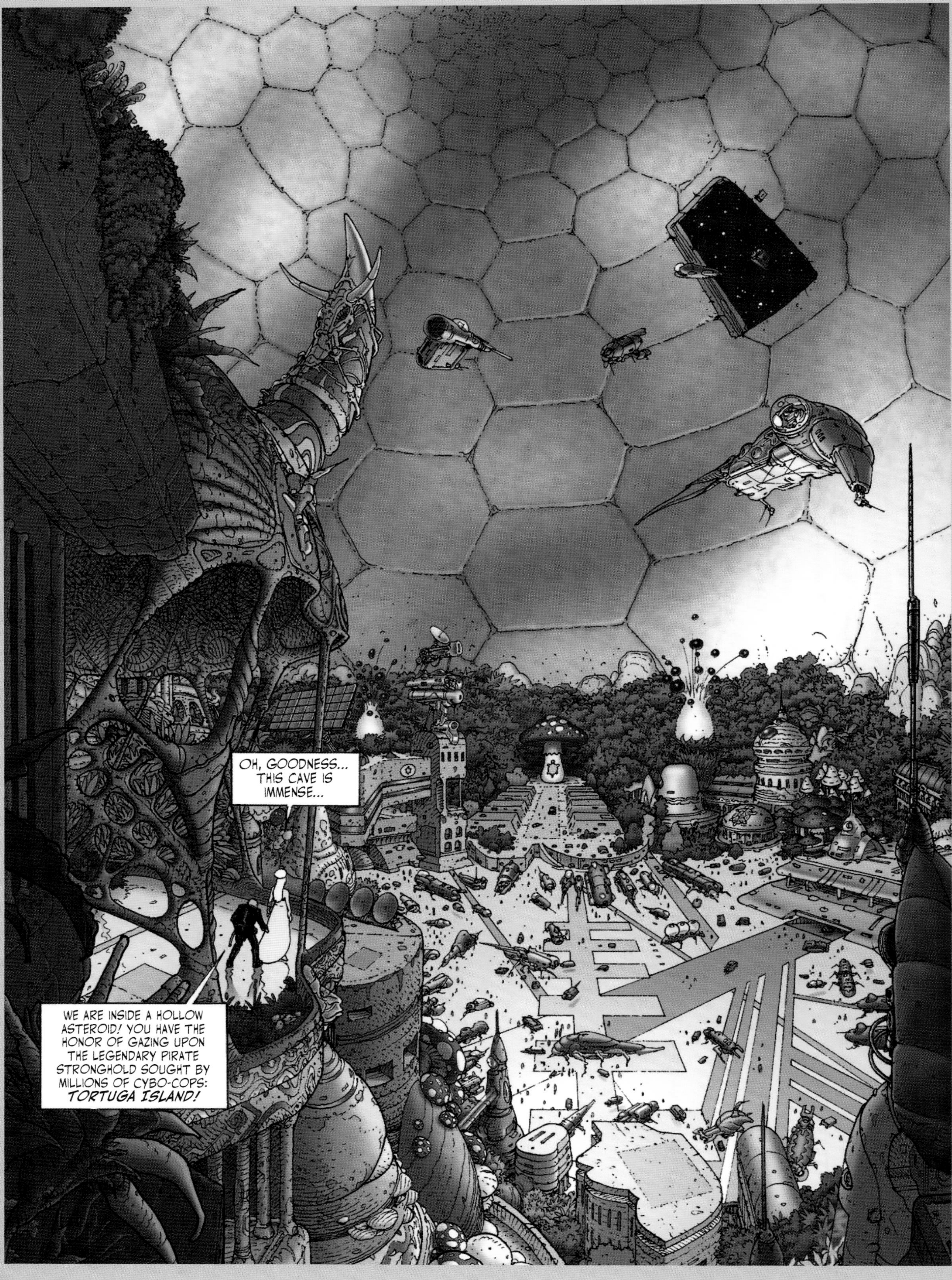
OH, GOODNESS... THIS CAVE IS IMMENSE...
WE ARE INSIDE A HOLLOW ASTEROID! YOU HAVE THE HONOR OF GAZING UPON THE LEGENDARY PIRATE STRONGHOLD SOUGHT BY MILLIONS OF CYBO-COPS: ***TORTUGA ISLAND!***

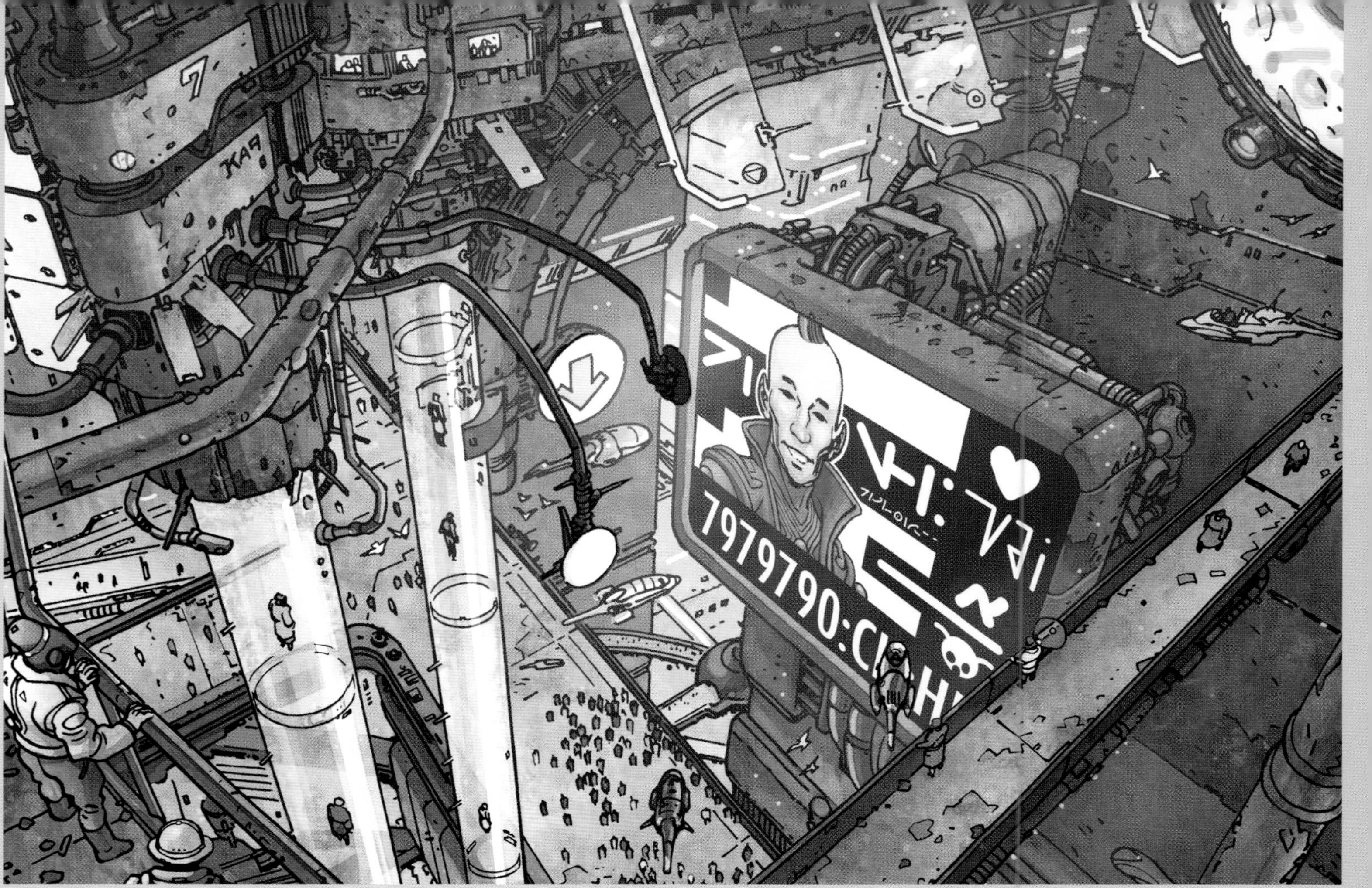
7979790:CI-H
KAP

of "Zelmatiodons" and other medusa flowers grow, while "Shadow Eggs" devour the suns and cover them in a layer of "solid plasma..." We could cite many more examples that blend the humor of Robert Sheckley with the lyricism of Cordwainer Smith, and also note the satire found in the intoxication of the masses via television, in a spirit close to Norman Spinrad's *Bug Jack Barron*.

The Incal is indeed filled with visual creations of all sorts. It combines pure formal inventions with references to our world: the aerial and delicate architecture of the Golden Planet, the complex metallic lacework of galactic fortresses, the sinister uniforms worn by the Technos, the endless stylized wardrobes of the female characters, and the traditional accessories of the space opera genre.

We could draw up a whole catalog of the different fashions, races, and types of technological design found in *The Incal* books, which would no doubt be more varied and abundant than those of any science fiction film with a multi-million dollar art budget. In addition, the sets in *The Incal* stand out for the way the visuals seamlessly move from one scene to the next. We go from the frantic urbanism of Terra 2014 to the magical atmosphere of the Forest of Singing Crystals; from symbolic worlds made of gold or water to the abstract spaces of metaphysics; from the wackiest extraterrestrial exoticism to the very earthy decay of the last portrayal of the Berg Planet.

In its own way, *The Incal* is a sort of living, breathing memory of the entire science fiction genre.

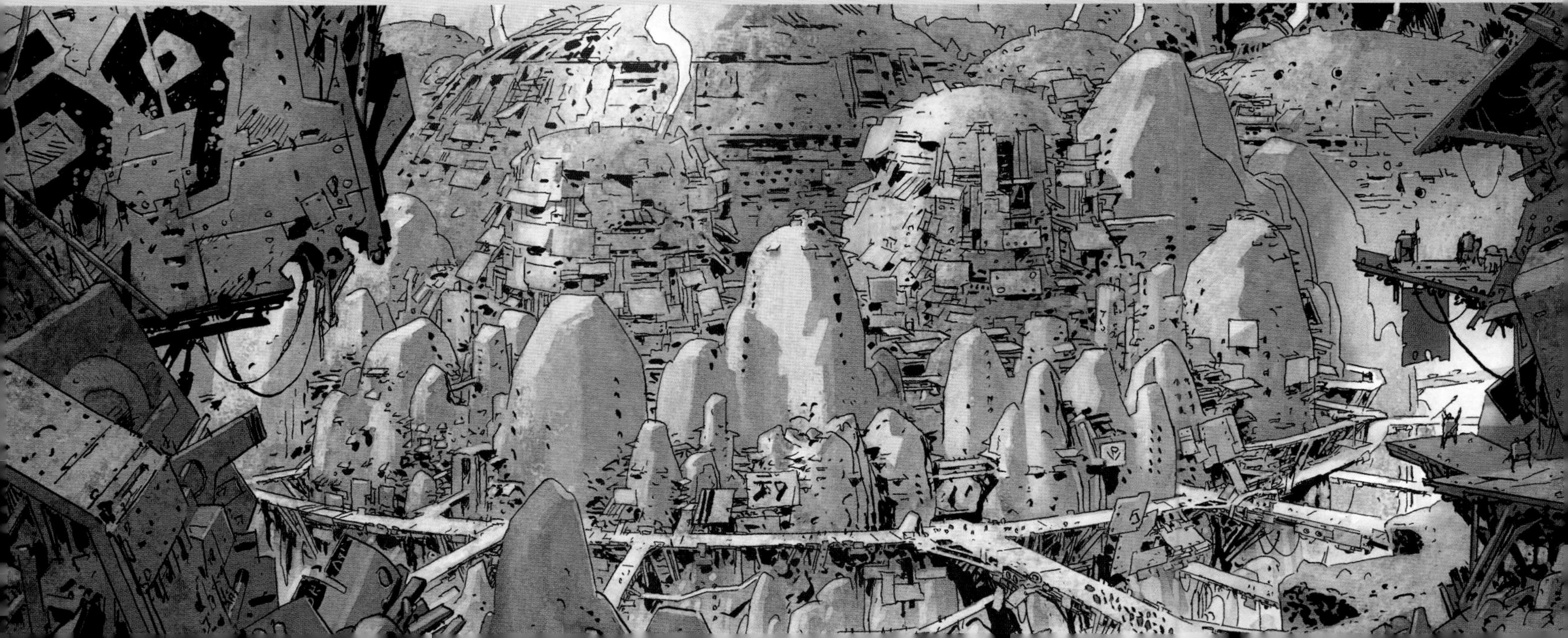

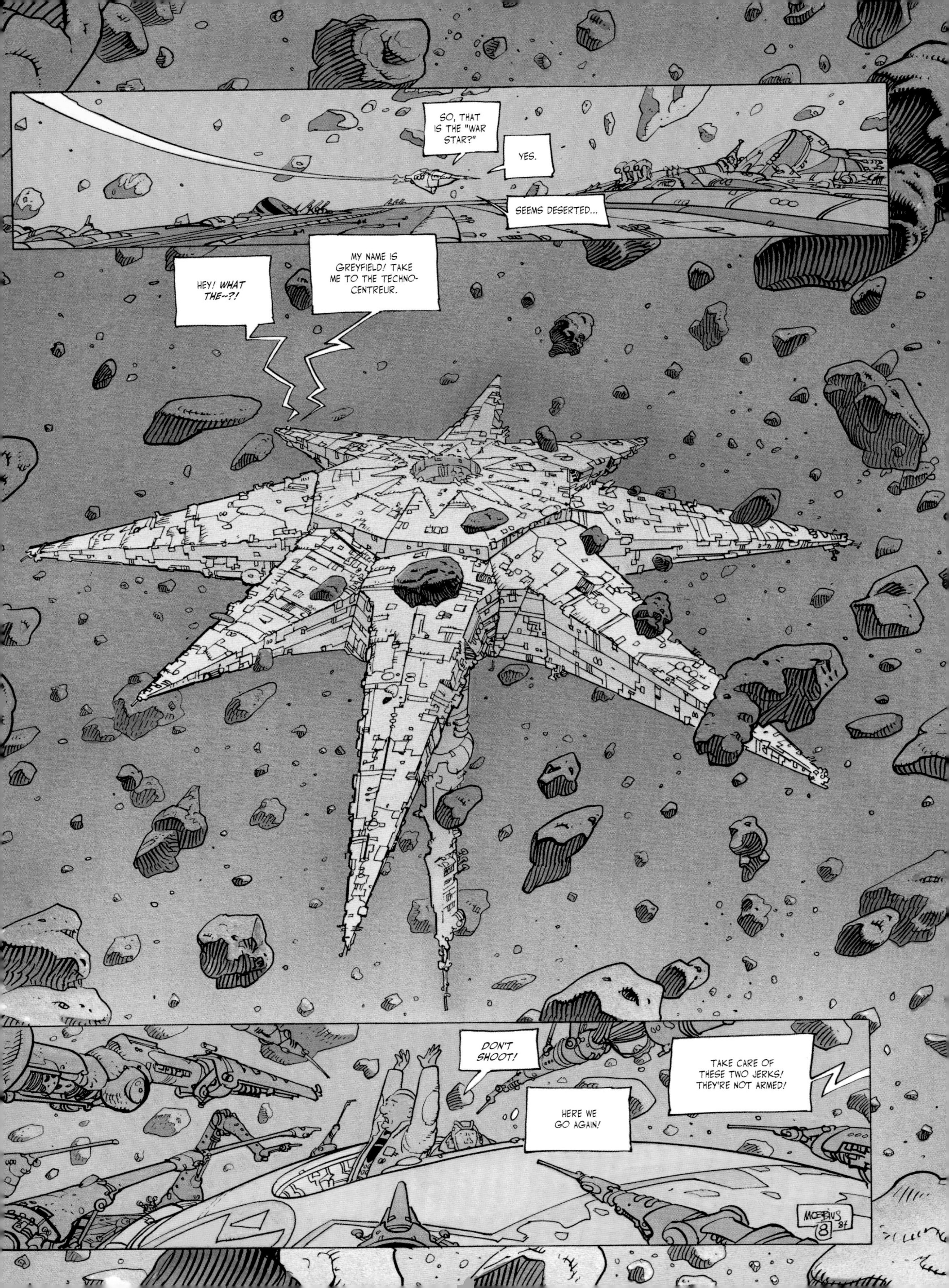
SO, THAT IS THE "WAR STAR?"
YES.
SEEMS DESERTED...
HEY! WHAT THE--?!
MY NAME IS GREYFIELD! TAKE ME TO THE TECHNO-CENTREUR.
TAKE CARE OF THESE TWO JERKS! THEY'RE NOT ARMED!
DON'T SHOOT!
HERE WE GO AGAIN!
MOEBIUS 8 87

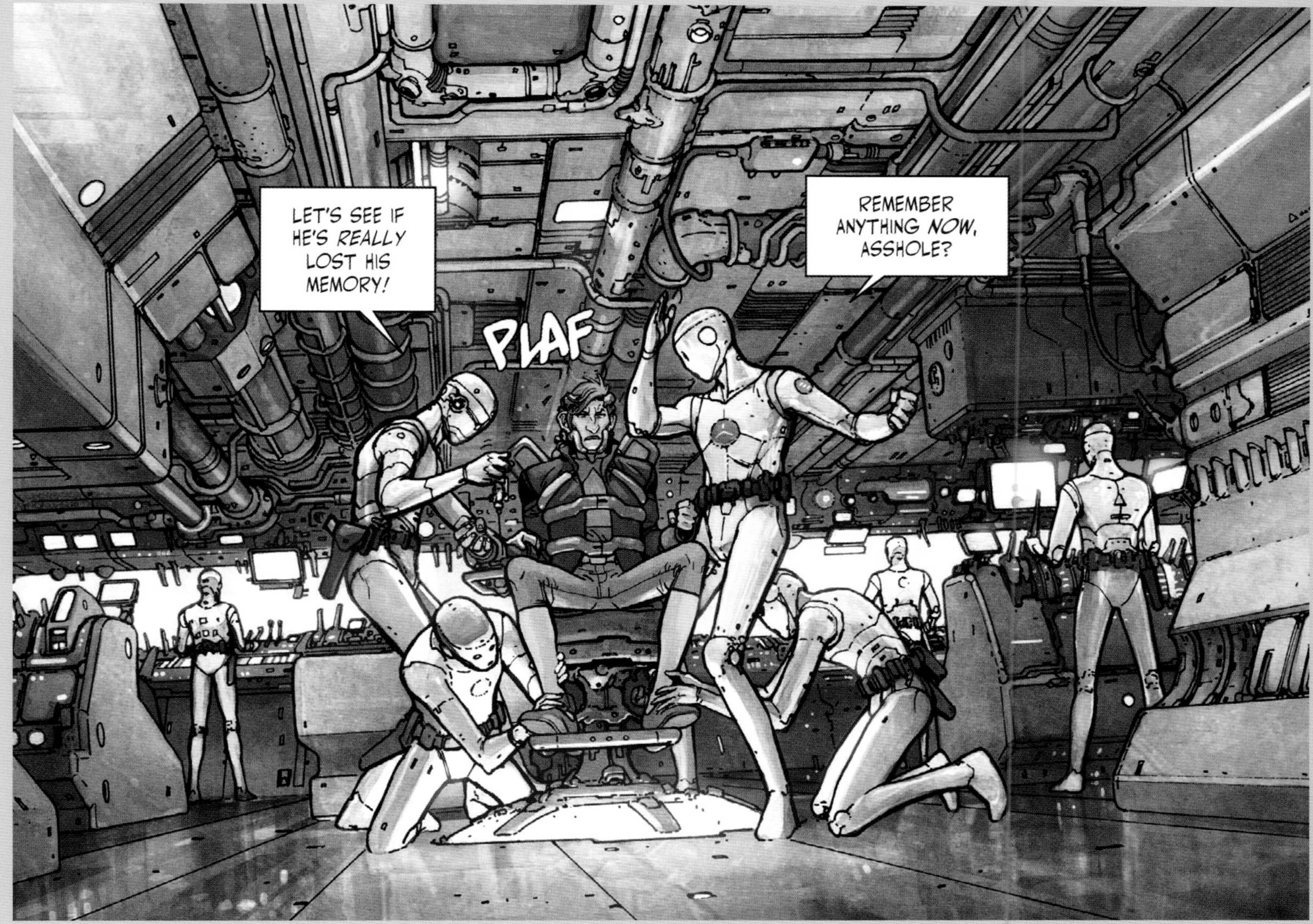
LET'S SEE IF HE'S *REALLY* LOST HIS MEMORY!
PLAF
REMEMBER ANYTHING *NOW*, ASSHOLE?

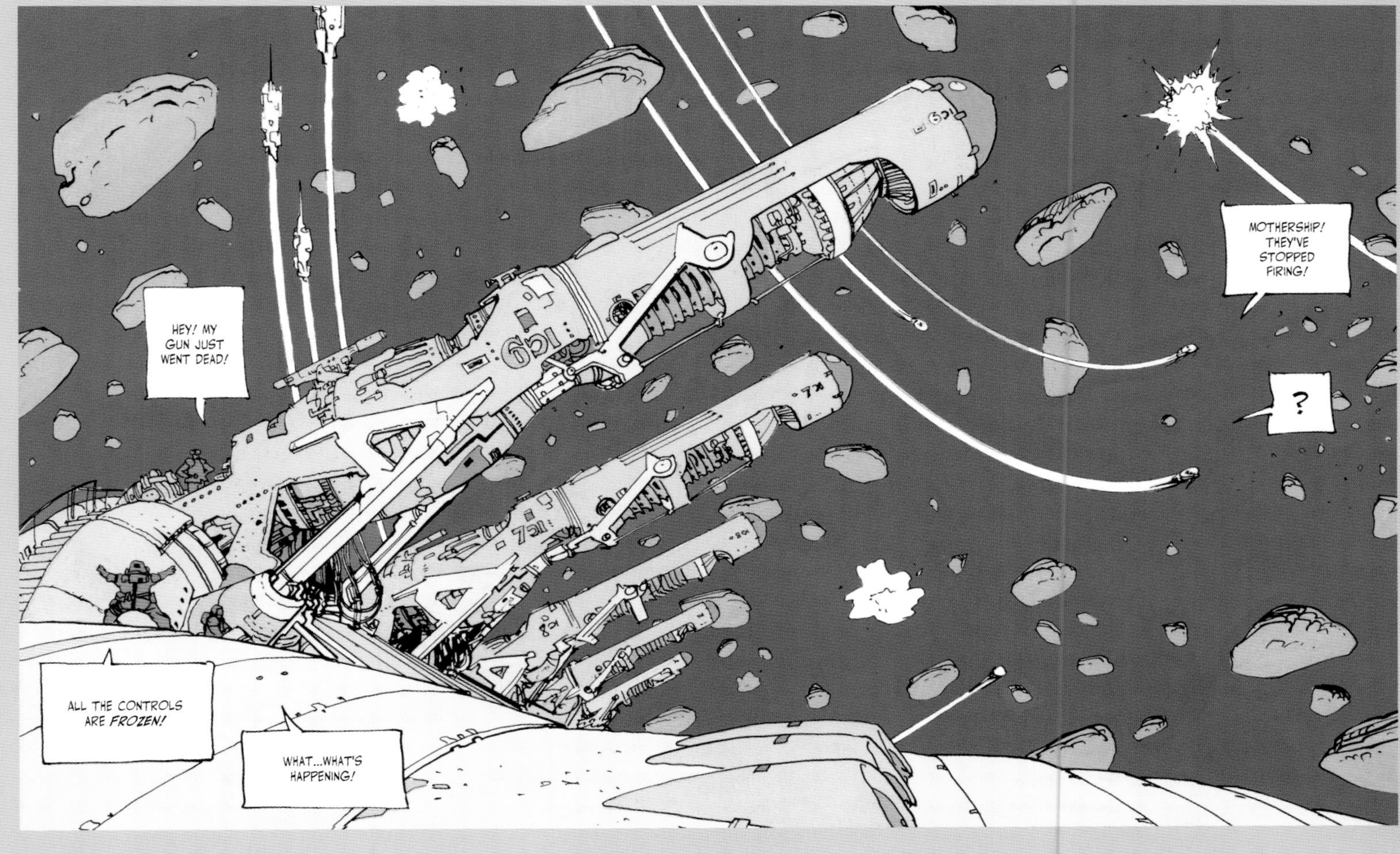
MOTHERSHIP! THEY'VE STOPPED FIRING!
?
HEY! MY GUN JUST WENT DEAD!
ALL THE CONTROLS ARE *FROZEN!*
WHAT...WHAT'S HAPPENING!

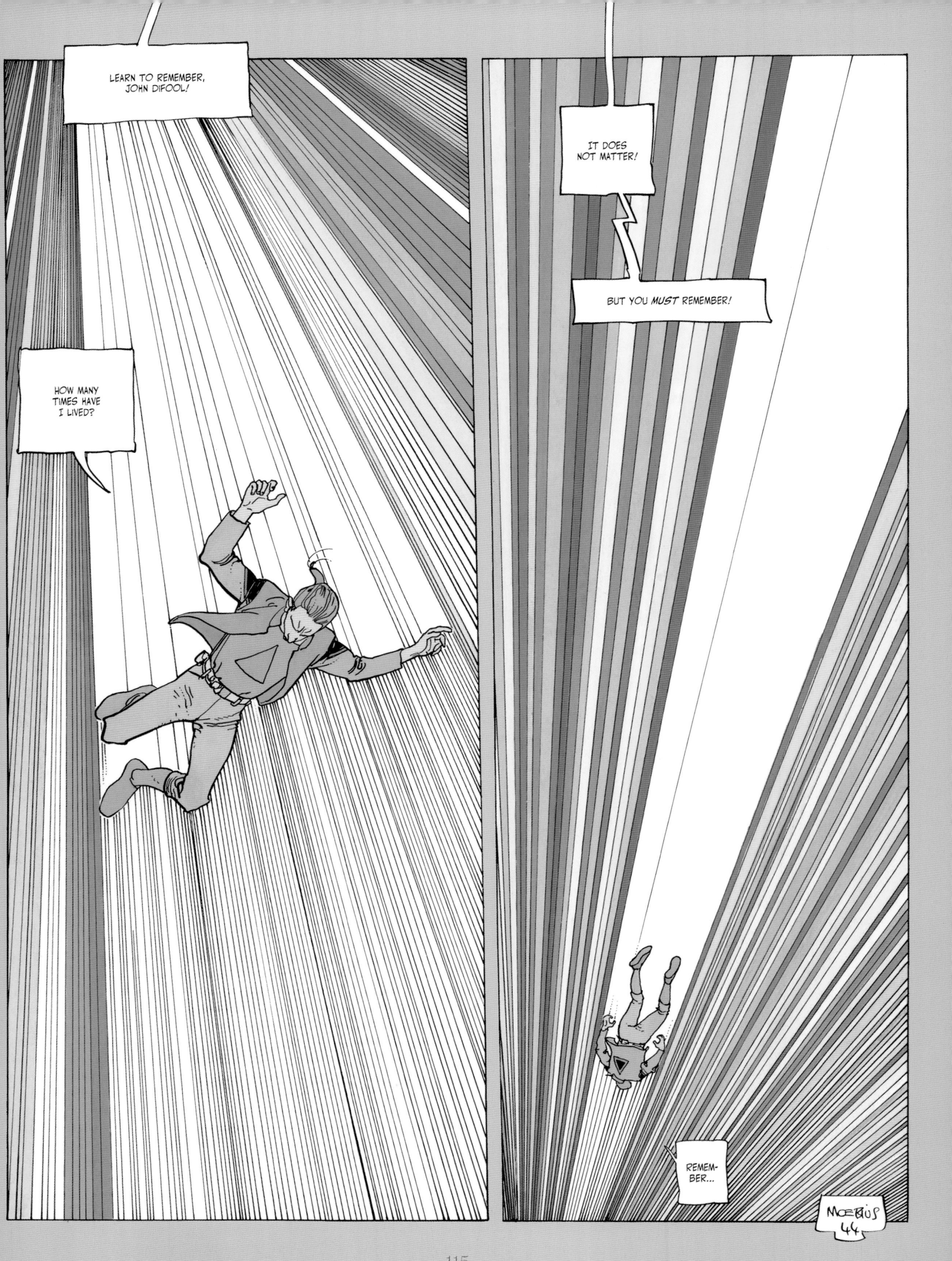
LEARN TO REMEMBER, JOHN DIFOOL!
HOW MANY TIMES HAVE I LIVED?
IT DOES NOT MATTER!
BUT YOU *MUST* REMEMBER!
REMEM-BER...
MOEBIUS 44

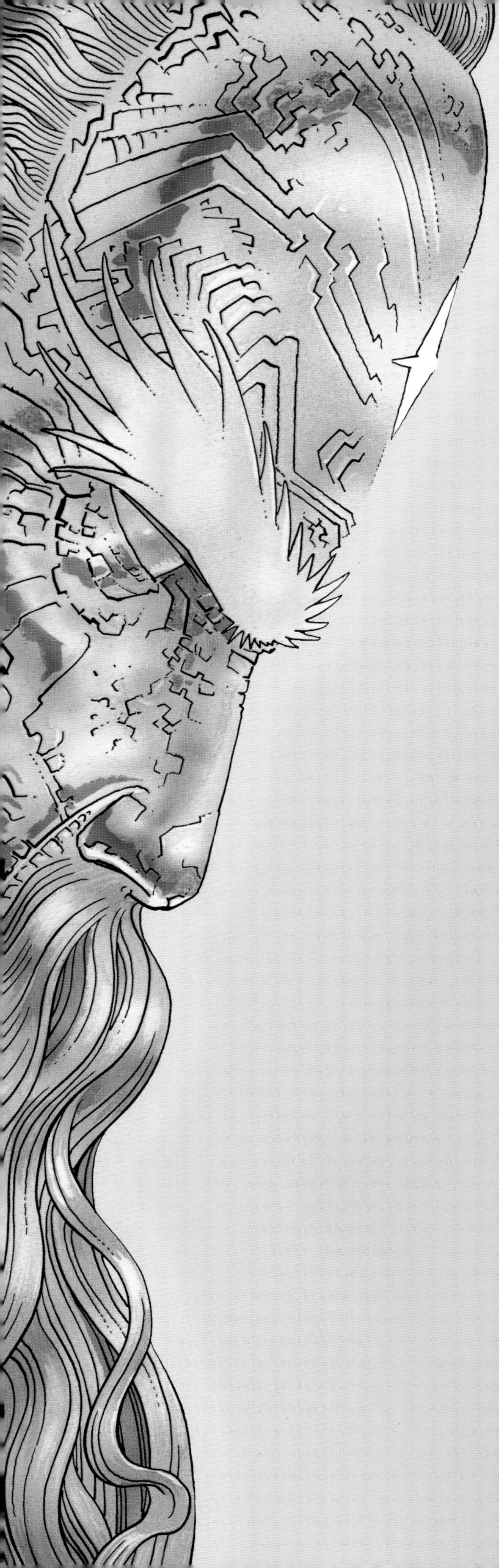

Illustr

Pages 1- 5: Mœbius.
Page 6: Left: Mœbius; right: Ladrönn.
Page 7: Mœbius.
Pages 8-9: Zoran Janjetov.
Page 10: Mœbius.
Pages 11-12: Ladrönn.
Page 13: Mœbius.
Page 14: ©Pascale Montandon-Jodorowsky.
Pages 15-16: Mœbius.
Page 17: Top: Mœbius; bottom: Zoran Janjetov.
Page 18: Mœbius.
Pages 19-21: Ladrönn.
Pages 22-30: Mœbius
Page 31: Left: Mœbius; right: Zoran Janjetov.
Page 32: Mœbius.
Page 33: Ladrönn.
Page 34: Top left and right: Mœbius;
center and bottom: Zoran Janjetov.
Pages 35-37: Mœbius.
Page 38: Zoran Janjetov, Ladrönn and Mœbius.
Pages 39-40: Mœbius.
Page 41: Ladrönn.
Page 42: Zoran Janjetov.
Pages 43-49: Mœbius.

tions Index

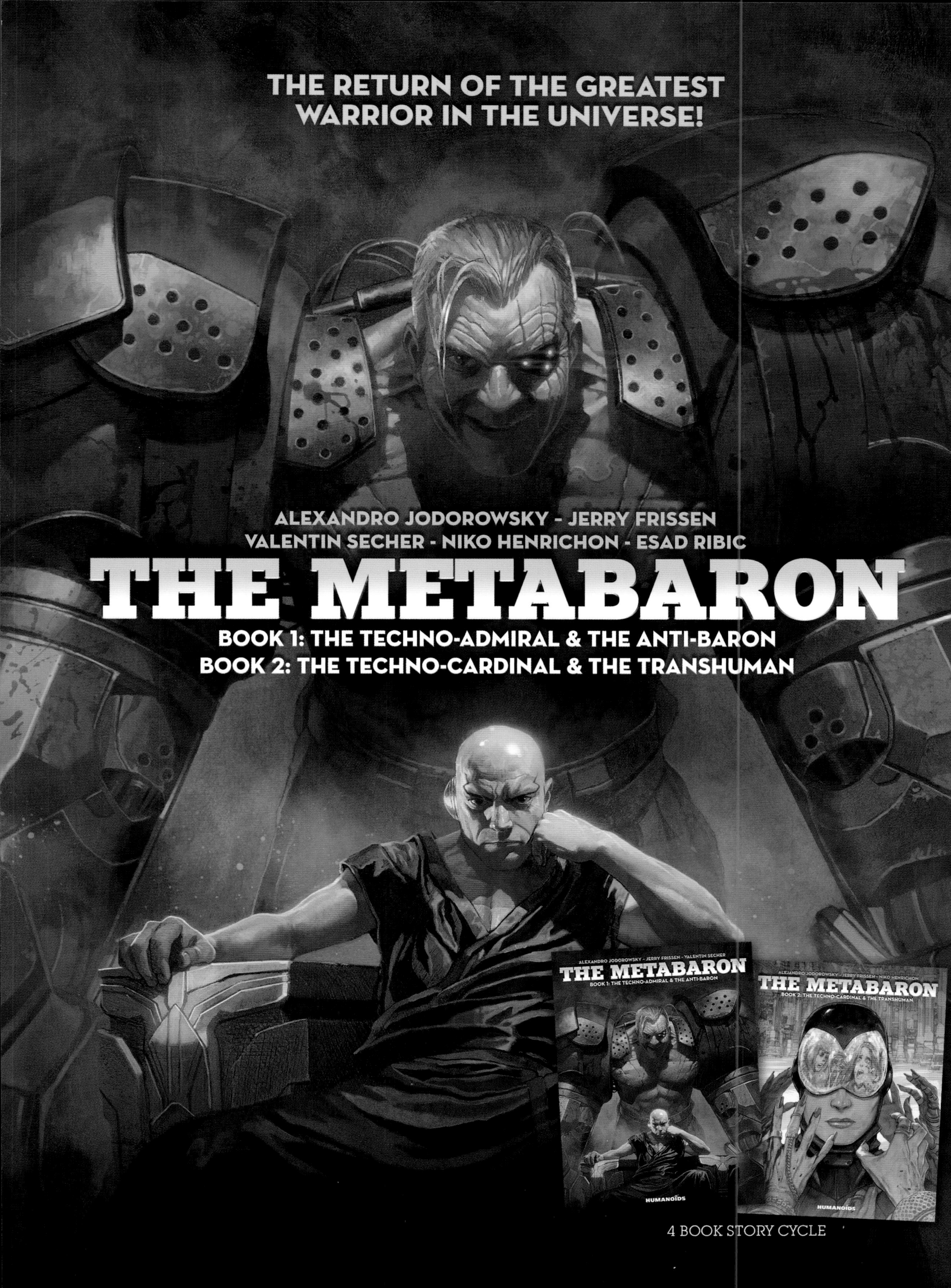

THE JODOVERSE

Created by visionary author, filmmaker, and philosopher, Alejandro Jodorowsky — along with some of the world's most singular and talented sequential artists — the Jodoverse is an incredible Sci-Fi universe, with each character and world complete with their own comprehensive backstories and mythology. Be it the hapless class "R" detective John DiFool searching for the key to the universe, the ephemeral Incal artifact; or the Metabaron, the greatest warrior in the universe. Themes like the battle of nature vs. technology, as seen in The Technopriests; or the blooming of the seeds of revolution against a tyrannical order, via an anomalous clone, in Megalex, are explored in topical and imaginative ways. These series have entertained millions of readers around the world, as well as influenced countless artists in all creative avenues, from filmmakers to writers. If you're not already one of them, this is your opportunity to get acquainted with some of these amazing stories and LOSE YOURSELF IN THE JODOVERSE!

"…Jodorowsky is our prophet. Our patron saint of imagination. A man with the mind of a god, where universes upon universes swirl and splinter, explode and coalesce, and wither and flower, all at once, all the time."

—Jason Aaron, Scalped, Southern Bastards, Thor, Star Wars

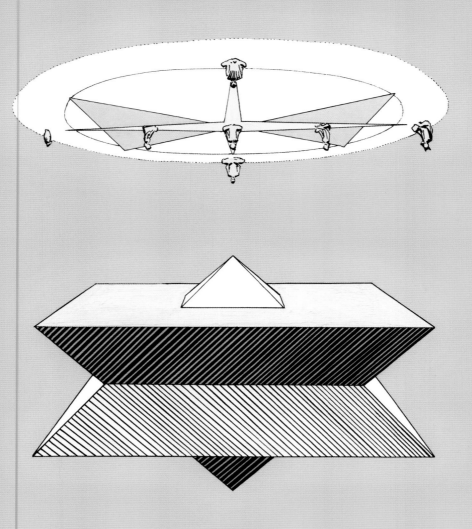